PRAISE FOR *Best European Fiction*

"Best European Fiction 2010 . . . *offers an appealingly diverse look at the Continent's fiction scene.*" **THE NEW YORK TIMES**

"*The work is vibrant, varied, sometimes downright odd. As [Zadie] Smith says [in her preface]: 'I was educated in a largely Anglo-American library, and it is sometimes dull to stare at the same four walls all day.' Here's the antidote.*" **FINANCIAL TIMES**

"*With the new anthology* Best European Fiction *. . . our literary world just got wider.*" **TIME MAGAZINE**

"*The collection's diverse range of styles includes more experimental works than a typical American anthology might . . . [Mr. Hemon's] only criteria were to include the best works from as many countries as possible.*" **WALL STREET JOURNAL**

"*This is a precious opportunity to understand more deeply the obsessions, hopes and fears of each nation's literary psyche—a sort of international show-and-tell of the soul.*" **THE GUARDIAN**

"*Readers for whom the expression 'foreign literature' means the work of Canada's Alice Munro stand to have their eyes opened wide and their reading exposure exploded as they encounter works from places such as Croatia, Bulgaria, and Macedonia (and, yes, from more familiar terrain, such as Spain, the UK, and Russia).*" **BOOKLIST STARRED REVIEW**

"[W]e can be thankful to have so many talented new voices to discover."
LIBRARY JOURNAL

"[W]hat the reader takes from them are not only the usual pleasures of fiction—the twists and turns of plot, chance to inhabit other lives, other ways of being—but new ways of thinking about how to tell a story."
CHRISTOPHER MERRILL, PRI'S "THE WORLD" HOLIDAY PICK

"The book tilts toward unconventional storytelling techniques. And while we've heard complaints about this before—why only translate the most difficult work coming out of Europe?—it makes sense here. The book isn't testing the boundaries, it's opening them up." **TIME OUT CHICAGO**

"Editor Aleksandar Hemon declares in his preface that at the heart of this compilation is the 'nonnegotiable need for communication with the world, wherever it may be,' and asserts that ongoing translation is crucial to this process. The English-language reading world, 'wherever it may be,' is grateful." **THE BELIEVER**

"Does European literature exist? Of course it does, and this collection of forty-one stories proves it." **THE INDEPENDENT**

BEST EUROPEAN FICTION 2013

EDITED AND
WITH AN
INTRODUCTION
BY
ALEKSANDAR
HEMON

PREFACE BY JOHN BANVILLE

BEST EUROPEAN FICTION 2013

DALKEY ARCHIVE PRESS

CHAMPAIGN · LONDON · DUBLIN

ISBN 978-1-56478-792-7
ISSN 2152-6672

www.dalkeyarchive.com

Funded in part by the Arts Council (Ireland) and
the Illinois Arts Council, a state agency

Please see Acknowledgments on page 459 for additional
information on the support received for this volume

Printed on permanent/durable acid-free paper
and bound in the United States of America

Contents

Preface

It is not only in French that the words *translate* and *traduce* bear a close affinity. Legend has it that John Braine's novel of ambition and opportunism in 1950s Britain, *Room at the Top*, in its Swedish version was very nearly entitled *Vinden*—'The Attic'—until a vigilant editor thought to double-check. It is also said that in a passage in one of Sean O'Casey's plays of Dublin working-class life where a character speaks of the 'little chislers', that is, children, an earnest Japanese translator rendered the colloquialism as 'small stone-masons'. One laughs, of course, but at the same time one does sympathise with the hapless traducer. Language is a sly and treacherous medium.

We are all familiar with Robert Frost's mournful contention that poetry is what gets lost in translation, but meaning itself can go subtly or grossly astray in the crossing from one tongue to another—not so much tripping lightly, one might say, as merely tripping. The problem, as any translator will ruefully remind us, is that in the original text meaning is not fixed, but is always more or less ambiguous. This is so not only in verse, but can be true of the most seemingly limpid passages of prose. You sit down to write a letter to your lover, or your bank manager, thinking you know exactly what you have to say, yet when you finish and read over what you have written you notice that the sense is not quite as you intended. Who speaks here, you wonder? The answer is, language itself, wilful, subtle, coercive. We think we speak, but really it is we who are spoken.

Even when language seems at its most docile, the sense, or nonsense, of a phrase can turn on the most innocent-seeming effect. Take that comma in the opening sentence of Wittgenstein's *Tractatus Logico-Philosophicus*. In the original the first proposition is written thus: '*Die Welt ist alles, was der Fall ist.*' Wittgenstein in his early work was fond of symmetry, and certainly this is a handsomely symmetrical sentence. However, the rules of punctuation in German are strict, and by those rules a comma is called for here, at the halfway point in the sentence, making for a nice caesura.

Yet the translators of the 1961 London edition of the *Tractatus*, Pears and McGuinness, flexing the looser muscles of English, render the line as: 'The world is all that the case is, as the German indicates.' Thus at the very outset of this tangled text the reader meets with uncertainty. Does Wittgenstein mean to say that the world is all, that the case is, as the German indicates, or, as the English seems to have it, that the case is that the world is all? These are, surely, two separate propositions, and though the difference between them may seem slight, it is not negligible, especially in a work that sets out to explore and even prescribe the limits of language. In the German version of proposition 1 the emphasis is on the allness of the world, while the English seems primarily concerned with what is the case or state of affairs in the world. Wittgenstein himself might have devoted a whole section of his later *Philosophical Investigations* to the effect of that apparently innocuous comma.

So who would be a translator?

Occasionally, of course, a translation chimes happily with the original. The poetry of Paul Celan is notoriously difficult to render into another language—indeed, it is a question whether the attempt should be made at all, given the poet's agonised relation to German, the language of the monsters who administered the Holocaust. Yet great and inventive translations have been made of his work, notably by Paul Hamburger and John Felstiner. In his search for a way of dealing with, if not expressing, the horrors suffered by the Jews in the Second World War,

Celan formulated a negative aesthetic—a 1963 volume of his poems is titled *Die Niemandsrose*, 'The No-one's Rose'—and again and again he inverts usages, twists and bends them, turns them inside-out. For instance in the poem '*Weggebeizt*', 'Etched Away', he speaks of

> *das hundert-*
> *züngige Mein-*
> *gedict, das Genicht*

which Hamburger renders as

> the hundred-
> tongued pseudo-
> poem, the noem

and Felstiner, wonderfully, as

> the hundred-
> tongued My-
> poem, the Lie-noem

In both these instances, 'noem', for '*Genicht*', is a stroke of genius. Compared to what Seamus Heaney has called Celan's 'tortuosities', or the knotty intricacy of the *Tractatus*, the novel, you might think, would surely present few problems for the translator. In fact, fiction is just as difficult to translate, if not more so, than verse. Here, too, the Frostian lament asserts its sad truth. The late John McGahern liked to make a simple distinction: there is verse, he would say, there is prose, and then there is poetry, which may be conjured in either medium. Thus the poetry of prose, no less than of verse, stands to lose badly when it is filleted from one language and fed into another.

For a novel or a short story even in its original state is already a translation. The version it presents of reality is as far from actual reality as our dreams are from the events of our lives out of which they propagate their lovely or malignant blossoms. In our lazy way we tend to imagine that a piece of fiction is a direct statement of a set of facts or factual images when in fact—in fact!—fiction is a kind of dream-metaphor, a moulded and mannered *traducing* of 'what really happened'. This is the wonderful fact about fiction, that we know it is all made up, a farrago of marvellous lies, yet we regard it as if it were somehow all true—which it is, of course, although the truth of fiction is not the same as the truth of life.

When we consider it at all carefully, we realise that there can be no such thing as a translation. What a translator produces is a new thing, and when he finishes, there are two works where before there was one. That is inevitable, given the nature of language, and given that there are languages. The Book of Babel is legion.

Who would be a translator?

Coda: Worrying that I might make a blunder, a thing easily done in this context, I consulted a Swedish friend on the matter of the word, or title, *Vinden*. Is not *vinden* the Swedish word for 'wind'? It is. But also it means, indeed, 'the attic'. But should the title, the mis-title, not have been *Den Vinden*? No, because *den vinden* would mean 'that [particular] attic'. Ah, the infinite undependability of words.

JOHN BANVILLE

Introduction

1

For some time now, I've felt compelled to convince the hypothetical reader—presumably ever-ready to grab the remote or download more shades of grey on the Kindle—that it is necessary to read difficult and/or translated works of literature. With considerable effort, here and there and everywhere, I've tried to build an argument based on the presumed benefits of such reading. For some time, being in that situation annoyed me terribly—to the point of my being tempted to say to the reader: take it or leave it.

What was bothering me, I realized, was that I sought confirmation in numbers. I strived to convert readers to my point of view so that they could buy the *Best European Fiction* anthology en masse, which would then confirm the utility and social value of the whole project. I was, as it were, marketing it, suggesting to small audiences around the world that they were an avant-garde of the great army of readers gathering just beyond the horizon, about to realize what they have been missing by not reading the anthology and translated literature.

And it turns out I don't care about the numbers anymore, even if they're pretty good, as the anthology has, over the past four years, introduced more than a hundred European writers to English-language readers, and generated a vast number of translations from more than forty European languages. The presence of those writers and their work is now indelible. The connection has been established and the flow of communication is ongoing.

2

For the past few years, every single review of the anthology brought up the question: What is European fiction? I am happy to report I have no clue. This is the fourth *Best European Fiction* anthology I've edited and I'm not any closer to a clear picture, let alone a definition, of what particular qualities of writing, other than loosely geographic, could be defined as European. True, there are intellectual domains or formal approaches European writers are conspicuously comfortable with, particularly when compared to their American colleagues: fragmentariness; dialogue with other writers across cultures and history; experimental cheekiness and love of absurdity; disinclination to entertain by deploying TV-friendly banalities masked as social commentary; presumption of the reader's intelligence; willingness to reach for the far ranges of both humor and seriousness; a firm conviction in the transformative powers of literature. But of course, for every piece that exemplifies one of the above, I could find—in the anthologies I've edited—a counterexample. Perhaps one constant and unchanging aspect of European literature is precisely its slipperiness—it cannot be collared, reduced to a marketable formula, or posited as the absolute opposite to American literature. The reason for that ought to be obvious: Europe is nothing if not an intricate entanglement of languages, histories, borders, and varieties of human experience. It is not only complicated—culturally, intellectually, geographically—but is ever in the process of becoming increasingly more so.

For the past few years, Europe seems to have been on the verge of collapse, due to the financial shenanigans rooted in the belief (so dear to

Americans) that the free market and capitalism would bring us endless joy and money. The European Union, which, like many an empire, appeared solidly eternal not so long ago, might not be able to outlive the ongoing debt crisis. Europe, as it were, might not survive itself. What heretofore seemed unquestionably real might turn out to be a foolish fantasy. The rule of apparent reasonability has approached its end and there is, shall we say, a widespread surge in absurdity. The reality of Europe is being renegotiated. If there is a need to reconsider—or indeed abandon—the intellectual and formal limits of realism, Europe provides plenty of justification. Perhaps significantly, the crisis of the European domain coincides with the crisis of the print form—the book and the related human project known as literature are undergoing a transformation with uncertain outcome. One should read European fiction not so much for the purposes of understanding it, but rather just to keep up with its accelerating history and to see how literature reinvents itself in trying to keep up with it. The understanding might have to wait.

3

When you come right down to it, no human experience appears translatable or understandable outside itself. The world looks different from each individual position—everyone is inescapably locked in a worldview. But it is precisely in overcoming that existential circumstance that humanity lives up to its potential; indeed, in transcending the biological and ontological individuation, humanity becomes imaginatively and conceptually possible. What allows for the ascension from the individual to the human kind is language—we are impossible as a species that recognizes itself as such without the belief that words can convey experience. Out of that belief writing comes;

without that belief literature—as the depository of the entirety of human experience—is impossible.

But language is far more than a code necessary for transmission of existential information. Language being merely a code would imply that the world is figured out before the words are spoken or written, that we can only speak and write what we know. As a matter of fact, language—and literature as the field of its actualization—serves us to negotiate the mysteries, to enter not only the unknown but the unknowable as well, and find ways to say what is unsayable or, even, unspeakable. Which is why imprecision is as essential to language and literature as precision. It is in the continuous search for the right word that we find meaning; it is in the failing to find the exact word that new interhuman spaces open. What great book or poem was easy to read or translate? It is in trying to grasp Proust that we fall in love with his work. Pursuing meaning in literature is the meaning of literature.

Translation is, therefore, essential to language and literature, as is the impossibility to translate exactly. "Poetry is what is gained in translation," Brodsky said, countering Frost's claim that poetry is what is *lost* in translation. Languages and literatures overlap, seep into, and contaminate one another, blocking—thankfully—the very possibility of purity. Literature is about nothing if not about continuously trying to say what is hard to say, to convey what is difficult to convey, translate what is impossible to translate. Those who harp on the impossibility of translation betray a belief in the superiority of their own language; as far as they are concerned, nobody can say it better than those who have already said it; our language is perfect for us as it is; the world is complete, in all its hierarchies.

Reading and inquiring about what is outside our experience means willfully adopting another worldview, putting ourselves in a position to look at things in a way that is, shall we say, displacing or even disorienting. But, as Graham Greene said, "When we are not sure, we are alive." Of course, there are plenty of books, writers, and readers who seek a confirmation for what they already know, who hope to cement the position from which it all looks solid, unalterable, and, therefore, bearable. If that is what you're after, stay away from this book. The *Best European Fiction 2013* anthology is proudly difficult and imperfectly translated.

ALEKSANDAR HEMON

BEST EUROPEAN FICTION 2013

space

BALLA

Before the Breakup

Miša discovered there was something in the apartment.

It was behind the TV set in the corner of the living room. But later in the evening when she phoned Jano, who had left on a business trip a few days earlier, she made no mention of her discovery. Why make him worry? He had other things to worry about out there in the Asian metropolis. Or maybe he didn't? Doubt started gnawing at her: only the other night she'd dreamed of her husband in karaoke bars and the things he was getting up to with sluts; though they might go by a different, fancier name in those parts—Miša couldn't remember the exact word—she was quite sure they were just sluts, engaging in slutty practices.

After the routine call was over she sat in the kitchen until late at night, and as the light of a small lamp above the freezer illuminated her hands and fingers, and long shadows crept along the floor and the opposite wall, Miša wondered why this had to happen to her, of all people. Actually, not just to her, to Jano as well—but Jano didn't have an inkling of it. Or did he? Was he lying in a hotel bed somewhere with an inkling? Was he on the twentieth or thirtieth floor of a skyscraper, in the middle of negotiations, with an inkling?

Miša had grown up in a family where nothing ever appeared

behind the TV set. Her parents had never even mentioned such a possibility to her, though they were happy to discuss in her presence the petty scandals involving their neighbors or people at work. But perhaps they'd had it in their bedroom too. Their daughter had never been allowed to go in there. Could it have been in their bedroom? Did they take it along when they went on vacation? On one of those outings they used to go on, leaving their daughter with her grandma in the countryside?

She went to the hallway and called a friend from the landline, for she felt the need to discuss this unexpected problem with somebody. A few sentences into the conversation she replied, baffled:

– You mean I should go and see a psychiatrist?

– Of course. You've got to. What if you're just imagining it all?

– You mean . . . hallucinating? You really think I'm hallucinating?

– But what if it isn't there at all? From what you're saying, it's almost the size of a wardrobe . . . Could something like that even fit behind the TV set?

– Soňa, believe me, it's there!

– I doubt it. Look, you know Dr. Monty . . .

– The one with the beard?

– No, the one who goes to the Irish Pub.

– Where does he sit?

– Right at the back, underneath the speakers.

– I don't know him at all.

– Well then you know the other one, what's his name . . . help me out . . .

– You mean Dr. Ráthé?

– Exactly.

– But he's not a psychiatrist, he's a psychologist.

– All right, all right, a psychologist might do for starters . . .

– What do you mean, for starters? It's as big as a wardrobe and you're calling this starters?

– I've already told you there's no way it could be as big as a wardrobe. Just calm down. I'm sure it's much, much smaller.

– So how big do you think it is?

– Let's agree it's the size of a matchbox, at most. It's absolutely tiny.

– Listen . . . How about you come and take a look?

– That's out of the question. I can't.

– Why? Look, come over! Please! Help me.

– But how?! What's this got to do with me? And anyway, I'm in a complicated situation.

– I don't understand.

– . . .

– What is it? Can't you talk?

– Uhm.

– All of a sudden you can't talk when I need you to do me a favor. Can't you even whisper?

– I can do that. But what am I supposed to whisper? You'd better go and check again . . .

– But I've been watching it the whole time. Actually . . . not the whole time, just now I was looking out of the window . . . and . . . by the door to the hair salon . . . you know where I mean . . .

– Of course I do. By the door. So what's there?

– There . . .

– C'mon, what is it?

– Nothing! Nothing at all! Don't you understand? It's not there. It's only here, behind the TV. Why don't I imagine it's out there, too, if I'm only imagining it? Let me tell you why: because it just isn't out there, only here. And you were lying.

– How was I lying?

– When you said you could only whisper. Just now you were so curious about what was there by the door to the hair salon that you started shouting. Out of curiosity. And the only reason you found it so fascinating was because you go to that salon yourself. So the only time you're willing to listen to me, without accusing me of being crazy, is when it involves you too?

The phone call ended on a rather uneasy note.

Miša sat down at the kitchen table, picked up a mirror, and examined the pale skin of her pale face. It shone in the kitchen night. The eyes, the nose, the mouth, the corners of the mouth. Thoughtfully, Miša went on to examine her shoulders, chest, and legs. It would have been almost impossible to distinguish the whole from other wholes of this kind. Or perhaps only sometimes, thanks to the clothes, the situations in which they were discarded, by a particular whole's way of being naked. Way of being naked? Yes: see yourself for who you are! Step in front of the mirror, get to know yourself from the outside, but intimately! Let the inside follow. Follow the inside!

Miša stood up and sat down again.

She was sitting on her backside in the kitchen again.

Jano came home a few days later, left his bags in the hall, took off his shoes, went to the bathroom, took a shower, and, after thoroughly drying himself with a big thick bath towel, headed for the living room. She was waiting for him by the door. Thinking of the sluts and the karaoke. And also of herself, her role. Was she supposed to float up into the sky now, all dreamy-eyed and happy? Or should she let barbiturates, medication, or a psychiatrist take care of everything? She stepped back a little to let Jano pass. He sat down in the armchair and switched on the TV with the remote. The flickering blue light carved objects out of the dark.

That's when Jano spotted it.

It was moving slowly, sinister and inevitable. Jano didn't say anything. His face looked like a mask stretched on a rack of bone. Only when his wife whispered hysterically to him did he respond, commenting that, in his view, it made the living room even cozier than before, covering himself with his statement as though it were a precious Tibetan rug. Miša ran out of the block and called Soňa on her cellphone. She was panting:

– I know everything!

– What do you know?

– It's turned up at your place too! That's why you can't talk! It's watching you! It's listening to you! It's growing!

– . . .

– Don't you have anything to say to that?

– I told you I can't talk.

– Well, whisper then.

– Yes, it turned up here too. But that was a long time ago. It's stopped growing now, although, I admit, it's not getting any smaller either. We've gotten used to it. As it is. Look, I know how you feel. It's not easy to come to terms with the new situation at first . . . But is it really new? Okay, I know you never counted on this. You didn't expect . . . didn't visualize it quite like this. What woman would expect such a thing? I was hoping it wouldn't happen to you—to you and Jano. Last time you called, I thought you might be exaggerating a little. Because in our place it didn't grow quite so fast! Petó and I had been together for six years by the time we first noticed it! But times have changed, life is moving faster . . . I know I'm probably not putting it well, but the fact is, the world's gotten faster, so that you and Jano . . . Even though you've only been together for two years—it's been two years, hasn't it? Or three? Anyway, for some reason it's happening faster. Oh dear, I guess I am just behind the times.

– Soňa, I love you, you're my only friend. But why did you have to keep this secret from me, of all things?

– I'm telling you: I was hoping it wouldn't happen to you!

– And what about your parents? At home, when you were growing up . . . Did they have a problem too? You know what I mean.

– Of course. Nearly every family on our estate had it. I remember the Kropáčs, they had to move out because of it: it simply pushed them out of their apartment. One morning it was sticking out into the hallway. Can you imagine how delicate the situation was? Actually existing socialism, and you've got something sticking out of your apartment door? And you and your children have to sleep on the stairs? Well, my parents took their children in for a few days, the kids stayed in my room, but I didn't like them, they cried all the time. By the way, it eventually turned out to be a blessing in disguise for the Kropáčs: it followed them everywhere; in the end they were staying in a workers' dormitory in Smíchov, in Prague, but one night, after it caused a scandal by swelling up, making the whole house burst, waking up half the city of a thousand spires, they took a radical step: emigration. Now they have a wonderful life in the West, she's living in Italy with the kids and he's somewhere in Switzerland. They split up as soon as they crossed the border. Don't you get it? It was a question of life and death. But actually, in cases like this, it's always a question of life and death.

– But why did Mom never even hint at it?

– That's what women are like: though we can see—right from the beginning, actually—how things happen and how they're going to end, inevitably, we keep hoping . . . and making the same mistakes. We just don't learn our lesson. Typically. Not even seeing the way that our own parents have ended up prevents us from letting the same thing happen to us and our children. From their earliest days we push them toward doing the same thing to their kids when the time comes. It's like some compulsion, can't you feel it?

– Soňa! I thought I was going round the bend!

– That's right. You are going round the bend, but nobody will notice you're mad. It's a collective madness. You're no different from anyone else. How can you diagnose madness if everyone is mad?

Miša had no idea.

For weeks she just moped around the apartment.

She could see it was watching her intently from behind the set. Or rather, not from behind but from underneath the TV, which by now was floating on top of it, swaying from side to side like a vacationer on an air-mattress.

Miša stood on the balcony.

Miša leaned against the stove.

Miša even dreamed of going for a hike in the genuine, unadulterated countryside.

And wherever she happened to be, she wondered what it was that she and Jano actually wanted from one another. Wherever she might be she also wondered how she could get into the closet where she kept her large suitcase from before she was married, because by now it was cluttering up the whole room, blocking the way to the closet. And when it got especially bad, between the thirteenth and fourteenth cigarette, between a wistful stare from the balcony down to the street and at the skyscraper opposite—into the windows of prison cells similar to her own—between calm resignation and quiet horror, in addition to other, more important and essential things, Miša also thought that you need a partner to close the clasp on your necklace, and that you need a necklace to find a partner.

TRANSLATED FROM SLOVAK BY JULIA SHERWOOD

ŽARKO KUJUNDŽISKI

When the Glasses Are Lost

It was a stifling summer outside when suddenly everything stopped. The faces of the little girl and her father went pale; maybe the father was even more terrified than the little girl. She wasn't able to recognize real fear, nor was she aware of the danger of the situation; she only felt that her father's grip had suddenly become tighter, and this caused her face too to turn white as a sheet. As for the others: the tall fellow—destined always to experience life from so presumptuous a height—was wobbling to such a degree that he had to lean on the inside wall with his elbow. Actually, he wasn't so much leaning as bumping against the wooden surface of the wall, taking advantage of its proximity to avoid collapsing onto the floor. The elderly couple were huddling together quietly and moving gradually into the corner, as if trying to conceal themselves. The remaining four—the soldier, the man with the beard, the woman in red, and the man in the suit—were dispersed in all directions; one fell down, the other hit his forehead on the edge of the panel with the buttons, the third tumbled onto the floor, and the fourth pulled at the tall man's sleeve and stumbled forward.

Out of all of them, the woman in red, with the pierced navel, responded to the event the loudest, letting out an inarticulate sound followed by a salvo of curses, but nobody objected—as they might have done under different circumstances. The man with the beard, who knew precisely what was happening, continued to lie soberly on the ridged, rubber floor, caressing the hairs of his beard with his fingers. The gentleman in the suit—a striped jacket and trousers of indeterminate color—quickly stood up again and looked at his expensive watch, demonstrating to everyone else that he was in a terrible hurry to get somewhere. The soldier was the only one with his fleshy hands on his forehead, in noticeable pain, although he had in no way admitted defeat. After the first wave of shock had passed, the father concluded that the elevator was indeed stuck. The rest of them neither confirmed nor rejected this conclusion. It seemed too soon for them to replace their usual formal head-nodding on stepping into the elevator or stingy salutations when exiting with alarm, sympathy, and unity in a common cause. But it wasn't long before it seemed that everybody, except the two silent old people, had accepted the reality that they would have to communicate and work together.

The man with the beard suggested pressing the emergency button, but, as was the case with all the other elevators in the town, nobody believed that it would actually work, despite what the law required. Maybe one of them even put his thumb on that big round circle, without the least hope that this would lead to an observable result. Wanting to determine the altitude at which they were stuck—as if that would solve part of the problem—they tried to guess the floor they were on. At first, the digital readout only showed two eights, indicating that the power supply had been interrupted, throwing off its calculation. The soldier smacked the number display and then rapped on it with his knuckles; perhaps we might see these attacks as the expression of some naïve thirst for vengeance on his part? However, not only did the screen still refuse to display their vertical location, it now lost even those few flickers of life it had retained.

The passengers began a verbal inquiry; the last person who'd come in, the tall fellow, who was sitting at the rear of the car—he'd gone to the back, since his destination was the top floor—confirmed that he'd entered the elevator on the tenth floor. Now they were all asking each other on which floor they'd joined the party, and where each had planned to exit the elevator, and concluded finally that they must be somewhere between the tenth floor and the fourteenth—the destination of the father and his little daughter.

The father, a doctor, holding the little fingers of his daughter tightly, went up to the soldier after a while and looked at his bruised forehead in the dim elevator light. The doctor examined the head of the man in uniform, and told the soldier that his injury couldn't be treated in these conditions, and all they could do was try to make him comfortable. They looked for a hard object to bandage against the soldier's bump, which looked like a small horn growing on a newborn calf. Not having too many other options, the doctor's daughter pointed to the soldier's belt where a gun hung in a white holster that would have been more or less level with her head. The soldier reached for his gun slowly and bashfully, checked the safety, and put the handle on his forehead. The sudden coldness surprised him and he dropped the weapon. It bounced off of the door and fell on the floor. Some of the passengers looked at each other silently—keeping their fears to themselves. The woman in red was the first to reach for the gun. But rather than give it back to the frightened and clumsy soldier, she went up to him and pressed the handle to his reddened skin herself. Yet, it didn't bring him relief; on the contrary, now he was embarrassed as well as in pain.

The old lady whispered something to her husband and he kneeled on the floor and started poking around the man with the beard (who, meanwhile, had informed the others that he was a painter); soon the old man was squeezing carefully through the other people's legs. The old lady explained that the sudden stop had caused her glasses to fall off, and she'd only just realized that they were missing. Some of the other passengers kneeled then too, wanting to help the old man, who was still on his knees, impressing the younger people in the elevator with his endurance and persistence. The number of people in the car blocked a lot of the light from the weak fluorescents, their silhouettes casting numerous shadows—a deep darkness on the floor that made their joint quest significantly more difficult. The man in the striped suit—a dandy, really—didn't pitch in with the search, but instead started calling for help. He started yelling various names, as if he knew important building personnel who were in charge of keeping the place running day to day. No matter the volume, it was all in vain. The building's elevators had only been recently installed and they were, as it was said, absolutely cutting edge. They had thick walls and solid insulation, which kept their movements perfectly quiet— an utter joy. Nothing like those rickety, terrifying, ancient elevators you find in older buildings, their decrepit mechanisms straining to pull vibrating cords tied to old tin cans up musty tunnels. No, these new models moved quickly and silently, and always stopped with the utmost gentleness. They gave the passengers a feeling of trust and security.

But everyone present had no choice but to accept the fact that the system wasn't working properly—perhaps a flaw in the installation process? Soon enough, when he noticed that his yells were useless, the man in the suit started to slam his open palms violently against the closed metal doors—something of a shock for everyone else. When he figured out that even this wasn't loud enough, he lifted his briefcase and he started to smack its tiny wheels against the silvery, mirrored surface. The echoes from this latest assault bounced all over the elevator car, occupying every plane and angle, and inciting even more unrest among his fellow passengers.

Suddenly, the tall fellow grabbed the dandy's hands. Having gotten his attention, the giant then pointed toward the little girl, who was covering her ears with her hands and looking at them both in confusion. Her father tried to convince the panicking gentleman to apologize to the girl for the scene he was making, but the dandy refused, explaining that he was doing what he was doing for the collective welfare and common interests of all the stranded passengers. The doctor didn't give up, however, but continued in dignified persistence until their juvenile bickering turned into a heated argument. This was the first actual fight of their ordeal, and it put everyone even more on edge.

Moments later, when he realized that he'd already missed his meeting, the man in the suit removed his jacket, holding it in one hand while still clutching his briefcase in the other, as though there was something strictly confidential in it. The other passengers began to indicate that the temperature, which should have been regulated by the ventilation system, was now increasing in waves, each even more unbearable than the last; they had to do something about that. Most of the men removed some layer of their clothes, and loosened their ties if they had one—or, if they didn't, like the painter, they rolled up their pants. The old lady pulled out an electric hand fan and started whirring it in front of her face, turning it to her husband's from time to time, letting her husband work it when she got tired of holding it up. Everyone else was wiping their dewy foreheads with everything within reach—their sleeves or facial tissues that they'd been keeping in their pockets, thinking that they would never need to use them—everyone, that is, except for the soldier and the woman in red, who were chatting incessantly now on various subjects. At that particular moment, the soldier was explaining to the girl how his gun worked, how to switch the safety on and off, how to aim and shoot—things that he wouldn't be talking about so nonchalantly in other circumstances. The father interrupted them, saying that it would be appropriate to try, for a change, to keep quiet and listen, in case anything was happening outside—whether the elevator next to theirs was moving, for example, or whether they might be able to hear any workers trying to fix whatever malfunction had stranded them all there. They were longing to hear the updates and instructions that rescue teams would surely be calling out, discussing their prognosis and planning the best possible way to get them out of there.

Except for the rumblings of their bodies and the clicking of the old couple's dentures, however, there still wasn't a sound to be heard. By now the old man had already stated his hypothesis that the tall fellow was the culprit. Despite everyone's reasonable rejoinders, the old man blamed the tall fellow and his capricious decision to force himself upon the collective in the elevator for stranding them in this situation; the elevator must have had a weight limit, and the tall fellow must have caused an overload. On account of his being the cause of all of their troubles, the old man then demanded that the tall fellow—who had since revealed that he was a historian—tell everyone some stories, which would put their own unfortunate situation into the proper perspective. So he presented their time in the elevator as historically inevitable and spoke about the old legends, for instance when the galleys of the Githiesh navy got lost in the Salzburg Sea and so couldn't take part in the battle of Getersburg, providing sea support to their infantry. Later, however, when the sailors worked together, and all the captains coordinated their movements, they surprised the enemy from behind, and thus defeated them utterly. The tall fellow would have certainly continued to dig through these musty catacombs if the well-dressed gentleman, who had been grinding his teeth all the while, hadn't suddenly—after ferociously mashing his cell phone's keypad—put his phone to his ear. Not a word was spoken, until this small cause for hope was extinguished as well: no signal.

It would have been one thing had the tenants in the building simply not cared about the passengers trapped in the elevator—that wouldn't have concerned them quite so much—but the fact that there had been no sign of life, that not a single sound had penetrated the car, and that the passengers had been unable to get a single message through . . . this seemed to threaten their assumptions and beliefs about the state of the world they'd so recently left. Time was passing, and soon the woman in red, who was sitting on the floor with her back against the wall and her hands wrapped around her knees, declared quite loudly that she was about to faint from starvation. The soldier had leaned his head on her and was already dozing off. Swallowing his self-importance, the well-dressed man addressed the group as a whole, concluding that the day must now be over: it was probably night outside. The passengers had long since begun licking their dry lips, hoping to relieve their increasing thirst, and it was then that the artist pulled a liter water bottle out of his bag, and, after taking the first sip, passed it on to the others. When he was first offered a sip from the bottle, the man in the suit politely—albeit with a grimace—declined; a little later he was quick to grab the bottle and fiercely drink down what was left. The water seemed to calm the passengers down, and now they all lay down on the floor—inasmuch as this was possible—which had seemed wide enough at first, but now felt much smaller. Except for the soldier, who would occasionally wake up to keep an eye on his fellow prisoners, and the little girl, who kept complaining to her father—even though he was doing his best to placate her by telling her stories, patiently and quietly—the others soon fell asleep.

The snoring and the deep sighs that came from the passengers on the floor mixed with other bodily sounds, until the entire group sounded like a small, joyful band. Some of them bumped their heads together accidentally, or pushed aside their neighbor's belongings, but overall there was no hostility, no angry shoves. This temporary respite didn't last long, however: their peaceful dreams were interrupted by a jarring bang. Almost everyone jumped to their feet, save for the artist and the man in the suit, who—as if stuck to each other—didn't budge. With messy hair and bleary eyes, they rose toward the light of the elevator's ceiling; this time they looked at each other not with suspicion, but terror. Now several of them mentioned that they had to answer the call of nature. For a while they were wondering just what to do about this, until the tall historian came up with the idea to use the empty water bottle while the rest covered their eyes or turned their backs. Then they all fell asleep for the second time.

There were no outbursts of desperation come morning, only the gurgling noises of their empty stomachs, like abandoned kittens mewling on someone's porch, permeating the car. Their shared vulnerability had turned into a mutual compassion and softened their lonely hearts. The woman in red went on and on about some recent events in her neighborhood. Reminiscing remorsefully about her lack of sympathy for a stray dog that had been playing in front of her building, she promised she would mend her ways once they got their lives back. Now they all started to evoke similar poignant memories from their lives, as if standing in front of some invisible adjudicator who would soon make a final decision about their destinies and allow only a few to go back to address their errors. Through these recollections they felt they were somehow guaranteeing their futures, giving evidence of their own worth—or their pretentions to superiority. After the soldier explained what had brought him out to the building the previous day, his companions concluded that he shouldn't have been there in the first place—he'd gotten the wrong address. But squeezed between the bodies of the father and the woman in red, who every so often was taking out a book and pretending to read attentively, the soldier didn't regret his mistake for a minute. The businessman, on the other hand, suddenly turned toward the old man and his wife, saying that he'd never liked old people and almost never let them cross the road, when he was driving—he'd zoom right into the crosswalk and cut them off. He demanded then that the old couple apologize in the name of their entire generation.

After they'd all purged their souls, they went silent again. The painter dozed off, snoring loudly. When they began to stir again, they noticed that the heat coming from the ventilation system had been replaced with cool air. It was blowing steadily from above and now everyone started to put their clothes back on and lie closer to each other. Some of them switched their seats, depending on their ability to tolerate the chill. Some time later, you could hear a sort of chewing sound coming from one of the elevator's corners, shortly enough followed by a loud smacking of lips. Those who were closer to the old man and woman could see for themselves, and those who were farther could simply sense that they were chewing candies without sharing. The woman in red crawled closer to them and begged for some. At first the old woman held tightly to her bag and wouldn't give in. She relented soon enough and opened her bag to give the woman a single nicely wrapped candy. This only served to reaffirm dislike of the old couple, especially given the way the doctor's young daughter was staring with watery eyes at the woman eagerly munching her prize.

A new ray of hope emerged when the elevator suddenly restarted, moving down one stop. And yet, they were all certain that—if, for some reason, the elevator resumed its travels—it should go up, not down. Still, this development reassured them that their ordeal—which had lasted more than twenty-four hours now—was nearing its end. The well-dressed businessman and the tall historian jumped to their feet and again started to yell out to their invisible saviors and bang uselessly on the doors with the soles of their shoes. This time no one complained. This supposed glimpse of light at the end of the tunnel made them increasingly impatient. For a while now, the painter had been scribbling lines on the smooth walls of the car, using a pencil he'd taken out of his pocket. He claimed to be an artist, but, in fact, his drawings seemed more like imperfections being introduced onto the surface of the hitherto spotless elevator, which, until then, had been shining like a crown jewel. But such purity was lost on the car's current inhabitants, who were staring at the painter without complaining or criticizing his sketch. The painter was scrawling from the floor to the ceiling, slowly turning their dungeon into a sort of scribbled whirlwind that they all felt they were being drawn into as time went by. To them it seemed that these lines were the only thing expressing their situation—cold, hungry, thirsty, tired—forced to contend with all the fallacies that their current ambiguous state brought into relief. It was because of this that the painter—who hadn't said a word since beginning his drawing—became an object of renewed suspicion, since the passengers would have dearly liked to find someone to blame for their predicament. Spitefully, though with curiosity as well, they began to question the bearded man. The old woman accused him of stealing her misplaced glasses when she'd been unable to find them on the floor. The historian, who'd previously blamed everything on the inevitability of history, questioned the painter's decision to keep his water bottle a secret for so long. And the old man concluded that only the painter seemed as though he'd been fully prepared for this incident. The soldier, the woman in red, and the father and daughter all refused to take part in this new trial, only mumbling quietly on occasion, as if trying to douse this fire. It was the father who eventually succeeded in calming everyone down by saying that it was useless to worry about who was responsible for the accident, and how it would make more sense to do so afterward, when they got out. But—they realized he'd said "when" instead of "if." This was somehow the final blow. Exhausted and tired, they all gave up on the idea of being rescued. The soldier and the woman in red were hugging each other; he was playing with her belly-button ring while she was tracing the tattoo on his left forearm. The little girl finally calmed down and sat in her father's lap, while the painter gave up on his drawings and dropped his blunt pencil onto somebody's shoe, without checking whose.

The old man was exhaling into his wife's hands to warm them up—the least he could do. Although it was cold in the car, the man in the suit had already begun to make himself a bit too comfortable; he'd dropped his suit jacket onto the floor, loosened his tie, unbuckled his belt, and even taken off the expensive watch that he'd been staring at so often in the dusky elevator light. Almost half-naked, he then leaned back, stretched out across the elevator's door like a gatekeeper. They were all petrified, just waiting for his performance to end and the curtain to fall.

The following morning, the elevator finally moved up. As if some mysterious crown wheel had finally loosened, the elevator cut silently through a thick layer of air. At first, the passengers who were awake— or who were only half-asleep—thought that they were imagining things, that they were hallucinating, and that this meant they were on their last legs. Soon enough they realized that they were actually moving, but they couldn't decide if the elevator was simply moving up to the next floor, where they were initially supposed to stop, or if it was headed for the very top of the skyscraper, or if perhaps it was about to drop back down into an eternal abyss. Regardless of what was happening—as the elevator rapidly accelerated—no one had any intention of detaching themselves from one another; their bodies were more or less glued together. Likewise, they had no intention of preparing themselves to make their long-awaited reentry into the civilized world with dignity. All they did was sit still, with no expectations at all, just sitting quietly and breathing heavily.

They only moved when the doors opened in front of them, but

only to close their eyes, or cover them with whatever was at hand. An emergency team jumped right in, making sure everyone was okay. The passengers clung to the elevator's walls as if caught on fish hooks and grabbed onto each other's arms, making it difficult for the emergency team to coax them out onto stretchers. Even as they were exiting one by one, the paramedics couldn't help but notice that the members of the now disbanded group were all trying to reach out to each other, perhaps waving weakly, as though hoping to schedule their next meeting as they passed each other in the hallway. Indeed, the presence of all these newcomers evoked a look of fear, uncertainty, and suspicion in the passengers' eyes, as if the emergency crew had been sent with the express purpose of separating their little band from whatever invisible and mysterious feeling that their captivity had created, and which was now likely to be taken away from them.

When there was no one left in the elevator, and the ambulance sirens could no longer be heard, a lady with various soaps and detergents, a rag, a scrub brush, and a bucket full of water walked into the empty car. With her wet rag, she started to wipe away the thick, full lines of the drawings that covered the interior of the elevator like unobtrusive armor. Once she saw how tenacious the pencil marks were going to be, she tried to scrub them with her thick brush and some whitish powder. While bending over to rinse off her brush, she saw an old pair of glasses in the corner, seemingly abandoned, but she didn't make any effort to pick them up.

TRANSLATED FROM MACEDONIAN BY
NIKOLCHE MICKOSKI AND ELENA MITRESKA WEISS

DRAGAN RADULOVIĆ

The Face

Winter in a seaside town like Budva has one advantage that makes all its shortcomings look ridiculous and insignificant—winter reduces people, things, and events to their true proportions, brings everything to light and makes it a topic of conversation. I know people who don't like the winter, who are bored; but they don't do anything to give meaning to their lives and instead wait for someone else to do it for them. Since that doesn't happen, their time becomes hungry, and the emptiness in their lives grows until nothing can fill it anymore. Those people feel winter is merciless: in summer they manage to hide away, but in winter that becomes impossible, and they show themselves just the way they are—unfit for life.

In winter the men of Budva fish, booze and play cards, work on their houses, discuss politics, renovate bars and cafés, lend money and charge extortionate interest, seduce other men's wives, and worry that their own might cuckold them . . . When you think about it, the "metropolis of Montenegrin tourism" only lives, in its own unique way, in winter. Whoever doesn't fit into the rhythm of the town is condemned to vegetate on its margins—same as they would be anywhere else. But in order to fit in they first have to master a parlor game that people are very fond of in Budva: gossiping. They're obliged to discover the attractive side of this sport and participate without worrying about the outcome. Petty souls see gossiping as something bad and unworthy, while connoisseurs of human values consider it an activity that brings people together and makes the town a more agreeable place to live. One local theoretician of winter social life, the freethinking Sniper, saw gossip as an inseparable part of the media landscape:

"Winter is a time when the men of Budva realize the ideal of direct democracy: everyone has a voice and the right to shape the sphere of public discourse through participation. And when they open the town television station everyone will get their own few minutes of fame on the screen," he stated categorically.

Waiting for those promised few minutes, one harsh December evening I found myself in Budva's best-known underground restaurant, Kod tužnog Tulipana (The Melancholic Tulip). Together with a few other card lovers I was playing round after exhausting round of Lora, drinking red wine, and waiting for the famous specialty of the house—Octopus Risotto in Mist. (Mists are actually extremely rare and short-lived in Budva, so this mist had nothing to do with the meteorological phenomenon; rather, it referred to the whitish film that covers people's eyes when they get mindlessly drunk and pass out.) Malicious tongues claimed that the culinary skill of Tulip, the restaurateur, began and ended with this dish, and there was nothing apart from the mysterious name to distinguish it from any other risotto—but no one ever complained. On the contrary, since Tulip only prepared this dish once a year, it was a question of prestige for the people of Budva to be seen in his restaurant on the occasion.

All the tables were occupied that evening. I saw many familiar faces—the cream of local government, business, and the culture scene; there were also some people I didn't know, ugly mugs who gave me a bad gut feeling. According to an established custom, dinner was served after midnight. As we ate we chatted casually, listened to the blues, and enjoyed the intimate, almost familial atmosphere of the restaurant—all up until one idiot (who Tulip then asked unambiguously to leave the premises) called on Gonzales to tell us all what happened to Geiger and why he died so suddenly.

As much as we adored gossiping about one another, there are some stories that one just does not tell: any inquiry about them is interpreted as an indecency, and the pryer loses his place in society and is branded untrustworthy. The story about what happened to Geiger had topped the town's list of forbidden topics for several years. A fellow I know confided in me while we were fishing for mackerel off Sveti Nikola Island that he'd heard the tale from Gonzales, but he wouldn't repeat it for me, even when I insisted. He said I wouldn't believe him, and he couldn't tell it well enough because he didn't understand everything. And again, I know several people who got a fistful of salt in the ass for having hassled Gonzales; he kept a sawn-off double-barreled shotgun without a buttstock under the seat of his wheelchair (which was the basis of the morbid joke behind his nickname—he was anything but Speedy). One barrel of the shotgun had a buckshot cartridge and the other was loaded with coarsely ground salt: just which barrel he discharged depended on the type of idiot who was giving him a hard time.

The question about Geiger made Gonzales flinch in his wheelchair; he hissed several curses to himself and in the direction of the overly curious fool, but when he saw Tulip give the fellow his marching orders he acted as if he hadn't heard and kept eating.

The evening went nicely, and when people were starting to go home, satisfied with Tulip's risotto, Gonzales asked Tulip and me to help him to the toilet. He was an athlete at drinking but disabled when it came to negotiating the urinal. When he'd finished and wheeled himself back to the table, he ordered a bottle of wine and invited me to join him. Tulip was busy clearing away the cutlery, a drunk was snoring at the lowest point of the restaurant with his head on the table, and Gonzales filled our glasses and took a deep breath.

"Fucking jerks! As if they were really interested in what happened to Geiger—they don't even deserve to hear his name!" Then he tilted his head to the side a little, gave me a probing glance through half-closed eyelids, as if he'd never seen me before, and asked:

"Does your brother stay in touch?"

"More or less," I replied, realizing it would be best not to show how much I disliked talking about my brother.

"How long has he got left now?"

"Seven years."

"What does he say? How are the jails in Australia? Does he have to kill kangaroos or make shoes for the Aborigines?"

"He doesn't complain."

Gonzales laughed. "A good guy, your brother. A bit of a hothead, and too harsh, but definitely good. We went to elementary school together, you know."

"He told me about that," I answered.

"What else did he tell you?"

"That if ever I needed anything, or got into any trouble, I could ask you for help."

"And so you can, whatever it is. Just tell me, and I'll sort it out."

I nodded and muttered a scant "Thanks."

"But you don't get into trouble—they say you're not like your brother at all . . ."

"No, I'm not," I replied.

"What do you mean you're not?" he asked.

"I don't get into trouble and I'm not like my brother at all." I probably repeated those words with a tinge of resentment in my voice, and Gonzales didn't fail to notice.

"Hey, just a bit of fun, sonny—no hard feelings. I like to tease people. It's all I've got left. And now pour us each another glass of wine and let's bury the hatchet, all right?"

I nodded and did as he suggested. For a while we drank in silence, then he asked out of the blue:

"Are you also interested in what happened to Geiger?"

I felt awkward because, by asking that question, he was putting me into his category of fucking jerks, but I simply couldn't say no. I was itching to find out, just like everyone else in Budva, so I aimed for the middle of the road:

"I'd like to hear, but if you don't want to talk about it—just forget it."

He withdrew into himself, evidently satisfied with the company he'd found, and showing no sign that my words had registered with him, and after a while he asked me what time it was.

"Ten past four," I replied.

"Do you need to go home? Are you late for something?"

I shook my head.

"Good—" said Gonzales, "I'll tell you what happened to Geiger. I feel like I need to tell someone tonight, and right now you're my best choice." He inhaled deeply several times, as deeply as he could, like a diver filling his lungs before the plunge. Then he reached into his shirt pocket, withdrew an almost new pack of cigarettes, took one out, and began:

"Geiger was in a particularly bad mood that evening. I could tell by his voice when he rang and suggested we meet at Kaktus Café. I was tired and not sure I really felt like going out at all; I'd spent the day trying to repair the boat's motor. But in the end I decided to go out—I needed a bit of company. Geiger was sitting out on the terrace at a table next to a big cactus and sipping his whiskey; his mobile phone lay blinking with its green cyclops eye next to his pack of cigarettes. After we'd said hello he stewed in silence; he only waved to the waiter, and when the fellow finally lumbered up to the table he ordered 'two doubles.' I didn't object, although I would have preferred a beer. But, ultimately, what did it matter? It didn't make any difference what I got blasted on that night. Several attempts to engage in conversation with Geiger simply failed. Whatever I asked, he'd reply curtly and unwillingly, and when what I was saying didn't demand a direct answer, he didn't listen at all.

"'Have you seen Kefir?' I asked.

"'I called him shortly after talking with you. He promised he'd come later.'

"Good, we'll wait for him, I said to myself—maybe he'll be less grumpy and more in the mood for a chat. I'd hold out for a bit longer, I thought, and then if Kefir still hadn't arrived I'd go home for a bit of shut-eye. I felt weariness creeping over me and was starting to feel sick of it all. Just as I was beginning to sink into gloom and despondency, Kefir turned up at the gate and yelled jovially:

"'Whereya been, ya freaks?'

"I couldn't think of what to say back, but Geiger obliged:

"'Up shit creek. Whereya been yourself, ya moron?'

"The question was part of the standard repartee and didn't require an answer, so Kefir didn't reply; he just said hello, looked at the table to see what we were drinking and, satisfied with what he saw, signaled to the waiter to repeat the order—this time with one more glass.

"Kefir's arrival enlivened the conversation, if you could call it that at all, since he talked incessantly, while Geiger mumbled to himself and I expended the last of my energy trying to stay awake. And I definitely would have fallen asleep if there hadn't suddenly been an uproar: a blockhead passing by our table with a few mugs of beer and a glass of tomato juice tripped on a bump in the floor, lost his balance, and spilled the drinks all over Geiger's shirt and pants. Geiger didn't quite realize what had happened at first, but when he saw the red stains on his clothes he smiled and slowly began to get up from the table with an expression on his face that seemed to say: Oh, never mind, these things happen: just apologize and everything's fine.

"But Kefir and I knew very well what was brewing: Geiger had decided to beat the cretin up; he just didn't want to frighten him with a yell and have him run away before he got his thrashing. We saw it coming: the cretin fumbled around at our feet, muttering a paltry apology, trying in vain to clean the blotches off Geiger's pants with a tissue. Kefir held onto Geiger while I urged the poor fellow to move before it was too late. But he didn't listen and bent down to reach the patches on Geiger's lower trouser legs—just in the right position for Geiger to deliver a mighty kick in the head. We heard the sickening thud of the shoe connecting with his face. He recoiled and fell down on the floor, and the waiter reached for the phone to call the police. None of the cretin's buddies showed any inclination to stand up for him. Kefir went up to the bar, paid the bill, and impressed upon the waiter that he keep this to himself. Then we left the café.

"We loitered around town for a while and peeped into a few bars, but there were none that took our fancy. As glum and silent as Geiger had been earlier, he now chattered incessantly and laughed just for the sake of it. Kefir and I looked at him like he was loony at first, but soon we started laughing too, especially when he imitated the cretin bending down and fumbling with his tissue. All in all, it had been an eventful evening out.

"It was getting toward the wee hours and we were tired of walking and complaining that none of us had come into town by car. Just as we were about to go our separate ways, Geiger suggested we spend the rest of the evening at his place.

"'But it's late,' Kefir objected.

"'Come off it—you call this late?' Geiger argued.

"'Shall we?' Kefir asked me, not wanting to decide.

"'If the idiot wants to listen to our whinging and has a bottle of whiskey on offer—I'd say we go!' I resolved.

"Every time I went to Geiger's place I was surprised, as if I'd never seen it before. The space he lived in didn't appeal to me at all. Back then I didn't know why I felt so uncomfortable, and when I finally found out it was too late to do anything about it. Geiger had studied architecture and was one of the best students of his generation. People who understood the town's needs predicted a successful career for him, but unfortunately nothing came of it. In the early nineties, every turd from Podgorica and Belgrade who'd made it rich had to have an apartment in Budva (it was a question of power!), yet the developers' mafia didn't find my friend a suitable associate. Once I asked him why, and he replied that their interests didn't square with any serious definition of architecture. 'Any silly bugger with a diploma can design those sterile holiday hovels,' he spat, and added after a moment's reflection: 'I hate this town from the bottom of my heart, believe me, but I don't hate it as much as they do!'

"After his father's death, Geiger sold off several plots of land and used the money to build a four-story building in the center of town. He designed it himself, in fact I think it was his only building. He used every square meter rationally: the first floor was reserved for commercial use, and the floors above accommodated offices and luxurious rental apartments, where his skill found its fullest expression. But his apartment at the top of the block confirmed a side of his personality that was completely incomprehensible to me and that I long considered the capriciousness of a wealthy man. This penthouse was a single, huge space of over one hundred square meters, with walls seven meters high. The kitchen installed in one corner was fully equipped and always immaculately clean, as if never used. The bathroom and toilet were housed in a rectangular room of dark glass at the other end of the main space. On the northern wall there hung six large graphics on one and the same theme—they showed different stages of the birth of a monster. They were repulsive and painful to look at but you couldn't take your eyes off them. On the opposite wall were shelves crammed full of books from various fields, mostly architecture as you'd expect. Beneath the shelves were several armchairs, a richly inlaid mahogany table, and a stereo. In the middle of the penthouse stood a table of hewn stone, which, to be exact, was more like an altar than a desk or table. Five pillars were arranged in a circle around it and supported a dome, also made of stone, with an oculus one meter in diameter in the middle, directly above the table. It all looked stupid and useless to me, nothing but an ostentatious waste of living space. But now I'm convinced that Geiger had the house built for the sole purpose of erecting that dome on top of it.

"Kefir and I slumped into the armchairs while Geiger pottered around at the fridge, trying to ferret a few ice cubes out of its innards. Presently he came up carrying a bottle of whiskey, a pot of ice, and three glasses. For an hour, or an hour and a half, we listened to music, Nick Cave and Swans, and smoked one joint after another. We talked about life, the universe, and everything to a constant flow of alcohol until one of the two idiots opened a Pandora's box of questions—it must have been Kefir because he was browsing through the books in Geiger's collection. One of the titles probably induced him to start a highly intellectual discussion on a metaphysical topic: Did evil exist in the world, and if so, what was its nature? Was it something fundamentally and substantially separate from good or just a paucity of good—when the quantity of good tends toward zero? If God was our guarantee for the existence of good (as the ancient books say), did evil also have an authorized representative on earth? If so, was this representative on a par with God? If not, if he was subordinate, was this because of his inability to create, given his limitedness, meaning he could only spoil what had already been created and turn things into their opposite? If that were the case, didn't good ultimately have to give its prior consent for parts of creation to be unmade, which would clearly mean it was abandoning its prior nature? Or was that not necessarily so? So how much freedom of will was involved, and in what way?

"The discussion gradually began to turn into a battle and they engaged in polemics about whether good could change its scope and quality or whether it was eternally immutable, unlike evil, which possessed the power to grow and transform. Accordingly, if we note that evil has prevailed, that doesn't mean good has diminished or disappeared—it remains constant—but only that evil has amplified its possibilities on an enormous scale and fully obscured good. But there's another side to the coin: that which possesses the power to grow so quickly and completely conceal its real nature, without any visible trace to counter that impression, is, inevitably, quickly expended and vanishes. But the breaking down of demonic simulacra is a process that often lasts several human lives, so the 'quickness' of the process is no consolation.

"I knew that evil is fascinating, can charm people, and is absolutely entertaining; I also knew it's much more interesting than good, which can be so bland and banal as to make you sick; but I'd never thought about good and evil as seriously and with the passion that my friends did that evening. The matter is much simpler for me: I do good when I can and bad when I have to, which I suppose is a weak excuse, but I have no other, so it'll have to do. The discussion they were having therefore didn't interest me, and soon I didn't understand anything they were saying anymore. Only later—to be exact: after Geiger bequeathed me his manuscripts and books—did I develop an interest, and then every new realization acquired in the light of what had occurred that evening only added to my anxiety and fear.

"Geiger was quick-witted and excelled at debate, I knew that, so it greatly surprised me how well Kefir countered him, and on several occasions his clever remarks undermined Geiger's argumentation. I could tell this by the way Geiger had to struggle to defend his position; Kefir would immediately see how flawed it was and shoot it full of holes. I tried to interrupt them but that proved impossible. The discussion was of great significance for them both, although the reason escaped my comprehension, and, realizing I could do nothing, I went out onto the terrace so at least I wouldn't have to hear them anymore. I wondered if we'd made a mistake by not simply separating and going home to bed, or if at least I had, seeing as I needed to keep repairing the boat the next day, and being tired and drunk like this I'd sleep all day and everything I'd planned would come to nothing. But at one point there was quiet in the house and it drew me back inside. The two had finished philosophizing, so I could return. I heaved a sigh of relief.

"I found them sitting in their chairs, empty-eyed and tired.

"'It's time to go,' I said, but they didn't hear me. The words passed through them without a trace. 'Okay, guys, as you wish, but I'm going to get moving,' I threatened, yet I couldn't get up. A strange, leaden heaviness filled my body and weighed me down. This attack of weariness will soon pass, I thought. I reached out for my glass on the table, but halfway I changed my mind and slumped back into the armchair, my shoulders bumping against the backrest. I felt a dull emptiness in my head and the irresistible urge to vomit. I was sick of it all.

"Suddenly Kefir spoke, completely without warning:

"'You say they're always here: whenever two people are together, one of them is present as a third. That's what you said, isn't it?'

"Geiger raised his eyes: his face showed clearly how hard it was for him to reply, but he summoned the strength:

"'Yes, I used those words . . . You understood me correctly: wherever there are people, *they* are also present.'

"Kefir didn't give up: 'Does that mean we're not alone here this evening?'

"Geiger tried to smile but his smile turned into a canine grimace: 'We shouldn't overestimate our own importance—there's probably more interesting company than ours here tonight.'

"But Kefir decided not to relent: 'What would happen if one of them was here now? How would we recognize his presence?'

"While Geiger was thinking what to say, words shot out of my mouth without any prior thought: 'What would happen? What do you expect, Kefir—the end of the world?'"

At that point Gonzales looked around as if to make sure that everything was in the same place as when he started his tale. Tulip had finished the washing up and was now sitting behind the bar filling in a crossword, the drunk hadn't moved, and the fire in the hearth had burned to embers.

"Put on another log or two—" Gonzales said, "the mornings are terribly cold." I got up and did as he asked. When I sat down again I expected he'd continue the story but it seemed he was no longer inclined. We sat there in silence for a while, and when I started to get bored I decided to prompt him:

"And? What happened after that?"

He looked at me with a wry smile in the corner of his mouth.

"Nothing—" he said, "the light went out."

The expression on my face must have been pretty asinine because the gentle smile on his lips grew into a guffaw. How stupid of me, I cursed myself: Gonzales had found someone to pick on tonight. I was angry at him, but I didn't say anything. He did:

"I think my words were still in the air when we suddenly found ourselves in the dark. We couldn't see anything for a moment or two, but when the lights outside began to come in through the windows there certainly was something to see: in the middle of the room, right beneath the dome, there rose a regular-shaped cylinder of pulsating darkness. It moved quickly within the space bounded by the pillars but stopped and hovered next to each of them for a few seconds, as if gathering strength. Geiger got up and went toward the darkness, only to be stopped three yards from the closest pillar. He stood there utterly still, looking into the darkness before him, and then seized his head in his hands and fell to the floor without a sound.

"As soon as the light had gone out, Kefir had drawn his pistol and loaded a bullet into the barrel. That was evidently his habitual reaction to unfamiliar situations. He pointed his gun at the hovering darkness and muttered, 'Sweet, bloody heart'—his favorite imprecation.

"And me? I didn't budge from my seat. I wanted to flee but didn't have any control over my body. Imagine—I couldn't even close my eyes! It was as if I'd been destined to be there and see everything. I was a witness in this story.

"When he saw Geiger fall, Kefir fired two shots and was instantly thrown back against the wall; he slid to the floor and didn't get up. I heard laughter and growling, which grew louder with every passing second, and then I saw it—actually I only saw its face, eyes, and jaws, which exuded a colorless slime. The face (if that formless mass deserved that name) consisted of disarranged clumps of what looked like cooked meat. Bloated and stillborn, it changed its shape, while the eyes remained the same: filled with a cold gleam, and in their depths I sensed an inkling of satisfaction. The face was enjoying itself, as least inasmuch as we were interesting objects for its gratification. Soon I felt a terrible pain in my head—and then I heard the song: the meat of the face issued sounds and words in a language I'd never heard before. It sounded tender and ominous at the same time, intimate like a lullaby but incongruous with the horror that sung it. I lost consciousness, and now I'm so glad I did, because if I'd listened to that singing meat for one second longer I think I would have lost something much more valuable.

"Day had broken by the time I regained consciousness and gathered my wits. Geiger was lying on the floor and trembling with spasms that washed through his body in waves, while Kefir crouched next to him and moistened his forehead and chest with water. We didn't say anything: we waited for Geiger to come to so he could tell us what had actually happened.

"It was late afternoon before Geiger spoke, and what he said didn't please us at all:

"'If I'm right, and if that thing is what I think it is, we're in big trouble and aren't going to get out of it easily. I'm going to seek the help of someone who understands this sort of thing better than me, and until then it's best that the three of us not meet. When I find help—I'll let you know. I'm sorry.'

"We parted with insults all round, and even today I burn with shame when I think of it. But that's not important; what is, is that I realized that the apparition we saw wasn't a surprise for Geiger as it had been for Kefir and me; later—reading the documents he left about the dark side of architecture, specifically about the connection between space and the demonic, which he admits he started to delve into in the final years of his studies—I became convinced that what we saw was the result of his experiments: he'd invoked that creature on previous occasions only to meet it that night unprepared and suffer the consequences, as did we who were with him. Whether we were innocent or to blame doesn't matter a scrap now. We all bore part of the burden and paid a price commensurate with our stake in the game."

"What was the price?" I asked Gonzales.

"In a nutshell: Geiger died in hospital three months later, as dry as a stockfish, with the doctors unable to tell why his body kept losing fluids so quickly, what was draining the life from him. They played around a bit, tried this, that, and everything else, and came up with the craziest conjectures, but in the end they could only watch as he shriveled before their eyes. Kefir, on the other hand, was found on the beach six months after the event with two bullets in his body, his heart torn out, and minus his right hand. A friend who knows a few guys in the police said they all wondered why Kefir ended up like that, but when their surprise wore off they concluded that he'd probably gotten mixed up in the drug scene, made a mistake somewhere along the way, and ended up on a hit list.

"And me: one morning, nine months after that ghastly encounter, I discovered I couldn't get out of bed. My legs had gone numb. And since then I've been a modern version of a centaur—half human, half wheelchair."

"Didn't you want to know what was behind it all?" I asked him.

"There's no *behind*, sonny. *Behind* doesn't exist," Gonzales snarled, waving dismissively. "Everything is surface; it's just that a few places are terribly deep, and if you look too long, you think you see something there."

TRANSLATED FROM MONTENEGRIN BY WILL FIRTH

reality

LASHA BUGADZE

The Sins of the Wolf

"It's taken me ages to find your number. Two days I've been trying to call you."

"What can I do for you?"

Silence.

"Oh God, this is so embarrassing . . ."

"What was it you wanted?"

"It's embarrassing. Should I just say it?"

"Yes, go ahead."

Silence.

"You sound different on the phone."

"Do I know you?"

She laughs. "No, but I know you. I've seen you on TV."

I'm getting tired of this. "Right . . . What was it you wanted again?"

Silence.

"I really liked your book."

"Thank you. Which one?"

(Silence again—has she forgotten the title?)

"*The Sins of the Wolf.* I've read it twice already . . ."

"Thank you, that's very kind."

"Who are you talking to?" my wife asks.

"It was just so true to life, so realistic . . ."

She sounds like a young girl, and I can't work out what she wants. Does she want to be my friend? Does she want to send me something she's written? I mean, girls are always calling me to read me their poetry.

"Thank you."

Maybe I should hang up? Pretend we've been cut off?

"I feel really bad asking . . . Oh God, I'm sorry, but look . . ."

Down to business, finally!

"Yes, what is it?"

"I wouldn't normally bother you, but I just didn't know what else to do . . ."

"Who is it?" My wife pulls a face.

"Please, go on. I'm listening."

Silence.

"It's Bakar Tukhareli. I really need to see him. Can you put me in touch with him? Or give me his number?"

(Did I hear that right?)

"Sorry? I didn't catch that. Whose number?"

"Bakar Tukhareli's. You know, Bakar the Thief."

(She's having me on.)

"This is a joke, right?"

"What do you mean?"

"You're not serious?"

"What? Why?"

"Well, how am I supposed to introduce you to Bakar Tukhareli?" I look toward my wife and smile. But really I'm already starting to get angry.

"Why, don't you know him?"

"Okay, kid, you've had your fun. It was a good joke, very funny . . ."

"I wasn't joking . . ."

"Good-bye," I say and hang up.

"Who was that?"

"Some kid, wanted me to hook her up with the Thief."

"Which thief?"

"Mine, Bakar."

"Oh boy . . ." She laughs.

I was working on the third part of my trilogy. I needed to kill off the Gypsy Baron as quickly as possible and get my heroes safely to the coast. One dead body should have been plenty this time. In the second part (*The Sins of the Wolf*) there were so many bodies I almost lost track. In the end I actually counted them: 134 deaths in a five-hundred page novel. But no, that was too few for my publisher—he pretty much asked for one per page. Talk about bloodthirsty. His motto: new page, new corpse. When I took him the manuscript for *The Sins of the Wolf*, he asked me—and I'm not kidding—"How many are there?"

Almost as if he was joking. But he was actually dead serious.

"How many what?"

"Don't 'how many what' me. Bodies!"

"Loads."

"What do you call loads?" He wouldn't let it go.

And it was then that I knew that if I'd had eighty-six bodies in *The Pig Skin*—the first part of the trilogy—then this time I needed even more.

"Throw in another ten, some incidental ones," he said when he'd finished reading the manuscript.

He was still smiling at me. He was worried I'd laugh at him. But we talked about it anyway (again, almost jokingly), and he seemed absolutely convinced that it was because of the eighty-six bodies that *The Pig Skin* was such a bestseller. What could I say? Perhaps he had a point.

This time around I had a big surprise in store—the third part of the trilogy, *Children of the Sun*, was going to be completely different from the first two parts. Maggie was about to write a letter to absolve the criminal . . . and declare her love.

There were two things I was supposed to be doing that day: writing Maggie's letter and taking my twins to their first guitar lesson (my wife wouldn't back down on that one).

There she was, standing by the entrance to my building, smoking a cigarette. She was dressed like a boy, in jeans and a denim jacket, a black Charlie Chaplin T-shirt underneath. She wore a silver ring on her thumb.

As we came out of the building she called over to me:

"Excuse me!"

And she ran over. She looked like an angry dyke. At first, I actually thought she was a boy. Her gait seemed strange, somehow—almost ape-like. She hunched her shoulders too, like some street-corner hoodlum bending forward in the cold.

"I'm sorry to bother you," she said. "I phoned you the other day about Bakar . . ."

I realized who she was, but I asked her anyway, instinctively: "Bakar who?"

"Bakar the Thief. I asked you for his number . . . ?"

"Oh come on, honey," I said angrily, and shoved the twins toward the car. "Go take the piss out of somebody else."

"I swear on my brother's life, you've got it all wrong." She stood in front of me, her arms outstretched. "You said that to me last time too. You hung up on me before I could speak . . ."

There was a hidden camera somewhere, surely? I looked around again.

The twins were staring at me in astonishment.

"What do you want, kid? Have you got a bet with someone? Is that it?" I had to bite my tongue to stop myself swearing at her.

"The Baron did let him go, didn't he? He's not in hiding anymore and—I mean, that's what you wrote, isn't it?"

She was insane. It suddenly hit me. Her face was deadly pale, her lips were twitching nervously. She wasn't taking the piss; she was out of her mind.

My anger vanished. For a second I was afraid; I grabbed the twins' hands. Then I started to feel sorry for her . . .

"What did I write?" I asked her, almost sympathetically.

But she laughed. "No, I mean, what I said about him needing to be in hiding, it wasn't a question. I was just saying—I know that much at least . . ."

What was I supposed to do?

It was pure fantasy. Unfortunately, I had to disillusion her.

I spoke to her as a parent would a child. Tactfully. Warmly, even. "Listen, my dear. Bakar Tukhareli doesn't exist. I made him up. He never lived with the wolves and he never stole for the Baron. I made the Baron up too; he doesn't really exist either."

Silence.

"I'm sorry."

Do you know what made me say sorry? Her face. Her already ashen face had become even paler. She pulled back, as if I smelled bad. Strange as it may seem, she was looking at me with fear, irony, and compassion in her eyes, as if *I* was crazy—in other words, the same way I'd looked at her just a moment before, when I realized she was crazy.

And that's how we left it. Neither of us said another word. In fact, I just walked off. She never moved from the spot.

And I thought to myself that if there were two kinds of crazy people in this world—those who were wise with it and those who were just stupid—then she was probably the second kind.

I was sure I would never see her again, but I was wrong; I saw her again the very next day and in the very same place, right outside the entrance to my building.

"You think there's something not quite right about me, don't you," she said, "following you around like a spy? But I swear on everyone I know, living or dead, I really need to see him . . . What you said to me before—about him not existing—I've realized now why you said it. I'm not stupid. I'm not the first person to come to you asking for his number, am I? I bet they drive him mad . . . but I'm not like that . . . He just doesn't know me . . . How can I make you understand?"

(Well, do you understand?)

What was I supposed to do now? All I could think of was:

"Have you read *The Three Musketeers*?"

"What's that got to do with it?" Once again she looked offended.

"Answer me. Have you read it, yes or no?"

"Yes, I think so. I don't know."

"What about *Otar's Widow*?"

"What?"

"Didn't you go to school?"

"Why are you making fun of me?"

"I'm not making fun of you, honestly."

"Well, what's that got to do with anything, then?"

"Look, did you go to school?"

"So what if I did? Is there something wrong with that?"

"No, precisely the opposite."

"Okay, yes, I went to school. What's your point?"

"Well, did you do *Otar's Widow*? Or—I don't know—*Othello*?"

Silence.

"Do you think they're real, those people? You think Giorgi actually existed?"

"Which Giorgi?"

"Giorgi, the son."

"Whose son?"

"Otar's."

"What?"

"The son of Otar's widow . . ."

She looked at me with a smile on her face. She seemed to be more and more convinced I was mad.

And you know what? That made me angry again. But somehow I managed to just laugh.

"How old are you?" I asked her.

"Twenty."

(Well, that was a lie; she looked younger.)

"And do you know what it is that writers do?"

"What?"

"They make things up, don't they? You've read *The Sins of the Wolf*, right?"

"Yeah."

"I made it up. From start to finish. There's not a single character in it who really exists."

"Well then why did you write 'This is a true story' at the beginning?"

"It's just what writers do, isn't it . . .?"

(How could I explain?)

She smiled again. A sympathetic smile. A pitying smile.

But eventually my patience ran out. I was old enough to be her father, at the very least, and so with as much authority as I could muster I said to her in a low voice, "I swear on my own life that Bakar Tukhareli is not a real person, and may I be struck down if I'm telling a lie."

She actually jumped. She was dumbstruck . . . but only for a moment. Then she squinted at me again, suddenly, suspiciously.

"He should've played his ace. Then he wouldn't have needed to go into hiding."

(Even swearing on my own life hadn't done it!)

And then I realized she was referring to chapter seventeen, "The Casino Affair," where Bakar trumps Neron Pilpon's Jack of Hearts with his joker, and the Baron beats his ace with a second joker.

And now she'd made me angry with myself; I should have just laughed in her face! There's nothing worse than a reader with blind faith. She really would have believed anything I'd written.

Fine. If she wasn't going to believe me, what could I do?

There was no reasoning with her, but I still had to get away somehow. There was nothing else for it—I was going to have to pretend my character did exist after all.

I needed to draw a line here. Calmly, with no fuss, no irony . . .

Like this:

"Okay. There's nothing else for it. I'll tell you everything . . ." I paused. "I don't know where he is. I haven't heard from him in over a month."

She actually sighed. Oh my God, I'll never forget how she sighed, with such relief.

"Has he sold the car, the Opel Vectra?" she asked me, seriously, like some weary co-conspirator.

I nodded.

"Did Maggie call him?"

And then I saw it: she loved him, my Bakar Tukhareli, my thief. She was scared to ask that question more than any other, but she asked it nonetheless.

How her heart must have pounded in her chest, the poor thing!

I don't even know how to describe what I was witnessing; she was like some terrible enigma, this teenager, full of life, standing right in front of me, jealous of the lover of a man who existed only in my novel.

It was the stuff of fiction.

I felt sorry for her. I wanted to protect her.

"No, she never called. Edishera went to western Georgia instead."

She wasn't exactly pleased to hear this. Edishera was no less of a threat than Maggie (in *The Pig Skin*, he had shot Bakar three times, because while he was alive Edishera couldn't become a thief), but it seemed to calm her down anyway.

All she asked me was this: "So why did you swear a minute ago that he doesn't exist?"

She was right, that had confused things: neither she nor Bakar the Thief would ever have sworn such an oath unless they were certain it was the truth. What had I done? I had committed an unforgivable sin—the Gypsy Baron would have given me a beating for that—and cheapened the very act of swearing an oath, casting doubt upon its worth . . .

I suspect she just couldn't understand how Bakar had ever trusted *me*—such a faltering, inconsistent, and deceitful man. How could he have let someone like me write him, how could he have told me his story?

I don't know whether it was this or something else that made her look at me with that air of disgust again, as if I smelled bad. I was starting to rattle her, and her nerves were going to pieces.

But I wasn't about to push this child too far, was I?

I said nothing. I just smiled at her like an idiot and went on my way. Once again I was sure I would never see her again.

Some time afterward I was appearing as a guest on a radio show, talking about literature, and I recounted the story of the girl who'd believed the hero of my novel was real.

"I don't think she was really that naïve," speculated the presenter, who wrote novels himself. "She must have been a bit strange . . . a bit crazy."

"That's what I thought at first, but then I started to question that. There was something really unique about her. I've never come across a reader as gullible as her before . . . She was as trusting as a newborn baby."

I spent almost the entire show trying to convince him how naïve my teenage reader really had been. Yes, I was laughing along with him, but if I'm honest I was angry: first she wouldn't believe that Bakar *didn't* exist, and now he wouldn't believe such a naive reader *did* exist . . .

I really don't understand how it could be so difficult to believe in the nonexistence of one or to entertain the notion of the other.

"That could only happen with someone who's never read a book in their life," one caller argued (there was a phone-in as part of the show). "It sounds like your novel was the first book she'd ever read."

Well yes, it's not impossible. But so what?

"Or maybe she was actually the ideal reader?" one woman argued. "Maybe that's how people read the world's very first books? So here is a pure, untarnished reader, a virgin reader if you like, and we sit here with our erudite skepticism, drunk on our own intellect, and assume she has psychiatric problems . . ."

And so this real-life event dragged me into a discussion about the education—or lack of education—of society at large. But regardless of how naïve or insane Bakar's admirer was, we all agreed on one thing: there was no way you could describe this girl as a "quality reader"—we all felt it was completely impossible for a book to have an impact like that on a reader with any level of competence.

"You should write a novel about it, you know," the presenter said to me after the show had finished.

A novel? I don't think so.

I'd say it was more suited to a short story.

And if I do write it, I'll finish it like this:

I see the girl again (in a crowded place, like a station, or at a demonstration, or the airport, or a sports stadium), but this time I just watch her; she doesn't see me. Standing next to her—or is he sitting?—there's a young man. He has black hair, a tattoo on the back of his hand, and the yellowed face of someone with hepatitis C. I can't believe it: it's Bakar Tukhareli. The Thief, the one and only. Exactly as I described him in my novel.

TRANSLATED FROM GEORGIAN BY ELIZABETH HEIGHWAY

PAUL EMOND

Grand Froid

This evening a play was performed at a little theater in suburban Brussels, one of those curious productions in which the actors mix so intimately with the audience that the latter wind up believing they're part of the cast. Before the performance began, extras had been installed in the auditorium, scattered here and there among the seats. When the audience began to enter, usherettes dressed up in black conducted them with great ceremony to their assigned places, while around them the extras sat hunched and immobile in heavy fur coats covered with snow, or a sort of white powder that imitated it precisely. Surprised, certain members of the audience couldn't prevent themselves from emitting a few *sotto voce* comments:

– See that? They look like they're frozen.

– Like cadavers, almost.

– They keep it horribly cold in this theater.

– It's scandalous, they *could* warm it up a bit.

– Look, look at that one, there's a little icicle hanging from his nose!

– That's not an actor, it's a mannequin.

– No, no, it's an actor.

– Touch him, you'll see.

– I wouldn't dare.

– Remind me who wrote this play?

– It's another one by that Damploune, whose pieces are playing almost everywhere these days. They're never very cheerful, but this one sounds promising!

– If I'd known . . .

– *Grand Froid!* You can see where he got the title!

– It's even colder in here than outside.

– They're saying it's minus twenty tonight.

– Let's hope this doesn't last too long. My teeth are chattering already.

The lights had been lowered, but the performance failed to begin. A fine white powder, a sort of light sleet, perhaps even genuine sleet, or a feathery, almost impalpable snow, like that which covered the extras, or mannequins, had begun to sift down from the ceiling onto laps and shoulders.

– You can't see where it's falling from, they've snuffed out all the lights up there.

– It's as cold as real snow.

– But it *is* real snow, I assure you.

– Let's not exaggerate.

– My feet are already frozen.

Very quickly it became almost impossible to distinguish the extras from the spectators, unless one of the latter happened to fidget a bit, so that there slid from his lap or his shoulders a minute amount of that frozen powder, that sleet, that almost impalpable snow, which had gradually covered everything: the extras and the audience, the seats, the floor, the carpeting in the aisles, everything, all of it now veiled by a slightly glimmering layer of white, while the stage remained in darkness. Several spectators, in increasingly timid whispers, exchanged a few more words:

– We've got to get out of here.

– It isn't possible.

– Yes it is, no one could stop us.

– I wouldn't dare.

– I'm so cold, I'm going to get sick.

Finally, after what had felt like an interminable wait, there came something like an enormous silent rupture. Up front, where the stage should have been, a street appeared, a street with slightly melancholy lamps, a street covered with snow, a street where it was still snowing, where it never stopped snowing, a street empty and cold and of seemingly infinite depth; out of which there emerged, to the great stupefaction of the audience, squealing across the snow, all of its ancient metal rattling, an almost antediluvian streetcar, slowly advancing toward the auditorium: an antediluvian streetcar likewise skinned with snow.

– Do you see that old tram? It's magnificent!

– Unbelievable: it's a real street, not a set.

– Are you sure?

– Don't you feel that wind?

– I can't feel much of anything. I'm still too cold.

– In theory, there shouldn't be wind in a theater.

– In theory . . .

The old streetcar looked so exhausted, it seemed to have come from the farthest of far-flung *faubourgs*, from those frozen and deserted suburbs where the avenues dwindle and lose themselves in almost infinite extension. It crept toward the audience, magnifying little by little, like some strange white caterpillar crawling out of the depths of time, and finally halted a scant three meters from the first row of spectators; its windows were flocked with frost, nothing of its interior could be distinguished.

The streetcar had stopped, but its doors did not open. In the auditorium and on the street that had taken the place of the stage, another long silence descended.

– It's just like Damploune, that.

– All the same, it's crazy!

– I don't want to stay here. I've been sitting in the cold, at a show I don't understand at all. Let's go.

– Impossible, how can you want to leave?

– I'm afraid.

– That's absurd, there's no reason.

Then, approaching the front of the stage at a slow trot—at a pace so dragging, so seemingly fatigued, that one might have imagined they too were emerging from the depths of time—there came a group of men dressed in heavy fur coats identical to those worn by the extras in the audience, coats whitened by snow, or that white powder that so perfectly imitated snow. At irregular intervals, and according to some quite unguessable logic, each of these men would stop for a moment, draw a revolver from the pocket of his coat, aim with an extended arm, fire in the direction of the old streetcar, and then resume the chase.

When the first of these pursuers had arrived within about ten meters of the vehicle, they stopped; they were soon rejoined by their fellows, and a few moments later stood side by side, forming a line which blocked the whole breadth of the street, each of them motionless in his heavy fur coat covered with snow, or white powder. Once more a silence invaded the street and the theater, a deathly silence, descending on utter immobility.

– Do you think this is going to last long? Nothing's happening.

– I don't know what they're waiting for.

– That's enough. This time it's certain, I'm going.

– How are you going to do it?

– I don't see how they can stop me from leaving the theater. I'm going, that's all there is to it.

– Me, I wouldn't dare.

– Your mistake. *Bonsoir.*

The audience member had risen, was requesting with a gesture that his left-hand seatmate shift a bit to let him pass, when an echoing voice rang out from behind him:

– Halt! Where are you going?

It was the extra seated to his right, who had risen as well, causing some of the white powder or snow that covered him to fall. He'd drawn a revolver from his pocket and was threatening the fugitive, who, at the sound of his voice, had stopped cold.

– Where are you off to? Answer!

– But . . . Monsieur . . .

Again, there was a murmuring some three rows up:

– They've hidden actors among the *audience* as well.

– The runaway? No, no, I know that fellow, he isn't an actor, he's a tax official.

– Are you sure . . . ?

– Yes, yes, I'm telling you.

The whole theater had turned toward the man attempting to leave, and the one who was threatening him—not just the audience but, even more surprisingly, the extras in their fur coats as well, who had risen to their feet as one a few moments after their colleague, letting a bit of the snow or white powder that covered them sift to the floor. Each of them held a revolver, also pointed in the fugitive's direction. The extra with the echoing voice repeated:

– I told you to answer.

– I wanted to leave . . . the other began in a hesitant tone. But he did not continue.

For at that precise instant the sound of a violin became audible—a marvelous music, an air of such exquisite purity that it seemed to be emerging from another world. Two steps from the old streetcar there appeared to the spectators a young woman dressed in a superb white fur coat, followed by a violinist playing as he walked. Perhaps they'd stepped from one of the tall houses lining the street, whose gray façades gleamed softly in the cold. They advanced toward the audience; then, leaving the street, they entered the theater, finally reaching the row where the man who had wanted to leave, and the one who'd prevented him, were still standing. The violin's tone quavered like a magic crystal in the frosty air of the theater.

– You desire, Monsieur, to leave our show, said the young woman in a slightly histrionic tone. It's possible, of course—but you should know that it will entail certain risks, certain dangers. Follow me, if you will.

– Listen, I . . .

– Since you've expressed the wish to leave our show, follow me. I'm here to attempt to satisfy you.

– It's so cold, and I thought . . .

– Your reasons don't matter, Monsieur. Your name, please?

– Traumont, Michel Traumont.

– You want to leave our show. Very well—follow us, Monsieur Michel Traumont. I beg you, my friends, put your weapons away and sit down again, she added, addressing the extras, who immediately obeyed: Monsieur Traumont will follow us without your assistance, I'm certain of that.

– But I mean, I . . .

– Follow us, Monsieur Traumont. This way.

Accompanied by the violinist, who hadn't ceased his playing for a moment, and followed by Michel Traumont, who didn't dare protest, the woman once again traversed the theater, stepped back into the street, and approached the old streetcar.

– Halt! Where are you going?

This time the violinist's bow stopped short, and that sudden cessation of music ran like a shock through the audience. One of the streetcar's pursuers had left the line formed by his companions, and advanced a few steps. He brandished his revolver at Traumont.

The young woman stepped between them:

– Monsieur Michel Traumont has expressed the desire to leave our show. It's my role to show the exit to whoever does so.

A burst of applause rang out from the extras in the theater, and the pursuer holstered his pistol, took his place once again in the line.

– This play is truly curious.

– And you're sure Traumont isn't an actor?

– Impossible.

– My nose is going to freeze.

– Cold blood—you would've done better to stay at home. Much warmer.

– You don't find all of this a touch unsettling?

In the first row of the audience, a man, still young but with a severe expression, rose with evident haste, as if propelled by too stiff a spring. One might have imagined he'd only just realized what role he had to play—unless, of course, it was all just a part of the show. In a voice marked by emotion—unless, of course, it was merely a sign of that nervousness that attends a first performance, and particularly a performance for which one hasn't prepared—he delivered his line:

– It is *my* role, this evening, to administer the exit exam. Take the violin, Monsieur Traumont.

Traumont looked down at him with an indecisive air. Then he glanced at the young woman, who waited, still smiling. Then at the musician, who was offering him the violin. Then, once more, at the man who had called out from the first row. He addressed himself to the latter:

– Look, this whole thing is completely insane. I was cold, I just wanted to go home . . .

– *Cher* Monsieur, the young woman broke in, I told you, your reasons don't matter at all. Don't speak anymore, don't say a single thing, you can be sure that nobody here is interested.

And as if to emphasize these last words she gently shook her head, communicating as she did a particularly graceful motion to her long black hair, which cascaded down upon the brilliant white of her fur coat.

– I told you to take the violin, repeated the man in the first row, in a slightly more confident voice.

– But I don't know how to play, stuttered Traumont.

– Go on, it's not so hard, added the violinist, smiling and pressing the instrument on him a little more insistently. A bit of good will and the job is half done.

– Take it and play: those are the rules, said the man from the first row, who seemed more and more at ease.

– And if I refuse?

– I'd advise you not to refuse, Monsieur Traumont. I wouldn't advise that at all.

The extras in the auditorium seemed to titter in unison. The spectators whispered to each other:

– But why are they laughing?

– I don't see anything funny about it, myself.

– Well, you know Damploune's sense of humor . . .

The young woman took a step in Traumont's direction, smiling at him with an almost angelic expression:

– If you don't take the violin, you won't leave, believe me, Monsieur Traumont.

Traumont raised his hand to take the violin, then snatched it back.

– What a fantastic actor! Look, he seems more and more indecisive.

– But I'm telling you, I know that Traumont isn't an actor. He's the one who audited my brother's tax returns last year. Made him pay through the nose, the swine!

– He doesn't *look* like a bad guy.

– Sure, but just wait till he gets his claws into you.

The man from the first row had stepped into the street, and now seemed perfectly at ease. In an almost threatening tone, he once again repeated:

– Play, Monsieur Traumont. I'm telling you to play.

– But I've explained, I don't know how. This whole thing's absurd. Besides, it's too cold, my fingers are completely numb.

– Play!

– Well . . . since you insist . . .

With a resigned, a timid gesture, Michel Traumont took hold of the violin and bow offered by their owner. He placed the instrument against his left shoulder, imitating as best he could the standard pose, and then, with his right hand, lowered the bow toward the strings. But he paused, and lifted his head again, looking around with a grimace, as if to say: No, this is too stupid, don't ask me to do what I don't know how to do.

– Come on, Monsieur Traumont, play!

This time it was the young woman who insisted. With elegance and vivacity, she indicated the theater, to make him understand that everyone was waiting. Whether he liked the idea or not, he was part of the show now, wasn't he?

So he played. Or rather, produced a frightful screech, as anyone would who was scraping a bow across the strings of a violin for the very first time in his life. All the extras seated in the auditorium burst out laughing, and then loudly booed, before once again ceasing abruptly in unison. As if an invisible conductor had given the signal.

– That wasn't brilliant, said the man from the first row.

– But I told you, stuttered Traumont.

– Make a bit of an effort, insisted the young woman in the fur coat, her smile still seraphic.

– But what do you want? responded Traumont, in a despairing voice. I've never played, I never learned how.

– Come, come, just a little effort, Monsieur Traumont, repeated the young woman. We aren't asking the impossible.

– But that's precisely what you're doing! protested Traumont. Stop this nasty joke! Let me go home.

Once more, as if with a single breath, the laughter of the extras rang out, and cut off.

– Do you want to try one more time? asked the man from the first row, who now seemed to have his role by heart.

– It's no use, you can see that.

– Is that your last word?

Traumont acquiesced with a nod of the head.

– Pity. We would have loved to see you board the tram without our assistance. Bon voyage all the same, Monsieur Traumont!

A gunshot rang out, causing a number of audience members to jump. It was impossible to say straight off just where the report had come from, for, apart from Traumont, who crumpled to the ground, everyone in the auditorium, everyone in the street, remained perfectly still. A moment afterward the applause crackled out, then stopped dead, replaced all at once by the music of the violin. But it wasn't the musician who was playing anymore: they could all see Traumont stretched out impassive on the ground, his left hand still clutching the instrument's neck. It seemed to be coming from everywhere at once, this music, from the depths of the theater, from the receding walls of the houses in the street.

– It's impossible . . .

– I don't understand this business at all.

– To be forced to play an instrument you don't know! To be shot right down!

– Wait! You don't actually believe . . . They're actors! They've shot him with a blank!

– You're saying he isn't dead?

– He'll get up to bow at the end.

– But I'm telling you, I know him. He isn't a professional actor, he's a tax official . . .

– He plays his part so well, it's obvious he's a professional . . .

– Believe me, he works for the fisc—

– Whatever you say. For my part, I prefer to wait till the end of the show to leave.

It had stopped snowing. Above the street the sky had cleared, and the scene was now lit by the brilliant silver of the moon. The fur-clad man who had shot Michel Traumont slipped his pistol into his pocket and stood motionless. Two of his comrades stepped forward and scooped up the corpse. The old streetcar's front door accordioned open. The two men stepped into the vehicle, deposited their burden there with a bit of difficulty, and exited again. They had barely descended when the door slid shut and the ancient streetcar, rattling all of its antediluvian metal, began to move off, to roll slowly away. The men who'd pursued it as far as the theater now followed it off at a run, each of them stopping an instant, at irregular intervals, according to some unguessable logic, to draw their pistols from their pockets, aim in its direction, and fire, before continuing the chase. When the streetcar was so far away that one could no longer distinguish its pursuers or even hear their shots, the young woman turned to the auditorium and saluted with an elegance out of another century. After a few moments the music stopped. The extras in the theater broke into violent applause, and then, as a single man, laid their hands in their laps.

None of the spectators dared to move. A leaden silence descended on the theater, and all sat motionless in the cold.

TRANSLATED FROM FRENCH BY AARON KERNER

KRIKOR BELEDIAN

The Name under My Tongue

The laser spot

kept appearing, disappearing, flickering, leaping from place to place, skipping, beaming in short, quick blinks, returning to its point of departure, suddenly calming down, almost sweeping across the illuminated surface, to the left, where it would rest; the tip of the long, thin plastic pointer would stop for a second, quivering in the dust that slowly turned into a half shadow, then caught by a sudden fever—a growing, dancing tongue of flame—it would blaze from one side of the map to the other, withdraw all at once, then move forward again as if exploring something, now more hesitant, cautious, it would seem that it had disappeared, but it would reappear, flying like an arsonist setting fire to a field, or like erupting gunfire, exploring the void, the shadow, or more precisely—the light layer of the shadow;

the woman standing at the podium went on playing with the pointing stick with one hand, while she leaned against the table with the other, resting her body, her torso outlined in the half dark, her widely opened collar showing yellow alabaster skin where soon a bead of sweat would appear, the muscles of her neck and throat, taut with tension, kept straining then relaxing, reaching up to the restless chin and its complex working machine;

meanwhile the staccato voice, zigzagging, rising suddenly, forcing itself into higher notes, was pushing out words that were barely separable, that didn't fit into one sentence, but became an open slope, a surface, a plateau, unraveling around a panting breath that tried to say everything at once; it wound around itself layers of details, digressing from the main path, it expanded, extending into episodes, then with a thrust of the tongue muscle, hitting the hollow of the mouth, it returned, finding again its previous force and depth, a kind of subtlety in its sharpness, it would bend the medium, exposing the sullen, hermetic amphitheater to something jolting, something disturbing for a moment; but without lessening its vehemence, it suddenly stopped; an unexpected caesura, while the echo was still reverberating in the distance;

as someone who has stepped onto a dangerous ledge and automatically draws back from a head-spinning precipice, I woke from my doze; it was a late afternoon relaxation, a numbness or stupefaction that would allow my mind to err, to wander aimlessly from one image to the other, involuntarily jumping from one scene to the next; the more I focused the more I exhausted myself, falling into utter helplessness, it seemed as if I were taking refuge behind a neutral, invisible screen, and the more or less fragmented segments of reality passed, along with the inevitable voids that separated them;

I was half reclining, my legs stretched underneath the chair in front of me, perplexed, having lost the sense of place and time—was I searching for something that wasn't there, but that seemed to be there nonetheless? my writing journal was still on my knees, open, the first page was scrunched, a little dirty, marred with ink, and there were even a few sentences illegibly scribbled on it . . . just as, when I went on a plane trip, after putting away my handbag and camera in the compartment above the seat, I would settle in with the calmness and contentment of someone who occupies his seat without paying a slight attention to the flight attendant, and with the enthusiasm of someone about to do something very important, I would take out my journal with the intention of writing down a random thought that had just crossed my mind, start by jotting down the date and place, as if that in itself would mark the entrance into a new world, but then gradually the sound of the engine, and the time that failed to pass, would diminish my excitement, I would slowly drift into a restless drowse filled with noise, following the panting sound of a fireplace that spread its radiating glow and warmth in the distance, while the ghostly images forming on the walls would turn, disappear;

they had been speaking for a while in dull, monotonous tones despite the diversity of languages, people with thunderous names; I had heard about them from the papers, announcement leaflets, anecdotes circulating among the intellectuals; they would get up from the big long table that was nearly as wide as the blackboard, place their notes on the podium, leaf through the pages, sometimes turn left toward the Chair of the panel who was sitting at the other end of the table, a man with a slightly ragged, dirty beard, his head resting on his hand, deep in thought or perhaps already half asleep, who made hand or eyebrow gestures to this or that person—there was still time, the speaker could continue with his paper, twenty minutes, five minutes, after which, predictably, the Chair would have to interrupt—

nearing his conclusion, the speaker would raise his voice, take a deep breath, look at the audience, immediately accelerate, utter the last sentence or what seemed to be the last sentence in one breath, the dynamic young woman sitting next to me, who was either busy with her notes or with the recording machine, would occasionally glance up from beneath her eyelashes, as if somewhat indifferent, while the wave of fragrance from her loose hair and armpits diffused into the air, conquering, discomforting even, I would feel I had to write down the final conclusive statement: there is a history ... memory, historical truth, duty to memory, free interpretation of historical events, what is history without memory? everything could have been razed to the ground, lost, disappeared, etc., etc., something along those lines, generalizations that sounded more like aphorisms, descriptive, elementary maxims, capitalized words that, with their luminous aureole, would define, concretize, deepen a vague, undefined, unstable reality;

all the speakers had tried to gain the fluctuating attention of the audience; sometimes they would depart from the paper's main topic in the last part of their speech, they would try wearing memorable clothes, apparently they entrusted the role of impressing the crowd, of keeping their audience awake, to the outfit, noting the inevitable finale, at which their voice, having reached a certain pinnacle, would bow down; this was followed by several more or less sparse rounds of applause, erupting, then ceasing;

each speaker would leave the podium and sit down behind the long table, pour some mineral water from the plastic bottle into a paper cup, raise it to his mouth, clear his throat; he would watch the audience from the distance of his half closed eyes as people moved, dared to change the position of their bodies, cough, whisper a few words to their neighbors, sneeze, smile, shake their heads or simply stand up and leave the room, go to the bathroom or out for a cigarette break, disturbing the others, saying hello to acquaintances, friends, sometimes distant relatives whom they would meet only at such places,

ah, you're here too, isn't it interesting?

sure, indeed, certainly ... certainly ...

meanwhile, the Chair was inviting the next speaker, standing ceremoniously behind the podium with the orderliness of a pontiff whose main mission is to guard the economy of time, making a few appropriate, polite remarks about the previous presentation, noting that it was indeed a truly important work in the context of the conference, leaning toward the audience with the feigned intimacy of a salesman, as if conversing with each individual person,

everyone in the audience certainly agrees with me, bon, without exaggerating . . . we can say, very . . . important claims . . . we are most . . . grateful to the Professor . . . or esteemed Counselor,

there were variations in his tone, a few minor observations, which could have been easily dismissed despite the obvious effort to complicate the speech; he would slightly raise his neck with the persistence of someone who has valiantly agreed to carry a heavy burden, gesticulate a greeting with his hand to someone familiar, smile indulgently, the solemn smile of a national benefactor,

hey, là bas,

there is a crack of alcohol, a greasy hiccup in his voice,

please, turn off your . . . cell phones!

he would raise his right hand, tired as if from repeating, pointing to the greenish board, wasn't it written there, please turn off your cell phones? some people would lower their heads, their hands searching for their phones, checking the settings, while the Chair addressed the group of people who had been crowding in front of the door at the back of the auditorium, those who were standing, helping them find seats, over there, to the right, come near, come closer, proposing that some of them go up to the mezzanine, there's lots of room, there are seats, always the same old confining seats made of oak with backs that have faded, lost their varnish;

we were required to follow the analysis for several years, one or two hours per week, happiness, according to . . . , creation and its forms—thought and space, the happiness, *hic et nunc,* that, which every . . . will refer to, the scholar sat in the dark cell, partly illuminated by the light coming from the narrow window, his head bowed, thoughtful, while the winding staircase next to him spiraled up, as he continued his meditation, heading to new places, the screen would turn into a mental stage that widened as we learned how to connect, moving beyond all the axioms, pieces of evidence, proofs, conclusions, in order to enter another world, completely different from the one that I had entered when I heard, for the first time, the sound of the metro in the labyrinths of an underground station;

and there was still the end of History, after which everything returned to the beginning, a kind of recorded fairy tale, which every living person would read, and the events? they were more or less colorful incidents,

the bald man was elucidating it, coloring it with contemporary hues; a system of sound beneath the city—the endless, continuous process that had its own course and that had undergone a gradual inflection, a thesis, an antithesis that had been repeated in the previous century, had drowned already; he was collecting his papers, the unopened books that he had produced from his worn satchel, rare, heavy books that made an impression, as would a hermetic Hegelian sentence; as soon as the noise erupted, the almost invisible door at the front, to the right, would open and the custodian in his white apron would appear, examining those who were present through his myopic glasses, moving back and letting the professor disappear with thundering footsteps in the hallway; then we would hurry, a few of us would fall behind—tying a tie, filling a tobacco pipe—we would all head to another hall just like this one, but slightly different, a colonnade with a row of statues of forgotten philosophers at the entrance, windows that opened into collateral yards but that were always shut tight, an idyllic fresco on the ceiling above the pushing and jostling crowd, the same smell of mice, of antiseptic, of knowledge, the smell of a place that has been kept locked, a thick, oily smell that lingers on in every corner and that goes deep into the crevices of the same seats and stairwell, the wide, amphitheater-style stage, on which one day a student—an imposter—would jump and make noise with his feet,

friends .. !

a heavy smoker's cough, a fist banging on the table asking for attention,

comrades .. !

according to an unprecedented decision made . . .

the girls on their feet had taken off their coats a long time ago, they were whispering, beautiful, sometimes really beautiful girls, with very little makeup on; an imbecile who was wasting a seat, emptying his pockets, taking out a small notepad and throwing it on the table, people crowding in,

the banging fist,

. . . by the Ministry of Education . . .

the same banging again,

. . . the University . . . is closed, the Student Council . . . has organized a demonstration, the situation . . . is serious,

he would come down and start disseminating leaflets, black on white, big black flags, explosive slogans . . .

GENERAL STRIKE / REVOLUTIONARY ORGANIZATION / POLITICS / IS IN THE STREETS

now, a few people, following the proposition, were going obediently up along the narrow, spiraling stairwell, looking like medieval pupils ascending the stairs; it was very different from our wooden, terribly slanted stairwell that went up to the roof, the steps of which were mostly dislocated and cracked, rotten from rain and dampness, ready to collapse under anyone who dared step on them, but still working with a strange durability, and with the agility of a tightrope walker I would step on the most stable parts, at times leaning over the banister to peek into the window of Sĕt Janet, who would yell curses in Arabic as if frightened, while I'd jump two stairs at a time, playing with my anxiety, flying up to watch the neighborhood from above;

the street branched off from the main avenue into a small triangular square, or more exactly a place that for a moment belonged to no one, as the people who had paved the street had left it open by mutual agreement, where the slanting shadow, like an umbrella, stretched up on the hill, here—the roof of Arev's house, the pergola, the strings of pepper, dried eggplant, and across, under the eastern white pine, Mr. Garbis who sewed trousers, a headscarf tied around his head like some Arab woman, was tying the vines to reed stakes so that they'd climb up to Simon's clothesline, a little lower Nano was sitting on the edge of the balcony, the eucalyptus that shimmered under the sun right in front of her would extend, as it were, and touch the olive trees and the empty houses on the hill across from her, partially covering the gardens on the river bank, the sea in the distance, and in the evenings, when the sky turned a deep azure blue, when the last airplanes descended into the city from the east, on the far mountains, the embers in the ashes would slowly grow into flames;

the banisters, two of them, formed a helicoid labyrinth, they turned, as if you were approaching an inaccessible place, an open area, a vaulted sky, and here were women with small handbags, men out of breath who emerged at the entrance of the mezzanine, moving to its edges and conquering the hall for a moment, above its confusion and noise, catching their breath, wiping their foreheads and temples with handkerchiefs, scanning the audience below;

from there, from the front row, leaning sometimes against the low banister, sometimes against the seated people, moving, as if we were walking along a dangerous mountain path, we would head toward the center where now a young man with a moustache had arranged his tripod, focusing the lens of the camera on the stage, one eye closed—a black spot, the other—a pink circle, like a director who was pleased with his film, and was following the recording from another screen, which, with an automatic regulation, seemed to be progressing independently, while next to him, behind him, to his right and to his left, on the top seats of the mezzanine—men, women, old and young, chins resting against hands, hands resting on knees, were listening, or perhaps merely trying to listen, periodically moving their heads, listening to the presentations as if without comprehending, following with eyes that expressed complete boredom or total loss, immobile, detached like the empty eye-sockets of Greek statues, as if following the speech but surrendering to its tumble, its rhythm, being carried away, I suppose, to a different place where events were occurring that were not apparent here in this hall, but which formed a muffled, omnipresent noise, an unconscious tumult like that of a city's unremitting, underground breath; a leaflet would spiral down from one of the upper rows, someone had written *Je vois aime* on it, captivated we would clap and smoke, spellbound by the new word that belonged to no one, to no one side! it had no owner, you'd get up from your seat, stand up and like a lover in the night, it would be yours for a second, and we, like the Renault strikers, were the actors of history who had been called to change life . . .

the Chair was now inviting the last presenter of the panel, whose works were familiar to everyone,

he was holding the watch in his palm, weighing it, as it were—what was time? it was gold, no, it was nothing! nothing, but sand, nonexistence, and there were things that never passed, things that were eternal, everlasting, he was scratching his beard, smoothing it with his fingers, and turning to the woman sitting at the very end of the table, protected from the semidarkness,

so . . you are this panel's last presenter, ahem, bon, bon,

gesturing with his right hand—

shall we start?

his voice would all of a sudden rise, now he was trying to make a joke, as if it were necessary to bring some sort of merriment to the atmosphere, he not only had to preside over the panel as a small, local tyrant, giving it a more invigorating air, but also had to make it lively, favorable, effectively making use of the breaks, the indefinite moments between presentations, *et c'est pas facile,* one had to maintain the seriousness, the circumstances of the material and place, avoiding at the same time the boredom that such materials, such analyses might cause, proceeding as traditional narratives do, long, winding, weaving into each other, as if the same mood had been recurring in different forms and voices from the beginning of civilization, and laughter introduced a personal note, conjuring up a noble, intimate atmosphere, as a few minutes ago, during the break, in that interstice of time when the Chair approached the woman, took her hand, but then kissed her on the cheeks, whispered a few words in her ear, then kissed the hand of the other woman standing next to her, a proof of my respect, in a loud, ironic voice, stepping away, smiling, showing his red gums and a row of uneven teeth,

so . . . we'll see you in a little bit . . . ahem! . . you look very nice today . . . but . . .

almost grunting, as if to thwart, to kill his eager exclamations, yet at the same time asserting them,

try . . . to speak, briefly . . . ahem! . . you'll be more effective . . .

there is an affirmation in his emphasis, an order, that perhaps registered in my mind only later,

agreed? . . I beg of you,

he had already said everything, there shouldn't be any surprises, everything was set right from the beginning;

we were descending, hanging on to each other, the noise, the laughter, the slogan of the day was rising from the front rows, beaming, splitting into fractions, like pigeons excreting on everything, bouncing off the screens, the red and black letters of the dancing, exhausted, crumpled, reforming sentence

L'IMAGINATION PREND LE POUVOIR!

it hung across the façade of the grand theater, from the huge columns, art is dead, and death is counter-revolutionary, really, why should one die? idiot! keep walking!

hand radios were blasting in the distance, people were whistling from the front rows, there were small red and black flags, young, always beautiful girls in the back rows, then a huge slab of stone would hit a police van, bombs, tear gas, sobbing, red swollen eyes, the long and winding siren of an ambulance,

but the crowds kept moving forward, *merde!*, they kept walking, with steady pace, confident, the smell of gas was everywhere, spreading underneath the trees, the sound of the spiraling helicopters, we would stop, close our mouths and noses, the photographer was taking photographs when the baton hit his head, I saw those batons, he says, but I was sure, this was France, they wouldn't dare, he was rolling on his back, getting kicked in the face, they were rolling shutters down over the display windows, the shops were being emptied out, the batons were coming down fast, I was suffocating from the smell of gas mixed with the smoke of burning plastic and tires, we were running, people were running behind us, they kept pushing, groaning, we were going through the entrance of some building, while up above, the eternal good-for-nothings, the pensioners, the philistine officials, watched from behind their curtains, shaking their fists at us occasionally, you'll see! tomorrow you'll see! they were waiting for all of this to end, they'd had enough, the riots had to be crushed; leaflets were being dropped in the police station, people were being hand-cuffed, they were being thrown into dark cells, others were being beaten, punched in the stomach, in the back, in the ass, a little blood from the nose

imbeciles! assholes! castrates! freaks! ... youth thus ... repulsed ... young people who dreamed of changing life . . . heh! words that would kill and curse life . . . me or chaos! reforms now! yes . . . a new program! end to injustices! no more masquerades! . . .

the woman got up from her place, smoothed her dark-colored skirt, touched the scarf around her neck that came down to her chest, she was thin but had wide hips, promising calves, she walked toward the podium in her red summer stiletto shoes and her toenails were painted bright red, her shins were savagely white, she tried to raise the microphone, which seemed to have the tendency to slide down the stand: every speaker had to do it, draw his or her mouth close to the microphone to check the volume, then withdraw, look right, left, toward the Chair, to whom everyone was obliged to smile a fake, automatic smile;

the woman glanced in that direction too, questioning, frowning a bit, looking behind the Chair, into the dark booth where a lamp shone and where the head of the interpreter moved in a regular cadence; after every twenty or twenty-five minutes, as the speaker changed, the door of the booth would open, a man or a woman would emerge, there were two of them, the entering and exiting persons would exchange a few words with one another, the exiting person would cover his mouth with his hand making a smoking sign, since smoking was prohibited and a nonsmoking sign with bold red letters hung on both sides of the stage

that's what they had tried to change years ago, the revolution was dislodging cobblestones, hurling them into the air in its final throes, weaving barricades, the radios were blasting, roaring, three thousand, three hundred thousand people in the streets, the law was retreating, abandoning the square, passions were spilling over, flowing, blossoming, burning, squandered, May was marching off the avenues, love was flirting from the sidewalks, people were unanimously revolting, rebelling in a tide, overflowing their shores, putting an end to the chewing of watered-down words, to smoking opium, getting fucked over, no ringleaders, no slogans, we were on top of the wave, loose, free, completely free, dancing, clapping, a Gitanes in her mouth, a masculine girl was writing on the blackboard as if in a calligraphy class—

IT IS FORBIDDEN TO FORBID

the hall was rumbling, thundering, roaring, the coils of smoke were everywhere, ascending, infiltrating the air, forming a thick misty dome, while the Chair, red, raging, as reported in the press, was trying to institute silence, so his colleagues could speak, one of them had Mao's Little Red Book in his hand, another held Lenin's tract: put an END to police brutality! END to civilization! SOON, SOON, the flames will materialize THE FUTURE!—and we only wanted to live, we wanted to unlearn everything that we had learned, the green or red or blue or black night, while the mezzanine was gradually emptying out, everyone was descending from the top rows, joining people in the front, coughing, wanting to speak, wanting to piss, the hall too would soon be empty, the footsteps would die out, dust, the smell of cigarettes, soon everything would be in ruins, and so everything is a question of language, of cultural revolution . . .

raising the stipends . . . until the Pentecost, until the victory of law,

    when gasoline opened the way to vacation

    and Paris threw off its mask of fear

    the rats descended back into the cellars;

a woman was going into the interpreter's booth, the people in the audience had barely had time to take off their earphones when the light, metallic whisper recommenced, the head of the interpreter kept moving like that of a cow being herded uphill, with stooping shoulders, she was trying to follow the speaker's rhythm, stopping, waiting for the sentence to end, after which she would start forming the same sentence in a different language;

the woman standing at the podium was holding the pointing stick tightly in her hand in the half shadow, with the other she kept adjusting the projector, searching for the right position; she was coquettish, slightly pale even before reaching the podium,

I have some transparencies . . . maps,

meaning that after so many long, boring, abstract presentations there would be images, concrete things projected on the screen,

finally!

she was smiling at the Chair, while the technician was fussing with the projector in the back of the stage, going back and forth, trying to operate the machine, checking the electric cords, switching on the light, switching off the auditorium lights; the atmosphere in the room would suddenly become familiar, safe, almost unreal, the classroom slowly descended into the evening darkness, allowing the dream to emerge, like at the beginning of those "sword-and-sandal" films that I used to like so much with hundreds of actors and expensive sets showing military action, wars, easing into the story with a simple pipe melody, history framed by a bucolic setting, as though every detail had its place there, every voice its command, every person his calling and his role, and it was possible to flirt with melancholy then;

her hand kept turning on the overhead projector, as if outlining two invisible intersecting circles, her fingers or, more precisely, the enlarged shadows of her fingers were projected on the screen, turning on one another, weaving into each other, inventing a jostle, a tumult of luster and shadow, a devouring mass, that would suddenly become clear when she removed her hand from the glass surface, leaving the transparency lightly trembling, with various tedious details, which nonetheless would be so important later;

did she cough, clear her throat, smile coyly? but I noticed immediately that her voice was heading toward the distant mountains, on the border of which the flame kept flickering endlessly, there should have been a mountain range in the north, a rough mottle of lines, circles of waves that doubtlessly marked the sides or the planes; her voice oscillated, she couldn't find the right words, while her left hand moved to join the right hand on the pointing stick, then abandoned it; the mountain range formed the border of a historical province,

yes, an almost impenetrable natural barrier, that's what all the historians and the travelers had said,

at the same time, the flame followed another invented, winding direction marked by a bold dashed line, as an upward path on the ribs of the mountain, excavating those inaccessible lands, one of the images of which was drawn from memory by someone who had once lived in those places and was fond of that geography and had published it in some book,

that's that,

the professor would say, a heavy-set man, he would take off his jacket and put it on the chair, roll up his sleeves, light up a cigar, his squint eye would switch from presence to absence in a dialectical shift, with the drive of someone in a continuous monologue with himself—

I think that . . . we . . .

he would try to visualize the words, puff out smoke, clear his throat,

we can't not be part of . . . the movement, it's absolutely necessary that the intellectuals . . . help the workers and unite the students, we need . . . a general front,

he would place the cigar on the edge of the table,

. . . our action showed that the people's . . . outburst had its place in the social movement . . .

he was evidently waiting for his words to sink in, expecting perhaps to leave an impression on his audience, but a voice from the back, it could have been any one of us, neutral, arrogant, ironic, almost spelling out each letter—

you're so well-read . . .

he was shaking his head in silence, blowing out smoke,

. . . and such a bad politician,

the man was leaning against the table,

comrades!

get back into your hole . . . you philistine!

history had turned a page, on the walls, side streets, statues, pedestals in red letters, the crowd kept walking, taking over the alleyways, sidewalks, the square, it would erect barricades, red and black flags, and "The Internationale" thundered along the entire length of the avenue again and again: FREE THE PRISONERS / CHAOS IS THE LAW / GASOLINE IS FREE / WHY DIE, STUPID? KEEP WALKING / FUCK THE PAST / THE OPERA BELONGS TO THE PEOPLE, the banner was hanging on the building's façade, swelling from the warm spring breeze, bit by bit tearing and draping over the statues of Haydn, Rossini, cursing them . . . THE MORE

YOU PHILANDER, THE MORE YOU REVOLUTIONIZE, THE
MORE YOU REVOLUTIONIZE, THE MORE . . . / YOU WANT TO
LOVE / HAPPINESS HERE AND NOW . . .

here and now . . . I was at the starting point again, in the same
place or almost there, as if it had all returned, I too had come full
circle and could watch the marches over and again, in front of a box
of old photographs, like mother's bundle, where all the unnamed
were revealed, here and now or nowhere

TRANSLATED FROM ARMENIAN BY SHUSHAN AVAGYAN

KIRILL KOBRIN

Last Summer in Marienbad

To GD

He was waiting for his wife by a mineral water spring. She was late but that didn't cause him any aggravation. It had been a few years since he had stopped being aggravated by her late arrivals, her vulgar manners—befitting the common Berliner—and her pragmatic Zionism. He stayed calm even as she dug her enormous teeth into a steak with a succulent chomp. During the last couple of years, acting with a doctor of law's carefulness and consistency, he'd removed her from himself, installing her in a special room at the far end of the corridor of his life. There she stayed, never sticking so much as her nose outside; his body would occasionally sink into hers with reluctance, but even during those shameful moments his thoughts would remain elsewhere, sometimes at yet another labor litigation committee, sometimes in one of his recent dreams: painful narratives, long and disgusting as worms. True, he respected and valued her: she had, after all, saved his life by making him marry her—he'd been coughing up blood by then—and then curing him, one could say nursing him to health in that magic Swiss sanatorium. Indeed, she had spent six months sitting next to him, holding his hand, on that balcony—he would never forget those tartan plaids and wooden chaise lounges, those ostensibly cheerful voices coming from the consumptive maidens in the dining room, those coffins carried out of the hospital building in secret, under the cover of darkness. Or he might forget them—what does it matter. He had already forgotten many things, including those that had constituted his whole life for years and years; his officious friends; his writing, compulsive, pathetic; even his long-established habits, such as his silent walks to the green hill crowned by a squat copy of the Eiffel Tower. Now there was little left but dreams. They weren't exactly gone—on the contrary, they would unravel their infinite threads nightly, entangling his mind, which was tormented, half-deaf, half-blind by now, and in the morning he would resurface, exhausted and breathless, in their huge conjugal bed, his wife's large head resting next to him, birds making a lively noise outside, the maid already rattling crockery in the kitchen, well, time to get up, have tea, go to work. In the office, while dictating a letter to his secretary detailing an industrial accident in Nymburk, he would close his eyes and slip into the images of the most recent dream retained by his memory: there he is, being dragged by some businesslike men through a four-story house in Vinohrady; as they pass the second floor his arms are ripped off; by the time they reach the basement the assailants have only his head in their hands, yet he's talking to his torturers in an animated manner, even apologizing for splattering their gray suits with his blood. That's fine, they tell him, we've worn our aprons for the occasion. Very well, he says to them, closing his eyes and slipping into the next dream, where he is conscripted into the army and, being the most educated, is made to write letters home for illiterate soldiers. He zealously throws himself into this work but is faced with an insurmountable problem: his battalion consists of Croatians, Hungarians, and Poles, and he doesn't speak their languages. He offers to write in German and have the letters translated afterward; an elderly lieutenant with a moustache, who looks like the late Emperor Franz Joseph, commends his resourcefulness and appoints him the head of a special correspondence unit. He spends every day composing letters, while several privates sitting next to him diligently translate these into the many languages spoken by the Empire's subjects; his subordinates work so fast he can't keep up with them, so instead of writing up his messages he starts simply dictating them. Then he opens his eyes and finds himself in his director's chair, the office flooded by the spring sun, the secretary drumming away on her typewriter; it's May 1923, the Empire hasn't been at war with anyone for fifty-five years, he's about to finish his dictation and head to a vegetarian restaurant for lunch. Tonight he is going to the opera with his wife.

Still no sign of her. He shifted his position and looked around. This summer, Marienbad isn't as crowded as the previous year: there are fewer Germans, fewer Russians, the rich Istanbul merchants in their red fezzes nearly gone. Political squabbles proving stronger than people's desire to be rid of their physical ailments, the Russians are now taking the liver-curing waters at their German allies' resorts, while rumor has it that the Turks, with their radiculitis and gout, have flooded the Caucasian spas. As for the Germans, they need no medical treatment at all—the Germans, according to their Kaiser's recent statement, are made of steel. Instead, the French are here in record numbers, cocking their bowlers and soft American hats (the latest fashion, that), drinking a lot, and not mineral water either, curling their theatrical moustaches, threatening to give a good beating to the Boche, the Cossacks, or the Turks if they should lay a finger on "la belle Autriche," "the land of the divine Beethoven and the sublime Rilke." Swashbuckling show-offs. Smug nonentities. They only mention Beethoven to refer to their own Napoleon, while Rilke once had the good fortune to serve as a secretary to their pompous Rodin, if you please. And where is he now, anyway, our Rilke? Not in Paris, you can be sure of that. He recalled visiting that city, so foul and full of bad food, with Max some ten years ago. Max himself was foul too, flopping on his companion's bed in the morning just as he was, in his dirty clothes, waking him up, urging him to forgo his ablutions, to hurry. Where to? What was so very special about Paris? Still, the two of them would stroll grandly, take in various new sights, having agreed to write a novel together; they would pay diligent visits to cafés, the Opéra-Comique, parks, the Louvre, the brothel. That is, The brothel he liked best of all. Even though the way that big-mouthed blonde manipulated his body was fairly routine, the order that reigned in the place, that solemn and rational order, almost redeemed all the chaos of Paris. The French were classed as the enemy back then, so Max with his usual fussiness even printed a little article in *Prager Tagblatt*, titled "Militant Paris"—one wonders if he remembers about that now? One wonders, indeed, what he's even up to these days? He'd come across Max's articles in newspapers recently, something along the lines of the goals of world Jewry in the Triune Monarchy. He hadn't read them, cautious not to read anything at all that might remind him of his past life and all its paraphernalia: Max, their bachelor trips to Paris and Weimar, Wolf the publisher, Löwy the actor, Zionist leaflets, Greta, all that writing, the dull headaches, the insomnia. These days, thank God, he slept every night.

Marienbad was, indeed, full of Russians only last year. Army types, their hair close-cropped, accompanied by ladies; lawyers' families with children so numerous he shuddered at the thought of the amount of energy and money required to bring them all up; authors dressed in a true liberal fashion, in French-style jackets; girls not wearing bustles, holding books in their hands, sweet, dreamy

Russian girls. When it came to Russian girls he was knowledgeable, having read a lot about them in his time, in books by the severe Tolstoy, the gentle Turgenev, the terrible Dostoyevsky. The year he met Felice he also discovered that famous Russian revolutionary with a German-sounding name. Herzen, that's right. Missing a beat momentarily, his heart resumed its normal rhythm. Oh yes, it was Herzen he happened to strike up a conversation about, with a young Russian lady, here in Marienbad, last summer, on a bench by the white, fretted gallery, white hats and umbrellas all around them. He was here alone, his wife having gone to Berlin to deal with some family affairs. The already familiar marital routine broken, he came back, quite unexpectedly, to what he used to enjoy so much, all that wandering around and staring at things. There was a time when he cultivated that stupid habit, telling himself that a writer, above all else, must be an observer. Now that his writing was reduced to business papers, he took to it again out of sheer boredom. After his medicinal water and breakfast, he would walk to the gallery, sit on a bench, open a newspaper, and, while skimming through the usual exchange of cantankerous notes between Petersburg and Paris, Vienna and Berlin, Belgrade and Istanbul, he would glance at passing saunterers, taking in their awkward stances and comic gestures, and listen hard to their multi-tongued conversations, trying to grasp their meanings. So he sat there for days, watching the Turks complain to the Russians, the Russians demand explanations of the Austrians, the Austrians ask the French for support, and the latter shake their republican fist at Emperor Nicholas and his cousin Willy, while agreeable bourgeois strolled around, emboldened by the half-century-long continental armistice, reassured just enough to start spending their leisure time and substantial amounts of money on cures for gallstones and gastritis. Once he noticed a girl on the bench opposite; for some reason her features reminded him of his wife, so he rose to leave. As he was getting up, he caught her intent stare. He walked up to the Kurhaus and back again, hoping to find her gone. But she was still sitting on the same bench, spying on passersby over the red cover of her open book. He strolled past, noting her clothes, the same as Felice's in that memorable photograph, a white blouse and a dark skirt. He also noticed that the only resemblance between her and his wife was in the large nose; the rest—her lips, the shape of her eyes, the hue of her skin—being different. She kept watching him, which made him angry. He decided to say something biting to her, in German, hoping that the Russian wouldn't understand and he would be able to retreat safely, his revenge exacted and no harm done. How did he know immediately that she was Russian? It was because of the book—he recognized Cyrillic letters on the cover. There was a time when he used to think about Russia often, to the point of dizziness; he would dream of the sentiments he found in Dostoyevsky and Herzen, even imagine himself living in some Russian backwater, in a hut by railway tracks going nowhere. After that unfortunate Serb killed the Archduke, a war with Russia seemed unavoidable, and he had been terribly worried, tormented by his desire to join the army in order to put an end to the hell his life had become, to finish it all in one swoop. He started reading French memoirs about Napoleon's Moscow campaign, savoring the idea of the most powerful army in the world being swallowed by huge, snow-covered Russian plains. Perhaps that was why he wanted to go into the army, to march upon Moscow and vanish forever on the outskirts of Asia. He could no longer remember the exact reason. However, Rasputin persuaded the Czar not to declare war, and the Serbs, very bitter at Russia, accepted Austria's ultimatum and so changed patrons yet again. He remembered his distress, shortly afterward, at the news of Austrian sleuths looking for conspirators in Belgrade. Back then, in the summer of 1914, everything seemed lost to him: he had been sentenced by Felice, a conviction she herself was to quash later, as it turned out, and his plan to take Napoleon's route to Russia failed. Nailed to himself, he began to write a novel but never got past the first sentence. "Someone must have slandered him, for one morning, without having done anything wrong, he was arrested." He had memorized this phrase, the only one he could now remember from his writings, having given all the papers, notes, and diaries to Max after the wedding, telling him to burn everything. The treacherous Max asked, acting innocent, why he didn't destroy them himself. What could he say? He said nothing. A few days later, Max telephoned to inform him that he had fed his scribblings to a bonfire at his friend's allotment in Nusle. The choice of the place was ideal: he used to work on that allotment himself, trying to harden his soul-tortured body. He never saw Max again.

He managed to make out the lettering on the girl's book, having learnt the Russian alphabet eight years ago. The cover had the name "Herzen" on it. Approaching the girl, he faltered: "I could hardly stay here with your spying on me. So there." With that, he turned around and, already starting to walk away, heard a reply, in immaculate German, "You started spying on me first!" He stopped, turning back. She was looking at him, cheerful and composed. "I thought you were too busy with your Herzen to notice." It was time for her to be surprised then, but she gave nothing away, retorting, "And I thought you were too occupied with your paper." "Not at all—I was just contemplating what that misanthropic Socialist might have said were he to witness a parliament emerging in Russia, with the government led by that liberal Mr. Nabokoff." "Do you think he would have been pleased?" "Unlikely." "I think you're right." They laughed. They introduced themselves. She was proud of her Greek name, Lydia; she was proud and independent all around; she studied at Marburg, where her teachers were serious philosophers; she appreciated Marx;

she was translating into Russian a French novelist who had, she told him, undertaken an epic work to eclipse Balzac. Although her parents, who still lived in a seaside town in Russia, supported her financially, she saw her dependent status as a burden and wanted to stay on in Germany, to teach. He felt a pang of envy—cupidity, even—in the presence of her young vitality, her posture never bent by a six-hour workday in an office, her carefree attitude to geography, her seriousness. Despite being seventeen years younger than him, she was more knowledgeable and talked with more confidence. She even saw her Jewish origins differently; when he recalled seeing a famous Chasidic Rebbe from Beltsov here in Marienbad six years ago, she listened to his story and remained indifferent, apparently having little idea of who that was, and when he asked her if she was going to Palestine she replied with an ironic smile that she preferred to be a subject of a Russian emperor than a Turkish sultan. And so the conversation went on, he telling her about Werfel and Meyrink, the "Falcons" and Kaiser Karl; she telling him about Rasputin and Plekhanov, Gumilev and Kuzmin. Ah yes, of course, it's all coming back to him now, he read that novella once, in his previous life, it was by a Russian author, what was his name again, about Alexander the Great. Of course it was, there were crocodiles in it, whose urine was capable of burning a hole in a piece of wood. He caught himself too late, one doesn't talk about such things with young ladies. "What, about crocodiles?" "No, no, I didn't mean those, I'm sorry." They chatted about everything and anything, even politics—she was well-versed in international affairs, suggesting at one point that when it came to the Aegean problem, Russia would always stay on the side of its ally, Turkey. "Then you and I will be in opposite camps," he offered sadly. "It may be for the best," she replied, somewhat awkwardly.

They finally parted in the evening, after dinner, as she hurried home to translate her French author, having agreed to meet the next day by the gallery; he, too, went home, to write a letter to his wife, finish reading his paper, calm his suddenly rebellious heart. Around ten, already in his pajamas, he went to bed intending to browse through Goethe's travel diaries before falling sleep, the only book from his previous life he still allowed himself to touch. Outside it was a stormy night, the weather so inclement it would be best to stay indoors, yet for some reason he leapt out of bed, dressed quickly, and went outside. There, in the street leading to the town center, dark and empty, he experienced a feeling of loneliness, so unusual for Europe that one couldn't help but call this feeling Russian. The town center was still smoldering with the usual resort activity, but he wanted no noise or light, so turned into the very first side street instead. Walking past low houses, he kept looking in their windows, as was his old habit. Although most of them were shuttered, he could still see through some: in one of them there was a woman sitting with her sewing in a yellow circle of light; in another a fat man in braces, reading a newspaper, looking somewhat aggrieved; in a third a chambermaid making a bed. The street was a cul-de-sac. He stopped, caught his breath, and went back. Drawing level with another window, he peered inside through the partially drawn curtains. He saw a girl at a desk with her back to him, writing something. Or rather, not so much writing as copying something from a book, and not just copying whole pages—she was being somewhat selective, from time to time leafing through a huge volume fixed vertically on a special stand. For a moment he imagined that the girl must be writing a commentary, perhaps to some Talmudic text, but he drove that absurd thought away. Next to the books on the desk he noticed a photograph of a young man with large sad eyes, his head resting on his left hand, the index finger sunk into his cheek. The young man looked Italian or French, but could just as well be Jewish. He came closer to the window and stood there for a while. She kept working with great concentration until another girl came into the room, probably German, a petite blonde with an amazingly large bosom. The scribe, as he dubbed her, dropped her pen, annoyed, and turned around. As he recognized Lydia it dawned on him that she was neither copying nor commenting but translating the very Frenchman she had mentioned. Perhaps it was the novelist himself in the photograph. He thought it apt; let the translator's labors be blessed by the author's presence, his benevolent gaze. Meanwhile Lydia must have said something very harsh to her friend, who became weepy and dabbed her eyes with a handkerchief. He would never forget what happened next. Lydia went up to the blonde and kissed the neckline of her dress. The blonde looked up and embraced her. It was a long embrace, long enough for him to realize he was awake. The lovers were kissing, whispering something to each other, then finally Lydia waved the blonde aside, went back to the desk, put the finished pages in order, closed the dictionary, and stole a glance at the portrait before going to the window, very quickly, giving him just enough time to step back. He was already walking away at a brisk pace when the screech of the drawn shutters scraped through his hearing. Early the next morning he packed his suitcase and took the first train to Prague. The day after that he was standing in his office, dictating to his secretary a letter to Phoenix Bohemian Insurance Company.

Still his wife did not come. The crowd around him was getting thinner, time to go, to have tea and talk to the other guests sitting at their table-d'hôte. He shook away the memory, so reminiscent of one of his dreams, and made a few circles around the pavilion with the mineral water spring. The relentless August sun burning through his dandyish light-colored suit made him take refuge in the shade again. And then he saw his wife at the end of the alley. She was walking fast, nearly running, her long bony face full of dismay and extreme anxiety, her large mouth askew, some terrible word she had to deliver struggling to come out of it, so he started toward her, a little frightened, her ugly face and awkward figure causing a wave of forgotten pity and tenderness in him, and as he grasped her hand with a thumbed newspaper tightly gripped in it—my God, what's the matter with you, Felice my dear, what's happened—she looked at him, her eyes full of fear, and said: "It's war, Franz."

TRANSLATED FROM RUSSIAN BY ANNA ASLANYAN

art

VITALIE CIOBANU

Orchestra Rehearsal

When the professor of linguistics went to see who was knocking on the classroom door, interrupting his soporific discourse from the lectern, I had a presentiment that the person out past the threshold had come for me. There wasn't anything to justify this feeling, unless we are to believe that the longstanding expectations you nourish within yourself, often accompanied by a diffuse sense of guilt, are able to convey unmistakable signals from the outside world. A few moments later, after engaging in a short dialogue in the form of curt whispers, leaning half into the corridor, Mocreac turned on his heel. Above his thick lenses, his myopic eyes wandered over the class until they fastened on me. "Aristide, step outside for a moment: there's someone here who wants to talk to you." With an even gait, I made my way to the door, haughtily ignoring the indignant eyes of my classmates, all envious at my opportunity to avoid, legitimately, as it were, the monotony of an insipid and somnolent lecture. But only I knew, as I approached our professor's mysterious collocutor, what anxieties undermined the aplomb I had been trying to project to the rest of the class. It was Porfirich, the head of the student folk music ensemble, the man they also nicknamed Quasimodo, out of the kind of malice that is always prone to monstrous exaggeration, because he somewhat resembled the famous character from Victor Hugo: squat, with a bulbous head and an unnaturally large mouth that looked out of proportion to the rest of his swarthy, deeply wrinkled face. It's worth lingering for a few moments on that face: from the corners of his eyes the wrinkles spread out in a fan, which the mouth, acting as a spring, corrugated whenever he smiled or laughed, for he was constantly quipping, flinging innuendoes left and right, such as, "Natasha, stop blowing that clarinet on the stairs," to the delight of his listeners. Because, after all, what else is an ambiguous wisecrack, spoken by the right person, but an invitation to indulge in a vicarious sexual fantasy? Porfirich liked to foster an atmosphere of merry complicity around himself, in a wholly natural way, the same as other people might exude a particular musk, and his entourage, it goes without saying, enthusiastically joined in his game. Of course, Porfirich lacked the cathedral to be a genuine Quasimodo. It would have been more apt to say that he had access to infernal *bolgie*.

He ushered me over to the window with a conspiratorial and concerned expression. If anyone had been watching they would have seen a comical duo framed by the window set deeply in the thick brick wall of the faculty building, gesticulating disproportionately, like actors in a silent film.

"What are you trying to do, Aristide, make a fool of me? Are you coming to any more rehearsals or not?" Ignoring my sudden discomfort, he went on in an irritated voice: "We couldn't wait for you. We're leaving for Italy and we have to get the paperwork ready. You know very well how long the whole business takes! The boys kept asking me about you, because you're down on the list, but you forgot to come and see us!"

"Porfirich, I'm sorry, please excuse me," I mumbled, conscious of the dual effect of the feeling that was suffocating me—made up of undermined self-assurance and self-esteem resuscitated as a result of being needed. "I haven't had any time for the violin lately. I've been up to my ears in coursework, and other problems. But I'll come. I promise I'll come."

Quasimodo shook his head.

"That doesn't explain anything. It's been more than six months since I last saw you. Do you think I like having to track you down, to yank you out of lectures and ask you what you think you're doing? Do you think I like having to put off the decision all the others are waiting for? Look, we're having a rehearsal the day after tomorrow, on Wednesday. If you don't show up, then I'm striking you off the list. You've been warned. It's up to you."

And with that he turned his back on me, melting like a vampire into the gloom of the corridor.

You will never learn to read the signals fate is sending you. Or else you'll read into them exactly the opposite of what they're actually saying, because, out of some juvenile delusion, you still assume that fate will always pile gifts at your feet. Porfirich. What made him come looking for me? He might just as well have ignored me, or found someone to replace me, especially given that I was hardly indispensable to the ensemble. Quite the opposite, I would say. My encounter with Porfirich discomfited me, but more so the news that the ensemble was going to Italy, which was entirely unheard of, an event more fantastic than my flying to Mars or climbing Mount Everest. I felt all the more troubled by this given that the news came after a failed first attempt a year before. We had been due to go to a festival organized by the *L'Unità* newspaper in a number of cities in the north of the peninsula. This sortie into "enemy" territory, even under the cover of ideological allies, Enrico Berlinguer's communists, still required lengthy preparations; everything still had to be sifted down to the smallest detail. It had seemed that things were bogged down somewhere in the upper echelons of the political machine, or else that our Italian comrades had had second thoughts, and so without caring about betraying my philistine, mercenary motives, I had given up going to rehearsals, fed up with the pointless efforts involved in that time-consuming and unrewarding "hobby." I had looked on it as a blessing in my first year as a student, when all the freshmen had been corralled and sorted according to their "secondary" aptitudes, but the hobby had soon turned into a thankless chore: I played the violin, and so I had a talent that somehow set me apart from the gray mass of my fellow students; in their eyes, it lent me a kind of ludicrous aura. It was an artistic form of communal socialization, different from the usual panoply of drudgery to be borne by a journalism student in Soviet Moldavia. It didn't mean that I wasn't sentenced to punishment like all the rest, but it did offer me a way to spend my time differently, to alleviate the universal, withering tedium; it was a dram of entertainment, a refuge.

I was able to treat the folk music ensemble as an alternative to the kind of forbidden and perilous relationships that had been beckoning to me ever since I moved to this city. I took part in an unseen auction, without knowing that I myself was the lot under the hammer—the coveted trophy, the promised fulfillment of so many sustained efforts—and I had to learn how to root out and repress my own inclinations as I let myself be pulled now in one direction, now in another. Yes, it was something like the "redemptive alternative" magnanimously proposed to me by that secret policeman during our little talk in the caretaker's room of the students' hostel where I lived. He had asked me about the writer T., showing an especial interest in this leading figure of the intellectual world, who had a reputation for being a nationalist/dissident and was frowned upon by the official "organs": "It would be a good thing if you didn't see him anymore. You'll make things complicated for yourself. What are you trying to do? Get kicked out of the university? Why don't you find yourself a healthier pastime? Sports, for example. What about hang-gliding or parachuting? I know somebody at the club in town, if you're interested. It's very good for the health, you know. Much better than reading books in Romanian. I'm not saying you shouldn't read them if it gives you so much pleasure, just don't pass them on to other people."

The agent had an elongated, doggish face, beveled brows, and the almond-shaped eyes of an odalisque. He stared at you unwaveringly, without any embarrassment—a long-honed skill—rummaging through your brain to see what you were concealing from him, what you were trying to avoid, implanting a sense of guilt into your soul. I admit that my hatred for this particular species of villain was acute. I didn't know how to comport myself with them. I hadn't learned to look at them as human beings, no matter how perverse. I knew only that I despised them, grimly, tenaciously, and out of a firm conviction. And that was why I overdid my hate, ascribing them monstrous physical traits to match the abysses lurking beneath their invisible uniforms. I let myself be manipulated by clichés, swayed by bile. It was impossible for me to imagine such a specimen shaving in front of the mirror every morning, like a conscientious functionary, or playing with his three-year-old daughter on the brightly colored rug in the living room. I could never have believed he visited his mother on happy occasions, bearing a huge bunch of tulips; or pictured him pausing to catch his breath, leaning on the banister between the fifth and sixth floor of his apartment block, asking himself whether he had forgotten anything from the shopping list his wife had put in his pocket, for the party they would be throwing that evening.

Evil, the man wanted me to believe, was not all that terrifying. Nor was its scout, the secret policeman. It would be much more advantageous to regard him as a friend, as a counselor in times of trouble. I was being granted a privilege: "You can read them, but don't pass them on to others." Miron, who was accustomed to splitting hairs, something he took great pleasure in doing during our vesperal discussions, told me frankly:

"Be careful about this feeling of being 'chosen,' this privilege you were granted of being spoken to openly. Don't let it go to your head. They'll be keeping an eye on you, the same as they do on all of us. They just haven't got you for anything serious yet. They can't accuse you of anything just for having had a few meetings with T., meetings at which you could have spoken about anything at all, not necessarily anti-Soviet subjects. But they've made it clear to you that they're doing you a favor, and that when the time comes you'll be in their debt. Congratulations! You've joined the game: the game of cat and mouse."

His words were like a bullwhip. I felt the need then to spool back in my mind through the entire film scene of my interview with the officer and recount the entire sequence to my more worldly-wise friend . . . after an awkward pause, granted: the secret policeman had asked me to sign a slip of paper to say that I would keep our discussion confidential.

"Come on, don't be naïve," said Miron. "We've all gone through the same thing. It's their usual procedure. They ask you to sign in order to frighten you, so that you'll think they've placed the noose around your neck. Nonetheless, it's better if you don't open your mouth. There are certain things you don't discuss aloud, and certainly not with just anyone. But it's all right that you told me: that's so I could help you, so that you won't make any more mistakes in future—that is, if you've made any mistakes so far."

My colleagues in the ensemble (that makes it sound too pompous— it would have been more accurate to say, "my colleagues in getting drunk" or "my colleagues in delinquency") welcomed me back calmly, demonstrating that they were possessed of a delicacy I would never have suspected in them; allowing me to feel (what sublime largesse!) as if I had never been absent from their midst. Perhaps I ought to have judged them in a more balanced way and not have let myself be fooled by their coarse appearance and gutter talk. I used to go to rehearsals three times a week, tapping my black violin case against my flared trousers to the rhythm of the melody I was always humming inside my cranial cavity—between perambulations I had stacked up a repertoire rich in musical scores, learned by heart, firstly because I liked them and didn't want to forget them, secondly because they helped me fill in the blank intervals of my walks across the city, during which I would play them back, like magnetofon tapes, varying them according to my mood, whether spirited or solemn, but mostly serene and idyllic. My walk to the student culture club agglutinated into a symbolic canvas, which could be surveyed from the bird's-eye viewpoint of the huge obelisk of the heroes of the Communist Party in front of the university's student residences. First came the jail they called "The Baby," with its white walls, like a hospital, sheltering stripy-uniformed, proscribed elements of humanity. This I knew. But the invariable silence of the penitentiary signaled a mystery deeper than any I could have imagined: there was never any sound, no matter how small, not so much as a screech from the wheels of the truck that delivered food to the prison and took away used receptacles . . . perhaps with a few prisoners hiding among them in an attempt to escape. No sound ever came from that gloomy parallelepiped for the length of the three minutes it took me to pass by its three-meter-high white wall, so I would have been perfectly justified in regarding the frightening building as a piece of stage scenery designed to discourage infractions, or a film set erected at that intersection temporarily but then forgotten because of unexpected budget cuts.

In the next ten minutes, my tour took in two other sights. The Friendship Between Nations student complex, also known as "Little Istanbul," but populated mainly by Arabs, the offspring of lesser-ranking chiefs or bloodthirsty revolutionaries (since the postcolonial presidents, bloated with Marxist ideology and Soviet armaments, always sent their progeny to Moscow, Kiev, or Leningrad), who were now privileged students in Kishinev. I don't know what sort of education those individuals took back with them to their desert lands, but in the Moldavian Soviet Socialist Republic they made their presence felt with drug-trafficking and the deflowering of virgins, which was rather like training for the paradise promised by their prophet. I always looked enviously at those brown, solid, permanent-looking buildings from the inter-war period, comparing them to the shabby, ramshackle buildings in which we, the aboriginals, dwelled, and tried to imagine the orgiastic scenes that went on behind the green curtains, which, under normal circumstances, ought to have been the backdrop for the vocalizations of muezzins, their eyes rolling upward piously. The next piece in the symbolic jigsaw puzzle I traversed was the huge seashell of the national stadium, where we did our running in our physical education classes, under the guidance of a rugged Russian woman (a former biathlon champion, who had gone into teaching after she was discharged). The structure was like a middling-sized Roman circus, wherein the football team of Soviet Moldavia eked out its existence: Dniester F.C., the eternal "red lantern" of Soviet league football, manned by drunken and mediocre players, famous above all for the humor of the team's supporters, with their favorite battle cry of "Dniester! Drown them in puke!" The jail, the brothel, the stadium, and the cultural house: behold a synthesis of the human passions, concentrated over a surface area of three thousand square meters, the mainstays of every political regime, of every form of societal organization, from antiquity down to the present day.

The ensemble rehearsal room was on the second floor of the culture house and to reach it you had to cross the auditorium, interrupting all kinds of festivities and theatrical performances. It was an unpleasant feeling to run the gauntlet of the irritated stares of the people seated in the hall, whose noses I was rubbing in our musical gatherings, blocking their view of the stage. In time I had learned to put up with the exclamations of "Those idiots from the ensemble again!" I would even fling back venomous pleasantries, making faces, but I have to admit that the label stuck: we were, it goes without saying, "idiots," oddballs, fit only to be placed in a glass display cabinet as objects of curiosity. And, since I've raised the notion of a bizarre exhibit, it might be worth taking a snapshot of our group, and zooming in on four faces in particular—anodyne at first sight, but with whom I shared the ordeal of afternoon rehearsals. Leaving Porfirich out, naturally, since he was described above.

First there was Simona, the violinist and ensemble bruiser. She was brunette, chubby, and had vaguely Asiatic features. But her pigmentation was white. Porfirich was always coming on to her and, given the aplomb with which she would give as good as she got— either entering into the game of innuendoes or snapping at him, casting indecent words back in his face with practiced skill—it may be that something had indeed happened between them, that this was conquered ground; otherwise she wouldn't have displayed her rights of possession with such assurance. The rest of the ensemble would follow their scuffles with amused resignation, from the sidelines, spectators not allowed to participate in the events unless they paid the modest entrance fee.

Orthansa, the ensemble's prima donna, was a literature student, a prim and professorial girl with a languorous, indulgent smile for the conductor's smutty jokes. She didn't dislike them, but she made a point, at least when I was around, of conserving, out of a sense of propriety, her reputation for being a bluestocking. She was noble and urbane, a diamond in a basket of knobby pebbles. Toward me she had an attitude of sympathy and complicity. Together we were part of a mésalliance with the others. We wore our difference like some token of belonging to a different caste, to a waning species, which the times had forced to submit to a ritual of humiliation and survival in new, motley social circumstances, without any hope of a comeback in the foreseeable future. In fact, we had no concept of the future. Stirred into the swill of conviviality for the length of the rehearsals and during the blessed breathers decreed by Porfirich, when everyone would smoke and gossip, I used to exchange hurried words with Orthansa, and above all meaningful glances, "looks with hidden drawers," as she liked to call them. And in the brief moments when we were alone together, or on the way home, as far as the intersection by the "40 Martyrs" cinema, where our paths separated, we used to get back at our band mates by joking about them, laughing at the never-ending amorous war between Simona and Quasimodo, but not daring to start our own war, which, naturally, would have looked more like a reading-room idyll by comparison.

With Silviu the accordionist I struck up a composed and protective friendship from the very first. He was a stereotypical Moldavian, with a moustache framing his delicate mouth, eyes as limpid as a mountain spring, black wavy hair, and a contagious laugh that burst out at the slightest provocation. A friend. A man who understands you and helps you when you're in trouble without asking for anything in return. Surprisingly—because he had no pretensions and automatically placed me in a privileged position—I could communicate with him more easily than with Baciu, the ensemble's panpipes player, my colleague from university and collocutor in "nationalist" discussions.

Baciu regarded himself as being superior to the other band members. He wasn't the only wind instrumentalist, but the pipes of Pan were simply on a higher plane: his notes in the silken fabric of the folk melodies resembled the sensuous intrusion of a young lady from the city into a rustic ring dance: they gave them suppleness and elegance, they imbued them with intrigue, they made the audience dream. The panpipes were an individualistic, self-sufficient, self-worshipping instrument. You couldn't imagine a whole ensemble of panpipes players, whereas there's nothing more banal, more easily ignored than a gaggle of trumpeters—and, indeed, nothing more easily heckled when they begin to get on one's nerves. At the same time, the relative distance that Baciu and I had placed between ourselves—by mutual consent, I might add—was amicably fostered by our mutual awareness of belonging to the same circle of friends outside the ensemble, within which we had chosen to have strictly formal relations. Soldiers on the "ideological front" of the press, we read banned Romanian books and listened to folk songs from the other side of the Prut, secretly transcribing them on magnetofon tape in the university's recording studio. Moreover, we lived in the same student hostel, even if we had begun to bump into each other ever more seldom. Baciu, of course, had other places of shelter.

■ ■ ■

Those were the characters, or at least a few of them, and that was the atmosphere in which, four times a week, we gruelingly rehearsed Moldavian folk melodies to seduce Italian communists. Once we were joined by the dance troupe, the rehearsals increased to twice a day, so that we would synchronize. By the time I went to bed, I was unable to get rid of the sprightly melodies still resounding in my head.

By the end of May, we had mastered the music and all the travel documents had been authorized and stamped: the list of students and their chaperones, the passports, the medical insurance certificates.

I don't know which of my fellow band members the University's KGB man had recruited, but there was no doubt that arrangements had been made. Maybe he had recruited more than a few, because, surprisingly, he had left me alone. I was hiding under my shirt Miron's letter of recommendation to Feretti, the writer from Bologna who was to help me apply for political asylum in Italy.

As we left, my friend gave me these words of encouragement: "I hope that the orchestra . . ."—here he hesitated, and then went on: "I think that all those torturous rehearsals will come in useful. You'll be ready for the performance now, and you won't make a fool of yourself." I embraced him and assured him in the same complicit tone that all would go well.

On June 3, we got off the train at Bologna Station. I recognized Feretti on the platform, having pored over photographs of him night after night. But before I knew it was really Feretti, I had spotted his orange scarf, which was wrapped around the collar of his navy blue long-sleeved shirt. He didn't come near, but I knew that he had seen me and would find me the next day.

TRANSLATED FROM ROMANIAN BY ALISTAIR IAN BLYTH

TOMÁS MAC SÍOMÓIN

Music in the Bone

I dream of myself sitting in that chair. One year ago to the day. In my clinician's white coat. Switching on the tape recorder beneath my desk. Scribbling notes into a rough jotter while Mrs. X, the woman behind the desk in front of me, talks. Meanwhile, my partner in our psychiatric clinic in the dead centre of this city examines Mr. X. Mrs. X is tall, middle-aged, vaguely good-looking, of medium build. High cheekbones, an almost Slavic face. Carefully thinned eyebrows shaped to give an inadvertently vague look of permanent surprise. Her black dress sets off a white pearl necklace. Where have I seen this lady before. In another life? Is she a ghost ? Nothing ghostly, however, about that inexplicably familiar fragrance wafting into my nostrils.

– And, apart from that small . . . idiosyncrasy, shall we say, you tell me that your husband is normal, so to speak, in every other respect?

Giving a self-conscious professional's omniscient inflection to my voice. It seems to me that I have posed a similar question a thousand times, at least. To other women. To other men.

– In every possible way, Doctor, she says. He is really the most normal man you could imagine. In every way. Apart from his passion for music and this "idiosyncrasy," as you describe the mad behavior he gets up to now and then. The way he rises to his feet when you least expect it and starts to conduct some imaginary orchestra that nobody else hears nor sees. Even in the presence of my friends. I really don't know what to do about my predicament, Doctor. That man has destroyed my social life.

– . . . ?, I ask, wordlessly. (The tilt of one eyebrow can suffice to express a question mark.) The lady's slightly nasal voice drones on as she repeats what she has already told me.

I listen carefully. For the heart of the issue is often revealed in the retelling. And as she rattles on, the unexpectedly familiar whiff of her perfume unsettles me in some inexplicable way. I ask the question of myself yet again: where and when have I smelled that fragrance before?

– It doesn't matter where in the hell we might be, Doctor, (if you'll excuse my French). In the house, the church, the shops, on the street, on the bus. Or during social visits to the houses of our friends. Even in his office, if what his work associates tell me is true. Nor does he care who might be looking at him or listening to him. When his "idiosyncrasy" expresses itself, other people cease to exist, as far as he is concerned. And it's as if their opinions, customs, social correctness itself have vanished like a puff of air. His movements and the flailing of his arms giving onlookers to understand that he is conducting some sort of band or orchestra. Just as I've been telling you.

– Now let us talk a little about yourself, I hear myself saying. How do you react while this imaginary concert, so to speak, is proceeding under the imaginary baton of your spouse.

– I try to speak to him, to reason with him, Doctor, but he gives me the deaf ear. Just as if he were deep in some sort of hypnotic trance. As if I and the real world cease to exist for him . . .

– Even if you become angry with him?

– I've tried to stop him, of course. Stop making a fool of yourself in public, you idiot, I would say. For all the bloody good that did, Doctor, if you'll excuse my language. He paid not the slightest heed to what I said. And me simply trying to get him to return to the real world! And he stares at me with unseeing eyes all the while. Or, rather, seeing through me. That was the hardest part to bear, Doctor, his looking through me as if I didn't exist. And that lost look in his eyes. That is what scared me out of my wits . . .

– Does he ever become violent when you attempt to interfere with, or stop, his . . . artistic endeavours, if we can call them that?

– Not up till now, at any rate. In fact when this "music," as he calls it, stops, he tells me, somewhat sheepishly, that he is totally powerless to resist it. The beauty of it is such that he simply must conduct it, he says. He tells me that he is constantly amazed that neither I nor anybody else can hear his music. It is so loud, he says, that it drowns out every other sound. But I hear absolutely nothing when he gets these mad fits. Nor does anybody else. Not a goddamn note.

– And how are you coping these days?

– I try to make believe that he is not with me, Doctor. Especially when he starts to "conduct" in some public place.

– Can you give me an example? I ask.

– Can I ever! There was that wet Sunday a few months ago— how could I ever forget it—when we were attending midday Mass. The parish priest, Canon Murphy, was preaching from the pulpit overlooking the congregation. Talking about the sacredness of the sacrament of matrimony, I remember that much very well. When suddenly my husband jumps to his feet. Imagine the start that gave me. And then away with him, in full view of the congregation behind us, frenziedly conducting some imaginary choir. The canon stopped preaching and fixed him with a look that should have turned him into stone. I just shrank into myself. Hoping against hope that nobody would think that I was with this madman. I could hear an angry buzz of complaints from the pews behind us. And the puzzled faces of people in the pews in front of us turning around to see what was the matter. I am sure that everybody thought he was mocking Canon Murphy. The ushers dragged him, with difficulty, out of the church, the congregation silently observing the whole sorry spectacle. A burly shaven-headed brute, with a snake tattoo on the back of his neck, tried to attack him outside the church gates after Mass. But for a vigilant Garda on duty there, there is no saying how that story might have ended.

– So it was this incident that impelled you to seek professional help? I ask.

The "orchestral conductor's" wife blushes, the sudden rush of colour to her cheeks accentuating her early autumnal charm. And as I survey this modest blush, the long elegantly manicured fingers with their rings resting on the table in front of me, that elusive fragrance in the air, I am more certain than ever that I have met this woman somewhere before. Professional discretion prevents me from pursuing this matter further.

– Not really, Doctor, she says, answering my question. But when these "concerts" started to interfere with . . . well, the most intimate aspects of our life together . . . I hope you will not want me to supply you with the details! But, as a married man, you will appreciate exactly what I mean, she says, glimpsing at my wedding ring out of the corner of her eye. Suffice it to say that when your husband leaves the warmth of the marriage bed in the dead of night to conduct a phantom orchestra instead of fulfilling his . . . marital duties, you can see my predicament. Not to mention my frustration. And you can understand that we are talking here about a marriage that could not survive without "professional help," as you call it. And so both of us have come, as a last resort, to your clinic, Doctor . . .

– And he came here willingly?

– Dragging his heels, Doctor.

When the consultation ends, I switch off the tape recorder under my desk. Mrs. X leaves the office, her cheeks still glowing, probably from the highly personal nature of her "confession." No sooner has she left, leaving faint traces of her scent in the air behind her, than Sheila, our chief secretary, enters and leaves a note from my colleague on my desk. I quickly scan it. It informs me that the musically inclined Mr. X has been subject to a full battery of clinical tests. His pulse, blood pressure, blood sugar levels, cholesterol are all indicative of that gentleman's rude good health.

Therefore I am not surprised as I observe, some ten minutes later, the man who is sitting in the chair vacated by his wife. He is middle-aged, of medium height, balding, and with a slight tendency to heaviness. Rather like myself, in fact. He is clean-shaven, somewhat conservatively dressed in a gray suit, a striped shirt, and a dark club tie. His overall appearance proclaims the essence of bourgeois decency, a clean-cut image of civic virtue that normal citizens strive to attain. A pleasant, slightly conspiratorial smile flits across his face before he opens our conversation:

– Quite frankly, Doctor, I am not quite sure why I'm here, he says. I do not feel that there is anything wrong with me. But in order to satisfy my wife . . . you know how annoying women can be sometimes . . .

Without saying anything, I switch on the tape recorder. Having delivered his opening gambit, the conspiratorial smile returns briefly to his face . . .

I still say nothing. Pretending to scribble a note, I survey my client professionally from the corner of my eye. Not a trace of any abnormality in the tone of his voice, in the confident ease of his delivery. A performance conforming fully to the correctness of his appearance. I cannot imagine such a sober citizen in the guise of a crazed conductor of the nonexistent choir in his local parish church. Could the mysterious Mrs. X be the victim of such a delusional fantasy? I have been long enough in this profession to understand that superficial appearances often belie the real truth of a case. After I note the firm handshake of Mr. Normal, we briefly discuss the impending deluge promised by the weather forecast and how it may cause Sunday's championship football game to be postponed. Man talk! After this warm up, I place my cards on the table:

– The condition that brings you to this consultancy, I understand from talking to your wife, is that you sometimes imagine you hear a brass band, or an orchestra, playing within yourself. And that nobody but yourself can hear the music they are playing. And then, she told me, you feel some sort of compulsion, as it were, to conduct this imaginary ensemble.

The bland countenance of Mr. X is creased momentarily by a cynical smile.

– She would say that, wouldn't she! That all I hear is imaginary music, as she tells anybody who bothers to listen to her. But I have told her a thousand times that my music can in no way be explained in such simple terms. For we are talking here about a magnificent orchestra that performs in the deepest depths of my soul . . .

– Hmmm, very interesting! But, let us get a handle on this, Mr. X, I say. If you imagine that you can hear some sort of music that neither your wife, nor anybody else, can hear—if what she tells me is true—can't you recognise that there is a problem here we need to address? A not inconsiderable problem, perhaps? That may need professional help. When did you first note this, what you refer to as, music? Perhaps in your early adolescence, with the first stirrings of your sexuality?

– Balderdash, Doctor! It is only a problem insofar as she, and you it seems, construe my music as some sort of undesirable deviation from normality. As a problem to be solved. I, on the other hand, see it as a special grace from the Muse.

– Really! And when was the first time you heard this extraordinary sound?

– It's just as if it happened yesterday. There I was, embroiled in the preparation of tax returns, when I heard a single note being played on a viola. Or on a violin. Just a single note on some stringed instrument or other being tuned by some unseen presence within the office. I searched high and low to find where this strange note was coming from. The only radio I had in the office was switched off. As I listened to it, the note gained depth and volume. My body seemed to melt and be absorbed into this note. Then, I suddenly realized that the note was coming from within my own flesh and bones, Doctor. As if sounding in some far distant place and, at the same time, in some cavern in the depths of my soul. That note lasted about a half hour according to my office clock. But it seemed to me to be without beginning or end.

– What happened then, after that half hour?

– Not a thing, Doctor. When the note faded away—or when I returned from paradise, to phrase it differently—everything was more or less the same as before I ever heard it. In the beginning, I thought—just as my wife still thinks—that my mind had been subject to some sort of aural illusion. A temporary blip created by a fatigued brain or pressure at work. But, how I longed for the return of that note that I felt would never return . . .

– Yet, this longing of yours appears to have been satisfied, by all accounts?

– It certainly was, Doctor. One week later, as I was walking to the DART station, that tax-return stress was a thing of the past. Yet, as I walked, I heard my music once again and it sounded even more beautiful than ever. But it was no longer just a single note. It took the form of a simple tune that I had never heard before. A product of the culture of some exotic clime, perhaps, with just a hint of Araby. But, to be honest with you, Doctor, no human culture could generate such beauty.

– Hmmm! And this music seemed to be coming from within yourself, you say? Music from the depths of your own soul, as you might phrase it?

There was hardly any need for me to intervene. For, it is clear from the animated features of Mr. X that he can hardly wait to tell his whole story. To make the full confession that does good to the soul. Like the bearer of some sensational tale who has just found his first sympathetic ear.

– At first, Doctor, I thought the music was coming from my stomach. That something I had eaten had upset my digestion, with this unexpected result. The couscous I had eaten in a Moroccan restaurant the previous day, for example. Although you would hardly expect such fare to generate stomach music. Internal thunder, maybe, but music? A little bit later, the music seemed to have moved to my spine. A little bit later again it seemed to be coming from my heart. Later again, all of my body was, well . . . a concert platform for this band . . .

– A band you say?

– A full orchestra, Doctor. I began to hear it more and more frequently. And at each successive performance, still more musical instruments joined in. A weird thought occurred to me, at that time. I told myself that maybe that music was within me since the very day I was born. But that its pure sound was muffled by my own ignorance and life's discordant symphony. Anyhow, I hear it more and more often these days. And when I least expect it. In the pub, in the office, on the train, at home . . . And, a strange thing, no matter where this band is playing, only I can hear it, playing there, sounding deep inside me!

– And can you identify individual instruments in this inner music, as you describe it? Or, would you say that this "music" is played on instruments hitherto unknown?

– Not really, Doctor. As soon as I mentally label an instrument I hear—an Arabic flute, a Japanese koto, a medieval lute, a Scottish bagpipe, an Algerian reihab, an Indian sitar, uileann pipes — then the music itself contemptuously rejects that label. As if it was mocking my feeble efforts to reduce its incredible novelty to known human terms. And although the same basic tune is being played continually by this orchestra, or band, the infinite variations it plays on this theme, sometimes makes the latter well nigh unrecognisable . . .

As I listen to this long spiel from the mouth of Mr. X, I detect a classic case of schizophrenia encased in that conventional gray suit that faces me from the other side of my desk. Experience tells me clearly that the voices and mysterious messages that patients of his ilk report are in the same category as his strange "music." But other practitioners of my profession will be certain to take a keen interest in my description of the unusual symptomatology of X's neurosis. I continue to make rough notes in my jotter as Mr. X gives free rein to his stream of consciousness:

schizophrenia—interesting and unusual case
music instead of voices in his head
great paper for the next convention will make my name

Mentally composing the first paragraph of this putative paper,

I ask X, somewhat diffidently:

– And do you detect the influence of the great composers on this "music?" a question to keep Mr. X feeding data into my recorder.

– As I've told you, Doctor, this music is unlike anything that you or I have ever heard. And, believe me, I know what I'm talking about. For I've listened to the music of all the great composers: Beethoven, Haydn, Mozart, Delibes, Rimsky-Korsakov . . . all the way down to the moderns, like Philip Glass. I have researched the Ceòl Mór, the Great Music of the Scottish pipes, the classical ragas of India, the various musical traditions of Africa and their influence on the music of the Caribbean and the Americas. Trying frantically to gauge the origin of this music in my bones, I ransacked every musical tradition beneath the sun. From the Sean Nós of Connemara to the gríhe of the Berbers. From the rocks of Cape Verde to the deserts of Mongolia, I have listened to the traditional voice of seldom-heard peoples. From Joe Heaney to Benny Moré to Victor Jara to Lightnin' Hopkins. And I know how to separate the grain from the chaff, the true voice from that of the phoney, Woodie Guthrie from Bob Dylan, for example. You would hardly believe, Doctor, the long nights I have spent till the dawn listening to recordings of every type of music on this planet. And this obsessive cosmopolitanism is nearly driving my wife out of her mind.

– Not surprisingly! And all of this study brought you no nearer to the root of your condition?

– My effort was all in vain, Doctor. For no music that I heard from whatever tradition came even close to the ethereal music that my orchestra plays . . . An eminent Professor in our National School of Music suggested to me that I learn musical notation. Knowing this musical alphabet, he said, I would be able to transcribe my music into a written form. And thus be in a position, maybe, to make a startling new innovation in world music. However, I discovered before long that the form of musical notation that is perfectly adequate to a description of classical European music, say, has no relevance whatsoever to the music that only I can hear. The pre-classical pentatonic scale is, likewise, unable to describe the music of my soul . . . But all of that was before I realised that I was a conductor, not a creator . . ,

– What exactly do you mean by that, Mr. X?

– Well, one day as I was walking on a beach near my home, I was confronted with something totally unexpected. And the word "unexpected" puts it mildly, indeed . . .

Mr. X's last revelations have the effect of suddenly awakening me from a pleasant reverie, in which Mrs. X, the scent of whose perfume is still faintly—but tantalisingly—perceptible in the consultation room, was playing a central role.

– How interesting, I said. Now, please tell me what you mean by "totally unexpected"!

– Well, as I was walking along, listening to my music, I started to imitate the gestures of musical conductors up there on the podium facing their orchestras. And then I suddenly realised that I was able in fact, with the help of the movements of my arms, to conduct the music being played by my internal orchestra.

– Or, rather, you were able to adjust the nature of your arm movements to the music to which you were listening.

– No, you've got it wrong, Doctor. It was the other way around. Because what I found out was that my arms were capable of determining exciting new variations on the basic theme of the music to which I was listening. And to direct the musicians within me, so to speak, to obey my personal diktat, as expressed through the movements of my arms.

– I understand, Mr. X, that this "discovery" changed your life. And not only your life? And not necessarily for the better?

As I slowly enunciate those words, I simultaneously scribble the following words into my jotter:

emergency case
admit X immediately
under no circumstance must he be allowed to leave the building

– Well, it certainly did change things, Doctor, continues Mr. X. From the ground up, so to speak! Every time my orchestra visits me—and this happens three or four times a day lately—they expect me to conduct them in playing new variations on their basic theme. This is both an intense pleasure and an enduring challenge. For there is no limit to the variations I can create by concentrating exclusively on the movements of my arms. Nor is there any boundary to the beauty I can now bring into being. By paying not the slightest heed to the rules and regulations, so to speak, that determine what is and what is not music as defined by the times in which we live . . .

X spends a period of three months with us in the clinic. But no medication or therapy, nor combination of both in the various treatments we try, manage to silence his internal orchestra, as he calls it. For said orchestra now appears to be in permanent residence in his bones. Things have gone from bad to worse, as he now spends all his waking hours, from morning to night, "conducting" his phantom "musicians." Nobody but X can hear their "music," of course. But there they are, he insists, playing away inside him. The other patients derive great amusement from observing him conduct a ghostly orchestra playing his Great Symphony of Total Silence on the lawn behind the clinic. Not surprisingly, they call him Tchaikovsky . . .

I am in a deep sleep late at night—at three A.M. to be exact—when the most beautiful music that ears have ever heard wakes me suddenly. I sit up in bed and think instantly of Mr. X. Is it from his room, just over mine, on the floor above, that this music is coming? He will wake up all the other patients in the clinic unless his music is stopped immediately. I wonder why the damned night nurses haven't suppressed it already. I turn on the light switch, dress hastily, open my door, and step out into the corridor. The decibels are even higher out here.

A night nurse passes me on the stairs as I climb them on my way to Mr X's room.

– From which room do you think that strange music is coming? I ask her.

– Are you having me on? she answers, with a tired smile. But to be honest with you, Doctor, this place could do with a bit of music to liven it up. It's as quiet as a graveyard here tonight.

Is this night nurse as deaf as a post, I ask myself, while this unearthly music pours down on us like silver rain.

As I place my hand on the doorknob of X's room, the music rises to a crescendo. Hundreds, if not thousands, of orchestras address themselves simultaneously to the same theme. Now I know where this music is coming from, with absolute certainty. As I open the door, the volume of the crescendo doubles. I place my hands over my ears. To no avail.

Mr. X is nowhere to be seen. It is as if he has never been here. His bed seems as if it has never been slept in. Then I open his wardrobe, and I detect again the fragrance of the perfume of the woman in the black dress in my nostrils. There is no sign of X's clothes or suitcase. Anywhere. Did he ever exist? Just then, I get the greatest shock of my life. For hanging there is the black dress of Mrs. X. My clinician's white coat, my gray suit, and my striped shirt hang beside it, where

X's clothes should be.

The music is welling up inside me now.

Mr. X was telling the truth, the whole truth, and nothing but the truth.

For, with an imaginary conductor's baton in my hand, I extract whatever music I will from this unearthly orchestra within.

TRANSLATED FROM IRISH BY THE AUTHOR

TIINA RAEVAARA

My Creator, My Creation

Sticks his finger into me and adjusts something, tok-tok, fiddles with some tiny part inside me and gets me moving better—last evening I had apparently been shaking. Chuckles, stares with water in his eyes. His own hands shake, because he can't control his extremities. Discipline essential, both in oneself and in others.

What was it that was so strange about my shaking? He himself quivers over me, strokes my case, and finally locks me, until the morning comes and I'm on again, I make myself follow all day and filter everything into myself, in the evening I make myself shut down and in the morning I'm found in bed again. Between evening and morning is a black space, unconsciousness, wham—dark comes and clicks into light, light is good, keeps my black moment short. He has forbidden me it: for you there's no night. Simply orders me into a continuum of morning to evening, evening to morning, again and again. But in the mornings I know I've been switched off. I won't tell about it. Besides, why does he exclude me from the night? I don't ask, but I still call the darkness night. There is night and day, evening and morning will come.

■ ■ ■

Today is a visiting day. A collecting day, an exhibition day, a walking-around day, a following day. He goes, and I follow, clop, I pound the floor but don't feel comfortable, I would prefer to be at home doing my things, following my settings, being directed. I am intended for the home, for one space, elsewhere I am surplus, unnecessary. Of course, there are others intended for elsewhere, to each his own.

The exhibition space is too cold, the temperature eighteen point three Celsius, to be accurate. I do not generally mind cold or heat, nevertheless I feel stiff and creaky—but is the temperature the cause? Maybe not. Maybe I actually feel something. "I'm so pissed off my head is splitting," he once said, at the beginning of time, and since then I too have sought in myself something of the kind, the union of emotion and body, this my one and only. Stiffness is a new thing, and is that a sensation of mind or body? Hard for me to understand such distinctions, the division between mind and body, mental sensations and bodily sensations are certainly quite different, although rarely in my case.

Bumps into me as he stops, I let myself be bumped into a little bit on purpose, because here he hasn't yet said a word to me. Doesn't say anything now either, looks pensive. Rests one hand on his temples and scratches his head. I would dearly like him to speak, but of course orders can't come from me.

What have I learned lately? It is one of the great purposes, learning—development.

He taught me to read, it wasn't even difficult. Closed me for a moment so that I was on a black break again, whamm, like a quick night, a click, then he appeared in the middle of light, the new morning was quickly over, he said he'd updated me, and so I had learned. "This will increase your value," he said and passed me a book. The shelf is groaning with them, side by side, flat, formerly unnecessary to me, although unpleasant because they gather dust. Now they are full of words, maybe he wrote them while I was in the night. The one that he passed to me was thick indeed, a total of 1,108 gram-units, I opened it—he directed me a little—I read aloud from the point that first hit my visual sensors:

> *In presence of that light one such becomes*
> *That to withdraw therefrom for other prospect*
> *It is impossible he e'er consent . . .*

He laughed so much that he doubled up in the armchair. He: no name from my innards, for I am not allowed to address him by name. Any kind of title, I tried once, but then too he began to shake, eyelids wrinkled. Stroked me more eagerly for a while, it's true. But when I said it again, he slapped me so hard that my side element was dented. Slap! I straightened it myself later on. "Let's not get too close," he said as the reason for this new practice.

■ ■ ■

So, about the exhibition: We are in a giant room, huge, we have been here before—that much I've managed to extract from myself—but that was a while ago. I do not consider these things important enough to record very accurately in my memory, even I have my limits, you have to prioritise. I walk behind him. Now and again gives me glances although he's been pretending not to notice me all day, his posture is straighter than usual, quite splendid, and his expression I would call proud. From time to time he makes me stop, goes a bit farther away but keeps an eye on me, I would recognize his eye among a thousand, I am confident of that. Speaks with a few people, males, I do not recognize them even though I have seen them before, I am certain. Many of them inspect me, one winks and looks me over slowly, first my feet and then upward. What do I care, clop clop I go on pounding the floor. An ugly floor here.

We have arrived early: The exhibition hasn't begun yet, men adjust their creations, as yet not a wholesome multitude of people around me. We are just looking, I am not going to be shown today, we circulate, and every now and then he tells me to wait and I don't hear what he says to the others. Once a man who almost passes me by, older and with more facial hair than average, touches my back. I smile, I am now programmatically, exemplarily friendly.

We do not stay long. He quickly gets bored, talks to me for the first time in ages. "I can't be bothered looking at these ordinary things." So he says. Reaches out his hand and I take it in mine; I'd squeeze it if I were more autonomous. If I'd had permission, I would have looked up. Never so beautiful before, exulting. Though this only out of the corner of my eye.

Later: acts unusually, very different. Does not want to read the new newspaper beside his food. The newspaper stops coming. The old one lies by the sofa, wrinkling. Appetite has decreased, says so himself, tells me not to cook anything but pasta. That is what he eats, by the bowlful, nothing else, doesn't want to buy anything else. Weeks go by, there are seven days in a week. No longer goes out in the evenings, instead buys big bottles of stuff and sits in the living room with one of them beside him. Once, I sniff the bottle, out of curiosity, because I have felt a twitch in the left side of my neck. He snorts: "That won't suit your plumbing." Then pours it into his depths.

Once I get scared. In the morning I have been on for as much as ten minutes and thirteen seconds, and then the lights go out. At first I think he shut me down again, but no, I can sense and move. There is understanding, it is not night but a dark day, whatever that may be. But the lamps have gone out, and not a change in my innards. He says very loudly: "Damn, now they've cut off the electricity!" I would scream if told to: I can't survive without electricity, not for long, the next day is my electricity day.

He telephones somewhere, through the wall I hear the voice but not the words. First he's angry, then amicable, to me he's never been so beseeching, so polite. Never. But the electricity comes back. Why, he is capable of anything.

After that keeps me on later in the evenings, strokes me more slowly than before, maybe he wants to smooth my lumps and bumps, remove the dark oxides from my case, maybe he wants to make me gleam. When it is already far into the night—I have never been on so late in the night—he sighs, touches my innards, and switches me off. As if he did not want to stop, to close, to be without. Things are necessary, and I am among them.

Everything I think feels to me as if my shoulder joint is loosening. I do not report the fault. Sometimes I find such astonishing little actions within myself.

■ ■ ■

Seventeen days ago, almost exactly, I experienced something new. Earlier in the day, I had been set to read a book again, far into the evening. Meanwhile, he sat in a chair with his eyes shut. The wrinkle at one side of his mouth tautened and relaxed from time to time, human skin is remarkably flexible. After, we went to bed.

Maybe he switched me off wrongly somehow, because I found myself in the midst of blackness but was present there too. My mind stayed on, I could not move but on the other hand I did not wish to either, I did not think about moving at all, or about my own parts.

I saw unfamiliar, impossible things: things that don't really exist, I know well—but I saw them move and be in the same way as all of us who exist, move, and be, myself among them.

These things I saw:

Men with horns growing in their heads.

A big bird with a human face.

A blank wall you can walk through.

Furniture—a table and stools that jumped around.

Among them all, myself, I flew and floated, although I have not been granted such capacities.

Then he must have switched me off, because next it was morning.

■ ■ ■

One morning he is more talkative, less red-eyed. Some of them are coming here, men from the exhibition, I remember shapes from their faces and their ways of walking, no one human being is the same as the others. First the telephone rings, beep-be-beep, and then they come, driving into the yard one at a time. Before he opens the door he puts me in my own chair in the corner of the room, telling me to be nice. But my being is always nice.

"Shall we begin straight away?" one down-cheek shouts, not even coming all the way into the room, just putting his head around the door, and I am not used to such half-and-half behavior. In all my programlessness I begin to click my thumb, I can't think of any other actions. There are three of them. They are happy, even merry, I would say, if I was asked. "Good shenanigans?" asks one, and I have to consult my vocabulary. Apparently we have not had a lot of shenanigans in our house. His cheeks glow red, this speaker's, and all of them have bright eyes. They negotiate in loud voices, louder than I would ever be allowed to speak.

They bring in the kind of devices—mediocrities, he would say—
that I have seen at exhibitions. But then from a distance, out of
focus, now close-up; I could make contact with them if this was to
be considered necessary. The things are silent: they take them out
of boxes and set them out side by side in the corridor. "Let them
wait their turn," one says, younger than the norm, then eyes me as
a continuation of the queue. "You must be part of the furniture,"
he goes on, and winks—I remember him, because he has winked
before. A funny person, male, I allow him to touch my case. One of
them hasn't brought anything, he just watches. Stares at me, too, but
I do not allow it to affect my settings.

When they aren't looking, I just turn my sensors toward the others,
when the men talk together loudly but with different words in the
living room and forget to monitor the world, I walk back and forth in
the corridor and inspect what they brought, the beauties.

The first: small and white as a mouse, would fit on my upper limb
and that is indeed where I would want it to sleep—its curled form,
its nose touching its back toes. I bend over it and stroke it, its coat
is enormously soft, and if I were really small, a tiny particle, I could
hide in it. The head, though, has no fur; it is as smooth a skin as my
surface, in that respect I am perhaps lacking. It has no eyelids, but
its eyes are closed. What my eyes look like closed I do not know.

The second: I cannot make it out, it is the size of a stool and so
full of protuberances and ends or wiring that it, too, looks furry. I
circle round it, crouch beside it, try to see what manner of being it
is. I find a little hole that could lead to its insides—for a moment I
feel like opening it and touching—but of course I do not. You are no
toucher of insides, he said to me once. Although I do know how to
fix things, a car even.

The third, to me, is the most beautiful: the size of a large dog, and
the shape of one too, because it stands on four paws and has a long

neck stretched out to the front and side. I have seen pictures, and once even a live one. At the rear is a thin and long tail, an animal's tail, it is curled round one of the back legs like a printer's cable on a desk. The nose is longer and narrower than the dog's I saw, its head was like a ball; on the end of the nose are two narrow nostrils. Ears I cannot distinguish at all, its big eyes are closed. Not everybody has ears, and some have only inner ears. Most beautiful of all in the creature are its color settings: the dark blue of the snout changes to the purple of the neck, the orange of the side elements and the bright yellow spot of the lower back, asymmetrical, and then through the red of the thighs and root of the tail to the bluishness of the tail-tip and paws, sky-color.

■　■　■

The men pour the last drops from a bottle and look very happy, although the bottle is proven empty. The funny man doesn't drink anymore, but walks past me into the corridor, does not want to touch my side this time, although I would allow such a thing. I guessed that the beautiful creature is his, the one that is as gaudily colored as the sky on evenings when the sun goes out and dyes the clouds. The creature does not appear to have any innards at all—the man bends down in front of it, strokes its side, breathes into its nostrils. At first nothing happens, the other men glance at funnyman but he just smiles. His forehead looks damp—perhaps he's the kind that is called a pantshitter. "Pantshitters don't know how to keep their nerves in order," he said once when he was watching TV, and laughed. Not at me, he didn't mean me. My nerves are very well-disciplined.

But then the dog-snake, that's what I'll call it, opens up. First the eyes: their brilliance is fractured, as if they were made up of a countless number of little red lamps. Then the mouth: the creature opens its maw for a second and from its throat comes a quiet cooing, and I feel my internal rhythm missing a beat, for I have a rhythm too, after all.

"Forma," says the man, "sit!" The creature has lolloped around him with its sides like fire, flaring, we once had a fire in the grate here, but now it sits on its tail very obediently, just as I would sit down if I were commanded to do so, and if there were a tail behind me. They are so proud, all of them: the uncomfortable man of his mouse creature, red-shirt of his tousle-fleece, and then this last, the one with the dog-snake. There is a tickling in my innards: I would like to know what pride feels like.

It is my turn last. He nods to me from his chair, is so relaxed, I've never before seen him like this. Doesn't come to get me as the others did, trusts in the fact that I'm no vacuum cleaner, that I don't need to be pulled from the cupboard.

I walk into the middle of the room and look pretty damn good.

■ ■ ■

They leave at last, when I have read myself to exhaustion and done all sorts of other things, showing off my talents. He is still sitting in his chair and does not look as if he intends to get up. Tired head nods onto the table where the empty bottles stand. In his hand is one that is not yet empty. Outside, the sun has been taken away.

"Creation," he says as if in thought, "makes a person into something sublime. Almost a god. If one can create, one can no longer be an ordinary person." Then raises the bottle to his lips again. Sighs as the bottle empties, and lets it crash to the floor. I hasten to pick it up as I was intended to. Grasps my wrist. The wrist joint has been playing up over the past few days, really creaking, creak-creak, is he going to mend it now.

But he pulls me to him, slightly into his lap and slightly onto the arm of the chair. Puts his hand on my face element and strokes a point on my temple where the casing is particularly smooth.

"Do you understand?" he demands, as if I thought about such things at all. "Because of you, I am not ordinary, I am something quite extraordinary." Suddenly he smiles again. Gets up from his chair, pushes me off his lap. "Stand there," he orders, and his eyes gleam; he presses his hands to my sides and raises my chin into a better position. So I stand there. He paces around me and chuckles about something else, in a low voice that eludes my senses. From time to time he taps my surface, bends my fingers, at one point opening my insides but then closing them again.

"You're some beast, you," he says at last, nodding his head. Although I am no beast, but a being of quite a different kind.

I begin to tidy up, and go on tidying even after everything is in order.

"What does creation mean?" I ask it casually, in passing, as I take the rug out to beat it, although I probably did that already. It is not my custom to question, to question anything, after all one would hardly suppose that I would take an interest in the nature of things in general. One would not suppose it, not of one like me, not even an exemplary one like me.

He mumbles something, at first I doubt that he has heard me. Quite often a fault in the senses, ears not very accurate. He raises his hand in the direction of where the empty bottle was, I have not taken it away. Can't reach it. I want to help, but really, why should I pass him an empty bottle?

"Gods create," he then says, his voice coming muffled as if he was shouting at other people from the other side of a wall.

"Are y —, are you one of those?" I ask. I would like to tighten a screw somewhere deep down where something must have been jerked out of place—I am almost making mistakes. He begins to laugh, laughing from a deeper place than before and sounding different. I could even believe that it is not mere tiredness that makes him so fatigued.

"Yes, people do create. Books, for example, which you also read. And paintings. It's quite normal." He leans his head back against the chair, is clearly pleased with me since he is talking so much. It doesn't happen often, that. "Creation is making something that has not existed before."

A car light from the street makes a red streak on the floor. I click my head back and forth and try to understand, all sorts of things. Later he falls asleep in the chair and I am left on all night, for the first time ever.

■ ■ ■

A long time ago when I first arrived, so shiny and smooth-cased, I was kept in a place where there were children, almost the same age, I spent time with them and learned to be. He thought it important. While the children drew, I sat on my chair by the table and was very charming. Sometimes someone came up and bashed me, but the dents only became evident later, at home, after he had fetched me back.

"Great, very clever, you should be proud." That's the kind of thing they said to the children, and I listened.

I read again:

> O how all speech is feeble and falls short
> Of my conceit, and this to what I saw
> Is such, tis not enough to call it little!
> O Light Eterne, sole in thyself that dwellest,
> Sole knowest thyself, and, known unto thyself
> And knowing, lovest and smilest on thyself!

He no longer laughs at what I read, just nods. Then does something strange—leaves me alone in my own company and goes away, saying he will come back later: "I'm just going to do a couple of things, you'll be fine alone for a couple of hours."

I fall into myself. First I stretch out on the floor, he encourages it because it straightens a lot of things out. When I've done it, I feel lonely and grease my bends. After that I walk around the house and look good, stroke my details and their permanence, keep stopping at the window for a moment, looking at the world as it happens to be at this moment.

I read to myself, trying to pronounce well:

> *Within itself, of its own very color*
> *Seemed to me painted with our effigy,*
> *Wherefore my sight was all absorbed therein.*

Then I take a pen in my fair hand and do something that I have never done before.

■ ■ ■

At least a week goes by, and I do not count the evenings when I see all sorts of things before I am finally switched off. I do not understand where this comes from—there shouldn't be anything new, no updates or anything like them in my systems.

One time he is actually like me, someone with an outer casing, we are equal.

One time the sky is full of terrifying things, wings, shadows.

One time I stand in the kitchen, but it is dark, so dark that I cannot find myself.

Fortunately these views never last long.

· · ·

One day he comes back from his trip and is silent. We are both capable of silence, that is the same in both of us. Outside it is cold, twenty-six degrees Celsius less than the interior norm, and the cold has entered him, I sense it as soon as I take his coat. Moves more slowly than usual—perhaps he is suffering from stiffness. Does not want his usual cup of coffee but leads me to the living room. Holds a hand to my side, I follow. He sighs.

He keeps me by him even as he sits down.

"You know—" he begins, but how should I know, "—lately I have been short of money." I have not thought about such things. I am stunned for a moment. Perhaps this is just part of listening. I pull myself back together, however, as one should. "I have decided—" he continues, but falls silent, this is so completely new that I do not remember anything similar. Then he takes up a defiant position, raises his chin and straightens his back. "I am going to have to sell you."

What I find myself thinking is, sell, that's what's done to things, because he often comes back from shops where he has been sold food and bottles and small objects.

"One of those men wants to buy you."

"Who?" he lets me ask—he wouldn't always have done so; now the situation is quite different and I sense it under my casing. I feel petrified now too—it starts gently in my heel and creeps from there through the groin joints to my innards. I think, and then ask further: "It's the pantshitter, isn't it?"

Stands up, furious: "Is that what you call my friends, you—" he doesn't finish his sentence but hits me, hits me really proper, BANG, so that my seams shudder. I fall on to the floor and clatter and have no understanding of how I have offended against my programming. My temples feel tight, there must be something wrong inside my head.

Then he says nothing, I continue with former commands at least until evening and do not know what happens after that.

■ ■ ■

Electricity is what I need, that and sometimes other things too, orders preferably, because otherwise my existence fragments and goes off the rails and I am no longer as I was intended. Volatility, that is the danger—I easily begin to drift if rules and meaning are taken away. My borders move too much. Everything spins in my head, all that I have read and all the things I have stored away, I have experienced too much and I have perhaps not edited it sufficiently.

But through the sight, that fortified itself / In me by looking, one appearance only—I fumble for a moment in my memory—*To me was ever changing as I changed.*

Men with horns on their heads, myself with wings, he with a case
and children who are proud of what they have done
and a funnyman who smiled his face in two
and he paces around me and polishes me
But my own wings were not enough for this, / Had it not been that then my mind there smote
I grow dark.
A flash of lightning, wherein came its wish
I shut down once more for the night.

In the morning the stakes are high. I am not intended for anywhere but here. Elsewhere I would be senseless, unknown. As useless as a house that does not offer shelter from the rain, a car with no room for passengers. It is necessary to have a reason, a task.

I begin the morning with perfection. I execute my routines like an automaton, with unprecedented accuracy. Surely he will be dazzled, for life with me runs so smoothly.

When I have finished all that is expected, I offer him a surprise. He doesn't expect anything of the sort, believes I am still the untalented beetle he manufactured for himself. Standing in the hallway, about to go out, I walk up to him, almost in front of him.

"I have become masterly," I say, but politely all the same. He smiles, just a little. He continues to think he will leave, but I stand very fast in front of the door.

"I can create too." That is what I tell him, and I smile as well, trying to look new.

"Oh, but you can't do that." I amuse him; he trembles now as he sometimes does while watching TV.

"Oh yes I can," I say, holding my head up straighter than ever. He notices it, his eyes flashing, although he doesn't know he's doing it. Allows himself to be led away from the hallway into the living room. There I sit him down on the chair and remember to smile all the time. Smile smile, be beautiful, he used to say it himself. Light floods in through the window, too bright, it forces him to screw up his eyes although I would like him to keep them open, more open than before. But that is how a soft-surface is, afraid of light. I open a drawer, in the desk, and stretch my hand inside it.

■　■　■

The smallest child said, "I drawed a horsey." "A horse," the woman laughed, "—that's lovely!"

I listened my surface off.

. . . *as I changed* . . .

No, it didn't happen until later.

I draw out my creation—in a moment he will be dazzled.

He raises his face and moves his eyes out of the sun's path. Laughs until he's doubled over, guffaws himself into exhaustion like a blocked drain I had to clean once. "I thought you were serious!" His words remain in the shade because the sound of his laughter is so loud, but I know all about shady things, I do. "That kind of scribble, you can't even draw a straight line!"

I turn my drawing toward my own visual sensors: it shows galloping dog-snakes, mouse-people, trees blossoming gaily, cloud-light birds flying in the sky. My arm twitches.

"It is the world's most beautiful picture. I created it." I speak slowly, for clarity. He does not always understand me if I get upset, my skill is to be quick and accurate. I step closer, perhaps the sun is bothering him again.

"You don't know how to create! Even babies can draw better." He grabs the picture from my hands, dropping it, torn, on the floor. The sun strikes my sensors, too, as I bend down to pick up the piece of paper. Something twitches inside me, in all my systems, no longer just in my arm.

"My creator," I cry in my steely voice, beautiful and piercing. I reach out my arm.

TRANSLATED FROM FINNISH BY
HILDI HAWKINS AND SOILA LEHTONEN

memory

MIKLÓS VAJDA

Portrait of a Mother in an American Frame

She stands in the kitchen, in a kitchen, not our kitchen, not the old kitchen, not any of our old kitchens, but her own kitchen, an unfamiliar one, not mine, and she cooks, stirs something. She is cooking for me. That's another new thing, a strange thing. But there she stands, repeating anything I want, anywhere, whatever I happen to want most, at the time I want it. I am still here: she is not. And there are things I do want. But even if I didn't want them she would carry on coming and going, doing this and that, entering my head, calling me, talking, listening, now in delight, now in pain, thinking of me or looking at me, ringing me up, asking me things, writing to me as if she were alive. I am insatiable: I am interested in all that is not me, in what is private, in affairs before me and after me, in her existence as distinct from mine, and I try to fit the jigsaw together, but nowadays, whatever she is doing—and I can't do anything about this—is always, invariably done for me, because of me, to me, with me, or on my behalf—or rather, of course, for me.

At this very moment I want her to stand there, in that kitchen, stirring away. Let's have her cooking one of those dishes she learned abroad, let her make a caper sauce to go with that sizzling grilled steak. But I often have her repeat a great many other things too: for example, I have recently taken to observing her secretly from my bed as she slowly removes her make-up at the antique dressing table with the great gilded antique silver-framed standing mirror before her, going about her task in a businesslike manner, applying cream with balls of cotton wool, her hands working in a circular motion, efficiently, always in exactly the same way, pulling faces if need be, puffing out a cheek, rubbing her skin then smearing it with, among other things, a liquid she refers to as her "shaking lotion" and which dries immediately so she looks like a white-faced clown. Then she wipes it off and I fall asleep again. The room is full of mirrors, each of the six doors of the built-in cupboard is a full length mirror.

My bed is there in her bedroom: my own bedroom is being used by the German *Fräulein*. Sometimes I wake late at night just as she enters from the bathroom, wearing her yellow silk dressing gown, and I hear her as she applies creams and lotions for the night before going to bed, as she moves around, gets comfortable, clears her throat, and gives a good sigh before falling sound asleep, her mouth open, contented, exhaling loudly, exactly the way I catch myself doing nowadays.

Or I am watching her at eleven in the morning as she steps into the car, fully made up, elegantly dressed, wearing hat and gloves and high-heeled shoes, as she throws back the fashionable half-veil, pulls out of the garage, turns in the drive, takes the left-hand lane—the traffic is still driving on the left—and sets off from our Sas Hill villa in the Buda hills into the city center to do her shopping before meeting her friends in the recently opened Mignon Espresso—the first of its kind in Hungary—or at the Gerbeaud patisserie where she might go on to meet my father who sometimes strolls over from his office to talk over their plans for the next day or whatever else is on their minds. Then they come home together and eat. Or I see her in Márianosztra, or possibly, later, in Kalocsa, at the end of the monthly visiting time, led away by a guard armed with a submachine gun, out of the hall that is divided in half by a partition of wire netting, leaving through double steel doors, overlooked by enormous portraits of Stalin and Rákosi, and I catch a glimpse of her as she is shepherded away in a procession of prisoners and guards, and she freezes for a moment, conscious perhaps of me looking at her, to look back over her shoulder, sensing me standing there, staring at her. The guard's flat cap is covering half her face but her slight squint, her nod, her faint smile, and her suspiciously shining eyes tell me more than she could say to me in the fifteen allotted minutes in the presence of the guard.

Never in my life have I seen her cry. She did not cry when my father died, nor when her sister died. She cannot, she could not, perhaps she never wanted or allowed herself to give direct expression to intense feeling, not in words and certainly not in wild gestures. When either of us was going away on a longer trip she would embrace me and give me a light, brief kiss while gently patting my back by way of encouragement, then drawing a little cross on my forehead with her thumb. That's how we parted in December 1956 at the Southern Terminal, both of us in ruins, like the town itself, silently, crying without tears, since we both knew we would not see each other again for years, maybe never. Nor did I ever hear her sing or hum. Or, and this is another scene I often conjure, the telephone is ringing there, at her home in New York, and she looks at me in confusion, pleading with me once again silently rather than in words to answer it again because she has difficulty, particularly on the telephone, in understanding the language. Most of the time, of course, the caller is Hungarian. She hardly knows anyone here who is not Hungarian. Nowadays I have her pull this pleading face time and again, as if repeating a scene on DVD; I torture myself with it, it is my punishment. I always regret it but once or twice I rebuke her rather sharply for not having in all that time learned the language properly. But no sooner have I said the words than I am already regretting them: I don't know what has made me say them, made me want to lecture and criticize her, what makes me want to assert my independence, to push her away from me time after time. It's some obscure, as-yet-inexplicable urge I have to prod her where she is most vulnerable and often I am unable to resist it. I see she resents it; that I have hurt her; that it saddens her, that it makes her suffer, and that she closes up, but, wisely, accepts the latest rebuke, generously adding it to the rest. Perhaps she understands this instinctively better than I do. Even in the years before prison I was subjecting her to these low tricks; she bore the pain, but maybe, at that time, she could inwardly smile at the thought that her biological destiny had presented her with such a difficult adolescent. Very quickly though we're back to the usual way of doing things. Her patience, her calm, her seemingly endless wisdom in understanding, spring from a source deep within her. But she will never be more demonstrative than this. There are no sudden embraces, no pet-names, no uncalled-for affectionate kisses, no light laughter, no playful teasing, no letting-one's-hair down, no messing about.

Nor was there ever. I myself lack the capacity for at least two or three of those. We live in conditions of withdrawal and reserve, which is not the same as living in solemnity or dullness or indifference, nor does it exclude—not by any means—warmth, kindness, solicitude, gaiety, and a sense of humor cloaked in delicate irony, something I am particularly fond of. I have instinctively grown used, to some degree at least, to seeking what was missing in her in others: ever since I was born I have received generous helpings of them from Gizi, my godmother whom I adore, and, in her simple, modest way, from *Fräulein* too. Later I look for these qualities in girls, in women, with wildly varying results. But all in vain, since anything you were not given by your mother, indeed anything she did actually give you, will not be found anywhere else. That is my definitive experience. I have been feeling closer to her recently, ever since she died in fact. For a long time I believed she was a simple soul: that she lived by instinct alone, was prejudiced, was incapable of articulating her feelings, impressions, and passions, or only doing so when she was forced to and absolutely had to take a position on something. Then I realised I was wrong. She had a complex, rich, many-layered inner life, consisting not only of immediate feeling but of the tastes and ways of thinking traditional to her family and class. Over and over again in my head I replay the most memorable things she said, examining and analyzing them, and I always come to the same conclusion. Her opinions were thought through, never spur-of-the-moment or improvised, but properly considered and, when called upon, she could present excellent, concise arguments for them. She had outstanding moral judgment, impeccable taste, and her understanding of human character was all but infallible. She was not a snob but open and kindly, never condescending even in the genteel role of "madam," as she was to the servants for example. She was no blue-stocking, of course, but was reasonably well-read. It was thanks to her that I was introduced to Balzac and Dickens in my early adolescence, at a time when I was still reading Karl May and Jules Verne. In her later years she enjoyed reading Churchill's memoirs. She had studied at a girls' grammar school in Arad, her Transylvanian hometown, and, after the Romanian occupation, when her family—a fully Hungaricized landowning family of ancient Serbian origin, some of whose members played important roles in Hungarian history—fled to Pest, she studied the violin with Hubay, as long as they could afford it, which was not long. The photograph of the long-haired, slender, beautiful teenage girl passionately playing her violin—if one can go by such evidence—seems to indicate that she was deeply imbued with the love of music.

When the money ran out, she told me, they presented the violin to a poor, blind child genius. In view of that, it's surprising that she never showed the least interest in music later. Might she have taken offence at the hand fate had dealt her? Not one concert, not one visit to the Opera. The program of classical selections on the radio at lunchtime on Sunday—it was always on while we were eating—represented the entire musical diet of the family. Maybe that was because my father had absolutely no interest in music. From childhood on I would pick at the keys of my godmother's wonderful Steinway grand—a present from the Regent Horthy—and was strongly drawn to music, but year after year they kept rejecting my plea for lessons, dismissing it as a passing, infantile fancy. It was the only thing they ever refused me. Even today I can't forgive them for it.

But what I chiefly desire is to have her tell me stories: I want her to answer my questions, to annoy her by making provocative remarks, to correct her, instruct her, occasionally to cause her overt pain, to punish her, to let her know that she is my intellectual inferior, to confuse her and mock her and, immediately after having done so, somehow to convey to her how helplessly mortified I feel, to show that I know I have hurt her; but I can't quite say it, cannot quite bring myself to apologize, not even to mention the thing that continues mournfully to rattle around inside me like a sheet of newspaper caught on the railings. Not even when she appears to have put it all behind her. Even today when I dream of those things as have passed between us, I experience such a sharp pang of conscience that it feels like a pain in my chest and I wake up in a sweat. But she is capable of retaliating, not out of revenge, but in self-defence, and she can upset me too as when, for example, I ask some question about the family and she retorts: fat lot you cared about the family back then! What did her aristocratic ancestry—which is mine too, by the way—the aristocracy of which at a certain time in my life I was so deeply and genuinely ashamed, those historical names, matter to me then.

I wasn't even interested in the legendary patriotic general who was executed by the Habsburgs with twelve others at Arad in 1849. And grandmother, who was a baroness, she couldn't help it, what was my problem with her? Today, grandfather's ornate family tree, hand-painted in bright colors on parchment with all the coats of arms going back six generations, hangs on the wall of my flat along with pictures of other famous ancestors.

Right now she happens to be cooking, cooking for me in that kitchen, and as she does so, she is half turned to me, in a slightly demonstrative pose as I see it, while merrily chattering on, a pose in which there is no little pride. Her tall slender figure is an elegant exclamation mark in the humble kitchen: see! I can cook! She wants to prove—she is always trying to prove something—that she has learned to cook, and not just any old way. Before, she could manage—when she had to—a soup or two, semolina pudding, an omelette, a slice of veal, a bit of French toast, and not much more. She tied a green-and-white checked apron over her cream-colored silk blouse, her string of pearls (a cheap yet pretty piece of bijouterie, the real thing having vanished into the Soviet Union), her smart beige herringbone skirt, her stockings, her elegant, narrow but, by now, not-too-high-heeled shoes.

She wore these things until it was time for bed (having discarded the apron of course), wearing the same clothes she wore to the office, not even removing her shoes, which is the first thing I do as soon as

I get in, here, as I do at home. Or rather there, as at my home. She can't understand why the shoes bother me.

Slippers are for wearing only at night before bed, or on waking up. During the day it's so *non-soigné*, she says, Hungaricising the words to sound: *unszoányírt*. I hate this verbal monstrosity with its German prefix and French descriptor domesticated for home use: it looks even worse written down, something like a mole cricket.

I had heard it in childhood from her sisters and my cousins. It must have originated in Arad, presumably inherited from a series of German and French governesses. Naturally, I tick her off, not for the first time, gently but with an obviously annoying superiority, and tell her how many different ways there might be of conveying the same idea in Hungarian, so there is no reason to use a foreign word, especially not one so horrible. She is offended, of course, but does not show it; I am sorry, of course, but I don't show it. We fall silent. We often find conversation difficult in any case or stick to small talk. We are not particularly talkative people, either of us. Not with each other, at least.

The veal with caper sauce turns out to be perfect. I had never tasted it before. Back home whole generations had grown up never having heard of capers. I must have eaten one last when I was a child, when it shimmered in the middle of a ring of anchovy, like the eye of some sea creature: that's how I remember it. The flavor is familiar and yet entirely new. She is watching me to see how I react to her cooking. Do I like the capers, she asks. I don't let her take pleasure in it: so what if you can get capers in America, you can get anything here we can't get at home.

Occasionally you can get bananas at home now, I answer on the spur of the moment with Lilliputian self-importance, and there were oranges too just before Christmas. One had to queue up for them, of course, I add for the sake of objectivity. Really? she asks in a slightly disappointed voice. In my opinion she should feel cheered by this. Could she have forgotten what a banana or orange means to us there? We carry on eating. I sense that the caper sauce, the grilled veal, and the whole baked potato in aluminium foil was a long planned-for surprise, one of many, intended for me. It's a real American thing. Later she lists all the other dishes she can cook, just you see. And it turns out that in her free time she sometimes bakes cakes too, for Hungarian acquaintances, and acquaintances of acquaintances, bakes them to order, for money. So far I had known only—and that was because she told me in a letter—that she occasionally babysat, chiefly for Hungarians but also for some American families, and that she'd had some amusing evenings with naughty children who did not speak Hungarian, who might, for example, lock her into the bathroom for hours. Most recently she made ten dollars baking a huge Sacher torte, she proudly tells me. She buys the ingredients and calculates her fee, which, it seems, is the going rate in Hungarian circles, makes up the bill according to the cost of raw materials and often delivers the cake directly to the house. It sometimes happens, she tells me, giggling, that strangers offer her tips. Does she accept them? Of course, why not? I have to take a deep breath. These earnings, taken together with the modest income she has scraped together, have paid for the parcels of clothes, chosen with exquisite taste, that would arrive at my home on the Groza Embankment, and later for children's toys and clothes at the flat in Vércse Street. And clearly my airfare too, as well as the ample pocket money she has been giving me while here in New York, come from the delicious torte as well as the soiled diapers. The People's Republic had, somewhat unwillingly, allowed me five dollars of hard currency for my three-month visit. It is my mother who keeps me; a rather disturbing feeling at age thirty-four. She bakes four or five different sorts of cake, following the recipe in the book of course, and all eminently successful bar the caramel-topped Dobos layer-cake, she tells me.

Caramel is hard to handle. She pronounces it *kaahraahmell*, with wide open "aahs," not long, in the regional Palóc mode, but quite short, like the German "a." This irritates me no end, I don't know why. It has been aah, aah, aah all the way—*aahkaahdémia, aahgresszív, aahttitűd*, right down to *kaahpri* (capers) and *kaahraahmell*—ever since I can remember. And *maahszek* too, the colloquial word for semi-private undertakings. This time I don't stop myself pointing out that this is not a foreign word, but a Hungarian portmanteau, combining "ma," pronounced "muh," from *magán* (private) and szek from *szektor* (sector). It is a form of what we call an acronym, I add; adds the conceited, repulsive litterateur, her son. She does not answer. She has no counter-argument. She carries on saying *maahszek* and *aahkaahdémia*.

We eat. As a child I used to enjoy watching her as she adjusted the food on her plate with great topographic precision, shifting it here and there with careful, tiny, sweeping movements of knife and fork, like the director on the set of a film, arranging the shots and instructing the cast before rolling the camera. She pushes the meat to the right side of the plate, the garnish being neatly separated and ranged on the left. Turning the plate one way or the other is common, an unspoken taboo. She cuts and spears a small piece from the meat, loads the appropriate amount of garnish on the round back of the fork, and so carries it to her mouth. This is a far from simple operation, as may be demonstrated now, since the caper seeds would drop from the fork were they not perfectly balanced there and flattened together a little, if the speared piece of meat or potato did not block their escape route, and if she did not lean progressively closer and lower over her plate with every bite so that they might find their way into her mouth all the sooner. When the garnish includes peas, which means that only a few peas succeed in remaining on the curve of the fork behind the meat, that is to say leaving a surfeit of peas on the plate, she is forced to consume extra forkfuls of peas only. But she has a strategy for coping with that too. Using the knife she spears a few peas that will support a few slightly squashed ones behind them.

I have seen others deploy this technique but while they shift and prod the peas about, creating a mess on the plate, she manages to eat them in an undeniably elegant and distinguished manner. It is all done with great skill and grace. She divides the meat, the garnish, and the salad so that everything disappears from the plate at precisely the same time, every piece of meat with its due portion of garnish and vice versa. She never leaves any food on the plate. Nor do I. She has lived through the meager rationing and starvation of two world wars, I only one.

Any sauce or juice left on the flat dish, however runny, is conveyed to her mouth with the fork. One simply can't imagine her using a spoon. She leans forward and makes rapid spooning movements with the fork, turning it up a little so there's still a moment before dripping and thus she can safely steer it into her mouth. This spectacular technique requires close attention and speed: it demands a lot of time and energy, but it works. She turns the obvious pointlessness of it into a display of elegance. I eat the same way myself, ever since being allowed to dine with the adults, as did the German *Fräulein*, the whole act having made a great impression on her. But to the two of us it is like a private second language, and while we often make mistakes, it is the equivalent of a mother tongue to her, it is what she grew up doing, quite possibly never seeing any other way of eating, only this. My father, whose education had been under quite different circumstances, ate differently. That which could not be speared, he swept into the hollow of the fork and stuffed into his mouth. If sauce remained on the plate and he liked it he was quite happy to spoon it up, if he didn't like it he simply left it. If there were no guests he would dip his bread in, sometimes on the end of the fork but sometimes with his hands! He was allowed to. He was the only one. In my first days at the university canteen I was laughed out of countenance as I was unmasked as a trueblooded bourgeois leftover from the old regime when, out of habit, I started employing my mother's technique. The class-alien aspect of the art must have been painfully obvious, a blind man could see it, you didn't have to be a Marxist-Leninist to recognize it. Ever since then, when it comes to eating, my strategies are somewhat eclectic, though lately, since I have been dining alone, I have fallen into decadent ways; she out there, on the other hand, alone, is almost certain to have continued using her fork to spoon the sauce till the day she died.

Silence. She clears the table. She starts on the washing-up while I watch, she having refused my help. Her hair still looks chestnut brown and though this is merely a matter of appearances, there is no gray there. Her face is animated, refined, gentle, very beautiful, her eyes warm though she will soon be sixty.

I understand why in the thirties the Budapest tabloid press referred to her as "one of the most beautiful women in town." The ritual of the nightly removal of makeup—though, of course, I am not watching this from bed now as I used to but walking up and down behind her, chatting to her, recounting what I did with my day in New York—is quite unchanged right down to the "shaking lotion" and the same old movements, it's only the lovely antique mirrors that are missing.

The face that looks back at her from the cheap mirror now is still a feminine face, all attention: she can still take delight in life, is still curious, still wants to see everything. There is no trace in her of the expression you catch on other déclassé immigrants, the cynical hanger-on's don't-blame-me look. She has not walled herself in, become a solitary, she has not been distorted by the enormity and the harsh bustle of the alien world that now surrounds her. She is just the same as she had been in prison when sharing a cell with eight others. Having made subtle enquiries and going by what is around her, I know she is alone, though I had hoped she might have a man in her life. There is no way of asking her this directly, as it is something we never speak about. Grandmother brought up her three girls, she being the youngest of them, to avoid even the most harmless romantic literature, even that in which the attractive, and in every respect impeccable, young suitor makes so bold as merely to touch the innocent maiden's hand in the long awaited last chapter, at the point of engagement. She would glue the last pages together or simply cut them out with scissors, believing such episodes to be unseemly. My mother addressed the issue in less radical fashion, in the way that best suited her: it simply didn't exist. My sexual education at home consisted of a single short sentence that I first heard at the age of about four or five when the words first issued from her lips at a time when I lay in bed with some infection, possibly influenza: You are not to play with your pee-pee. That was it. My father said even less. He said nothing. So I became an autodidact in the subject.

Her circle consisted of a few relatives and female friends, all Hungarian, two of them quite close to her. I suspect, I sense, I see, since she practically radiates it, that she lives entirely, exclusively, for me, and that this, for the time being, is as certain as can be. She wants to show me, to buy me, all she can of America, all that is possible to show or buy, whatever is obtainable in intellectual or material terms.

That is because I have chosen to remain there, because I chose not to come with her. That is why she scrimped and saved, that is what she was preparing herself for all her life here. Almost as soon as I arrived the first thing she did was to take me to a medium-range department store and, bearing my tastes in mind, equip me with several suits of clothes, from top to bottom, the way she might a child, that is to say her son, whom she has now had on loan for three months. There were certain items of my own clothing that I had to throw out: she absolutely insisted on that.

There is another photograph of her, some thirty years back in Színházi Élet, a magazine for theater lovers, showing her playing patience with Gizi Bajor, the actress. Gizi is dealing out the cards while she looks on attentively, smoking, turning the signet ring with her thumb the way she used to. And there it still is, miraculously, the golden signet ring, next to her engagement ring: she doesn't take it off, not even while washing up. When I was a little boy I desperately wanted to have one of those. Engraved into the deep-red ruby, under a five-point crown, a tiny knight-on-horseback galloping to the right holds high his sword, a moustached head, bald save a single wisp, obviously a Turk's, impaled on it. Patiently and wisely she would explain to me time and again that I couldn't have one because it was not mine to possess, because even my father didn't have one.

It hurt me, infuriated me, it brought me out in a fever: I simply couldn't accept that I was unworthy of it. I, I alone, unworthy! When I could get anything else I wanted! It was the first time I felt the limits of my world and I couldn't understand it, couldn't get used to it. Yet how fine it would be turning it round on my finger while talking, as she did! To answer questions in so careless a fashion!

Several years, some eras later, I upbraid her on account of the ring. Before the *gimnázium* is nationalised in 1948 and I am still at the Cistercian school—but have become an avid consumer of the works of Hungarian novelists, poets, sociologists, and historians, most of whom are outside the Church-approved curriculum, and am fervently committed to the cause of equality—I get embarrassed by my mother, not just to myself but before others too, precisely on account of the signet ring she is wearing, which I see as an emblem of feudalism.

She spends her evening removing, at my stubborn insistence, the embroidered five-point crown above the monogram from the remaining items in her trousseau such as tablecloths, napkins, bed linen, towels, kitchen cloths, and dusting rags, and she does it silently, willingly, with a glum expression. Then, something I really haven't anticipated happens: I have to identify with the onetime envied, later despised, signet ring. The dictatorship itself so to speak pushes it on my finger, as I too am a "class-alien." Now I fear for her and try to persuade her to remove it because she could get into trouble wearing it. She won't listen to me. She has worn it all her adult life, she will not disown her family, she is not ashamed of her ancestors, she tells me rather sharply. Pretty soon, in November 1949, they arrest her on a trumped-up, patently absurd charge of panic-mongering.

"Who are you fucking, you stuck-up whore?" asks her first interrogator at the notorious security headquarters building, 60 Andrássy Avenue.

There are things to take pride in and wonder at in the little kitchen. For example there is a never-before-seen gadget, the electric can-opener, and next to it, hanging on the wall, there's a square-meter-sized piece of thick, perforated pasteboard, painted white and framed with red insulating tape, from whose holes hang, at a convenient distance from each other, a set of useful hooks accommodating a variety of kitchen utensils. It is a brilliant example of American practicality in offering solutions so blatantly simple that it takes your breath away.

She had seen it somewhere, put the scarlet border round it, fixed it to the wall all by herself, and it is so handy and saves so much space. I don't recall in our previous life, or lives, rather, ever seeing her with a screwdriver or hammer in her hand. Now she is the owner of pliers, chisels, files, a range of screws and keys, measuring tapes and insulating tapes, keeping them all in a professional-looking toolbox, proudly setting them out and recounting what she fixed with what.

We move into the living room, though she uses the English term with a little apologetic smile, since she could hardly call it a salon, the word we used to refer to the spacious sitting room in the Buda villa of my childhood. This small space is dark even in daytime, darker than the whole inner-tenement apartment. With a peculiar— and to me entirely unfamiliar—giggle and twinkle in her eyes, she lowers her voice and tells me that, through the window overlooking the tiny yard, she can see into a neighboring apartment where the occupier, in fact the janitor, a corpulent black man—just imagine,

Nicky!—right by the open window, even with the lights full on, there on the sofa, regularly, ahem, caressing himself! You can even hear his heavy breathing! That's why I have to keep the curtains drawn, even in the daytime. There are a couple of engravings on the wall in slightly clumsily fixed ready-made frames. In terms of furniture I see two ancient, much worn, and in every respect dissimilar fauteuils that might charitably be referred to as antiques, and two, just as dissimilar, also mock-antique little tables, as well as a spindly baby-sized chest of drawers on barley-sugar legs, matching the rest only by virtue of imitation. These she has purchased, piece by piece, as and when opportunity afforded, from a thrift shop, that is to say a store where are sold all kinds of cheap things abandoned or passed on by gentlefolk for charitable purposes. Some ornaments on the table, a few minor antique items of bric-à-brac, of silver, copper, and porcelain, a photograph in a silver frame, a lovely old ashtray; most of them Csernovics and Damjanich family relics that I had brought from home on request. They obligingly made themselves at home here, as if, indeed, coming home. There are vases on the tables and, as has always been the case, there are flowers in them. The style is familiar: these are obvious signs of her refined taste, obvious only to me of course. I myself lived with her beautiful antique furniture, on Sas Hill, right to the end of the war. She used to collect the tiny bits of polished dark-brown veneer that had flaked or fallen off them and keep them in a tin cigarette box: from time to time a skilled joiner would come and glue them back on with surgical precision as if they were missing pieces of a jigsaw, and there the furniture would be: repaired, impeccable, brilliantly glossy and majestic once more. Let such things be about her even now, however cheap, however fake, if only to serve for atmosphere, as compensation for the world that was once hers, so she may feel at home. This desire has crossed the ocean with her, it and she are inseparable companions, they are what she is, like her past, like her ring, like those capers balanced on the back of her fork, like the *aahkaahdémia*. And all this moves me, though I don't, of course, show it.

ZEHRA ÇIRAK

Memory Cultivation Salon

Laura Zwist arrives punctually and in an especially good mood for her appointment at the Memory Cultivation Salon. As always, she comes on Friday at two o'clock for her appointment. And as always, she carries a small packet with fancy little cakes. Exactly six months ago, on her seventieth birthday, she received a year's membership from her girlfriends for this unique Salon. She takes care not to miss any of the twelve appointments, one per month, and looks forward greatly to each one. Today is the halfway mark. That's why she wants to celebrate with her Memory Cultivator, Frau Merk—because Laura's convinced that one should take every opportunity to make hay while the sun shines. Besides, she managed to remember something very special today; and she also brought Frau Merk three red poppies. These rest in her tote with the little cakes. And an especially sweet little cake is what she popped into one astonished young mouth on her way over.

It is a sunny early summer afternoon and quite warm, but a cool breeze is blowing. Inside the small shop in the middle of a quiet street downtown it's as quiet as ever. There isn't a single neon light to cast an ugly glare on one's skin, but rather a pleasant radiating glow, a slightly golden warmth and cosiness. The salon and its lamp are in a room at the back, separated by a white curtain from the front entrance and reception area, and even more comfy still. Laura's gaze falls first on the round bistro table in the middle of the well-appointed room. Coffee stands ready to be served. She glances out the two adjacent windows onto the tidied green of the back courtyard with its chestnut trees. Then her eyes move to the honey-colored floor of the corridor and the whitewashed walls. She finds particularly lovely the pictures by Jan Vermeer hanging there, framed behind glass on one wall, with a few by Hieronymus Bosch opposite them. The bookcase that takes up the entire fourth wall is filled with carefully chosen literature such as the novels of José Saramago and Ernst Weiß, which Laura has borrowed in the course of the past year and come to appreciate. And several volumes of poetry stand there as well, out of which she and her Memory Cultivator read aloud from time to time.

Other than a high, narrow glass case where old-fashioned yet tasteful dishes are arrayed, there is the bistro table with three comfy leather armchairs around it and a stereo on the little table near the deep red velvet couch.

As usual, indeed more or less automatically, the two women sit down at the table immediately upon exchanging their opening pleasantries. They pour themselves coffee and, while Laura opens the packet of pastries and arranges the goodies on a plate, Frau Merk settles the three rather wrinkled poppies into a vase and says in a low whisper that outdoes the powdered sugar on the littles cakes in sweetness: "Today's the halfway mark, I've chilled a small bottle of sparkling wine, dear Frau Laura—after coffee we'll toast to us and to your memories. Many thanks for the flowers. I love poppies, especially these deep red ones with the black. The blossoms look like lingerie, don't you think? And when I sniff them I think of something made for feeling, not for telling, you understand?"

Frau Merk smooths her dark hair off her brow toward the back of her head, though its shortness doesn't really allow for smoothing, and certainly not for shaking. Nevertheless, she moves her head the way girls with long manes like to, the way Laura herself used to love to do when she was young. Lovely girl, long hair, the apple of the men's eyes.

Rattling the coffee spoon in the cup, Laura attempts to banish this image from her mind.

Frau Merk—who for certain reasons prefers not to be too informal with her customers, only allowing herself to be addressed by her surname, yet making fairly free with the first names of others—is considerably younger than Laura. Barely forty.

After numerous and varied jobs, which she pursued listlessly for some time, she'd settled determinedly on self-employment. On an impulse, not knowing what awaited her, she opened this store some three years ago, with this ad:

DO YOU RECALL? COME TO ME TO CULTIVATE EVEN THE MOST RECALCITRANT MEMORIES!

That's how it had read in the classifieds of a variety of serious magazines, on the local pages of the newspapers she deemed most promising, and on the fliers she distributed. On the reverse, nothing more than the telephone number of her shop, which she called the "Memory Cultivation Salon."

Frau Merk has accumulated many clients, mainly elderly women. For her, elderly means that these people are rich in experience and brimful of memories. She pays herself a by-no-means low but nonetheless affordable hourly wage; after the salon's overhead there is enough left to live comfortably. Most of the customers come once a month for two or three hours. Fifty to a hundred euros is what Frau Merk charges an hour, though the price is determined by her level of affinity for the client. She gives special rates to a few of the customers, the ones who can't pay much. But the best and most affordable option is, of course, the purchase of a membership.

Today Laura is wearing an elegant velvet suit that she knows Frau Merk finds particularly pleasing. It is of a simple cut, and black, and with it she wears a dark red blouse, just the thing to go with the poppies. Frau Merk notices right away, of course, and pays Laura not a few compliments. As usual, they tell one another about the events of the past month that they deem worth mentioning, assure one another of their friendship, praise the weather, and do not neglect the little cakes. And, at last, they come to the point: with the well-chilled sparkling wine Frau Merk has poured into simple but lovely glasses, they toast the half of the year that's over, as well as the half that still awaits them.

Finally, they settle in on the velvet couch. One leans on the left, the other against the right armrest. Laura tucks her legs beneath herself and makes herself comfortable. Frau Merk sets an ashtray between herself and her customer, who, in turn, immediately lights up a cigarette which she draws at quite pleasurably while bobbing her head up and down, and begins: "You see, Frau Merk, blowing this sort of smoke ring was something I could do even as a young girl. Rarely, though, do I manage to blow a small one through a large one. It's not at all easy, not everyone can do it. I happened to meet a man a long time ago who taught me how, after I was bold enough to ask him outright."

Then Laura demonstrates how well she can still manage it. A little group of smoke rings escape her lips, which twitch open and shut like the mouth of a fish, and float directly toward Frau Merk's face. Frau Merk blows them back toward her with quiet puffs, and the rings dissolve.

"Laura, today is the first time you've done that for me here. I didn't even know you knew how to make smoke rings like that."

"Yes, on the way over here I vividly recalled who'd taught me. The man was named Alfredo. I only met him once, but it was wonderful for a young girl like me, simply wonderful. It was on some Friday or another, I think it was Father's Day, when I'd just turned fifteen. My parents, some relatives, and I had stopped for a bite to eat at a popular local café during a day's outing. Everyone was still eating and talking animatedly. So I was able to go to the restroom and smoke a cigarette without anyone noticing."

Laura paused for a moment and explained with a giggle: "My parents were very sweet but a little strict, you know. If they'd even suspected me of smoking they would have been flabbergasted."

Then she returned to her story.

"For that reason I didn't want to stay away too long, and so I smoked rather quickly. After peeing, I stood in front of the mirror with the nearly finished cigarette in my mouth and watched myself puffing away. Then amid the sound of flushing, I heard whistling and giggling from the men's restroom beyond the thin wall. I examined the wall and quickly discovered a little hole next to the mirror. It was so small that a finger could have just barely fit into it, but it was still large enough to look through. I blew the last puff of my cigarette into it and heard someone on the other side curse. I waited with bated breath, curious. After a short silence, suddenly a whole series of little rings of smoke came floating through the tiny little hole. The last itsy-bitsy one flew—as if directed by the hand of a magician—through the next-to-last, bigger ring. I was very impressed and absolutely had to be able to do that myself. So I positioned myself right in front of the hole and said, 'Hello, could you please teach me to do that?' Well, I wasn't exactly shy, and more than that: I was curious. I said through the hole that I'd go into the restaurant's garden, and asked whether perhaps we could meet at the rear of the house. I'd have a cigarette behind my ear so he could tell who I was, and he should do the same. The man answered, audibly amused, that he would be glad to. And his laughter gave me the guts to go to this small, secret meeting.

"I told my parents that I wanted to walk around outside until they were through. So I stepped outside and around to the rear of the house. Leaning against a small shed, I only waited a little while before the man showed up with a cigarette behind his ear. I was startled because he was much older than I'd expected. He smiled and rubbed the eye that must've been the target of my smoke. He gave me his hand and said his name was Alfredo, I told him my name, and because I was rather impatient, I didn't even ask why he had been looking through that hole in the wall. I wanted to keep him in a good mood so he would hurry up and teach me how to blow smoke rings. I quickly lit up my cigarette, even lit his, and urged: 'Okay, let's go, hurry and teach me how I can make those rings. I haven't got a lot of time and I absolutely have to learn how.' The man looked very nice and he could easily have had a daughter my age. When he looked at me brazenly and said, 'Well, big girl, is it fun to sneak a smoke in the john?' I just answered him very cheekily, 'Well, Uncle Freddy, it must be fun to sneak a peek at girls through a hole in the wall!' We laughed.

"That sort of peephole was the first he'd ever encountered in a restroom, and who wouldn't have been curious? 'You would have looked through it, too, I think,' he said with a very friendly grin. And he was right. I admitted as much, and we got right down to the business of smoke rings. It took ten minutes, and I needed a number of cigarettes before I could manage halfway decent rings, and I got a little lightheaded from all the smoking. But then, when I was more or less able to manage it, the man asked me—can you believe it?—asked me outright for a kiss. He even said I certainly would not regret it. I kept thinking: 'Eyes shut, get it over with, just like blowing a smoke ring through a little hole in the wall.' Because the man was so likeable and good-looking to boot, and it seemed harmless to me, I let him. I just hoped he didn't have bad breath and would get it over with quickly. I stood up stiff as a poker right in front of him and closed my eyes. I thought he'd press a kiss onto my lips like you see in the movies, smush around a bit, and be done. But when he held me lightly by the shoulders and just as lightly pressed me back against the wall of the small shed and began to smooch with me at length—intensely, wonderfully—I wished he'd been teaching me to kiss these last ten minutes, rather than how to make smoke rings.

"First the man had opened my not too unwilling lips with his, ranging with his tongue deeper and deeper into my mouth. I was somewhat taken aback, but I liked what he was doing. He played with my lips and my tongue, explored the entire space of my mouth. I imitated what he was doing and found a great deal of pleasure in my new discovery. He must have noticed this, and became more insistent. I had closed my eyes and was hoping he would never stop. The man tasted good. Not like peppermint candies or anything, no he tasted like much more. The taste of 'I want more and more' spread throughout my mouth.

"On the one hand, Alfredo's kisses were like a form of anesthesia, on the other hand they were delicious slaps waking me up, as if I'd been a sleepwalker. I was uninitiated in that sort of kissing, and hadn't the least experience with such an active tongue.

"Now I was even more lightheaded, and my knees had gone wobbly. Man oh man, I thought aloud, and in my befuddlement even said thank you. All out of breath, I held onto his arm. I'd become quite dizzy, and I noticed he'd kissed awake something inside me. But I immediately felt ashamed. I believe my ears had turned all hot and red. That sort of kissing was something I'd never experienced before, and something I've never known since.

"Good thing I was standing against the wall of the shed, and that he still had hold of me. Otherwise I probably would have fallen over in my delirium of astonished pleasure.

"Certainly, the kissing had only lasted a few minutes. But it seemed like I'd been swimming for hours, that's how exhausted I was—though I also felt satisfied and excited and taller by several centimeters.

"Since then I have kissed many men, dear Frau Merk. I am still waiting for those sort of Alfredo-kisses today. Back then, when the man had finally let go of me and was looking at me silently but inquiringly, I felt like a small child caught with my hand in a honey jar.

"I heard my mother calling for me and flinched. The man took a big step backward and gave me his hand. 'Pity,' he said, smiling, 'I would have enjoyed practicing more ring-blowing and kissing with you, Miss. You have a talent for kissing, Halfpint.'

"'Yes, a real pity,' I said, and honestly meant it.

"We never saw one another again. I never told anyone about it, either. I thought of Alfredo often. But gradually, his image went blurry in my memory. Sometimes I thought I had only dreamed it all, but when I make smoke rings like these, I remember him again. And I know it wasn't a dream, just dreamlike.

"Do you know, Frau Merk, why I thought of it today, of all days? When I stepped out of the bakery with the packet of cake in my hand, I saw a fifteen-year-old boy leaning against a wall, smoking. He looked at me with a wink and made smoke rings, yes, several tiny rings blown through a larger one.

"I must have stared at him openly because the handsome boy said in a rather tauntingly impudent tone of voice, 'Well, Granny, can't believe your eyes, eh? No one can match me.' I don't know what came over me, but since no one else was around, and I felt as cocky as a fifteen year old, I handed him my packet of cakes, took the unfinished cigarette out of his mouth, and asked him just as impudently what he'd give me if I could match him. The boy must have been dumbfounded, and said 'Hey, Grannykins, you'll never be able to match this.'

"'And what if I do?' I asked him. 'If I do, then I get a kiss.'

"The boy made a face as if to say eww, eww. I closed my eyes, took a drag on the cigarette, concentrated hard, and blew a big ring, opened my eyes and puckered my lips in dreamy memory of Alfredo's kisses and sent several small rings right through it. My God was I happy that it worked. I hadn't done it in so long. Lucky try, I thought, and looked at the boy with a triumphant smile.

"The boy grew uneasy and shuffled from one foot to the other and said with a wagging head and sheepish voice, 'Man oh man that's cool, where did you learn that?' I thought he would turn and run away, but he must have been too nonplussed for that and I was fast enough to claim my prize. Without further warning, I held him by the shoulders and kissed him lingeringly on the lips. Greetings from Alfredo. The boy still held tight to the packet of cakes that I'd pressed into his hands. He was motionless, but nonetheless I sensed what he was thinking: Old woman. French kissing. Nasty business. I didn't kiss badly, mind you, but the poor boy was shocked anyway, perhaps even slightly revolted. He looked at me with enormous eyes. I quite calmly took the packet of cakes from his hands, told him to wait a moment, opened it quickly, and took out a particularly sweet tidbit. I held it under his nose and the boy opened his mouth quite automatically. He chewed on it with quick bites, visibly relieved. When he'd swallowed all of it, I asked him, 'Well, what do you say?' He shook his head in disbelief, mumbled, 'Thanks,' and ran away.

"'I thank you, my boy,' I murmured after him. Looking all around, as if I had done something forbidden, I took off. But I felt good nonetheless and couldn't help but think of Alfredo. Yes, dear Frau Merk, as if bewinged, I made my way to you today."

The Memory Cultivator had listened attentively to Laura, enthralled, and had smoked several cigarettes, all the while bobbing her head again and again in amusement. "Such a lovely memory," she said, smiling. "That is truly a very special memory, suitable for our celebration of this halfway mark. Let's toast to it with another glass of sparkling wine. I think our heads, both of them, have gotten quite warm, so that we're in urgent need of something cooling, dear Laura."

She brought the tray over to the velvet couch. On it stood a silver wine bucket cooling the bottle of sparkling wine and two glasses. She poured the bubbling liquid. The two women clinked their glasses a second time.

"One thing you still have to tell me, dear Laura," said Frau Merk after the first few sips. "Did this special kissing experience so influence you that you flirted with other older men in order, perhaps, to experience something like it again?"

Laura drank her sparkling wine in one swallow and said with gleaming eyes:

"Oh yes, it was just as you say, my dear. And I had wonderful kisses from many men who were several years older than I was. But nothing like those Alfredo-kisses. They were always lovely and always different. No one person, I think, kisses exactly like another. In such kisses there's always an interplay of souls, or of distinctive, individual thoughts. They are unique each and every time—the bodies that belong to these heads that are kissing with their mouths, experiencing something special. And that, dear Frau Merk, is why I think I'll never ever experience an Alfredo-kiss again. Unless I were to run into him again. But even if that were to happen, I can't imagine that I'd want to kiss a ninety-year-old man the way I did back then. No, that will remain deep within me as an especially lovely memory."

Frau Merk smiled, patting Laura's shoulder. Then she stood up and went to stand in front of the bookcase. "I think it would be appropriate today to read each other a few poems out of this volume. It's called *Die lieben Deutschen*. Frau Merk took the book from the shelf and handed it to Laura. The book was small but rather heavy. "645 Fiery Poems from Across Four Centuries" was written beneath the title.

Then she said, "Dear Laura, I'll loan you this little book; and as a farewell, I will read you these lines." As she spoke, she pointed to a poem by Kurt Schwitters on the back cover of the bound volume, and read with sparkling eyes:

My sweet dollface girlie
the universe goes swirly
when our lips go smacko
I feel simply wacko

TRANSLATED FROM GERMAN BY MARILYA VETETO REESE

DULCE MARIA CARDOSO

Angels on the Inside

To my friend Anabela, who gave me this title

We were coming back from the river and going up the path we always took. It was little more than a footpath. Very steep. The dirt was hard and faded. Hardly anyone ever took that path, but it was our mom's favorite route. We were coming back from the river. My brother on the right and me on the left, with our mother in the middle. Our mom was proud of us, more than she was of anything else in life.

The water was cold, even though summer was well underway. Above the most uneven parts of the river bottom the water turned white and bubbled noisily because of the strength of the current. The bubbles were so big that it seemed you might walk across the river stepping from one to the next. If we'd been able to do it, we would have arrived at the village we could see on the other bank in no time. It took hours in a car. Our car was old and the roads were in bad shape. We rarely went anywhere. Everything was too far away.

Our mom laid out my towel and my brother's on the flagstone and put our picnic basket in the shade of the umbrella pine. Our towels were identical, except for the color. Mine was orange and my brother's was blue. Both had white stripes. Our mom always bought us the same clothes and toys, or at least similar ones. I was a bit taller than my brother and had started to grow hair on the hidden parts of my body. Other than that, there didn't seem to be a big difference between us.

The flagstone was a little bigger than our lean bodies as we lay out in the sun, side by side. We always brought a wooden stool for our mom to sit on in the shade of the pine tree. She never did anything. She looked out at the river and the trees, at the sky and the village on the other bank, as if she were seeing it all for the first time. Our mom didn't like to talk. Sometimes she sang.

We were coming back from the river and going up the path we always took. Our mom's singing smothered the sound of the hard soil as it was crushed by the leather soles of our sandals. Wild roses grew along the side of the path. Sometimes daisies. But there were always rocks and broom shrubs.

As soon as we reached the river, my brother and I would take off our sandals, T-shirts, and shorts and run toward the water. Our little feet trod a path full of pebbles and thistles as if it was nice and smooth. We weighed too little for the pebbles and dry thistles to hurt us.

We could test out the water by going in just up to our knees. We had to wait to go swimming until we finished digesting our food. We never disobeyed. Since we had lunch at noon, we had to wait until three o'clock. With our feet submerged in the muddy river bottom, our legs as thin as twigs, we yelled as loud as we could, the water's freezing today, it's really freezing, ah, the water's colder than ever today. We said that every day.

Our screams broke through the tops of the trees and rose up to the clouds, then stayed up there yelling back down to us. Our mother said it was the echo. We imagined that an echo was another one of those animals that we'd never seen, but which lived up in the mountains surrounding the river. Just like wolves and snakes, the echo never allowed itself to be seen. But it made itself heard. It would even laugh with us. In a disjointed sort of way.

We also used to yell Dad, we're already at the river, or, we're going to launch a boat, Dad. We thought that the echo would get these messages to our dad.

Our dad was a technician at the dam, and every day he left the house early in the morning with a lunchbox in hand. He returned at the end of the day with his brow furrowed, as if he'd spent the day staring at incomprehensible things. He'd sit down on the best armchair in the house, and our mom would take off his shoes and serve him a glass of wine.

My brother and I liked to make up stories about the dam. Our dad was always the hero and he always defeated the horrible outlaws attacking the dam. We were sure that our dad had a gun hidden in his lunchbox. We invented a number of ways of obtaining the gun, but we never dared to put any of our plans into action. We didn't know if we were more afraid of handling the gun or of the possibility that it didn't exist.

The river flowed down to the dam and was the fastest way to get to it. However, nobody could take that route. Our dad had to drive through the mountains to get there and back every day. But the river ran directly to him and we were always awestruck when we looked down in the direction that it flowed. Even after it became hidden from view, down where there was a bend in the river, we knew that the water didn't stop until it got to the dam. My brother and I wanted to go down to that bend and then on to the next and the next, we wanted to go past all the bends in the river to see where all that water was going, to see the dam and all the dammed-up water. But our mom never left our spot. She spent the afternoon sitting on the wooden stool, and we had to stay close by. We weren't allowed to be out of her sight.

While we waited for our food to digest we entertained ourselves by building boats, which we launched in the water so that the river would carry them down to our dad. We'd make designs or write little notes that we hid inside them. We launched a boat, Dad, we'd yell, we launched another boat. But our dad never received any of the boats, nor did he ever hear the echo repeat what we yelled. The echoes and the boats break apart or run aground before they arrive at their destination, our dad would tell us when he got home. It seemed impossible to us that this could be the case every time. Lying on our beds, before we fell asleep, we blamed the horrible outlaws who attacked the dam for the disappearance of our boats. And on the next day we went back to making boats, yelling, we launched another boat, Dad.

Our chests expanded and collapsed whenever we yelled, but with or without air inside, our ribs were always visible. Our bodies still hadn't taken it upon themselves to grow. There was no way that the spurt our mother talked about was going to happen. It won't be long before you have a growth spurt, she'd say, it won't be long before I've got two men in front of me. But our bodies seemed to be deaf, and remained little.

We were coming back from the river and going up the path we always took. At certain points, the path became so narrow or the curves were so sharp that we could no longer see the way ahead of us. Since we already knew it by heart, this didn't prevent us from continuing on. Me on the left side, our mom in the middle, and my brother on the right. Far enough apart that we weren't touching one another. It was easier to walk this way, with some space between us.

We would have willingly gone without lunch, but if we didn't eat, we couldn't go to the river. Our mom used bay leaves in her cooking the way other women use salt. Our dad would say, dejectedly, even in the eggs, woman, you even put bay leaves in the eggs. But our mom kept frying a bay leaf in oil before she cracked the eggs on the edge of the cast-iron stove. The eggs, more than the excessive use of bay leaves, really intrigued me. The yellow sphere always in the middle, the fragile shell that served as its packaging, the transparent part that turned white over heat. It was all inexplicable. A real mystery. The kind of mystery that nobody has any interest in solving.

I spent a lot of time watching the hens. I tried to discern their knowledge of geometry by looking at their heads, especially their eyes, though they didn't even know the word. Indifferently, the hens kept pecking at whatever there was to peck at in the backyard, making haughty movements with their necks. Their indifference didn't bother me, since I considered them infinitely wiser than me. Aside from admiring their knowledge of Geometry, as demonstrated by their production of eggs, I admired the dignity with which they allowed themselves to be caught for slaughter on Sundays. The hens would scuttle around the backyard while our mom's hands pursued the one she'd chosen. I never understood how our mom chose, out of all the hens, the one that would be sacrificed. I also never asked her. As soon as the chosen one was caught there was a strange silence. Our mom would hold the chosen one by the wings, letting it dangle. The chosen one rarely shrieked or struggled.

We hated our mom for a time. We didn't yet know that the greater violence isn't what occurs after she'd chosen the hen. Or even the choice itself. The greater violence occurs before, well before, and it's this violence that makes the choice possible, or necessary. We hated our mom for a few seconds. No more than a few seconds. We still felt everything in a provisional sort of way.

Later, when I learned geometry at school, I didn't like it because it was all so abstract. Physics was more practical, but it didn't interest me either. I especially disliked the problem of the inclined plane. I disliked the guarantee that a heavy body placed on an inclined surface will stay in motion indefinitely and continually accelerate. I disliked even more the explanation that heavy bodies have the tendency to move toward the center of the Earth and only with effort are able to move away from it. The truth is I never liked school. I never accepted the fact that everything can, should, or has to be explained. Explained and communicated.

At three o'clock we'd run into the water. My brother's body became essential for all my mischief. Just as mine did for his. We liked to topple each other over. The more contorted we were when we fell, the better. Sometimes we smacked against the rocks on the river bottom and hurt ourselves. We also liked to race. Neither of us was a great swimmer, but we liked to believe we were. We asked our mom which of the two us was the better swimmer. You both swim well, was the answer she always gave. It was the same when we drew pictures and wanted to know which one looked the best. I like one just as much as the other, they both look very nice. As much as we insisted, we never got any other answer.

In the middle of the river, where we could no longer touch bottom, there was a tree trunk stuck between two rocks. It was like some kind of unattainable goal, as close as it may have been. We were forbidden to venture out there. Because of the current, our dad used to tell us.

Only once the skin of our fingers turned wrinkly, our lips turned purple, and we couldn't stop shivering would we return to our towels, laid out on the flagstone. We'd keep quiet as we felt our hollow, pulsating chests warm up from the heat of the air and the heat of the stone. As soon as we were dry we'd head back into the water. On those summer afternoons, time took longer to come to its end. And this I knew well.

We were coming back from the river and going up the path we always took. I carried the picnic basket, which was the heaviest item, and my brother carried the small wooden stool. Sometimes my brother would start slowing down, without noticing it. Our mom would call it to his attention, and the three of us would be side by side once more.

A car is a heavy body. The Opel Kapitan that the doctor owned was undoubtedly a heavy body. My brother and I liked that white Opel Kapitan better than all the other cars we'd ever seen. Even counting the ones in newspapers and magazines. There wasn't a single kid who didn't come over to the car whenever the doctor parked it on the street. We admired its brilliant chrome and held our breath so that we wouldn't fog it up. We'd run our fingers along the body. But lightly, since we were scared to scratch it. We'd peer inside it, marveling at the big, fancy steering wheel and the dashboard, which had three chrome gauges with numbers and symbols that looked like they controlled complex machinery. The seats were worn down and the stitching in the napa leather made very precise furrows in it. The headlights were round and hypnotic. It was a model from 1959, but so treasured that it felt brand new.

The motor of the Opel Kapitan made a growling sound that we all recognized. As soon as the doctor turned the key, the trademark growl of the Opel Kapitan could be heard for miles around. But on that day when, as we rounded one of the sharp curves of the path, we saw the Opel Kapitan taking up the entire width of the pathway, there was nobody at the steering wheel and nobody in the car. And nobody else anywhere near it. The Opel Kapitan was imposingly all by itself. Yet, nevertheless, it was moving. But no growl. Not even a single clicking noise. The Opel Kapitan was moving, and that heavy body was bearing down on us.

On that day the doctor had been called to attend to our neighbor, who awoke unable to remember where or who she was. While the doctor tried to discover the cause of our neighbor's illness, the Opel Kapitan inexplicably bore down on us.

We were coming back from the river and going up the path we always took. At certain points the path became so narrow or the curves were so sharp that we could no longer see the way ahead of us. Since we already knew it by heart, this didn't prevent us from continuing on. Me on the left side, our mom in the middle, and my brother on the right. Far enough apart that we weren't touching one another. It was easier to walk this way, with some space between us.

Our mom was also a heavy body. Even my brother and I, despite being really lightweight, were heavy bodies. Only with great effort could we move away from the center of the Earth, walk away from it. And the more tired we were, the greater the effort. When the Opel Kapitan inexplicably began to glide down the path, my brother and I were very tired from the walk up the hill and from playing in the river. Moreover, we became paralyzed when we saw that our beloved Opel Kapitan had chosen, of its own accord, to come find us. Advancing indefinitely, continually accelerating. It would take a superhuman effort for my brother and I to get out of the way of the Opel Kapitan, the beautiful Opel Kapitan, brought to life of its own free will, and also taking up the entire path in front of us, facing us. Close. Ever closer. Fast. Ever faster.

When my mom pushed me to the side, I don't know if I lost my balance or if it was her body on top of mine that made me fall. Our mom only had time to throw me to the side and protect my body with hers. I could see my brother, still standing in the middle of the path, the wooden stool in his hand, wearing a blue t-shirt and brown sandals, and the puffy shorts that we both hated, my brother, just a little taller than the glittering chrome of the Opel Kapitan. My brother, staring at the Opel Kapitan in front of him.

We were coming back from the river and going up the path we always took. Our mom's singing smothered the sound of the hard soil as it was crushed by the leather soles of our sandals. Wild roses grew along the side of the path. Sometimes daisies. But there were always rocks and broom shrubs.

The Opel Kapitan stopped suddenly before touching my brother. It simply stopped. No squealing of brakes or anything. As if it had forgotten the way things are. Or as if my brother had made it stop with some sort of machine-directed, targeted hypnotism. The beautiful Opel Kapitan, stopped by the eyes of my brother, who was still standing in the middle of the path, with the wooden stool in his hand, wearing a blue T-shirt and brown sandals, and the puffy shorts that we both hated. My mom's body off to the side, on top of mine.

We got up, and our mom went over to my brother, took the stool from him, and held her hand out to him. Almost reverently. My brother allowed himself to be led away from the front of the car. I waited on the side of the path. We went around the car and continued up the hill. It wasn't much farther to our house.

We never spoke about what happened that day when we were coming back from the river, going up the path we always took. We went on behaving as if nothing had happened. But everything was different.

We were coming back from the river and going up the path we always took. It was little more than a footpath. Very steep. The dirt was hard and faded. Hardly anyone ever took that path, but it was our mom's favorite route. We were coming back from the river. My brother on the right and me on the left, with our mother in the middle. Our mom was proud of us, more than she was of anything else in life.

Many years passed. Perhaps all this didn't occur exactly as I've said. But I'm certain that the day was coming to an end. And that the river water flowed gently.

TRANSLATED FROM PORTUGUESE BY RHETT MCNEIL

GUNDEGA REPŠE

How Important Is It to Be Ernest?

Spring, summer, and now autumn have passed, but Ernest is still living in the cabin in the woods. They had agreed that they would live apart for a while.

"You're not thinking straight," Maije had said to Ernest almost every day. For several years. Three years. Day by day he grew more and more miserable, and finally he calmly agreed, yes—okay, let's live apart for a while. Who knows, maybe Ernest would learn to think straight and everything would change. Maije says that everything, absolutely everything is determined by one's thoughts. Even the illness that will cause one's departure from this world.

Now here he is. And he doesn't even know if he thinks at all.

He has put away sufficient firewood, piled it up in lovely decorative rows to last him all winter. Because who knows if Maije will ever come back. And he thinks—he hasn't even given her a thought. The house is like any house. It's not important. Why do people bother to erect these walls around themselves only to suffer from isolation in the end? Everyone needs a home; everyone needs a home—so preached not only Ernest's grandma, but also his mama, his first wife, and Maije too. Perhaps you really do need one. But then you shouldn't complain that you need so many other things besides. Day after day. On and on. Endlessly. More and more. Yes, long, long ago he just happened to buy this cabin, but he'd neither longed nor hungered for it, he simply liked it. The spruce forest, the cowberry patch that he'd since turned into a javelin throw and track, the smell of the nearby bog, and the people who for some unknown reason had decided to live a life or part of a life together. Maybe children had once been born there. Yes, that's how it usually happened. Though children also liked little houses, toy blocks, and towers. Ernest's children were born in the city, because Annette, his first wife, had found the country terribly depressing, and even he himself had only come here to escape, until now. Now it is different. Ernest doesn't pour new wine into old wineskins.

Nature, nature. To hell with nature. For Ernest it's no cataclysm, no book of revelations, he doesn't need to get close to it, or keep his distance from it either; he doesn't need to race to the sea to be energized by the force of the wind, or cry out against self-destruction while sitting among the moss. He himself is nature. On occasion. No need to salivate for it. Yes, rabbits, dormice; yes, cranes, whose call makes you want to take off for hell-knows-where; yes, red clusters of cranberries and a spider's macramé; yes, copper sunrises on the silken trunks of birch trees, fine, fine. Titmice chirp chirp in November's unrelenting dampness, clamminess, fire—in place of a woman. No, nothing like that, none of the predictable reasons for living in the forest, no special desire to commune with nature. In any case, nothing extraordinary, nothing that would be worth mentioning. In general, there are very few things that Ernest wants to discuss. Well okay, maybe there was that one time when lame Juris brought back the liver he'd cut out of some beast he hunted down. Juris had fired up the wood stove, hopping on one webbed foot like a ballerina, flipping over that bit of game, fat crackling, his face as happy as a Catholic's at Easter, but it was only liver, after all. Fine, he'd eat it, had to eat it, but why all this bullshit talk about peppering, tenderizing, how a stag's differs from a wild boar's. Lame Juris, of course, knows all about it—so let it be. Then the two of them drank reddish-black wine as thick as motor oil, and soon thereafter you couldn't shut Juris up. He launched right in on the subject of art. A potter, he was. That's it. Now, Ernest likes his neighbor, and he likes pots, and he likes wine and a full stomach as well, but all his life, all his short thirty-nine-year-long life, Ernest has known that life is much more beautiful than it seems to be for Juris, Maije, Annette, Mama, and Grandma—more than for the majority of people, or so it seems. Then why so much angst about it? Why?

Because you don't think straight.

Ernest, grumbling, had spent the entire autumn creating a clearing in the woods to set up a little javelin throw and track there. For Maije. If she should come back and want to practice. Maije is a javelin thrower. That, you see, is really something. And the fact that he now likes his women with muscular legs, women who can run faster than he does—that really is a miracle. Before Maije he had only liked fluffy, soft, small sugared cupcakes of women, the kind you want to take in hand and protect from the pitfalls of the world, but—look who he ended up with! Maije.

Eating that liver had offended Ernest's imagination. Despite the fact that he wasn't picky. He could survive on pea soup, fried eggs, and stale bread for days, but as he and lame Juris ate, the thought hit him that the two of them were dining on Prometheus's liver. Who knew what his neighbor was really feeding him—or out of what sort of animal the liver had come. Ernest suddenly felt so sick to his stomach that he chased lame Juris home. Another year, another winter. Yes, yes. Go with God, go with God, the one and only. It was good that Juris listened to him. Ernest cleared the table, flung open both the door and the windows to air the house, but he still couldn't rid himself of thoughts about eating. About Maije. No matter how much he liked her, no matter how much he liked everything that made up Maije, Ernest couldn't stand how the woman talked with her mouth full. For example, he remembered how he couldn't take his eyes off the red tomato slice rolling around on her likewise red tongue, slithery slop being bitten into by small, sharp teeth, but through which, incredibly, flowed the twittering streams of Maije's voice. As if the voice was an independent phenomenon, as if it had no connection to the gluttonous human being through whom it flowed. It was incomprehensible. The sucking of chicken bones, the chewing of eelpout skin amid laughter and happy chatter. A human voice in a beast. That was Maije.

Now, out of nowhere, thoughts of sex popped into his head. How blushingly lovely and alluring were Maije's curves, her peaks and valleys . . . how wisely and well she had been created in the most perfect proportions. And what a symphony of fragrance, by God! All this despite the fact that, when making love, Ernest felt totally alone, felt himself being rough-hewn into a merciless, solitary concreteness. Nothing to complain about, he liked it, it was good, glory be, but Maije had filled his ears full of nonsense about how it was supposed to be some kind of cosmic flight, with myriad explosions of light within light, and it had occurred to him that she was enjoying it more than he was. Was that so? No, it wasn't true. Ernest hadn't been thinking straight. About the warm flesh in brothels, about the sense of fucking. But now there was nothing. Neither the valleys nor the cosmos. He wanted his Maije dreadfully.

Spattering raindrops, the wet autumn hobgoblins were now creeping in a gray mass across the windowsills, so the windows had to be shut. Before he latched the door, Ernest heard an angry snarling in front of the cabin. Having turned on the outside lights he went to see what was up.

It was like this. A few steps from the door there was a dog with his paws clamped firmly into the ground, chest thrust aggressively forward. An irregularly shaped head, with prominent cheekbones and round, sulfur-yellow eyes. Ernest knew for a fact that the dog's ancestors were Asiatic mastiffs: it was purebred—a Turkmenistan Alabai. Lame Juris had often told tall tales about a cutthroat dog who now and then was seen roaming the neighborhood hunting for rabbits and other fresh meat. He had bitten or frightened or something the child of some distant forest resident. Such foolishness. The dog was like any other dog. It was just the animal's bad luck to have had an irresponsible master, and now he was all alone in the world. The same as Ernest.

"Hello Pavlov!"

The dog lowered his ears and, straightening his forelegs, stretched slightly forward. His cropped tail twisted into a letter shape. A low growl.

"Don't bother putting on a show! When you're in a stranger's yard, you ought to keep your mouth shut!"

Annoyed, Ernest went back inside, latched the door, and sat down by his woodstove. A drop more of the oily wine, and the day would be done. Was this one of those days that Ernest had every so often, when he felt like his body was the body of the entire Universe, not just one discrete form in a cabin in the woods, the body of someone who had been separated from his loved one? Probably not. But on those days he felt happy. And he knew what the feeling meant. That not one of his cells would disintegrate into dust, that he was himself but at the same time the Universe, which included not only Africa but Russia too, not only wars and starvation but also stars and nebulae, and what humanity knew as "existence." But he had made the mistake of telling Maije about this feeling from the start. And what did the woman say? Well, what could the woman say? She laughed and accused Ernest of being enormously conceited.

"Oh, is that how it works? And on what part of your cosmic body is my own little microbe existence to be found, oh Father of the Universe?"

Maije was being coquettish, which wasn't at all becoming. All that was missing was for her to throw herself into Ernest's lap and begin to fool around.

When she left him, Maije had scoffed, since Ernest was the Universe, he could neither lack anything nor need anyone—he was already everything, so how could anyone abandon him? That's how it was and how it had remained.

Yes, Ernest had always known that at any moment something decisive and significant might happen. He learned to be vigilant and patient, and he'd had some successes, but he couldn't, even by force, be made to feel at peace. This constant waiting for a revelation got on his nerves, and he would short circuit from time to time, hissing like a bouquet of sizzling snakes, until the tablecloth, the table, and finally the whole house caught on fire . . . well, in his imagination, anyway.

"Please take me to the Mediterranean!" she had begged. "Please? Please! Please."

That too. So they went, they went.

"Brooding, Ernest, is a sin. You'll never become a yogi if you're always so sullen."

Ernest shrugged this off. "I've never wanted to be a yogi!"

Two weeks in the scorching sun completely killed his desire, but this brought with it the fear that he was hurting Maije's feelings. Ernest bought her a handful of pearls, telling himself off for being a tourist all the while, but Maije really did seem to relax, become calmer, more tender toward him.

"When you give me gifts, I feel important. Like you're investing in me."

Ernest shrugged once more.

"Do you really expect to win me over with this sort of attitude?" Maije asked again, as they were flying home.

"Win? What would I win?"

"Stop answering my questions with questions! What's wrong with you, anyway?"

"I was just asking myself the same thing."

Ernest thought—if it could be called a thought—that it wasn't right to live to the fullest, all systems go, just for one's own pleasure, just to feel good about oneself. Scratching and poking around inside him, there was some ancient—even sacral, it seemed to him—beast, some sort of ermine that kept reminding him that Ernest wasn't the most important thing in this world. There are bread trees and baobabs, tigers and queens, incarnations of Buddha, clairvoyants, thinkers, women giving birth—just like there are leaves fallen by the side of the road, hops, and marsh tea.

"You're not thinking straight! You can't accomplish anything, precisely because you aren't the most important thing to yourself! Believe that you're magnificent, and then you'll be magnificent!"

"Idiot," he had said aloud. How dreadful.

But one could make just about anything seem real, if one could get a certain number of other people to attest to it. Even better if they were influential people. What would Ernest do within such a reality? But then, isn't he already living in one?

Ernest pulls the remains of the fried liver out of the garbage and throws it out into the clearing in front of the cabin. Pavlov immediately pounces on it. Like Maije, Ernest thinks. He feels a sharp pain. The cosmos shouldn't feel pain.

He conjures up apple blossom season and a light breeze. And Maije, almost nude, starting to run through what had once been the cowberry patch. Maije's javelin soars and soars and they both can't wait for it to touch ground. Splendid.

It's her javelin that now pierces his chest.

"Pavlov, come and have a drink."

In the nighttime light the dog's cautious and vigilant eyes flash; he licks his own nose with a long, rosy tongue, and then enters the kitchen, shaking his thick, shiny coat. For a brief moment the two hesitate. Ernest and Pavlov. Then Ernest folds up a blanket for the dog and places it in front of the door.

"Good boy. Here we are—us two. Both alone in this world."

Ernest reaches out and scratches Pavlov behind his ear. The dog tenses up, but Ernest sees a tiny movement at the end of his tail. Friends.

Before falling asleep, Ernest thinks about his aversion to so many things. And he feels guilty about that, guilty with all his heart and soul. But what can he do about it? He avoids shifty men and superficial women, he's always given all the things that he finds repulsive a wide berth, because he doesn't want to collect stones in his heart, but now look at him, he's arrived at his cabin in the woods. He, alone with a bloodhound.

"You've consolidated all your assets in this one little cabin. Everyone else is going crazy about property."

He falls asleep with Maije's words sounding in his head.

The morning lies on Ernest with a dog's weight. Pavlov is licking his face.

Snow is sprinkling outside, the titmice are chirping, everything is as it was before, but Ernest now senses that something has changed. It's true that he wasn't awake when the decisive moment arrived, but it had arrived nonetheless. From where? And how? Through his nostrils? Perhaps his mouth had fallen open while he was sleeping?

He opens the door and looks all around, slowly and carefully. Ernest and the cosmos. Just think of the scale of it. The stars in their proper constellations have done their job; all he has to do is find a home for Pavlov. Maije would say that he was now thinking straight.

Someone is running toward him from the woods. A slender figure with flowing hair.

Pavlov snarls threateningly.

Ernest, arms joyfully extended, freezes on the threshold.

By the time he's tied up the dog, Maije has stopped breathing. She no longer has a face.

TRANSLATED FROM LATVIAN BY

MARGITA GAILITIS AND VIJA KOSTOFF

death

TANIA MALYARCHUK

Me and My Sacred Cow

1

I hated my cow and she hated me.

Even though we were like two peas in a pod: both of us crazy.

We competed with one another in mental abnormality, and the cow always won because she was the better runner. She had four legs, and I only have two.

Take this, for instance: we are walking across the village, it's high noon, the sun burns, the skin on my nose is peeling, the cow, black as tar, cautiously wobbles in front of me, now and then prudently glancing back, trying to assess my mood. I say to her:

"Bitch, now that it's all over, will you explain to me why you ran off into the woods?"

Daisy glances at me with a large black eye and doesn't say anything.

"Have you given a thought to how I feel?" I'm beginning to raise my voice. "You saw me reading a book. And the book was very interesting! Had you read even one book in your life, you'd know how it feels: when you're reading and some stupid cow you have to watch runs off into the woods!"

Daisy hopes that I'll blame the gadflies.

"What about those gadflies? They bite me too. Do you see me running off into the woods?"

We're passing the Volan household. Lyuba Volan is standing at the gate—a large deaf-mute girl, who's always getting raped in the pasture by her younger brother. She roars with laughter, and it makes me shudder.

"You know how much I wanted to kick your ass?" I continue. "A lot! But you run so fast I can't keep up! Wait till we get back to the barn—then I'll get you. I'll get you, believe me! With a broomstick! That'll teach you!"

We're passing Kamaykina's house. I'm hurrying the cow along because I'm scared to run into her—the old senile woman who's been after me for the past two years. Daisy's mother once knocked down her haystack while I was reading Hugo's *Les Misérables*.

We pass yet another house. Ours is coming up next. It's right next to the store. The store sells nothing but apple-flavored sparkling water, Turkish chewing gum, and matches.

"I'll kick your ass alright! Like there's no tomorrow!" The cow glances at me anxiously with a large black eye and lowers her head as if she's going to graze.

"Don't even try to make me feel sorry for you! I've pitied you before, for all the good it's done!"

Grandma's gate is wide open. Secured with a brick. Daisy will dive in and drink from a bucket under the ash tree, even though I'll yell to Grandma to give her some pesticide instead of water, because she's already managed to fill her gut at the puddle near the compost heap. Daisy will stare at Grandma sorrowfully, as if I hadn't tended her but tortured her with a hot iron rod. And I'll yell to Grandma to give her a taste of a whip, or to hobble her legs, or to tie her by the neck because she's mad.

Daisy slows down, hesitates. The gate is a few feet away. I can see the Basilyovskys' yard from here. A tall thin mother and her three girls, their hair as red as mouse fur, are sitting on the staircase of the brick house waiting for an old aunt to die.

"Come on now, don't worry. I won't beat you too hard."

Daisy makes a radical decision and picking up her pace, passes the gate and in an instant gallops away.

"You bitch!" I yell, running after her. "Come back! Where do you think you're going? You won't get away from me!"

The cow knows exactly where she's going. She's going to the store. Before I can manage to call her a bitch one more time, she enters its wide iron doorway and disappears into the stony coolness.

Once upon a time the store was the village elementary school. My grandma went to first and second grade there. Then she quit because she had to tend a cow. What's happening is deeply symbolic. Daisy ran into the schoolroom to pray for the redemption of all of Grandma's previous cows, especially the one on account of which she remained illiterate.

Auntie Ant sits at the store counter. She's an aged saleswoman, who thinks it's a matter of honor to remain in the empty store till the very end. She eyes my cow melancholically, and the cow pleadingly eyes Auntie Ant. If I hadn't come in right then, Auntie Ant would surely have said to the cow: "Hello! How can I help you?"

"Daisy! Come home! I promise I won't beat you," I say wearily. And, "Hello, ma'am," I address Auntie Ant. "How about slaughtering this cow? You'll finally have something to sell."

Auntie Ant is delighted, but quickly comes to her senses:

"Wouldn't your Grandma mind?"

"We won't tell her. I'll say that the cow has been taken to the insane asylum."

At last we two crazies come home. Grandma anxiously peers out of the gate.

"What took you so long?" she asks, and lets Daisy drink the cool well water out of a bucket.

"Better give her some pesticide!" I cry out defensively.

Daisy rubs her neck against my grandmother's thin torso. Just like a dog.

"My sweet baby," Grandma pets her. "Tired? Would you like some water?"

"I am very tired," says Daisy. "And she's the worst of all," Daisy nods in my direction, "How she torments me! When will her parents finally come get her?"

My parents will come in a few days. In a little while. I have to be thoroughly scrubbed before school. Especially my feet. And I have to be rid of head lice. They have to buy me notebooks and textbooks. So they could be here any minute now. Bitch.

2

Lyuba Volan hasn't always been a deaf-mute. She fell from a cherry tree as a child, when the owner of the tree caught her red-handed. She had such a scare she hasn't spoken since.

But some people say that she was born with no upper palate and has never spoken a word.

She wears long ragged skirts and walks barefoot in all seasons. To save on shampoo, her mother always crops her hair close to her skull. Lyuba is in a perpetual state of regrowing her hair. When she has her period, she's splattered all over with blood. Her younger brother Vulan rapes her daily in the pasture, and she laughs eerily. Sometimes, when it's over, Lyuba hugs him and kisses him on the forehead. Meanwhile, I keep an eye on Lyuba's cows. If anything happens to them, Lyuba's mother will order her son to lash Lyuba with a whip, and he will gladly do so.

Lyuba is his brother's first woman. Soon he will become her first and only gynecologist: to save money, he'll give her a home abortion.

She roars with eerie laughter, and sometimes I think this is her way of smiling.

3

The Basilyovskys, the tall thin mother and the three red-headed girls, sit on the staircase of a brick house and wait for their ancient aunt to die.

When she dies, the house will become theirs. They have no other place to live. Meanwhile, the four of them live in an old summer kitchen next to the house. They, especially the red-headed girls, are anxious to move into the luxurious quarters, mossy and moldy, just like the old aunt herself. They will jump on the mildewed embroidered pillows, sleep on the chicken-feather beds.

The youngest girl's first words were:

"Auntie, when will you die?"

The aunt's reply was:

"I will die, child."

The girls take turns bringing food and drink to the old aunt's quarters. They quietly enter the room, stand next to the bed, and keep silent for a while, hoping that the aunt will not wake up.

Their aunt has lived through the whole century.

Every day Mother Basilyovska takes the train to Kolomiya. She works as a security guard at the historical museum. When the museum personnel don't show up for work, which happens almost every day, Basilyovska locks herself up in the museum and doesn't let anyone in. The occasional visitors—lovers of antiques, or the tipsy Polish tourists—bang on the door, plead with her to let them in (because it's not a holiday and the museum has got to be open), and Basilyovska peeks out from behind a curtain, like a frightened ghost, like a sixteenth-century museum piece, and bobs her head, as if saying: "History is not available today, she is depressed, and I am only a Basilyovska, with three red-haired daughters and an immortal aunt."

The young Basilyovskys have nothing to eat. They wear bright colorful dresses given to them by the villagers. They wear bows in their hair, but no underwear. Their noses always run, and the girls lick off the snot. Their legs are covered with mud up to the knee.

The Basilyovskys are so red-haired and their freckles are so bright that each of the girls reminds me of a large sunflower containing an elf with a dirty face.

4

When the cow got sick, Grandma started taking her out for an evening walk.

Daisy's milk turned red and she mooed mournfully.

I am sitting at the gate, waiting for my parents to arrive. Grandma is walking Daisy in circles around the yard.

"Don't just sit there, child. It's getting late," Grandma tells me. "I don't think they're coming tonight."

"They may come late at night. It's not so scary when you travel by car."

"Or they may be busy," Grandma keeps thinking out loud.

"Hard, so hard!" Daisy adds. "There's blood in my milk."

I'm waiting for my mom, and I'm scared. I imagine her pressing my head to her breast, then suddenly pulling back:

"Tania, your head is full of lice!"

I pretend that I'm shocked:

"What are you talking about? What lice?"

"The lice are prancing around in your hair like horses! How did you let it come to this?"

"Mom, I don't have lice!"

"And what's this?" She pulls a large chubby louse out of my hair. "Do you ever brush your hair? Do you even wash it? Where in the world did all of them come from?"

"Mom, all the kids around here have lice! It's not my fault! They just leap from head to head!"

I am really nervous about my mom's arrival. Some time ago she reacted like this when she discovered I had worms. I hid behind the barn and picked the worms out of my turds to convince her that I didn't have them.

"Don't leave me at Grandma's for so long! Soon enough I won't be expected just to take the cow to the pasture, I'll have to milk it too."

Grandma pets Daisy on the forehead, and slowly walks her around the yard. Daisy obediently shuffles back and forth.

"Gran, why are you dragging the cow around?" I yell from the gate.

"She wants to walk around a bit. You're enjoying this, right?"

"Right," says Daisy.

5

Kamaykina has a beautiful young daughter, Lyuda. At one point, she initiated the transformation of the local children's library into a pool hall. The old portly librarian was forced to send some of the books to a library in a nearby village and to distribute the rest among the village children. That's how I got *The Adventures of the Elektronik* and *The Little Witch*. So I felt really good about the pool hall.

Lyuda was a brilliant pool player. She also played the guitar and sported a tattoo on her left arm. She had a Kolomiya boyfriend who came to see her on a motorcycle. The wedding was planned for fall. At the end of the summer, she went to Tlumach with friends and jumped from the third floor.

"Don't come near me. I'll jump," Lyuda told her drunken boyfriend, climbing onto the windowsill in the dormitory where they were staying.

Her boyfriend didn't believe her and kept coming.

Lyuda broke her spine and became forever wheelchair-bound. The village union bought the wheelchair. Her boyfriend came a few more times, made sure that Lyuda would never walk again, and the wedding was canceled with mutual consent. The last thing he said to her was this:

"I love you, and will always love you. If you ever get better, let me know. Even if I'm already married, I'll come back to you."

And right away he married another woman.

Lyuda quit playing pool, but she learned to embroider and to go without walking. Her arms became her legs.

That's when my cow, Daisy's mother, knocked down Kamaykina's haystack with her hoof. I lost sight of the cow because I was busy reading *Les Misérables*.

The old Kamaykina was immediately informed whose cow ruined her haystack. And right away she came by to pick a fight with me. I muttered something in my defense, but I had nothing to say to the last thing she kept repeating. She screamed:

"Who will pile up the hay for me now? Who will pile it up?"

6

And then there is Little Riding Hood, a boy of about eight years, who is always being sent to foster care by his mother, and who always escapes. The mother also escapes. A few times a year. To Odessa. With lovers. But she always comes back.

Little Riding Hood suffers from epilepsy. When you say something to him, he answers: "Wha?"

I go to the cemetery, which I call "the fruit and berry medley," and Little Riding Hood follows me there. Everything I love most grows at the cemetery: huge wild strawberries, the size of a fist, sweet cherries, sour cherries, apples, pears, and plums of two kinds, yellow and purple. You can pick anything you want, gather it into the folds of your shirt, and then go for a pleasant stroll among the tombstones and study the inscriptions.

Little Riding Hood breathes down my neck.

"Little Riding Hood, I'm going to the cemetery. Are you coming along?"

"Wha?" says Little Riding Hood and takes a step away.

"You'd better watch the cows. They'll kill us if the cows get into their vegetable gardens."

"Wha?" says Little Riding Hood, and comes one step closer.

"Aren't you scared to go to the cemetery, Little Riding Hood?" Little Riding Hood doesn't know what to say. He wavers between "Wha?" and "I'm not scared." Finally he says:

"I'm not scared. What's to be scared of? When I die, I'll lay there."

"Maybe you won't. By the time you die, there won't be any room left for your grave there."

"Why not?" Little Riding Hood dives indignantly into the bushes.

When Little Riding Hood's mother escaped to Odessa yet again with yet another lover, Little Riding Hood went to the Beremyan lake, swam five feet from the shore, and drowned. His disease caught him in the water.

"Little Riding Hood," the angels at the heaven's gate asked him, "why did you go for a swim at the Beremyan lake? Didn't you know that your disease might catch you in the water?"

"Wha?" Little Riding Hood replied.

"Watch out, Little Riding Hood. This isn't foster care. You can't run away from here."

Little Riding Hood didn't know what to say. He wavered between "Wha?" and "I will too if I want to!" Finally he said:

"I will too if I want to!"

7

Some pears are best left unpicked. They grow right out of the graves. These pears are large and juicy, they resemble human skulls. But I am not superstitious and can easily eat a dozen.

Suddenly I see Lyuba Vulan and her younger brother.

"Climb the pear tree," the brother orders Lyuba. Lyuba roars with laughter and tries to kiss her brother on the forehead.

"Climb the tree, I'm telling you!"

Lyuba starts climbing. Right under the pear tree is the grave of Basilyovsky, the father of the three red-haired elves. Basilyovsky says to Lyuba:

"Lyuba, don't climb the pear tree. You've climbed the cherry tree before, and look what happened to you."

"Keep climbing! Move on!" Lyuba's brother hurries her up.

Lyuba has climbed onto the first thick branch and is roaring with laughter.

"Climb higher," her brother orders.

"Lyuba, don't!" Basilyovsky persists. "Your brother is evil. He wants you to die. Or at least for your baby to die."

Lyuba has climbed higher and reached the next branch up. She hangs over all of us and smiles. Her skirt flares up and I see that she is not wearing any underwear.

"And now jump, Lyuba!" her brother yells. "Jump down to the ground!"

"Lyuba, don't jump!" I roar. "Don't jump, no matter what!"

Basilyovsky sorrowfully shakes his pear-shaped skulls in the branches.

"Jump, Lyuba, jump!"

"Don't jump, Lyuba!"

"Jump, Lyuba!" Lyuba is getting ready to jump.

And that's when my cow makes an appearance. Daisy. Her milk is red, and she moos mournfully. Soon she will die. But right now she knows whose side she is on.

Daisy bellows like a bull, shoots fire from her nostrils, stamps her hooves on the ground, and attacks Lyuba's brother with her horns.

Lyuba's brother doesn't even have time to get scared, hurled as he is into Little Riding Hood's freshly-dug grave.

Daisy waits at the grave for a few more minutes, watching Lyuba's brother. Then she goes back to the pasture to graze the withered grass and moo mournfully.

"Lyuba, why do you listen to this freak?" I ask, helping Lyuba down from the tree.

"Because I love him," Lyuba replies.

"Listen, you fell from the cherry tree, right? Or were you born without an upper palate? Is that why you are a mute?"

"I don't have an upper palate." Smiling, Lyuba opens her mouth to show me.

I give her my underwear.

8

My parents arrive on Sunday morning. They bring me chocolates and apricots. Mom presses me to her breast, then abruptly pulls back and starts yelling about lice. Just as I imagined.

"Mom, the people here are so miserable that they don't worry about lice. Everyone has lice around here, even the chickens. How was I to stay away from them?"

In the evening, the parents are getting ready to leave.

"I am going with you," I say.

"Stay another week. The cow died and Grandma is heartbroken. How can you leave her here all alone?"

Grandma sits by the summer kitchen, stares at my dad's car, at the dog in the doghouse, at her lousy chickens, at the empty barn, and doesn't say anything.

"I can't stay here anymore!" I cry out on the verge of tears. "I just can't! Who knows who else will die this week!"

"Stay," Mom insists. "There's stuff to eat here. There are pears and apples. The grapes will come into season in a few days."

"Yes, child," Grandma says, "stay. There's this and that to munch on."

"Wait for me," I start crying. "I'll go get my things! I'll be back in a minute! I'm going with you."

I run into the house and quickly gather my shorts and tank tops into a bundle. I grab my toothbrush, books, an outdated Soviet tape recorder, and some other stuff.

I hear my parent's car, an old Zaporozhets, starting.

"Wait for me!" I run after them, almost breaking my neck. I come out just in time to catch a glimpse of their car disappearing in the distance.

"Why did you leave me here?" tears are rolling down my cheeks, like large peas.

Suddenly my cow Daisy appears. She bends her front legs and I jump onto her back.

"Go Daisy! Run after that car!"

Daisy gallops like a good horse. I am bouncing on her back, the wind tussles my hair and dries out my eyes. I look like a louse on horseback.

"Daisy, we can't stay here! It's a graveyard, not a village! I can't help these people!"

The little Basilyovskys run out of their yard doing a little happy dance.

"She died! Our aunt died!" they yell.

"How nice," I say to them and ride on.

"I'm ready for a snack," Daisy tells me, turning her head. "I won't catch up with the car unless I have a bite to eat."

I tear off a piece of my thigh and toss it into Daisy's mouth.

The parents notice us approaching their car. Mom says to Dad:

"Go faster! They've almost caught up with us."

"I can't go faster," Dad answers irritably. "The gas tank is leaking."

"Daisy! We can do it, sweetie! We can pass them!" I yell victoriously. "Turns out it feels really great not wearing any underwear! Come on, Daisy! We're leaving them behind! We're running away!"

"Oh, Tania," Daisy giggles flirtatiously, "we're so crazy! So crazy!"

TRANSLATED FROM UKRAINIAN BY

OKSANA MAKSYMCHUK AND

MAX POPELYSH-ROSOCHYNSKY

ELOY TIZÓN

The Mercury in the Thermometers

Oh my sweet, sweet, sweet aunt from out in the provinces, my aunt of gauzy curtains always drawn, of lovely delicate needlework, treats from the confectioner just off the square, and missionary nephews in Africa, oh my dear aunt, with her parish Masses, her well-ironed petticoats, her balconies overlooking the main plaza with its convents and children dressed up for their First Communion, and the sun shines equally bright on children and convents, a small round table, little to eat, little to drink, much suffering, the little foot of widowhood, and the framed photograph of her treasurer husband in a factory where they made porcelain boxes, forty years of selfless, devoted marriage to Uncle Roque, that gentleman, oh my aunt, always on Sunday, so tiny, so hardworking, a merit badge, candied fruit, tidy cupboards, and rice pudding. Her eyes were always moist and she always seemed to be sniffling about something. Why? Nobody knew why. She was tidy. Sensitive to the cold. Smoke-colored hair. She survived on practically nothing, a grape, a tiny glass of mistelle, a sliver of cheese under a glass bell, on the mystery of her own age. She belonged to a congregation of the Sisters of Charity who organized benefit raffles and living nativity scenes. She was the only one who remembered the exact date of each one of our birthdays, and every year without fail she sent—by mail—a package to our house in the city, prepared with loving care, with something sweet and oily inside, a box of shortbread dusted with powdered sugar, or a whole selection of those little iced cakes called mantecados. After a few reluctant nibbles, they sat for months and months getting stale in the pantry, until suddenly someone got sick of seeing them there and tossed them into the trash can.

Oh, my sainted aunt, we had her address and we knew that she lived on that exact street, above that pharmacy, and one cold, sunny winter day we decided to visit her in her provincial home, and we showed up unannounced, and you didn't seem surprised to see us and received us on the threshold, chewing on something small, my dear aunt, I think it was an apple, smaller than normal, half an apple, or even less, a third, and extremely round. So there you were, Auntie, among your spare, spindly furniture, gnawing on your strange fruit, just as if you were gnawing on your provincial existence, and quietly clucking your tongue. On the floor, the doormat said *Welcome*. We took turns wiping our feet. We exchanged kisses at the door. Come in, come in. And in we came.

Her house. This way. The hallway. Careful. Oh. We bumped into each other. We apologized. Doors opened and closed, doors that seemed, how to put it, like married life. Cushions embroidered with cats. The sound of clocks ticking. Chimes, ringing, tinkling, whirring, it was almost embarrassing to speak out loud, our aunt leading the way, we tiptoed along the hallway as if in fear of never arriving or of disturbing the air, of profaning it, and all the knickknacks danced happily around us as a sign of welcome, lace tablecloths, photographs, sideboards, china cabinets, mirrors, like dogs crowding around to sniff at our hands.

And one room led to another, and the ceilings slid smoothly backward, each moment more quickly, more slowly, with their heavy drapes and clustered chandeliers, switched on or off, there was a pedestal table in our way, we had to dodge it, and a gelatinous light flickering at the end of the hallway. Or at least it seemed that way to us. We had to push through that heavy rarefied air, thick with oxygen breathed in days gone by, with overcoat sleeves, terra-cotta pots, lichens, carnivorous plants, Malaysian jungles, conifer forests, islands of melted lead, volcanoes in eruption, what an odyssey. And after all that: a wingback armchair.

Here it is, said our aunt. And added, by way of explanation: All month I've been wanting to buy myself a pencil.

Everything there was on a reduced scale, the chair, the table, the books (there were none). The cat, curled up into a ball on the carpet, looked like a mouse. Floating inside a bottle, suspended, a dried sea horse. A cuckoo clock (tick) pecked away at the time (tock).

We went in, ducking our heads, to the room reserved for receiving nieces and nephews. We took up the whole three-seater sofa and still needed more room. Squeeeeeze in. Next, our aunt asked us about our health and the four of us responded in one voice that we were all well, very well. And would we like anything to drink, and we asked for coffee, coffee. Then our aunt disappeared from sight, swallowed up by the kitchen, and after a laborious rattling and banging and clattering she came back bearing a tiny toy coffee pot, trickling stream, our aunt dragging her feet along the hallway as if hauling a locomotive on her back, hunched like a cyclist, pedaling like a drunken soldier, gibbous, her face twitching with tics. She stretched a cloth atop the lace table mat. White. She ironed it with her edge of her hand. Taking her time. Next, she took out, from who knows where, a little cardboard tray with four sweets, some tiny, sticky egg-yolk confections named for who-knows-what saint, as she told us, and a bottle of thick, monastic liquor, from which she poured out a thimbleful of nothing, a shadow of color, into some minuscule glasses.

There we were, face to face with our aunt. Our aunt staring back at us. In her provincial house above the pharmacy. Without knowing very well what to say to us, what to do, how to survive. We breathed with difficulty. We forgot to fill our lungs with air. We stared at our knees until we got dizzy: enough already. And we were starting to regret a little having come to pay this visit. We Fierros are like that. An inconsistent bunch. We want one thing, then we don't want it. We want something else. The same thing always happens to us.

The TV set's paunchy screen, switched off, showed a curved reflection of the room with us inside it. Our aunt scolded us: "None of you ever remember your old auntie anymore," she told us. And we—playing dumb—protested with our mouths full of marzipan cookies, well yes, well no, that the proof of it was that we were sitting right there on the three-seater sofa, the four of us together at that exact moment. We coughed. And, to banish any doubts, we held up our hands with our palms facing out.

Someone pointed to a painting of some fishermen hanging on the wall and our aunt settled the matter: "It's a sailing picture." Next question. We surveyed that cluttered multicolored mixture of planes, textures, surfaces, odors, and in the middle of it all: our aunt. Our provincial aunt. Dorotea Fierro. Seated with her back to the light. So far away. More remote than a lighthouse far out at sea. We located, after a certain effort, the teaspoons. We used them to stir the . . . coffee? We chewed the thick pulpy strands of candied pumpkin, called . . . angel hair? We swallowed the . . . liquor? After all that, we sat quietly, drifting in our thoughts, with a monastic flavor in our mouths, each one of us alone with ourselves, thinking about our own filthy lives.

Silence, as if an angel had passed through the room.

"Are you cold?"

"Hmmh?"

"If you're all cold?"

"No, no. Not cold. What makes you think that?"

"Are you sure?"

"Yes, yes, very sure."

"Ah, good. Because if not . . . "

Our aunt sighed. Our aunt always sighed, with or without a reason. Throughout her whole life, our aunt, Dorotea Fierro, had done nothing but sigh and cross herself over everything and step out onto the balcony and wrap herself in the fine light touch of gray wool and attend burials and religious processions and do needlework with a honeycomb stitch and be the widow of Uncle Roque, that gentleman, and chew efficiently, in front of visitors, little pieces of fruit. She didn't go out much. She only attended, on occasion, some choral and dance festivals. Our aunt said that she had no liking for buzzing about here and there for no reason, no, she wasn't like one of those pious women who spend the whole day in church, competing to see who can pray faster, none of that, she went to Mass once a week, at most, thank you. Not her. She went from her house to the market and from the market back to the house. You wouldn't get her out for any other reason. God is a very serious thing, not to be taken as a joke, said Aunt Dorotea, you must not try to wear him down, said our aunt, it's not good to test God's patience.

Other subjects. Age. The years. Time.

Oh, children, at my age the years fly by and time is unforgiving. We count coffins instead of birthdays.

Oh, she had been young once, too, what were we thinking, at one time she too had done some foolish things with her friends, like making prank phone calls to strangers or drinking carbonated beverages.

Silence.

That provincial city with its red cathedral. Black. Oblong. Slow. With towers that trembled against the watery sunset and gothic belfries filled with the sound of identical birds and amplified music. A cathedral that was not one but thousands, tirelessly repeated in the changing images on gaudy tourist postcards sold for a few coins at all hours, everywhere, along the damp archways and colonnades with drawings in schoolroom chalk and the echo of children's voices scurrying downstairs, toward the river, which is always on the left-hand side as you go down, you can't miss it.

And the cathedral grew and grew, enormous, it didn't stop growing taller and crashing down upon its stones, high as a tide, curved and wet, awash in the green waves of its stained-glass windows and its murmuring masses. Lamb of God who takes away the sins of the world. Its walls of living rock guarded, in an urn, the relics of some local martyr capable of working a miracle, of restoring eyesight to the blind, let's say, and there they were, in the urn, the martyr's tiny little bones.

And it smelled like wax (and a little bit like cocoa), the smell of the melted candles floated along the whole street, it permeated people's clothes and slipped into the shops selling salted fish and pickles, it stormed the Athenaeum, where an usher sat snoozing between plaster busts, it crossed the gardens made not so much of trees and plants as memory and the past, it filtered beneath the doors toward the convent tables set with a still life composed of a white tablecloth, a loaf of bread, a jar of water, and the very whitest hardboiled egg, as if just freshly painted: supper. And the whole valley ate supper at the same time, the kitchens bubbling with spirited activity and conversations and not a soul in sight on the provincial city's deserted cobblestone plazas, not one single passerby, the wind scurrying across them, hastening the flight of a newspaper page, a bandstand moaned with loneliness, nobody, only once in a while the sight of a cat's sharp cinematic shadow flowing along the wall or the last old pious churchgoing woman hurrying home, God help us, coming back late from the doctor, having her blood pressure checked. And after a little while the lights of some balconies began to flicker and go out and the creaking of bedsprings was heard and the dream that pulled down the sleepers' eyelids took possession of everyone and everything.

Our visit was drawing to a close. Our aunt stood up from her rocking chair, smoothed her completely white hair, as white as powder, and suddenly time pounced backwards like a lynx, and for an instant she was once again young Dorotea from the past, happy, tender, skittish, the young girl who was afraid of the mercury in the thermometers, with blonde braids and stockings, on her wedding day with Uncle Roque, that gentleman, and she was neither alive nor dead, the one who coddles us, who spoils us, who indulges all our whims and silly outbursts, who gives us presents, sticker albums and superhero comics, who teaches us to read and write and ride bicycles, who cures our cuts and bruises with iodine and saliva, be-cured-you-shall-of-frog's-bad-spell-if-not-all-cured-today-tomorrow-good-and-well, who dries the tears we squandered on an unlucky love, who consoles us, who makes us laugh, who blows our noses and then, with a slap on the bottom, sends us back out to the garden, upsy daisy, go get some sunshine, to go play with our cousins. But first she squeezes us tight in her perfumed arms, which produces in us the bittersweet sensation of being hugged by a wild rosebush.

During a flashing fraction of a second, right there, before our bewildered eyes, accompanied by a delicious tickling at the base of the spine, everybody was young and exchanged kisses, our mothers, our cousins, that milkman who knew how to whistle through his nose, the music started to play in the garden, there was a party with little paper lanterns, someone offered a toast, someone brayed like a donkey, the revelry flowed round among the tables, firecrackers exploded, couples danced all night wrapped in the tenuous glow of the fireflies and then got lost among the trees in the back, extenuated and happy, no one had gotten sick yet, and even Uncle Roque, that gentleman, stepped up out of his grave laughing cheerfully and brushing the dirt off his suit.

He died. All that died. Buried. RIP. A niche in the cemetery. A wreath of flowers. Rest in peace. A prayer for his soul. A flame that died out. Messy inheritances. Lawyers. Lawsuits. Battles between brothers and sisters. The land where the house stood was sold at public auction, acquired by a speculator, a pickaxe cut down the few remaining trees, and in the garden they put up a parking garage with a security guard. Today, our aunt, purblind, snoozes in a wheelchair, and we don't even know if she recognizes us. Oh, mystery of time. The hands of time creaked on. The clocks' soft tick-tock marked the time. We began to say our Good-byes. Good-bye to all this. We are ghosts of the past who have come to disrupt her routine. We realize this. It's distressing. And one day, far from everything, solitary and dignified in a rest home, she will lay her head on her shoulder and it will all be over, dear aunt, because it just won't do to try God's patience.

We sat back down on the three-seater sofa.

Nothing else happened. A change of light. Then we learned that our provincial aunt had fallen in love once, for the first and only time in her life, and it had happened suddenly. It happened one afternoon when she visited the office of a homeopathic doctor, looking for a remedy for certain, shall we say, feminine, ahem, aches and pains. Let's not get into details. The nurse opened the door to the doctor's office, and there he was. The homeopathic doctor was a sad man, with a cough, with sunken shoulders and resigned hands which in that moment were stealthily shuffling note cards and fountain pens. The doctor turned his large lazy blue eyes toward her and greeted her by way of asking: "How are we doing?" He said nothing more. Four words. That was enough. Enough—with such a small thing a heart can tear and bleed. Our provincial aunt fell in love all at once, so that she wouldn't have to repent it later on, and that very night she wrote it down in her diary, the diary that we inherited after her death in the rest home, oh my dear aunt, along with the urn containing her ashes, and that's how we learned it. They exchanged glances. And he said: "How are we doing?" She committed the indiscretion of falling in love right there, standing up in the middle of the doctor's examination room, in front of the nurse in her uniform, how embarrassing, body and soul, our Aunt Dorotea from above the pharmacy, hard to believe it, with her curved back, her dry skin, her facial tics, her muttered words, her little music boxes, her crocheted table covers, her silhouette like a chimney, her mantecados. To hell with the mantecados. Even those of us who are a bit ridiculous still deserve someone to love us. We all need a hand to close our eyelids when our hour comes round at last. For the first and only time in her life our aunt from the provinces fell in love with that homeopathic doctor, and it was a small love, homeopathic too, the minimum dosage.

After examining her, the doctor told her there was nothing wrong; it was just nerves. She returned home feeling relieved. Nerves, yes. That must have been it.

She saw him for the second and last time in the street, by chance, a few days later. He was standing in front of the window of a clock shop, and upon seeing her he tipped his hat in greeting. At his side, a young, pretty woman was holding a baby in her arms. She returned his greeting timidly, tilting her head slightly, then continued walking past with short little steps without saying a word. It was winter, the weather was quite cold, he was coughing. He had snow on his shoulders.

She was on the verge of succumbing. She sketched out a plan. She repented of it. The two of them were married. No, it couldn't be done, what a foolish idea. Uncle Roque lay sleeping in the other bed. Don't even think about it, no. In a small provincial town. In those days. Above the pharmacy. Everyone knew one another, everyone watched one another, it couldn't be done. She carried that adulterous secret with her for the rest of her life. Without knowing why, she felt dirty. She wrote convoluted letters that she never sent. She ate apples. She repented. Because she wanted to do something for that tall man with a hat, and she didn't dare to do anything more, she began to knit him a wool sweater, for the winter. Hospitals are chilly places. The war broke out and they hustled the homeopathic doctor up onto a truck and sent him off to the front, far away from there, among the living and the dead, and he never came back again. He came and he went. So much madness. The woolen sweater remained half knitted, with both arms still undone. It was not the moment to ask questions or seek advice. Unthinkable. It couldn't be done. Not to her confessor, not to anyone. Uncle Roque lay sleeping in the other bed. No, nobody ever discovered that feverish passion. She buried it in the deepest possible place. Better that way. Nothing came to pass. Time passed. For years she tried in silence to kill off that feeling, to drown it, to murder it thoroughly so that she could go on breathing. Our aunt unraveled the sweater she had begun for that sad doctor with snow on his shoulders, and with the wool she knitted an oven mitt, which turned out to be more practical. She ate baked apples. She helped run charity raffles. She went to choral and dance festivals. She became cold, with weepy eyes. Life, meanwhile, passed her by, indifferent, with its exacting caravan of noises, annoyances, toasts, obligations, illnesses, nieces and nephews, trips, lunches, coitus, bills, presents, Christmas processions, Sundays, births, and deaths. And after all that: a wingback armchair.

A wall of time, impossible to knock down, separated them. There were the two of them, both disconcerted and too shy, she was alive and he was dead, like two pale actors on stage, beneath the spotlights, twisting their hands in silence, incapable of saying a word, and the fact of having renounced a dream that was perhaps beautiful and central—the magnitude of that sacrifice—gave their trivial existences a phantasmagorical radiance capable of converting them into epic creatures. Where was the love? Stretched out in a cold tomb? It came and it went. Nothing came to pass. A breeze. Upon the cuckoo clock thirty years (tick) passed by (tock).

Order exists and chaos exists. Medicines exist that cure imaginary sicknesses, minor disorders of the soul, infections of the spirit.

Clothes hanging in the bedroom armoire, her own and her husband's. The clothes that they had bought together at sales and which would last long after both of them had died. And one of those dresses, chosen by herself, would serve as her shroud.

Oh, the mystery of time. Until one cold, sunny day in winter we decided to visit her in her house out in the provinces and our aunt welcomed us on the threshold gnawing on something small and vaguely startling—a live bird?—and her eyes slid from one side to the other like a polyp or ectoplasm. And one of us, it might have been me, pulled himself out of his stupor on the sofa, pointed with a nicotine-stained finger toward the shadowed window, and said emphatically: "It's getting late."

And then specified—I specified—more terrified, if possible: "Very late."

And then, we all saw it, our provincial aunt, very startled, made an odd movement, as if a chill ran through her, as if she was snuggling into her woolen shawl, shrinking her frame until it acquired the exact shape of her future coffin.

Oh.

TRANSLATED FROM SPANISH BY BRENDAN RILEY

SEMEZDIN MEHMEDINOVIĆ

My Heart

Today, it seems, was the day I was meant to die.

I was getting ready for work, taking a shower, when I felt a dull, metallic pain in my chest and throat, and the taste of cement on my tongue. I stepped out of the shower with a feeling of indescribable fatigue and wrapped my wet body in a bathrobe. Sanja was just about to leave the apartment to go to work, but then she caught sight of me through the open bathroom door. I told her I wasn't feeling well, I was going back to bed for a bit, this *weariness* would soon pass, and she shouldn't hesitate to go.

She stayed. Wet, my hair dripping, wrapped in the bathrobe, I stretched out on the bed. And I felt increasingly worse. She brought me cold tea, which didn't help, and then, having no choice, she called 911. After that, she stared out at the street impatiently, looking for the ambulance. I didn't have the energy to turn onto my other side to watch her by the window. I looked at the sofa where she had been sitting. I felt suddenly uneasy because she wasn't where she had just been. Then I looked at the photograph on the wall above the sofa . . .

Llasa. Early morning. A young Buddhist priest in a red robe had come out through a high wooden door in the wall of a stone building, and was now walking down a narrow cobbled lane, with a wisp of morning mist in front of him—a small white cloud, like a ghost that the priest was following. I let my gaze follow the white cloud above the cobblestones in Tibet.

Behind me, Sanja said: "Here they are." Then she came back into my field of vision. She opened the door and looked down the corridor, then anxiously glanced back toward me. And then our room was filled with strangers from the emergency services, settling themselves briskly around me on the sofa. I had never experienced such an aggressive assault on my privacy. Quite uninhibited and sure of themselves, they looked around the room, glanced at me, admired the floral pattern of the coverlet I was lying on; strangers in my room. A girl in a blue uniform had just opened my bathrobe, so that I lay before them naked, and asked: "How old are you, sir?"

"Fifty."

After the initial shock, there was peace.

I looked at everything around me without emotion, and so— without fear. And now that it is over, I remember the event as though I had seen it from a distance, just as though my mind had become separate from my body and had observed what was going on almost with indifference.

The shock did not come when the girl in the blue uniform said: "Sir, you're having a heart attack!"

That's when I felt calm. In films, when they are describing a critical state such as this, the picture is often left without sound, and sometimes they even make it slow motion. That is a technical evocation of the mind at work.

The mind behaves like a cold camera lens.

In my case, the shock had come at the moment when the ambulance arrived, especially when a bunch of strangers filled my room. This was something that happened to other people, not to me, and it was something I recoiled from. And here my fear of illness was expressed as fear of doctors and hospitals. I never went to hospitals, even as a visitor. And now, the girl in the blue uniform leaned over me on my sofa, and said: "You're having a heart attack!"

My first thought: She's wrong, it isn't my heart. Then I thought: I know this girl from somewhere. I tried to remember where from, but now there were a lot of human hands above me, attaching me to wires, turning me to the left, then to the right, disturbing my train of thought. I could not remember where I had seen that girl before. Through her blue blouse, I saw the outline of her breasts, but this wasn't erotic in the least. She was looking at me anxiously, as though accusing me of something.

And one other optical impression: the bodies of all those people around me were unnaturally big, while my body had shrunk. What was it I was feeling? Weariness. Weariness from the pressure in my chest, which was making me breathless, which had become the same as weariness with life. And I thought: So, is this it? Is this death? At that moment, in fact, I began to see everything not just as a participant, but also as an outside observer. And I thought: It's good, just let it all pass, I'm tired, I want to close my eyes and not remember. I want it all to stop.

The years I had lived through up to now were already too much.

On the way to the hospital, lying in the ambulance, my knee crushed by the weight of an oxygen canister, I watched the passing clouds, the green traffic signals that I had noticed up to then only as a driver. Through the back door of the ambulance, after we slowed down for something, I saw a sign on the façade of a brick building with the inscription LIBERATION BOOKS.

"What's the name of this street?" I asked the girl in the blue uniform leaning over me to fix my headrest.

Was my mind turning anywhere, just to forget the pain in my chest? The young man sitting by my feet kept shifting the heavy metal canister that was lying on my legs. He shifted it so that the cold metal lay uncomfortably against the bone of my knee, and for a while that became the dominant pain in my body. That made me silently furious with the young man, who was, perhaps, scraping the oxygen canister against my knees on purpose, intending to deflect my mind away from my heart to a different problem.

Then I turned my attention to the tops of the trees lining the street. In the autumn, the leaves here take on such dazzling, sunny colors that even on a cloudy day one has the impression of a surplus of light. Was it a sunny morning? Or did the colors in the treetops give me an illusion of sun? I had always been disturbed by the thought of dying in a landscape where deciduous trees grew. There was something unconvincing, something *obvious* about that.

It was somehow indecent to die in the autumn.

It was kitsch to die in the autumn, along with everything else.

The ambulance stopped in front of the hospital. In the parking lot, the first image I saw from my horizontal position was this: walking between the cars toward the hospital building was a girl in the red hockey shirt of the Washington Capitals. She was looking up, towarda window, or at a cloud.

I had only ever been in this parking lot once before, when the wife of the poet F. was giving birth to their daughter. I remember that he had bought a new Toyota Camry that day, and asked me: "Would you like to drive it?" "Sure." And I drove once round the parking lot. That was ten years ago. I can still remember the smell of the new car.

My oxygen mask began to mist up in the icy November air.

At the hospital entrance, I was met by a choir of smiling medical personnel. On my right, a nurse struggled to find a vein in my arm to take blood. On my left, two girls in green coats gazed and marvelled at the design of the coverlet I was wrapped in. at the same time, I caught sight of Sanja at the end of the corridor; a man (a doctor?) had just come up to her with some papers in his hand. She listened carefully to what he said and then began to cry.

The man was now leaning over me. He felt my pulse with cold fingers and asked: "How old are you?"

"Fifty."

I want to go back to my apartment for a moment.

What is the answer to the question *Who am I?* While strangers are examining my naked body in my own room? And among them is that girl I know from somewhere. What fills me with unease and muffled shame is not the proximity of death, but the realization that my body, at this moment, is an object without emanations. My corporality is asexual.

What is more, the ease with which these strangers shift my body through space creates an impression of my own weightlessness. I am what is left over of me, my mortal remains, as I lie in my bathrobe, under which I am naked.

All I know about the body I know as a poet, and that is pretty selective, limited to those characteristics in which the body displays its abilities and strength, and not its weaknesses and shortcomings.

About the diseases of the body, I actually know nothing.

The mind draws logical conclusions on the basis of data accessible to it, and when the attack happened, while I was standing under the shower in the bathroom, I immediately connected the pain in my throat and metal taste in my mouth with an article I had read in *Vanity Fair*. It was an account of an attack experienced by the author (Christopher Hitchens, who was later diagnosed with cancer). In that description he says that he felt pain in his chest and neck, and felt something like 'the slow drying of cement' in his chest (I'm quoting this from memory, but I think those were the words he used to describe his state, which was what I was now experiencing). And when I came out of the shower, and the pain in my chest increased, I was convinced that I had cancer.

Later, the emergency services arrived, and the girl (a doctor in a blue uniform) leaned over me and said: "Sir, you are having a heart attack!" and my first thought had been: No, dear. This can't be my heart.

My mind was so firmly convinced that my symptoms were like those in the description of Hitchens's attack that I favored the account from his article over the official diagnosis. In any case, at one moment I thought: this is comical! I'm dying thinking about Christopher Hitchens!

It was comical: my reality, at such a crucial moment, was being explained by a columnist in *Vanity Fair*, who did not know I existed, and so could not know, either, that I was, perhaps, right now ceasing to exist.

"How old are you?"

"Fifty."

This was a dialogue that kept being repeated today.

The number of years I had lived represented important information for the doctors. I had the feeling that, in this way, for the first time —in this long life—my time was being accurately measured. This meant that today all my illusions of youth vanished. We rationalize our experience of time, but beyond the givens of the calendar, we are not conscious of it. Because 'in spirit' we stay the same. 'In spirit' I was the same person I had been in my twenties. That's how it is, probably, with everyone; it is a characteristic of our species. That is how we protect ourselves from death. Western cultures see man in his asymmetry and disharmony, so they separate him into a body that ages, and a soul that does not age. Apart, presumably, from Dostoevsky.

Reduced to a body lying on the operating table, I communicated the whole time with my eyes and through a meagre exchange of words with various people who were working on my revival. This was a surprising number of people—those who prepared for the operation, and those who participated in it. They all struck up conversations with the dying person, and my impression was that the body (i.e. me) did not offer much information, even on the operating table. Apart from my unpronounceable name, the only piece of information about me was this coverlet with the floral pattern à la Paul Gauguin, in which I was wrapped when I came here; everyone commented on it, interested in the cultural origin of the drawing on canvas, presumably convinced that the coverlet had the same geographical origin as me.

At one point the surgeon who was operating on me, not knowing how to negotiate my complicated name, brought his face close to mine and explained, slightly alarmed, that he would have to communicate with me in the course of the operation and for that communication he would need a name to call me by. He said: "I'll call you Me'med. Is that all right?"

As for the coverlet, I don't know exactly where it came from, other than that it was some South American country. Perhaps from the same country as one of the hospital staff who took such an interest in it. In any case, these people treated my origin with great sensitivity, although they did not ask, nor, I presume, did they know where I came from. From my accent they knew only that I was foreign.

Does this mean that we all suffer from a kind of anxiety about dying in a distant, foreign country, a world where we are not at home?

This is the first time I see inside my body. On the left of the operating table there is a screen on which is projected an image of my cardiac arteries. What I see reminds me of a branching plant. One very thin, almost transparent twig had begun to grow and lengthen. Behind that *growth* was an unknown, delicate procedure that the doctor applied to my blocked artery, so as to break through the blockage and enable the normal flow of blood. Instantly, I felt indescribable relief. The same procedure was applied to the other artery: I watched as the branch grew before my eyes.

And that was all. The pain in my throat and pressure in my chest disappeared. The moment of liberated breathing was so refreshing that all trace of tiredness left my body. This made me want to straighten up, to get off the operating table and walk.

Full of oxygen.

The theater unexpectedly emptied, and for a short time I was alone. I heard a buzzing but didn't know what was making the sound. A machine?

Then the room filled up with human voices again. None of them took any notice of me. They were discussing the previous night's episode of a television series.

And they were laughing.

One girl, an African American, leaned over me and asked: "Would you like me to bring some water?' a Latino lad came after her and, as though it were part of an ongoing conversation with her, said: "you must!"

I said: "Yes, please."

And she answered him: "I can't. I won't!"

Someone else in the room was describing how he had spent half an hour that morning stuck in a lift. Finally the person responsible for the lift had appeared, and when they had freed him, he felt, he said, "like a Chilean miner who had just been brought out of the earth into the sun".

I drank water out of a plastic cup. And I couldn't remember when I was last that aware of the taste of ordinary, sweet water.

From the operating theater, lying on a narrow trolley, I went by lift to the ward. I was accompanied by two young people in hospital coats who didn't seem to be in a hurry to go anywhere; they were talking, laughing, and easily forgot my presence. They could have been lovers. Beside them, I felt my primary characteristics returning to my body. When we entered the lift, it turned out that my height in a horizontal position was such that they had trouble fitting me into the moving box of the lift. And when the doors closed, I could feel them rubbing against my feet as we moved.

All the people I meet today disappear. They vanish without my having a chance to say goodbye. These two young lovers who had been chirruping and laughing in the lift, as they took me from the lower to the upper floors, they too went away without my noticing the moment of their departure.

In my ward, a new nurse settled me in the bed and said: "Lovely coverlet."

I said I had brought it from home. She explained that I could by all means keep it here as well. Maybe she believed I had a childish emotional attachment to that rug.

Then I called Sanja, who had got lost somewhere in the depressing architecture of the hospital corridors.

If a line is drawn under Tuesday, the 2nd of November, 2010, this is what happened to me: as I was getting ready to go to work, I had a heart attack.

I was in the shower when I felt a dull, metallic pressure in my chest and throat, and when, soon afterwards, the ambulance arrived, the girl who examined me said, bluntly and without beating about the bush: 'You're having a heart attack.' Under an oxygen mask, I watched Sanja on the sofa opposite the bed where I was lying surrounded by strangers. Her face was contorted with fear. They hurried to take me away, wrapped in the cover on which I was lying; they took me to hospital, and then I had an operation. And after they had installed stents in my blocked arteries, I was settled into a hospital ward. It all took a little more than three hours, but during that time my world was fundamentally altered.

After the operation, the doctor looked for Sanja, but she was not in the waiting room. When they had put me into the ward, I called her on her mobile. She answered, she was on her way. She came into the room, pale as pale, her face swollen with crying. That face expressed uncontrolled joy and an absolute sadness that had overwhelmed her. Something in her was broken. She had an irresistible urge to hug me, but didn't dare for fear that an embrace might hurt. I asked her to sit on the bed, beside me.

"Where were you?"

"Outside the hospital."

"It's cold outside, and you're dressed like that . . ." I'd only just noticed that—in her haste—she had just put a little jumper on over her T-shirt.

"I didn't dare wait."

"What do you mean?"

"I was afraid the doctor was going to come and tell me . . .'

"Tell you what?"

". . . that you'd died."

"It hadn't quite come to that."

"When I was giving them permission to operate, they asked—did I want them to fetch a priest?"

"What did you say?"

"I said there was no need for that, and that you weren't going to die."

"You didn't tell them that a priest couldn't reconcile me to God . . ."

"No."

"You should have!" I said, joking.

She pretended to be cross (people were dying here and he was having a laugh!), then she slapped me gently with her open hand on my chest, then at the same instant remembered my heart and shuddered, she could have hurt me oh oh oh, she waved her hands in the air over me ohohohooo. Then we laughed.

I remember the rest of the day quite clearly as well.

When I was left alone in the ward, this is what I thought about:

Of course I had been thinking and all these years I had been developing my attitude toward my death, but I did not expect that it could come as a consequence of my heart stopping. all my other organs could stop functioning, but the heart was out of the question. It was here, I thought, to beat for me, just as long as I needed it.

I called my son Harun. He was now in St. Louis. At the airport.

"How long is it till your flight?"

"Six hours."

At midnight on 31 January 1996, on our way from Zagreb to Phoenix, Arizona, on our émigré journey to America, we had been at the St. Louis airport.

We were changing planes.

I remember rows of gray leather seats in the waiting room, and midnight travellers with Stetsons. In those days there were ashtrays on high stands beside the seats, and the stale air reeked of Jack Daniel's. There wouldn't be any ashtrays there any more. And now, as I chatted to him, I remembered a photograph from that journey. It was of him asleep, his head resting on his arms on a table in the airport cafe. He was thirteen then. I was thirty-five. He's twenty-eight now. Almost as old as I was that midnight, when we were wearily waiting for the plane to Phoenix. How long ago was that? Fifteen years.

"I'm sorry, son."

"What for?"

"That you've got such a long wait."

"You're comforting me, as though I was the one who'd had his heart stitched up!"

That *textile* image "stitched up" surprised me. As I thought about it, language became the only reality. I felt that every physical touch was freed of pain, and that was a nice illusion.

I'm really well, I feel cheerful, and it's easy to forget I've had my heart "stitched up."

Other than a dull ache in the vein they opened in my groin: in that soft area between my genitals and my thigh.

When I was lying on the operating table, at a certain moment I became conscious of that, that they were shaving my groin; a cold and quite disagreeable touch. At the time I didn't know why they were doing that. If my problem is my heart, I thought, why are they shaving my private parts?

A cold razor blade scraping over my skin.

And the image of a man condemned to death, being prepared in the morning for the electric chair, came suddenly to my mind.

And then this. Today Sanja said that was it. No more cigarettes.

"If you want to go on living," she said, "you have to stop."

And it was high time.

"There's a Bosnian, a doctor in Kentucky. I heard this story today. He had a heart attack, just like you, and while he was still in hospital, he asked his wife to park the car behind the hospital building. Then he'd go out, hide in the car and smoke a cigarette. Imagine! A doctor. His unfortunate wife refused to bring cigarettes, and she told his doctor colleagues about it."

In America everything is geared to stopping you smoking. Of all the nations on the planet, they are the most resistant to the tobacco habit.

Nevertheless, one of the finest sentences about the cigarette and dependence on it was written by an American, Laird Hunt:

When you smoke, other people come up to you and ask for a light.

The next day. I thought about how the news of her son's heart attack could affect my mother in Bosnia. In order to preempt any possible pain, I called her and explained that a rumor that I had had a heart attack was likely to spread through the Bosnian part of the world. I was calling, I said, so that my voice and cheerfulness would reassure her that this was not the case. She listened to me attentively, then there was a short pause before she asked: "So, how are you, otherwise?"

I clearly recognized her anxiety in that *otherwise*.

"Of all possible diseases, they hit on a heart attack," she said. "The Mehmedinovićs don't have them. No one in our family either on your father's side or on mine has ever had a problem with their heart."

So, that meant I was the first. Genetic degeneration had to start with someone; or else I—like all my relations—started out with the same heart, only I had carelessly filled mine with stuff that exceeded its capacity.

And when the call was over, I remembered a line of verse that I had last thought about perhaps in the late 1970s. It wasn't remotely worthy, metaphysical poetry, but a rudimentary line by the forgotten Bosnian poet Vladimir Nastić that went:

I nearly swooned, Mother, like you, giving birth to me.

Sanja came this morning before eight o'clock. On her way to the ward, she had bought me a decaf in the hospital canteen. The decaf was sweetened with artificial sweetener.

It wasn't coffee, it wasn't sugar, nor was I myself.

And she said: "You're looking well!"

I nodded affirmatively. Clearly I looked well, tied to the bed with all these cables so that I couldn't move, or sit up, or get out of bed and walk around the room. But that didn't bother me. I drank the coffee with great pleasure, just as though it was real coffee, with natural white sugar.

This morning a new nurse came. She said that it would be good for me to move, to walk around the room. I instantly dug myself out of bed, still plugged into hundreds of wires and with needles in my veins.

In the bathroom, Sanja carefully washed my whole body with a wet cloth.

Then I walked around the room. It was good to be walking again. This was what the experience of one's first step was like. I was walking!

But afterward, I was sitting in my chair and suddenly straightened up, and at that moment I felt something burst in my right groin (where they had shaved my private parts the day before with a razor). At the same moment I saw a swelling appear. I pressed the button on my bed to call the nurse, who came quickly, and looked at the swelling with interest. She measured my penis, which was lying over the swelling, against the outside edge of her hand. She was concerned. She measured the pulse in my feet and hurried out of the room to find the duty doctor.

Very soon, instead of her or the doctor, a young man appeared, a technician with a strange plastic object. In the center of the square object there was a half ball, which he pressed onto the swelling. The ends of the surface into which the ball was set had holes with a paper string drawn through them. He tied the string round my waist. But he moved slowly, all the time reading the instructions for installing this plastic object whose purpose was, presumably, to read impulses, or messages sent by the swelling near my genitals.

And it wasn't working.

He gave up.

He laid the plastic object down on the bedside cabinet, and left.

Was I now supposed to act like someone ill?

I didn't want to.

No.

In Chekhov's diaries there is a short note, a sketch for a story, about a man who went to the doctor, who examined him and discovered a weakness in his heart.

After that the man changed the way he lived, took medicines and talked obsessively about his weakness; the whole town knew about his heart, and all the town's doctors (whom he consulted regularly) talked about his illness. He did not marry, he stopped drinking, he always walked slowly, and breathed with difficulty.

Eleven years later, he travelled to Moscow and went to see a cardiologist. That was how it emerged that his heart was, in fact, in excellent shape. To begin with, he was overjoyed at his health. But it quickly turned out that he was unable to return to a normal way of life, as he was completely adapted to his rhythm of going to bed early, walking slowly and breathing with difficulty.

What is more, the world became quite boring for him, now that he could no longer talk about his illness.

A young African had come to photograph my heart.

On his index finger—rather than on his ring finger, like most people—he had a silver ring with a square stone, that is, a combination of two stones: a large turquoise in the form of a tear was integrated into a black square of onyx. For the next half-hour, as I watched him work, I looked at that ring.

In order to photograph my heart, he used a hand-held scanner, and moved the cold, egg-shaped object over my breastbone, on the left side of my naked chest. On the monitor in front of him, was he focusing on the image of my heart? Or some other visual content? I don't know, I couldn't see what he was seeing. I always felt a bit dizzy whenever I heard my own heart. My hand sometimes falls unconsciously onto my chest, on the left side, just as I am falling asleep, then I become aware of my heart, and that wakes me up. and now, as that young man was recording me, I was seething with discomfort. At one moment he pressed the round scanner hard down between my ribs. This was a moment of utter bodily discomfort.

"What are you doing?"

"I'm trying to make a bit of space between your ribs, so that I get a clearer image."

I can easily handle pain.

But this wasn't pain; this was separating the ribs right by the heart, this was far more than I was prepared to put up with. And that pressure between my ribs unleashed an uncontrollable fury in me. He had been scanning for half an hour already—had he taken any images? He said he had, but that it wasn't enough. And I told him that for me what he had already recorded was absolutely enough, pulled my pajamas over my chest and crossed my arms over it for good measure, to prevent any further approach to my ribs.

It was as the young man, confused by my reaction, was putting away the instrument and leaving the room that Sanja stood with a decaf in a cardboard cup. She noticed my agitation and asked—what happened? I waved my hand, never mind, nothing, the examination took too long and that was why I was irritated. But then, I was put out by the expression on the young man's face. While he was packing up his apparatus, I noticed a smile of mild revolt on his face. Did he think I was a racist? That was it! I could see it in his expression. That's what he thought. He thought that I reacted the way I did not because I didn't enjoy having him forcing my ribs apart, but because I had something against the color of his skin. I felt a need to talk to him, to put him right, but I knew that could only increase the misunderstanding.

So I didn't say anything.

Nor did he.

He left without a word.

Then Sanja appeared with a decaf in a cardboard cup. She told me some of my friends were calling and wanted to visit me in hospital.

No, no.

They wanted to assure themselves that the heart attack had happened to me and not to them, which was human and normal, they wanted the confirmation that the misfortune had passed them by.

I refused.

The third day.

I was moved out of intensive care into an ordinary hospital ward, where I shared a room with this old man. He was a Slovak by origin.

Lukas Cierny. That's what was written in blue felt tip on a little board on the wall, to the right of his bed. Nice name. Lukas Cierny. How old could he be? Eighty? Maybe more. He had Alzheimer's disease, and some chest problems, and his breathing was very restricted.

In the middle of the night he got out of bed and set off somewhere, and they brought him back from the corridor. "Where were you going?"

"I want to get dressed and go for a walk."

Old Cierny is much loved, there's a procession all day long of his children, grandchildren and great-grandchildren. They fill our room with laughter while they fix their father's, grandfather's or great-grandfather's pillows under his head, comb the sparse hairs on his skull and do whatever they can to please him. It is clear from the old man's vacant gaze that he doesn't know who all these people are. They turn to me as well, kindly, as though we'd always known one another and were related. The mere fact that I came from a Slavic part of the world gave them the right to that familiarity. Even though their own Slavic origin was pretty foreign to them. His daughter, when she introduced herself to me, said of Lukas: "He's from Czechoslovakia." She was a pure-blooded American, from Pennsylvania.

He, who remembered nothing any more, answered questions in English and then sometimes in Slovak. When he replied in Slovak, the people he was talking to didn't understand him. However, that didn't bother any of them, they weren't conversing with him in order to exchange information, but to simulate communication.

Someone had just come into the room and greeted Lukas with "How you doin'?", to which he replied: "*Dobro.*" It was a reflex response in Slovak, a language which at this time was evidently closer to him. The person to whom the old man directed his '*dobro*' did not understand the word. The old man had been separated from his Slovak language for some seventy years. And now the word came out of him, as it were, unconsciously. But this linguistic muddle had an emotional effect on me. As though now, close to death, the old man was preparing to face death in his own language. When he pronounced his 'dobro' it confirmed for me that I was in a foreign, distant land. Sanja was sitting by my bed, and when she heard the old man say 'dobro', as though in our shared language, her eyes automatically filled with tears.

Later, I heard Cierny breathing with difficulty, as though he were having an asthma attack. That lasted for a while, and then he calmed down, and I no longer heard his breathing. And each time that happened, I thought he had died.

In the course of the evening, the nurses who looked after the two of us changed.

That evening there was an African Muslim girl wearing a violet silk scarf, with full make-up, including bright red lipstick, as though she was going out for the evening, to a restaurant and not a hospital ward. She was quite cheerful and sweet, young. She may have been twenty, perhaps twenty-five, but she addressed Lukas Cierny and me as though we were children.

"Where are you from?" I asked.

She laughed, and asked back: "Where do you think?"

"Ethiopia?"

"Close."

"Sudan."

"Close," she said, and waited for the guessing game to go on. But I didn't feel like going on guessing, so, disappointed with my faint-heartedness, she admitted: "Somalia."

She stood in front of the board—on which she was going to write her name and mine—and asked, with a felt tip in her hand: "What's your name?"

After a brief hesitation, I replied: "Me'med."

From the perspective in which we found ourselves, the differences that are so fundamental to us became unimportant: whether she was from Sudan or Somalia? That mattered only to her; it left the entire continent where she now lived—indifferent. And the entire cosmos was indifferent to the differences in our identities. Seen from the perspective of death, it was a matter of total indifference which of the two of us was Slovak, and which Bosnian, Lukas and Me'med, patients stuck in the same room.

Just before midnight (she had come into our room to take blood samples), the young Somali girl asked the old Slovak: "What's your name?"

He said nothing. She asked: "And what year is this?"

"1939!"

That's what he said: *1939*.

What did 1939 mean to him? He must have been ten, perhaps fifteen then. That was the year before the big war. Maybe that was when he had to leave his home for good, and now, in his old age, it turned out that he had never left that year. Truly, what had happened to him in 1939? I would have liked to hear his story, but he was no longer in a state to tell it.

There's a year in my past I've never left as well.

1992.

Sometimes I'm woken by the clattering of Kalashnikovs over Sarajevo. I get up, make coffee and stay awake till morning. Through the window I look at the lights of Washington, or snow falling over the Pentagon.

During the night, Lukas Cierny got out of bed, and the young Somali put him back. "Where were you going?"

He replied: "To get dressed, I must go for a walk."

He didn't actually know he was in hospital.

Then in the morning, when she was encouraging us to get out of bed, he refused, and she ordered him loudly: "Get up! Stand up!"

"No!" said the old man.

And then—over the old Slovak who was refusing to get out of bed —she began to sing: "Get up, stand up, stand up for your rights!" Youth is beautiful in its arrogance.

The young Somali girl, with her turquoise scarf, with her new make-up, gleamed in the morning light, bending over the Slovak at the end of his life. She was happy because she was at the end of her shift, and singing.

I was waiting very impatiently to be let out of hospital. In fact I was afraid this wouldn't happen today. It was Friday, and that would mean I'd have to stay here over the weekend.

But the doctor appeared and asked me to walk down the corridors hooked up to all those sensors and sonars. I walked down the corridors while the doctor followed the behavior of my heart on the monitor in front of him. I enjoyed that walk: in an hour I'd be outside, beyond the hospital walls.

When I came back into the room, the doctor checked the working of my heart once again, this time with a stethoscope and, as he didn't find any sinister sounds in my chest, in the end he gave me precise instructions about how to behave—when I got out of hospital.

And then I could go home.

I looked at him. He was Indian, he was called Rayard. And I thought: this man saved my life and we're parting like complete strangers.

I said: "You saved my life."

He said: "Yes."

And left.

After that a smiling middle-aged man arrived, with a mauve bow tie ("I'm your limo driver"), and took me in a wheelchair through the corridors to the main entrance. This was a hospital ritual. Regardless of the fact that I could walk, a man I had never seen before was pushing me in a wheelchair out of the hospital. There was something childish in that ritual move out of the world of the sick into the world of the healthy.

I parted from the stranger warmly, as though we had always known each other, and was left alone in front of the hospital. The fresh November air startled me. I'd been impatient to leave, and now that I was on the street, waiting for my taxi, I felt a mild uncertainty, and fear.

When you come back from a journey, you find things just as you left them at the moment of departure. After all the days of being away, you are now back in your own room, perhaps there's an ashtray on the desk with a cigarette butt in it, perhaps a half-finished glass of wine, or a book you were reading on the day you left, open. Everything that retains a living trace of your presence in these objects becomes an image of the time that has passed and cannot ever be replaced.

I came back from hospital and the first thing I saw from the doorway was the nice cover on the bed, the one with the floral design à la Paul Gauguin, which had come home before me. Washed, it lay over the bed, and its textile essence was unchanged—there was no trace on it of the hospital, or of my illness.

Sanja had carefully removed from all the rooms most traces I had left of my previous life, which, according to the doctors' instructions, I ought to give up. There were no ashtrays. The smell of tobacco smoke had quite disappeared from the air.

I went into the sunroom, my covered balcony, my office.

I wasn't there either.

Erased from my rooms, now I could start over.

And then, reluctantly, I went into the bathroom, where it all began.

I undressed and stood in front of the mirror. I looked at the area beside my genitals. It was no longer a swelling but a bruise that was growing pale, with reddish edges, almost the color of rust.

I shaved.

Then I stepped cautiously into the shower, listening to the behavior of my body. The water was too hot. There was no pain in my neck, no pressure in my chest. Nothing hurt. The bathroom filled with warm steam. Water poured over me; was there anything simpler than this? a naked body with water pouring over it?

And I remembered a short film called *The Room*.

This is the story: a young man walks down the street as the light is fading, and through the open window of a room, above him, he hears the sound of a piano. And he stops. Then he sees the silhouette of the girl who is playing the piano. But the reason he stops is not only the music he heard, nor only the girl whose silhouette he saw. He does not know where that attraction comes from, he does not know the reason for his stopping, but he is aware of a strong magnetic pull emanating from that room, sensed through the open window. And years pass. He leaves that town and lives all over the world, then, as an old man, he returns. He buys an apartment, and lives out his last years in it. One day, after bathing, he leaves his room and hears the siren of an ambulance stopping in front of his building. It is night. And then he becomes conscious of everything. The room where he now finds himself is the room he had once seen, as a young man, while the sound of a piano reached him through the open window. And why had he felt such a strong attraction? The young man could not have known what the old man knows now: what he had seen then was his room, the one in which, when the time comes, he will die.

I came out of the shower; wrapped in a towel I walked through the whole apartment. Now I'm looking out of the window, and I say: "this is not *that* room."

Sanja hears me. She stands behind me, leaning her head against my wet back, and asks: "What did you say?"

TRANSLATED FROM THE BOSNIAN BY CELIA HAWKESWORTH

LYDIA MISCHKULNIG

A Protagonist's Nemesis

So why do you think furniture stores don't sell coffins? That's what the young intern asked me at the last office party. I raised my eyebrows. But when I tried to answer her, I couldn't think of a convincing argument. A coffin wasn't a piece of furniture, I ventured hesitantly; it was at best a container, a shell.

But a coffin is an essential part of the furniture at wakes, the young woman insisted. We stock the right furniture for every stage and purpose in life. It goes without saying that we supply everything for newborn babies, so why not everything for the dear departed?

It also went without saying that we supplied everything for our own midsummer picnic—our office party. We brought along our own brand of garden furniture, tablecloths, and tableware so that we could enjoy our day in the park in true company style. Everything was stowed in our capacious yellow-and-blue shopping bags, which look a bit like wide-bellied boats. We ferried our stuff along the avenues to the historic Lusthaus, the pleasure pavilion where imperial hunting parties found shelter and amusement in days gone by. In front of its baroque façade, we set up the furniture, laid the tables, and put out the food from our own delicatessen. Meanwhile, the employees' children cavorted on the grass.

We—the adults—ate and drank our fill and stretched out to relax on our own brand of rug. Then the intern asked, since we were used to having our office party outdoors, why couldn't we organize a wake outdoors too? And again I couldn't think of any good reason why we—meaning my company—had allowed ourselves, up till now, to ignore the very substantial line of business represented by funeral supplies.

I attended our staff parties in Moscow, Riyadh, and New York too. We're expanding in every direction and bringing a family ethos to consumer culture; speaking for the company, I welcome this, but not the shortsightedness of excluding death. It is my job to connect mundane episodes and form a unified whole. Just as a wreath needs a frame, life, which is a series of episodes, needs a scaffold, a skeleton. A firm needs backbone, and people need backbones, for all people are brothers, and for "brothers" you can also read "sisters," since they're just as subject to mortality. I see it as my ideological mission to globalize the concept that both living and dying are affordable and part of everyday family life. Using innovative PR and marketing concepts, I gave the company a frame of reference for human existence that is understood the world over, while to the world I gave a culture of cordiality and to our staff a climate of congeniality in which a person can not only bloom and grow but also fall ill and die. But something is bothering me and I can't put my finger on it. I keep feeling I've forgotten something, something that's almost within my grasp . . . Our furniture company is prolifically permeating every aspect of life.

In principle, a corporation is a body, but not bodily in the sense that a body can be arrested or locked up; the corporate body is defined by its function, its role being to put skin on our flesh and keep it all wrapped around our bones so that we can embrace our nearest and dearest without literally assimilating them, merging or decomposing into a shapeless mass. Indeed, this is why you might characterize a coffin as a sort of wooden skin for the deceased.

My company's branding is all about conveying a sense of security; we want our customers to trust that we are there for them.

I wanted to get to grips with my own self-deception too. What I'm saying right now sounds strange, as if I were merging with myself, my own plans and goals, and my own horror of death. Of course—death. Why didn't I think of it first, instead of that impudent intern? There's the room where the body is on view, the room where mourners are greeted or served refreshments, maybe another room where people can say a prayer . . . At the very thought of these spaces I could see before my eyes flat-pack coffins in pine, tie-it-yourself funeral wreaths, print-it-yourself sympathy messages, candles for the wake, lanterns for the cemetery, self-assembly crosses for the grave, in metal or wood. Of course, it would all have to be cheaper than the traditional undertaker's wares.

I faced Death and overcame my fear. I lay back on the company rug and surveyed the set: woodland clearing, historic pavilion, horse-drawn hearse.

The children were playing baseball. A cradle with the latest employee offspring in it was nestled in the grass to one side. Patterned textiles fluttered in the wind, like flags run up a mast. A successful business playing its part in conquering death. The crown in our company logo symbolizes our Corporate Eternity.

Man is, and always will be, mortal, the intern asserted. I turned away; I had no desire to discuss the finer points of a monarchic corporation versus a corporate monarchy with some young intern. She was neither a political scientist nor a sociologist, nor had she any other authority to be voicing opinions. With every word she spoke, it became more obvious that she simply wanted to be noticed. She was trying to hook my attention with her determined obsequiousness. Once she realized that her pretentious blather was boring me, she moved on to topics that naturally interested her. Some of these were quite interesting, and I built them into the model of our furniture company, which would embrace the generations entering this life as well as those on the way out. Seeking was a way of life for her, she told me. She sought meaning and purpose in every word. She found meaning bit by bit, she told me; and the purpose of words was to make reality speakable and readable. The word was mighty, it ought to be so mighty that it could call itself forth; the word was almighty, she said. She confided in me that she wanted to be a writer. She wanted to write right into power, and write all the way through power. That's highly ambitious, I replied patronizingly, and yawned. She apparently didn't believe I had what it took to take her ideas and make them my own. She wanted to grasp each individual word, she continued, clearly not getting the message. She wanted to command the spoken word; to have power and be able to communicate what struck her as powerful.

She sat down on the rug and stretched out. I think she wanted to make herself my reality; she said she was curious and wanted to see what reality looked like. I only hoped that I looked better than her image of power. I had to muster all my strength when she said that the only real power was death and fear of it, which could only be sublimated by celebrating death triumphantly. Whoever manages to banish your fear of death, to show you how life and death can be overcome, will be rich and powerful, I thought. Suggestions of immortality . . . resurrection! Now we're in advertising terrain. It's time, I believe, for the word to be made image.

I'm originally from Memmingen, in southern Germany. I knew very well that Vienna was famous for its cult of the dead, but unlike "dear Augustin" of the folk song, who fell into a pestilential pit during the Plague, I had every intention of landing in a gold mine.

For all her clever ideas, I was more experienced and quicker at bringing ideas to fruition than you would have thought from looking at the intern's funereal expression now. This afternoon she was being allowed to help out with the photo shoot for the pilot catalog.

I had to muster my strength. It had been a very trying year. I felt drained and didn't want to move around too much. Soon I would see whether power could create reality—if I had the power that I portrayed myself as having, that is—and then I would see whether adding the funerary line to our business was a success. I sprawled on my rug, arms and legs stretched out, while the others unpacked the coffin parts.

Dressed in several layers of black, the intern was playing the part of a romantic beauty, recently deceased. Like a princess in mourning surrounded by flattering courtiers (the heads of department), she busied herself fashioning a funeral wreath of pink roses, ligustrum, and ribbon for the camera. The cameraman was clever, and certainly good enough at his job to conjure just the right mixture of grief and composure into her expression. I waved encouragingly from the sidelines. I kept out of the limelight. I thought it fair that she should be allowed to play the corpse.

From a distance, our midsummer's party this year would have looked more than a trifle odd to passersby. The entire staff worked on the shoot. We were one big family, dealing with a bereavement.

Our furniture company will help you deal with your bereavement; that was the motto for our project, and this photoshoot was for the pilot catalog that would introduce our customers to the new line. We are setting an example, describing our vision of the affordable funeral of the future. We welcome more honesty in matters of life and death. We offer valuable tips, equipment and accessories, clever solutions. You will not be alone in this. We will help you. We will supply instructions. Invite your friends over and mourn together while you think up a few wise, comforting words.

The employees' children were playing baseball, badminton, football. The younger ones were playing pirates in the sandpit, or on swings and jungle gyms. They relieved some of the solemnity of the situation and symbolized renewal and the eternal cycle of life. The first funeral wreath was under construction: the intern was making it with the heads of department. The photographer snapped away eagerly while they worked. She rattled off the instructions, and they handed her ligustrum, then carnations, roses, ribbons. She made a floral crown out of the leftovers, which she was wearing on her head the next time I looked over. It was slightly cloudy, so I could look up without sunglasses.

A canopy of leaves. Wind. Dappled sunlight. Perfect lighting conditions for our model funeral.

The checkout girls were dressed in casual gear from our textile department—we consider clothes, which after all we put on and take off, as portable furnishings. They were working away, equipped with screwdrivers, demonstrating that our coffins could be easily assembled by women too. The intern looked proud as she stood there, erect, chin jutting out. She was the first to put her hand up when I was casting for the shoot, I remember.

The wind was blowing the black ribbons about. The apprentices, who had put them out too early, were cursing and throwing away the tangled ones, rolling off new lengths of ribbon from the spool and putting them on the tables where the golden lettering for our sympathy messages lay. The early summer light shone playfully on the apprentices' young faces as they enthusiastically rubbed the transfer letters onto the black ribbon.

The intern was busy chatting to the women screwing the coffins together when they began pointing excitedly to the other end of the grassy area. There, beneath the green shade of a tree, and between the green of the bushes, a woman dressed in white had suddenly appeared. She just stood there, a distraction.

I think my first thought must have been that someone had ordered an angel of death for the set. I was annoyed by this kitschy idea, which would have ruined my enlightened plan for an enlightened society. I was about to jump up and give the intern a dressing-down, but at the last minute I realized that the apparent angel of death was more likely a bride in her wedding dress who had accidentally wandered onto our set.

Meanwhile the intern was already running off in that direction, and before I could even raise my voice, she had already reached the little girls, whose innocent game of baseball was meant to illustrate how death is just a natural part of everyday life. Waving her arms, the intern shouted at the girls from the edge of the playing field and rounded them all up. Following her lead, the gaggle ran off blithely toward the woman in white.

I no longer remember whether the carriage that I'd spotted in front of the pleasure pavilion was our horse-drawn hearse or a wedding coach. The horses were whinnying, tossing their heads back and forth. The coachman was in traditional dress: black trousers, black cloak, and black bowler. We had even purchased a background banner that said "Horse-Drawn Hearse."

The horses headed off, the coachman roaring unintelligibly at them. He kept shouting and yanking the reins as if to force the horses to a halt. But all his shouting and roaring only sped them up, and they broke into a trot, whinnying all the while. The coachman pulled on the reins again and the horses started to turn. Another yank on the reins, a crack of the whip, and the horses started galloping around the pavilion as if racing one another. The grown-ups were laughing; the children were getting a little scared.

The coachman disappeared behind the pavilion. He shouted for help. The horses stomped, then the carriage clattered off along the main avenue into the forest, the sounds fading as it grew more distant.

The excited children ran over to the grown-ups. The grown-ups reassured the children.

Had anyone seen what happened the bride?

And where had the intern got to?

At first I just scanned the area from where I was. Maybe she was behind the bushes?

We couldn't go on with the shoot if the deceased had up and left with the bride.

I waited a bit, then stood up and went looking. The photographer took a break. I was fuming. The intern was sabotaging my project. Out of revenge, because I had stolen her idea. The first place I looked for the little bitch was behind the bushes. That's where the pond was. A murky green. A few leaves floating motionless in the middle. Water lilies in flower. Water striders skated jerkily across the still surface. I spotted a few toads on a small spit of land along the shore, but no sign of my chief mourner. Farther on there was nothing but scrub.

I went back to the park area. The children were playing *Who Wants to Be a Millionaire?* As I listened to them explaining the rules of the game, I was struck by the careful way these kids, who had all grown up with two languages, chose their words. Everyone had forgotten about the bride, and the intern was still missing. Which of them had abducted which?

All the staff were sitting in a circle, finishing off the food. The half-assembled coffin lay abandoned on the grass. A few of the children were trying to put the crosses together. I took the screwdrivers away from them so that no one would get hurt.

Later on I had another good look around all the paths in the park. The intern had vanished into thin air. I had to take her place. Otherwise I might as well dig my own grave. We quickly finished assembling the coffin, completed the wreaths and ribbon-lettering in a flash, fit all the bits of the candelabra together, stuck in the candles, distributed the crape, and took up our places in a casual, free-standing formation around the coffin, in which I lay as the corpse, *the piéce de résistance*. The photographer clicked and clicked and clicked. I think we managed to get the whole thing in the can.

The midges arrived as the sun began to set. The toddlers grew cranky. The baby was hungry again. The children wanted to go home.

We started to break camp. The adults took care of the furniture and the heavier things; the photographer took care of his camera. The children folded up the tablecloths and collected the dishes. I took care of the trash, collecting the ends of ribbons, the scraps of crape, the bits of ligustrum and wire. Where had the intern got to? The women wrapped plates and glasses in foil and banners so that the insides of our bags wouldn't be smeared. I stuffed what was definitely waste into an ordinary trash bag.

I carried the trash over to the large bins behind the pavilion. I walked right around the circular building.

Maybe the intern's still hiding out with the bride and waiting to ambush me, I thought, because she feels robbed of her idea.

Not a trace of the carriage. Nothing but the wind and the avenue.

I went to the bins and stuffed the refuse in. Then I went along the avenue for a bit and from there into the bushes again. I found a piece of cloth. White and black. I pressed on into the thicket. Found what were perhaps shreds of ribbon or crape, and footprints in the softened ground. My heart pounding, I bent branches aside, broke off twigs. Snapping. Splashing. The pond. It was all darkness above the water; nothing to be seen.

I beat my way back through the undergrowth and hit upon the bins again. The tarmac shimmered a silvery color. I opened the lid of a bin and lifted up the bag I had thrown in, to see if any bits of bride or intern were lurking underneath. But the only thing under the picnic refuse was my funeral refuse. I walked around the building again and wanted to head back to the grass. But I couldn't budge. I tried to lift first one leg, then the other, but I was glued to the spot. I pulled and strained so much that my muscles and ligaments began to burn. I couldn't move, and finally became exhausted from all my exertions. I fell to my knees, breathing heavily, bobbing my head like a horse, and then looked up.

I was alone. I hadn't even noticed the others leaving. My colleagues, the apprentices, the checkout girls, the photographer—all gone! They had left me behind. Where the hell had they got to? Why hadn't they waited for me? How long had I been running around after the intern? By now it was pitch black.

There was one bag left on the grass. Where was the coffin, where were the crosses and flower arrangements that had been scattered across the grass? Only this last bag was still there, glinting in the dark. They would have waited for me, I was sure, and wouldn't have dared leave a bag behind if I had exercised more authority with my staff and hadn't stood in as the corpse.

Maybe they had stayed behind and were watching me from within the pavilion. In the darkness the round building had become a watchtower. I felt as though I was under observation, and that was enough to scare me. I didn't want to feel scared. But I started to panic all the same. The only thing that seemed at all reassuring was the plain company bag on the grass. The crown in our logo gleamed kitschily at me. The bag had no handles, just a zipper. Surely I didn't design this type of bag, I thought to myself. But I didn't want to add to my confusion and ask questions that I couldn't answer. All that mattered was that the bag was one of my company's bags. So I accepted it unquestioningly. It was much bigger than our other bags, the ones I knew, and longer than it was wide; it looked a bit like a boat from where I was, if I were at the helm.

The dew was already falling on the grass, on the trees, on the bag, on me. I didn't want to spend the night crouching there senselessly and getting wet. And I didn't want to be afraid. Eventually I undid the zipper, crept into the bag, and was going to crawl over the grass and onto the avenue, on all fours, with the bag on my back like a shell. I was pleased that I'd had this idea and that I could, as it were, wrap myself up in the idea of sheltering and hiding in the bag. I started crawling but immediately got so tired that I had to give in to it. I lay there in the bag and slept and dreamed. I could hear myself speak. I distinctly heard myself say "bag."

And at that very moment I realized that's it, that's what I've been forgetting. But now I don't even care. I'm not thinking at all. For I am a fictional character, and the writer who created me wants me to die, because she doesn't like advertising directors who steal her ideas. So she lets it become tight and dark and airless around me. I can already hear her closing the zipper, which can only be opened from the outside, of course. So I am trapped and doomed to die.

Now I'm shivering. I could do with a good stretch but I can feel my limbs growing stiffer and stiffer. I want to sink into a deep sleep again or else die quickly. I have a feeling I can still hear steps, but should I cling to disillusionment until my last breath? I think I am being carried. I feel the scratching of the pen that is writing: yes, you are safe.

TRANSLATED FROM GERMAN BY RACHEL MCNICHOLL

body

MARIE REDONNET

Madame Zabée's Guesthouse

My bedroom is tucked away in the attic, with a sink and a toilet hidden in the corner by a wooden screen covered with designs of lotus blossoms and birds. From my window, I can see the rooftops of Paris and the bell tower of the church, Saint Ursula, on the edge of the Quartier des Perles. Every hour I hear the bells ring. Pigeons and sparrows come and peck at my windowsill. The sky has been low and cloudy since my arrival, but when the sun comes out in the middle of the day, light pours into my room, which has a full southern exposure. For the first time I have a room of my own. It gives me a sense of well-being and freedom: I have a place where at last I can be alone with myself. It's a new experience. In Ama and Lili's home I slept in the living room, and in prison I always shared my cell with other detainees.

Madame Zabée lives, as I do, in the attic of her guesthouse. She insists on saving the loveliest rooms for her boarders. She has made up a very cozy little apartment for herself, with embroidered draperies on the walls and decorative objects from all over the globe displayed on shelves—souvenirs from her trip around the world. It's hard to guess her age because it seems to change throughout the day, from one moment to the next, depending on her constantly changing hairstyles and outfits. Her smooth face is always perfectly made up. She wears exotic clothes that give her a certain flair. She also likes jewelry; she has a whole collection, from all the countries where she's lived. Throughout her long trip, she always worked in hotels. She is proud to say that her guesthouse is her first home and that she worked hard to buy it and then fix it up the way she wanted. She wants her boarders to feel at home, too. Her guesthouse is very well maintained. She watches over everything, conscientious about the comfort of each tenant. She spares no effort and seems to live only for her guesthouse. She likes to play at keeping whomever speaks with her off balance, so that it's impossible to have a stable image of her. With her, I can be sure of nothing, even if everything appears to be so well established.

My schedule isn't very different from the one I kept in Loisy. I go back up to my room around eight in the morning after waiting for Madame Zabée to come and tell me that my shift as the night watchman is finished. She is usually punctual and respectful of my time. Then I sleep until the early afternoon. The boarders get up at the same time that I do, and I have breakfast with them at the host's table. Madame Zabée takes advantage of the sleeping guesthouse to do the chores, buy groceries, and cook. Always thrifty, she has no household employees. She wants to do everything herself.

After lunch, I go for a walk. I cross the Quartier des Perles and go up the boulevard as far as the Gare du Nord. Then I go down toward the Seine. I walk softly along the quays. I find it so moving to walk alone in Paris. I need to walk, to walk without stopping. I don't go far from the Seine, which is my landmark, much as the Canal Saint-Martin was for Amid when he lived in Paris. I don't dare to sit on a bench or go into a café. With my false papers, I feel as criminal as an illegal immigrant. But as long as I walk, I have a sense of security because I melt into the crowd. Madame Zabée insisted that I should always keep my papers on me, in case I'm stopped, to have my identity verified, but that doesn't reassure me, because the papers are forged. At Saint-Michel, I get on the metro and go up to the Gare du Nord, and then I come back on foot to the Passage du Soir via the most direct route, as it's time to go back for dinner, just before I begin the night watch. I almost always dine alone because by then the boarders are already busy in their rooms. The night for them begins earlier than it does for me.

When I get back from my walk, I take care always to greet Ali. He's finished his nap and is always in his shop at the end of the day. I buy what I need from him. You can find everything in his corner store. He comes from a small village located in the south of Tamza. What a coincidence that it was in precisely this town, in the teacher's house, that I was arrested while I slept peacefully in Ama's arms. I don't tell Ali because I don't want to remind him of my past. Unlike Madame Zabée, he has never been sympathetic toward the failed revolutionary movement that I was a part of. He made that very clear to me. According to him, there is no better regime than the one in Tamza. If he chose to live in Paris, it had nothing to do with politics, but with business. He tells me, laughing, that his shop is like a hive—it makes the best honey. I wonder what he does with the money he's made from his honey, as he works hard and seems to live modestly. Every man has a secret, and to penetrate this secret would be fatal: that's part of one of the Chinese poems that I meditate upon during my night watch, while I think of Mateo. It feels like he left a long time ago. I don't want to admit that I miss him. I don't want to think about the old train station at Loisy.

Ali always invites me to have a cup of tea in the back of his shop. He doesn't drink alcohol and doesn't offer any to his friends. He says to me: "I obey all the precepts of my religion. So far, I have had *baraka*, blessings. God is great and merciful. He protects the Quartier des Perles and its foolishness. Without Him watching over us, we would be lost."

I am friendly but reserved with Ali. I don't want him to try to indoctrinate me. It wouldn't work and he would blame me for it. I don't want to know with whom he spends his time in the neighborhood, aside from Madame Zabée. He lets me know that he is in contact with immigrants from Tamza who have been successful in Paris and to whom, if I wanted, he could introduce me. "They need a guy like you." I thanked him, declining his offer. Out of the question for me to meet the legitimate Tamza network, whose reputation is known even in Fort Gabo prison! I want to lead my life alone, even if I have to forgo certain protections and advantages. With Ali, I maintain good relations while keeping my distance. I've asked him several times about Madame Zabée, but he pretends not to hear me. He won't talk to me about her.

Madame Zabée's guesthouse lives for the night, like the aptly named Passage du Soir—the Evening Passage. I understand now why Madame Zabée is so demanding of her night watchman. The boarders need me constantly. They call me incessantly. I have to bring them coffee or a drink, go buy them cigarettes, or maybe medicine, or oils with which to massage their backs, I have to fix sandwiches for them, comfort them on the nights that work weakens them and when one or two are sick or having a nervous breakdown. I learn to be a jack-of-all-trades: errand boy, waiter, counselor, psychologist, nurse. There are often little incidents that need to be handled carefully in order to keep things from going sour, such as a dishonest client with demands that can never be satisfied, and who starts threatening one of the boarders. Then I have to come and help the boarder so that his client can leave the hotel without doing him any harm. I must never call Madame Zabée unless there's a serious incident. She only works during the day. At night I take the baton. So far I've managed to avoid any real trouble. I've had to be smart and cunning. I've discovered talents in myself that I didn't know I had. I've entered into an unknown world that seems mysteriously familiar to me. The boarders are satisfied with me.

But why did I say "his" client, when I should have said "her"? As a matter of fact, I call them all by their nicknames, which are always feminine. There are seven men, or rather women: Sophia, Ingrid, Macha, Jeanne, Greta, Lauren, and Marylin. They keep their true identities secret; only Madame Zabée and the inspector know. The inspector tried all of them before deciding on Marylin as the only one worthy of taking care of him. I can tell that having been rejected by the inspector is a relief for the others. At the guesthouse, nobody ever says his name, as if to allow him his anonymity. They just call him "the inspector." As a client, he has a terrible reputation. As an inspector, though, the girls have nothing to complain about. He lets them work without any drama. He's too attached to Madame Zabée to risk spoiling the relationship with her. It's impossible to tell who is more indebted to the other.

Each boarder has a painful history, and each one lives in unstable circumstances. Sophia is originally from Mozambique, Ingrid is Lebanese, Jeanne is from Brazil, Greta comes from Ukraine, Macha from Turkey, Lauren grew up in a Palestinian camp, Marylin was born in the Caucasus. Madame Zabée's guesthouse is a temporary refuge for each of them. They dream of changing their lives and living somewhere else. They feel close to me since they know my background, even if they lead such different lives. I may be a stranger in their world, but I am nonetheless a part of it since I am the watchman. I never could have imagined that such a thing would happen to me. Before becoming night watchman in Madame Zabée's guesthouse, I had never met a transvestite. In the Movement, nobody even joked about that kind of thing. And in prison, a transvestite who revealed himself as such would not have survived.

Even when they exasperate me, I feel fondly toward them. I find them funny, imaginative. They like to act out scenes inspired by cult films whose scripts they know by heart. Their nicknames are a wink to the actress of their dreams. They were born for the stage. I like the provocative way they dress and make themselves up. I like their gestures, their glances, their hoarse and seductive voices. They all borrow one another's dresses, accessories, and even accents, vocabulary, and roles. They play at resembling one another so that the clients mix them up, or else they'll change their nicknames just to create pandemonium. They take stimulants and soft drugs to give themselves the courage to face the nighttime clients of the Evening Passage. They certainly don't work for their own pleasure, I can attest to that. The clients allow themselves total license with the girls, at least to the extent that this is permitted. They spare them nothing. The girls are left to the clients' mercy. Despite their toughness and their cynicism, they are fragile. And yet, they expose themselves to danger, as if to scorn their own lives.

Madame Zabée has forbidden hard drugs in her guesthouse. Any boarder who violates the ban is immediately thrown out. She repeats the rule regularly in a solemn tone: "No hard drugs in the guesthouse." She asked me to keep an eye on the clients and to throw out anyone who's shooting up, because the serious problems always start with them. It's on account of this prohibition that the inspector turns a blind eye to the nocturnal activities of the boarders. And if one of the boarders should happen to go into withdrawal, she has only to leave. There's no shortage of similar guesthouses in the Quartier des Perles. I pretend to enforce Madame Zabée's orders, but I have no illusions. The residents and their clients do what they want in their rooms; I'm not there to watch them. The important thing is that there is no evidence, and no drama.

To amuse themselves, the boarders try to seduce me. Marylin is my favorite. She invites me into her room whenever she has a break. She needs to unburden herself. She talks to me about the village in the Caucasus where she was born, which no longer exists because it was bombed on the pretext that it was harboring terrorists. She lost all of her people. Now she has nowhere to go. She goes where chance takes her. Playing at changing her sex is her way of responding to the drama of her life, of mocking her life, all the time. That's the only thing you can do, she says, shuffle the cards and throw off the game, get dizzy and pretend, and never stop, because that's when everything would crumble. I never get bored listening to her repeat her stories. I find her magnificent in her sequined dress and the boa thrown around her neck, with her false eyelashes and her platinum hair, lying on her bed where she takes breaks as she waits for a client to call. She rolls her *R*s outrageously and everything about her is excessive and alarming. She spends all her money on having dresses made for her that are copies of the ones that Marilyn wore in her classic movies. She wears them for her clients who are Marilyn fans. But she also goes out of her way to botch her impersonation, to ridicule her clients. Deep down, all the way deep down, there's a small lost girl, softly crying. Marylin may eventually come to identify with her heroine, even if she pretends the contrary. She intimidates me, so I stay in my role of attentive and protective night watchman. I don't want to take advantage of my position to gain her favors. I also don't want to incite any jealousy among the other residents. They love each other even as they hate each other. Their complicity does not exclude cruel rivalries.

Madame Zabée respects them, and perhaps more than that. I don't know exactly what kind of rapport she has with each of them. She never unveils her true identity, even in her moments of abandon. The boarders are grateful to her. Thanks to her, they can work in good conditions without being harassed by the police. Certain mornings, when the clients have left, and there's been some small, happy reason to celebrate (a birthday, a holiday, a gift offered by a client, an upcoming trip), there's suddenly a festive atmosphere at Madame Zabée's guesthouse. Ingrid and Macha play music to accompany Marylin and Lauren, who take turns singing songs about their villages. Marylin's was destroyed by a Russian bomb, and Lauren's was scratched off the map after being razed by Israeli tanks. Their voices rise miraculously, bearing no relationship to their regular tones. When they sing, they seem like twin sisters. Sophia dances a little apart from the others to a melody that she alone can hear. Greta and Jeanne mimic the grotesque mannerisms of their nighttime clients. Madame Zabée appreciates these moments of intimacy with her boarders. She reserves special tendernesses for each girl, like a suitor. She loves spectacle and revelry. Despite my fatigue, I join the party, dressing myself up as the Queen of Sheba and offering extravagant gifts to Greta and Jeanne. Madame Zabée likes my little number. She feels I've adapted well and quickly to my work at the guesthouse. It's been a success; this probationary period has been conclusive. I'll do just fine as the night watchman.

When there's a moment of calm and nobody needs me, I turn on the TV and flip through the foreign news channels. I try to understand the state of the world from which I've been severed since my detention at Fort Gabo. What I see is total upheaval, as if all our ideas had drowned in the sea, and the Movement, like an old ship that's rotted from the inside out, had sunk into the bottomless depths. I feel like I no longer understand anything that's happening.

Like Madame Zabée and the other boarders, Marylin is interested in my plans to become a filmmaker. She wants to be an actress in my film. She says that she would prefer acting in a movie to playing the role of Marylin with her clients. Playing around, she begs me: "Please, Diego, write a part for me so that for once in my life I can appear on the screen just as I am and I won't be forgotten. All the roles that I play here are false. I want finally to play a part that's mine and that's still unknown even to me. Please, do it for me."

I hear Marylin's request, which is the same as all the boarders' and Madame Zabée's as well. But for the moment I am unable to respond. How could I invent roles for them when I haven't even started to write my screenplay? As soon as I start to think about it, my mind goes blank. Marylin's request has come too early. She'll have to wait. My response saddens her. She tells me that she can't wait, that she's in a hurry.

I am deeply troubled by living surrounded by men who seem to be women. I want each of the boarders, especially Marylin, even if I don't let myself act on it. All night, I'm highly aroused. When I see women walk on the streets of Paris, I find them bland. Not one of them holds my attention. Women for me at this moment in time are Madame Zabée's boarders, and Marylin is their queen.

Madame Zabée has noticed this attraction. She hasn't forbidden me from having relations with the boarders, but she does warn me, "Above all, don't get attached to them, you don't know where that will lead. I love them all; I wouldn't rent my rooms to them if I didn't. But I also know that they're unbalanced, and that most of them will come to a sad end. My guesthouse is only a way station for them. They stay here for a few months, a year, then they leave, attracted by this or that enticing proposition and by the desire for change. None of them is able to stay put. When I hear news of them, I could cry. But I'm like you, I'm under their spell—I have to endure their appeal. I can't live without them now. I'll give you some advice: Make a movie in order to become yourself; if not, you risk losing yourself. Your life so far has hardly been a success. It could finish badly if you don't take control of it. Nobody can make your film but you. It's up to you to give yourself the means to do it."

Madame Zabée spoke openly with me. It was up to me to think about what she said.

The inspector comes once a week. He arrives at eight P.M. sharp, when the bells ring eight times at Saint Ursula. He always wears the same outfit, a severe three-piece suit, and everything about his approach is composed, as if none of his gestures were natural and he was afraid to show who he really is. He tries to deceive me. He greets me with a glance, as if I was his accomplice. Accomplice in what? I respond politely but without being friendly. I am instinctively wary of him. As soon as he arrives, the atmosphere in the guesthouse changes, though no one could say exactly how.

He dines with Madame Zabée in her apartment and spends a good deal of time with her. Then he's received by Marylin, who keeps him in her room until morning, something she never does for anyone else. When he leaves the guesthouse, he looks disheveled and haggard. It makes me uneasy all day. I try to talk about him with Marylin, but her lips are sealed, undoubtedly because the inspector is a client that Madame Zabée referred to her in particular. Marylin doesn't call me, the nights she spends with him. She doesn't need anything. There's no noise from her room. Everything happens in utmost secrecy. The inspector acts like a man obsessed.

I told Marylin what I think of him, at the risk of displeasing her. She shrugged her shoulders and replied, "Soon it will all be over. What good is it to stick your neck out and cause trouble? Take advantage of the time that I'm here, instead of thinking of the inspector." I don't know why, but her response saddened me deeply.

One day, at noon, I wake up a little earlier than usual. Without thinking what I'm doing, I knock on Marylin's door. She had still been sleeping. She opens the door for me, half asleep, and she takes me in her arms without saying a word, leading me over to the bed. I close my eyes and give myself to her as if I were a man in the arms of a woman in the midst of becoming a man while I in turn am metamorphosing into a woman. Marylin, she's like Cinderella's glass slipper that I somehow lost. She fits my foot exactly. But unlike Cinderella, I only wear a single shoe.

From then on, I continue going to wake up Marylin and make love with her just before breakfast. She doesn't give me a lot of time, as though she's on the clock, or as though she just didn't want me to get too attached to her. She's happy to give me pleasure, she likes my company, but she certainly isn't attached to me. For her, I'm only a friendly and kind night watchman, nothing more. She never speaks to me again of her desire to act in my film, as though she no longer believes in my plans. How could a night watchman at Madame Zabée's guesthouse manage to make a movie? It's just a dream that he has to help him get through life. I try not to think about anything other than the moment that I spend with her each day. It's a singular experience, calling everything that I've ever been into question.

TRANSLATED FROM FRENCH BY KATINA ROGERS

IEVA TOLEIKYTĖ

The Eye of the Maples

It was my parents who brought me to the house of the Davydas brothers. My mother found out about the Davydas brothers from my aunt. It was already well into autumn, in the mornings the fields were flooded with a sticky fog, and the light quietly glided through it to the damp August grass. I had just turned nine—my father, hiding in the kitchen, would cry at night, as they thought I would not live to see autumn. My sister started to be afraid of me, and even avoided touching me. No one knew yet if Clavin's disease was infectious. I often remember the wet, velvet eyes of my mother—"Our child isn't going to die, she's just scaring us." It wasn't clear how I'd gotten sick. Clavin's disease is one of the most mysterious maladies on earth. The blue disease—an old friend of mine. It's very hard to catch in time, or rather, it's very hard to convince yourself that you're sick in the first place. I only realized in January that my neck was turning blue. Slowly. At the beginning it just seemed like a bruise, like blue streams were flowing under the skin. It didn't hurt at all.

When they brought me to the Davydas brothers, my neck was as blue as an azure stone, as if my it had been soaked with ink. I remember that I was calm, that day. During the trip, Mama let me sit in the front seat, and Vijolė, my sister, was angry because of that.

We always fought over the front seat. There the road opened up right in front of your eyes, and you felt almost grown-up.

■ ■ ■

The house of the Davydas brothers is outside of town. It's a wooden, three-story house painted yellow, drowning among hundred-year-old, bluish-green larch trees. Next to the walls of the house, the blossoms of huge, reddish hollyhocks swayed, and the grass was mowed. I can still see it: in the windows there were many white, thin children's faces. I saw that my mother was afraid; after stepping out of car she said cheerily, "It's really very beautiful here," but she tried not to look at the windows.

We went inside, and my father was carrying a small suitcase; he didn't let me carry it. I got angry, I didn't want anyone in this house to think that I was weak or spoiled. Two graying men met us, Paulius and Matas Davydas. They were dressed simply, in jeans, and at the beginning I thought that they were also someone's parents, but they introduced themselves to my parents, and I realized that I was mistaken. Inside it smelled of sage and wood, everything caught my eye because it was new, unknown, and I almost didn't hear what everyone was talking about, until the thinner man said, "Goodness, what a blue little neck," and shivers ran up my spine when he touched my bluing skin. The Davydas brothers, my mother, father, and even Vijolė smiled. Looking at them I thought that I would certainly die.

Saying good-bye, my father kissed me on the forehead, and I felt ashamed. He'd never behaved like this before. I saw that my mother didn't want to go, she was afraid to leave me here, but my father took my mother by the hand unequivocally, and they left.

■ ■ ■

The Davydas brothers were the only ones who treated children with Clavin's disease in our town. As far as I know, they weren't doctors. They were herbalists, Paulius and Matas, with dark blue eyes, and black hair going gray. It looked almost silver because of the white strands. The brothers reminded me of shriveled wolves, forever stuck in winter. And then I was unnerved when I found out that the other children called them the Wolves, in private.

Paulius brought me to the attic room. There were two narrow wooden beds, a small table, a lamp, an old and small cabinet that had absorbed the smells of the past, and a small white bookshelf with a few books on it. A soft light flooded through the window. You could hear children playing in the yard. My new roommate was reading a book in bed and acted as if I wasn't even there.

"Vainius, say hi to your new roommate, Kasparas," Paulius said happily.

He shut his book, looked at me for maybe half a minute, and I remembered that my mother called those kind of eyes amber—she says, "Look, that child has amber eyes like a bird's!"—Vainius looked very weak, so thin, pale, but in those eyes were the little flames of a strange insolence. The feet sticking out of his jeans were bright blue.

"Welcome," he said.

■ ■ ■

That August there were thirty-nine children being treated in the house of the Davydas brothers: thirty boys and nine girls. All were about the same age. Some of them had spots that were quite small, while others frightened even me with their scars. "My poor little blue children," Matas would repeat, while rolling a cigarette,

but on the first floor, in the room with the window to the apple orchard, there was an eleven year-old girl with blue palms. Blonde, with small bones, with extremely thin wrists, watery eyes, she amazed me with her indifference toward everything. It was as though she didn't see the blue skin. She hardly talked with anyone, and sometimes the boy they called "the Leader" would make fun of her, but she, Ofelija, simply didn't react. This fascinated me to no end.

One day I asked her why she wasn't afraid of anything. She told me:

"I was in the Eye of the Maples, nothing's scary after that."

I had no idea what she was talking about, but I understood that if I was worth something, I had to get there.

"Maybe you could take me there?" I asked.

"Me? I can't. The Leader will invite you, when he decides that you can go." She smiled strangely. "But at that moment you probably won't want to go there anymore."

"Of course I'll want to go there!" I said. I couldn't let her think that I was a chicken.

"They all say that."

■ ■ ■

The children called Saulius, the oldest boy in the house of the Davydas brothers, the Leader. He had just turned fourteen. He was the only one of all the children who was tan and not too thin. Saulius had a single blue spot on his forehead. He looked as though he was the chosen one. The first day, when I had just arrived, Saulius came up to me in the garden and asked with a inquisitive look:

"Your name?"

I looked back at him, confused.

"I asked, what's your name?"

"Kasparas," I replied suspiciously.

"Hello, Kasparas. I'm the Leader here. You can come to me for everything. You understand?"

"Um, okay," I said. I didn't really understand what was going on. He was already turning away, but then he turned back, as if remembering something, and said, almost mockingly:

"Your parents lied to you, you know."

"What?" Nothing was making sense to me.

"You'll never leave here. Children are left here at the house of the Davydas brothers to die."

"No way," I said.

"I know what I'm talking about."

And he left. I walked around the garden for a long time afterward and chewed on the juicy white sour apples. I was certain, somehow, that he was telling the truth. I suppose that's why I respected the Leader from the very first day.

■ ■ ■

The Eye of the Maples, the yellow one, my old friend,

I remember like it was yesterday. Already on my first night I noticed that something was going on. Around two in the morning I heard thumping steps down below. On the fifth night Vainius went out again. He quietly dressed in the darkness, and afterward, almost without a sound, slipped out of the room and went downstairs.

I didn't sleep, I was waiting for him to return. It was maybe half past three when he slipped back into our room. The air was filled with a pungent, unfamiliar smell. I opened my eyes for a second and our glances met. A cold eye glowing in the dark. His blond hair wet, Vainius was shivering all over. I don't know why, but I closed my eyes then and pretended to be asleep, pretended that I hadn't seen anything, or heard anything—if there was anything to have seen or heard.

In the morning we didn't even discuss it. He was very happy. His eyes simply glowed with an incomprehensible light. I was itching to ask where he'd gone at night, but I already knew that you didn't do that sort of thing at the house of the Davydas brothers. I just needed to wait a little longer—the Eye of the Maples would show herself.

■ ■ ■

We were given strange medicine. Three times a day we had to drink one glass of it. "The brown water," Ofelija called it. And it was indeed a translucent brown liquid, like tea. I still feel its sweet, acrid taste now.

I had just finished my last glass of the day as the Leader passed by in the cafeteria. He put his hand on my shoulder, looking at nothing in the distance, and whispered in my ear:

"This night you will come with us to the Eye."

And then he left, as if nothing had happened. Vainius looked at me conspiratorially and said, "It will be interesting."

■ ■ ■

And she came,

we woke up at the same time and dressed quietly. Then we left, our steps thumping, we went downstairs, and the Leader took out a key and gently opened the door. It was cold outside, and there was steam coming out of our mouths. It was almost like an autumn night. Someone said, "Faster, faster." We ran, and my heart was beating as loudly as our steps in the night.

The Leader stopped running, and we slowed down to a walk. No one spoke. There were ten of us, and Ofelija was not there. Only boys. The smell of bonfires wafted from the fields, and we stepped into a fir grove. I was barefoot, and my feet were aching from the dew and sharp fir needles. You could see the Milky Way, and the forest was full of the pale light of the night. However, as we went deeper into the black foliage, there was only one thought running through my mind—"Fool, where are you going?"

My jeans were already wet to the knees,

the fir trees began to thin out, and a forest of yellow maple opened up in front of us. Like a park. The ruins of a house and a well could be seen. I still avoid abandoned houses now, because I always feel as though I've broken in, as though I'm soiling something holy with my presence.

It was already there, waiting for me, the Eye of the Maples,

smaller than our little room in the attic. I don't know another word—not a lake and not a pond, an eye, an eye, an eye,

black water surrounded by yellow maples.

Then the Leader said:

"Tonight, Kasparas will dive."

■ ■ ■

My heart sank. I didn't understand what he had in mind.

"You have to dive to the bottom and take a handful of sand," he said, as if reading my mind.

"But Leader, it's his first time here," Vainius interrupted.

"Do it," he said curtly.

I had never been so scared in all my life. It's hard to explain. You'd need to see that black water, you'd need to feel that ice, freezing your bones. I felt entirely alone. Everyone fell quiet, watching expectantly. There was *nowhere* to run to. I had to dive,

and I dove in, I jumped with my head down. I opened my eyes, but it was so dark under the water that I could only grope around. But there was nothing to grope. I swam deeper still, but was running out of air. Even then I knew that if I didn't want to drown, I'd need to turn around while I still had enough air to swim out again. But there was no bottom. Just black water. My head started to spin, and after giving up, I began to rise to the surface. I climbed out gasping for air, there was that terrible sound, lungs hysterical, *aaaaa aaaaa aaaaa aaaaa aaaaa aaaaa aaaaa*. I got sick. Almost crying, I said:

"You tricked me! It's bottomless!"

"If I'd said that it was, you wouldn't have dived in so deep. But, in fact, it does have a bottom." His calm tone infuriated me even more.

"Then show me, if you're so smart!" I yelled, the disgusting taste of forest water in my mouth.

"One night, one dive," he said curtly, and everyone turned to go home.

I tried to understand, why, what all of this meant, but I couldn't. I'd never been so angry in all my life—and maybe I'll never be that angry again. We went quietly, and when I saw the yellow house and larches, suddenly I understood: "But I didn't die! I'm still alive."

■ ■ ■

September was already creeping up. With mist, painfully green fields, people's glances getting browner, the drumming of the rain on the roof, the children staring out of the window unthinkingly, the softly dancing dewy white spiderwebs on the junipers and harvested fields, the bloody rowan berries, the smell of putrid leaves, the smoke of bonfires, the sound of falling apples,

when they fell like that the smell of the grass changed, it blended together with the damp smell of reddish fruit. Everything smelled of autumn, the horizons spread out, the blue contour of the forest and the misty sky passed by slowly, like lazy, even brush strokes in the landscape. It was then that the coming autumn began to scare me.

I had been at the house of the Davydas brothers receiving treatment for three weeks now; a few days later, the children back home would be starting school. Everything here was so different from what I'd known before: no parents, no sister, no relatives, no friends, no home, no school. Nothing. Though some of the most wonderful and important days of my life were spent in that house. It was as though the house of the Davydas brothers was under a spell. *You won't ever return, you won't ever return* rang in my head.

And one morning Vainius woke me up, he was so excited that I could hardly understand what he was saying. Only his eyes were clear: burning like they never had before, as if triumphant following some victory. He was holding a bottle in his hand, full of some kind of liquid, and I, having just awoken from sleep, didn't understand at first what it was.

"Kasparas, they duped us! There isn't any medicine! Look, it's identical to the stuff in the pool, the Wolves have been giving us the damn water of the Eye to drink!" It seemed like he had twenty birds flapping their wings in his lungs, and he might explode right there.

The smell of water from the forest thinned out in the room, and I understood that Vainius was telling the truth. We started to laugh. We laughed so hard that it seemed like our last joke. Vainius fell onto the ground and simply rolled around from laughter, doubled over. He repeated, "I'm going to die, I'm going to suffocate, I can't anymore," tears were running down my face, but I couldn't stop either, hell, it was the same damn water from the Eye, and every time, when I laugh, I remember Vainius, my old friend, his loud, triumphant laugh: *eye eye eye eye eye eye eye eeyee.*

■ ■ ■

He was punished. There was no other way.

That same evening the Leader invited both of us to go to the Eye. Wading through the pine forest I was hounded by the thought that tonight Vainius would have to dive in. I don't know why. Both of us had been feeling guilty, though no one else should have known about our discovery; and yet, it seemed that the Leader knew everything, and would now discipline us.

We stood in a circle around the black, glimmering eye, and after a good long silence, he said ceremoniously:

"This night Vainius will dive in."

I hated the Leader for those words. My heart was beating, my legs were shaking, it wasn't in my power to stop it. I wanted to shout, "You bastard, you're doing this on purpose, you want to kill us," but I kept quiet. I apologized to my friend in my thoughts; I knew that I couldn't help him. *Vainius, forgive me, you understand, I don't have the right to help you, you are alone. You have to jump.* That silence. And the black water.

Vainius turned to me, smiled, and said:

"Bye, friend."

He dove in so gently. This was the second time that I'd been to the Eye. It's only now that it's clear to me how horrible it was to see what I saw. I counted in my head: one, two, three . . . thirty, thirty-one . . . seventy . . . ninety-two . . .

I don't like this, I wanted to shout to Vainius, but I understood how stupid that would have been . . . one hundred thirty . . .

I was about to jump into the water, but the Leader wrestled me to the ground. I could feel the damp grass on my face, and hot acrid blood ran from my lip. He said, "Don't you dare."

Silence, the kind of silence you can only hear near the Eye of the Maples. About five minutes had passed. I was already sobbing, my whole body was shaking, I dug into one phrase and repeated it obsessively: "We killed him, we killed him, we killed him." I didn't see anything around me. It started to rain, I returned to my empty room in the attic completely soaked. I howled the whole night. I hated myself. I hated everything.

■ ■ ■

I woke up well after noon. There was a sweet, yellowish autumn light that filled the room. I heard voices outside, someone was crying out joyously over and again, "Come, come here, look at this, a miracle, a miracle, my God, a miracle, *heyyyyyyyyyyyyyy, eeeeeeeeeeeveryoooooooonneee.*"

I stuck my head out the window. I thought that I must be dreaming. There was a maple with yellowing leaves in the yard. I ran outside and was struck dumb. I stood bolted to the ground, entranced. A huge, beautiful yellow maple. Vainius sat on a branch high above. He was naked. Smiling. He was swinging his legs. He was so thin and pale. He was white now all over, even his feet.

I was speechless. "Vainius, my old friend, the Eye of the Maples took my voice . . ." The Davydas brothers came, and I heard, "What on earth . . . ?"

By the afternoon many people had come. "It's a miracle," they said, "that maple was never there before." The parents of all the children came. Only the Leader's parents weren't there. My crying mother hugged me: "My child, you're healed," she shouted. It was only then I saw that everyone was as white as Vainius. As if that night the autumn mist had wiped away the sad, blue wounds.

Paulius lifted Vainius out of the tree and wrapped something around him. I never saw him again. Just that last glance. Paulius carried him away thrown over his shoulder, because he was struggling, not wanting to go. I still hear now how Vainius triumphantly exclaimed:

"Friend, there are only rocks on the bottom!"

■ ■ ■

Afterward, a sudden, happy return home followed, but in reality it wasn't all that much fun—I still thought about Vainius, sitting in the tree, about the confused Leader, looking at the parents of the other children, about Ofelija, so calm and courageous, about our strange doctors and the house where I spent so much time, where you could hear the thumping steps of the children in the night and the whispers near your door, where laughter and clinking glasses echoed in the cafeteria, where we drank the sweetish water of the Eye, where everything seemed strange and mysterious, where your past life didn't count, and the only thing that could help you survive was the strength that was hidden inside you.

My thoughts went on living in the house of the Davydas brothers for a number of months. I wanted to find Vainius and Ofelija, but I didn't have a thing to work with, no telephone numbers, no addresses, no last names. Later it started to seem that none of it had happened, but even now, after many years, I sometimes wake from my sleep at two in the morning, as if about to be summoned to the Eye. I am sitting in a dark room, heart pounding. I can still see the black water, and fear shackles my bones.

I was in the Eye of the Maples.

TRANSLATED FROM LITHUANIAN BY JAYDE WILL

RUMEN BALABANOV

The Ragiad

1.

As she was dusting in the kitchen, Nevena Krusteva heard a voice:

"Oh, woe is me, thrice accursed!"

Nevena transferred her rag to her other hand, listened carefully, but hearing no more, she continued the job into the entrance hall. The coat rack was massive and collected a lot of dust. Then the voice welled up again.

Nevena Krusteva listened frozen, cast a frightened glance at her husband's raincoat, but the wail was not repeated, so she went to dust the living room. The television was white with dust, you could have written your name on the screen, so she went to the kitchen to wash out her rag before proceeding.

As she wrung it under spurting hot water, the voice cried out again:

"Ow! It's unbearably hot!"

Now Nevena was really scared, she threw down the rag with a shriek and took refuge in the corner. The rag splashed in the sink and cried:

"Brrr! You couldn't care less! Straight from boiling hot to freezing cold. I'm not made of steel, you know!"

It slid up the metal surface of the sink and in one jump landed on the kitchen table, right by the vinegar bottle.

At last Nevena Krusteva got a grip on herself and managed:

"How on earth . . . ?"

"I don't know," the rag replied sadly and practically shriveled on the tablecloth. It fell silent a moment and then asked, "Can I have a sip of the vinegar? I'm parched . . ."

Nevena didn't answer and the rag slithered up and pushed its way down the bottle's throat. Several noisy sucks later, it swelled up like a sponge.

"Hrrrrrrrr!" it purred with pleasure. "That's better now!"

Nevena remained in the corner, clenched tight, watching the talking rag with staring eyes, not daring to take a step closer.

"My dear lady," it continued serenely, "I'm not used to heavy physical labor! And so I would beg you to treat me with more care. I'll have you know, I'm not just any rag. Until yesterday I was Petraki Nikolov!"

This last revelation proved too much for the woman, she clutched her chest and fainted, having first made sure to place a protective hand on the arm of the kitchen chair.

The rag was not unmoved. It spent some time wondering whether it ought to jump onto Nevena's forehead. It had heard that vinegar helped with fainting spells . . .

2.

The rest of the day Nevena Krusteva didn't set foot into the kitchen. She locked herself in the living room and swallowed valerian every hour, waiting for her husband.

Her husband didn't grasp the situation immediately. Only after he'd calmed his wife down and got her to sleep in an unfastened dressing gown on the sofa did he open the kitchen door to find the rag hunched defiantly over the sugar bowl.

"It's not my fault—what happened!" the rag defended itself right away. "All I said was that, up until yesterday, I wasn't a rag, I was Petraki Nikolov. That's the whole truth!"

With trembling hands Nevena Krusteva's husband took a bottle of rakia from the fridge and drank two hundred grams in one gulp. He waited for the spirit to flow into his veins before quietly asking:

"So . . . Petraki Nikolov?" he lifted his hand and pointed his finger. "It's you, is it, my friend?"

"I say, steady on!" the rag was hurt. "Don't call me friend! After all . . . I do deserve some respect! And another thing . . . It's not good manners to drink on your own when you've got guests!"

The husband thought this over, sat down at the table, and poured a few drops over the rag.

"Ah, now that makes all the difference!" It relaxed and prepared for conversation.

While he was listening to its confession, Nevena Krusteva's husband took so many gulps from the rakia bottle that he scarcely remembered any of the rag's revelations. He only managed to write down Nikolov's old address on a scrap of paper.

Around midnight, the two of them said goodnight. The husband went to lie down in the living room, after locking the kitchen door, just in case, and the rag stayed draped over the sink.

3.

The next day Nevena Krusteva's husband left work early and went to the address he'd written down.

The house was enormous, with a small front yard and an overgrown arbor in the bushes. The yard and arbor were empty so the husband rang the front doorbell. For a long time no one answered, then steps could be heard, creaking on the wooden stairs, and a woman appeared on the threshold. She was well preserved, Mongol-eyed with raised cheekbones and rouged face.

"Does Petraki Nikolov live here?"

"Nikolov?" the woman pondered. "He was living here, but I haven't seen him for a long time."

She managed a discreet yawn and shifted from foot to foot, throwing a quick glance over the empty yard.

"Where did he work?"

"He was the head of the Institute, but they kind of dismissed him . . ."

"And you, what are you to him?"

"It's like, I was his wife . . ." she sank into thought again.

"And you haven't looked for him?"

The woman stared at him questioningly.

"Why should I look for him?" She crossed her arms, tired. "Haven't I just told you what happened?"

Nevena Krusteva's husband didn't know what to make of this. The woman in front of him looked too self-possessed to be lying.

"Do you realize that your husband has become a rag?" he at last found the strength to ask.

"It was in the cards!" The woman sighed. "I mean, that's what happens once you get fired . . ."

This time she made no effort to hide her yawn and pulled on the wire buttons of her dressing gown.

"Please forgive my disturbing you!" Nevena Krusteva's husband gave a slight bow and left. Behind him the door gave a lazy click.

4.

As soon as he got home, Nevena Krusteva asked him:

"Well?"

"It's true!" Her husband shrugged his shoulders.

Nevena Krusteva flopped onto the armchair and burst into tears, wringing her hands.

"What a horrible story!" She couldn't calm down.

"Yes, indeed," sighed her husband. "I never knew that people could turn into rags. It must be the result of some biological mutation . . ."

"What sort of mu . . . tation?"

"Biological! This rag used to be the head of the Institute. You don't get to be head without being some kind of weasel."

"That's all we need—spies in our house!" Nevena's sobs grew louder. "I'm scared, I'm scared . . ." Her whole body shook in the chair.

"There's nothing to get upset about!" Husband reassured wife. "We'll keep him under lock and key for a bit . . ."

He pondered a moment before continuing:

"Don't do the dusting with him. It hurts his feelings."

Nevena Krusteva jumped up:

"Let's throw it out. Throw it out right now. It'll do us some harm otherwise, you mark my words!"

"What do you mean throw him out?" her husband protested. "We've got to help him."

"It's always us doing the helping!" Nevena yelled. "Always us . . ."

Her husband fell silent. He was already planning what he would do. He had a good heart and, what's more, a fatalistic sort of feeling that the same thing could happen to him, which nudged him toward heroic action . . .

5.

The next day was Saturday; he went again to the familiar address. He rang three times and the same Mongol-eyed, tired woman appeared at the door.

"It's you again?" she asked and wrapped her dressing gown more closely round her body as if feeling the cold. "Come in!"

The rooms were dark, with small windows and old furniture scattered about. Thick carpets covered the floor. Their feet sank as if into fine sand.

"Sit down!" the wife said and pointed him toward a disemboweled couch covered in real leather.

"Yesterday I told you," said Nevena Krusteva's husband, "that your husband has turned into a rag."

"I remember now," his hostess interrupted him. "He sold himself to the devil!"

A canary broke into song in the next room.

"To what devil?" Nevena Krusteva's husband asked, stunned.

"There's only one devil," the woman calmly corrected him.

"When did this . . . happen?"

"When was it . . . ?" she thought for a moment. "It was five years ago! The devil came around one night and asked us if there was anyone looking to sell. He was out canvassing the neighborhood, collecting volunteers. I refused but my husband wasn't so sure . . .

I think that he agreed that very night."

The woman listened to the canary's singing from the murky room nearby.

"The devil was very convincing!" continued the woman, lost in her memories. "He said that anyway lots of people were turning into rags, but without realizing it, without getting any benefit from it . . ."

"But the benefit, what was the benefit?" Nevena Krusteva's husband interrupted, unable to restrain himself.

"I don't know," the wife sighed. "They arranged to sign the contract the next day at the Institute."

She lay back.

"But I can guess at the benefit . . ." she continued. "From then on, things went well for my husband. Quick promotion, I mean. We hardly saw one another, he was fantastically busy . . ."

There was a pause.

The canary stopped singing. No doubt exhausted.

"Even so, he tricked him!" she sighed.

"Who?"

"The devil! He didn't spell it out that becoming a rag meant exactly that. My husband somehow got the idea that the devil spoke in metaphors. You know how people say, 'Look at that wet rag!' . . . And it's no big deal . . . People think up all sorts of nonsense . . ."

"You don't happen to know where that contract is now?"

"No, my husband didn't want us to talk about it! He insisted I'd dreamed the whole thing . . ."

Nevena Krusteva's husband shifted his weight noisily on the sofa.

"And why did they dismiss him at the Institute?"

"They threw him out . . . They didn't dismiss him! That morning the cleaner saw a rag lying on his desk and threw it away. She didn't realize it was Petraki Nikolov!"

Above their heads a cuckoo chirruped. Ten times.

"Don't you want to see him?" Nevena Krusteva's husband asked timidly.

The woman gave him a frightened look.

"No, no! I've got a weak heart . . ."

"Even so, I could bring him around one day . . . Maybe he would feel better in his own home."

"Hardly," the woman exclaimed. "He felt at his best in meetings."

Nevena Krusteva's husband stood up.

"If there's anything new, I'll get in touch again!" he said and offered his hand.

The woman stood up too.

"I can give you some advice!" she announced. "Don't give him anything to drink . . . his liver's swollen enough already after all those meetings . . ."

6.

In spite of this, Nevena Krusteva's husband decided to go to the Institute where Nikolov had worked. On Monday, dressed in his best suit, he took a deep breath and slipped under the entrance arch.

The porter stopped him. He was sitting in a glass cubicle, in a heap of newspapers, folders, telephone wires, and scattered scraps of everyday paper.

"I'm looking for Petraki Nikolov!"

"It's not his day for appointments," the porter muttered darkly.

"I'm his cousin! I've just flown in from Paris . . . I'm bringing him a parcel from the sister Institute . . ."

The porter eyed Nevena Krusteva's husband suspiciously. He even rose from his comfy chair to look the visitor over from head to toe.

"Petraki Nikolov isn't here!" this guardian of propriety concluded in the same gloomy tone.

"No, no! I know he's at work! I spoke to his wife . . ."

The porter settled back in his chair and said:

"Nikolov is in a meeting!"

"It's a question of national importance!" Nevena Krusteva's husband said in a sharper tone. The porter got up to look at him again.

Once back in his chair, the porter reached for the phone and demonstratively pressed three numbers. The phone gave a set of quick beeps.

"Petraki Nikolov?" he drawled.

"Petraki Nikolov is at a meeting in the center," a strong female voice rang out.

"Well, you see, they've brought a parcel here from the sister Institute . . ."

"Let them bring it up!" the voice sang.

The porter gently replaced the receiver, then thought the matter over, but eventually reached a decision:

"Leave your identity card here! Third floor, room twenty-five . . ."

The secretary was very charming.

"Leave the parcel!" she smiled.

"Can't I hand it to him personally?"

"Nikolov's abroad!" she said.

"But didn't you say he was in a meeting . . . ?"

"Either he's in a meeting or he's abroad!" the secretary smiled again. "He's terribly busy. I haven't seen him for half a year . . ."

"In that case I'll take it by his house . . ." Nevena Krusteva took a hesitant step backward.

"I doubt you'll find him . . ." The secretary's response was not quite as friendly now as she tapped at her keyboard with all her fingers.

Her visitor closed the door behind him and set off down the corridor. A clerk appeared hurrying toward him.

"Excuse me, I'm looking for Petraki Nikolov!" Nevena Krusteva's husband said.

"He's in the lab." The clerk didn't want to stop. "No, no . . . Actually, there's a committee meeting today . . . Or else he's abroad . . ."

The clerk slipped into an office.

7.

As soon as he got home, Nevena Krusteva's husband decided to begin a frank dialogue with the rag. Nikolov wasn't sitting over the sink but had climbed up on to the sideboard, where the Krustev family kept its water glasses.

"Don't touch me!" the rag shrieked and gazed in horror at the rest of the rags lying in the cardboard box underneath him.

"Silence!" shouted Nevena Krusteva's husband, hoping to restore a semblance of order to the kitchen.

He sat down at the end of the table, poured himself a glass of grape rakia, and drank it. "The way things are going with this rag, my liver's going to be in trouble too," he thought, and filled up his empty glass.

"What's all the noise about?" he asked.

"They want to make me dirty!" the rag Nikolov explained hoarsely. "They want to force me to wipe the dishes. I mean to say, I've worked in the Institute, after all, and I'm not going to let them treat me like a . . ."

He was going to say "like a rag," but swallowed instead.

"I had an official car . . . a secretary . . ."

He's got good reason to cry his heart out, thought Nevena Krusteva's husband . . . I've never seen a rag sobbing.

Nikolov got a grip on himself and continued:

"And stop pouring yourself that horrible drink. Haven't you got any vodka at least?"

"I have," the host replied mechanically. "I save it for guests!"

He got up and from the living room brought a brand new bottle of Zubrovka and opened the top with a snap.

"Pour me some!" implored the rag and flopped on to the table.

"How's your liver?" asked the host, as though in passing.

"Can't you see?" Nikolov answered angrily. "It's like an old rag."

Nevena Krusteva's husband sighed and poured fifty grams of vodka over the rag. He judged it a sufficient dose to loosen any inhibitions.

"See here," he began. "I've been looking into your situation. I've gotten to know you, so I'm doing away with any formality. Your situation is really serious, friend, but you've got no one to blame but yourself!"

The host waited for his words to sink in before continuing:

"You're the one who signed a contract with the devil!"

The rag Nikolov quivered.

"How did you find out?"

"They told me at the Institute!" his host lied.

"So they've found out there?" Nikolov let out a heartbroken sigh.

"Most of them guessed long ago that you'd sold your soul to the devil."

"So they found out about Nichev?"

"Yes about Nichev and about . . ." The host continued to lie out of his noble feelings of sympathy.

"And about Boyanov the former deputy director," Nikolov murmured even more quietly.

"Yes!" his host nodded emphatically.

The rag fell silent.

"It's all over with me . . ." He let out a heartrending sigh and asked for more vodka.

Nevena Krusteva's husband did not refuse him.

8.

To find the devil is devilishly difficult.

After he'd taken a physical description from the rag Nikolov, Nevena Krusteva's husband went out to look for him.

But he couldn't find him.

Exactly the opposite happened. One evening the devil himself appeared in front of the man.

He didn't look at all like the devil, except that his skin was dark. He was wearing a tracksuit with a silk scarf round his neck.

"You've been looking for me," said the stranger. "In connection with the rags?"

At first Nevena Krusteva's husband didn't catch on. He wondered if his wife had sent an old mattress to be reupholstered—but then, his guest didn't look like a workman.

"In connection with the rag Nikolov," the stranger clarified.

Only now did his host understand. He invited his guest into the living room: his wife had gone to visit a neighbor, and Nikolov, daydreaming in the kitchen, could not be allowed to overhear their serious conversation.

The devil lit a Kent cigarette and crossed his legs.

"I'm really pleased you've come!" the host began. "I couldn't find you anywhere!"

"I know," the devil waved his hand. "I've been very busy recently."

"I think we can work something out."

"Yes?" The devil perked up.

He took a form out of his attaché case.

"Sign this and everything will be okay!"

"What's this?"

"A contract! You sell me your soul, and in return . . ."

"In return for fast promotion, luxury . . ." the devil's host finished the sentence . . . "We're not on the same wavelength, I'm afraid. I was looking for you because of Nikolov. Nikolov worked in the Institute. He was the boss!"

The devil smiled.

"But he still works in the Institute. And he's still the boss!"

"But I checked," his host exploded. "They told me in the Institute that . . ."

"Nikolov's abroad," the devil helped him out.

"Yes!"

"Because he really was abroad."

"But his wife . . ."

"Says she hasn't seen him?"

"Yes!"

"Well, she wasn't seeing too much of him even before!" the devil laughed.

Nevena Krusteva's husband didn't understand anything.

"Well, and so what is that thing in the kitchen?"

"A rag!" the devil's answer was brusque. He put out his cigarette. "Look, the whole thing's not quite what you'd expect. I'll be frank with you! Recently we've fallen behind with the plan. With us there's been a significant shortfall, we just don't have enough souls. So, I'm sure you've heard how, these days, people are constantly getting caught up in self-improvement schemes. And what happens as a result? It's very simple. When they face the inevitable moral crisis, I appear and suggest they sign a contract. Then after a while I take their souls from their bodies. Recently we included a new clause which means we then turn the bodies into rags. It's less wasteful than just letting them die. You can bear witness yourself that there's no difference in the quality of the rags."

"Aside from the fact that they talk!" the host interrupted, a little sarcastically.

"A small defect at first sight, but just think: we've created sentient rags! That's nothing to be sneezed at . . ."

The devil fell silent a moment, was about to light another cigarette, but held back.

"Even so, please, I beg you, make him a human being again," the host pleaded.

"Human being?"

"Yes."

"He's never been a human being!" The devil shook his head. "How can I make something out of nothing? That's not in my power . . ."

The devil gave a guilty smile and finally lit his second cigarette.

In the growing silence, they could hear through the wall a sigh that was deaf to the world. The rag Nikolov was getting ready to sleep.

TRANSLATED FROM BULGARIAN BY CHRISTOPHER BUXTON

women

A. S. BYATT

Dolls' Eyes

Her name was Felicity; she had called herself Fliss as a small child, and it had stuck. The children in her reception class at Holly Grove School called her Miss Fliss, affectionately. She had been a pretty child and was a pretty woman, with tightly curling golden hair and pale blue eyes. Her classroom was full of invention, knitted dinosaurs, an embroidered snake coiling round three walls. She loved the children—almost all of them—and they loved her. They gave her things—a hedgehog, newts, tadpoles in a jar, bunches of daffodils. She did not love them as though they were her own children: she loved them because they were not. She taught bush-haired boys to do cross-stitch, and shy girls to splash out with big paintbrushes and tubs of vivid reds and blues and yellows.

She wondered often if she was odd, though she did not know what she meant by "odd." One thing that was odd, perhaps, was that she had reached the age of thirty without having loved, or felt close, to anyone in particular. She made friends carefully—people must have friends, she knew—and went to the cinema, or cooked suppers, and could hear them saying how nice she was. She knew she was nice, but she also knew she was pretending to be nice. She lived alone in a little red brick terraced house she had inherited from an aunt. She had two spare rooms, one of which she let out, from time to time, to new teachers who were looking for something more permanent, or to passing students. The house was not at all odd, except for the dolls.

She did not collect dolls. She had over a hundred, sitting in cosy groups on sofas, perching on shelves, stretched and sleeping on the chest of drawers in her bedroom. Rag dolls, china dolls, rubber dolls, celluloid dolls. Old dolls, new dolls, twin dolls (one pair conjoined). Black dolls, blonde dolls, baby dolls, chubby little boys, ethereal fairy dolls. Dolls with painted surprised eyes, dolls with eyes that clicked open and closed, dolls with pretty china teeth, between pretty parted lips. Pouting dolls, grinning dolls. Even dolls with trembling tongues.

The nucleus of the group had been inherited from her mother and grandmother, both of whom had loved and cared for them. There were four: a tall ladylike doll in a magenta velvet cloak, a tiny china doll in a frilly dress with forgetmenot painted eyes, a realistic baby doll with a cream silk bonnet, closing eyes, and articulated joints, and a stiff wooden doll, rigid and unsmiling in a black stuff gown.

Because she had those dolls—who sat in state in a basket chair—other dolls accumulated. People gave her their old dolls—"we know you'll care for her." Friends thinking of Christmas or birthday presents found unusual dolls in jumble sales or antique shops.

The ladylike doll was Miss Martha. The tiny china doll was Arabel. The baby doll was Polly. The rigid doll was Sarah Jane. She had an apron over her gown and might once have been a domestic servant doll.

Selected children, invited to tea and cake, asked if she played with the dolls. She did not, she replied, though she moved them round the house, giving them new seats and different company.

It would have been odd to have played with the dolls. She made them clothes, sometimes, or took one or two to school for the children to tell stories about.

She knew, but never said, that some of them were alive in some way, and some of them were only cloth and stuffing and moulded heads. You could even distinguish, two with identical heads under different wigs and bonnets, of whom one might be alive—Penelope with black pigtails—and one inert, though she had a name, Camilla, out of fairness.

There was a new teacher, that autumn, a late appointment because Miss Bury had had a leg amputated as a result of an infection caught on a boating holiday on an African river. The new teacher was Miss Coley. Carole Coley. The head teacher asked Fliss if she could put her up for a few weeks, and Fliss said she would gladly do so. They were introduced to each other at a teaparty for incoming teachers.

Carole Coley had strange eyes; this was the first thing Fliss noticed. They were large and rounded, dark and gleaming like black treacle. She had very black hair and very black eyelashes. She wore the hair, which was long, looped upward in the nape of her neck, under a black hairslide. She wore lipstick and nail varnish in a rich plum colour. She had a trim but female body and wore a trouser suit, also plum. And glittering glass rings, quite large, on slender fingers. Fliss was intimidated, but also intrigued. She offered hospitality—the big attic bedroom, shared bath and kitchen. Carole Coley said she might prove to be an impossible guest. She had two things which always came with her:

"My own big bed with my support mattress. And Cross-Patch."

Fliss considered. The bed would be a problem but one that could be solved. Who was Cross-Patch?

Cross-Patch turned out to be a young Border collie, with a rackety eye-patch in black on a white face. Fliss had no pets, though she occasionally housed the classroom mice and tortoises in the holidays. Carole Coley said in a take it or leave it voice, that Cross-Patch was very well trained.

"I'm sure she is," said Fliss, and so it was settled. She did not feel it necessary to warn Carole about the dolls. They were inanimate, if numerous.

Carole arrived with Cross-Patch, who was sleek and slinky. They stood with Fliss in the little sitting room whilst the removal men took Fliss's spare bed into storage, and mounted with Carole's much larger one. Carole was startled by the dolls. She went from cluster to cluster, picking them up, looking at their faces, putting them back precisely where they came from. Cross-Patch clung to her shapely calves and made a low throaty sound.

"I wouldn't have put you down as a collector."

"I'm not. They just seem to find their way here. I haven't *bought* a single one. I get given them, and people see them, and give me more."

"They're a bit alarming. So much staring. So still."

"I know. I'm used to them. Sometimes I move them round."

Cross-Patch made a growly attempt to advance on the sofa. Carole raised a firm finger. "*No*, Cross-Patch. *Sit. Stay.* These are not your toys."

Cross-Patch, it turned out, had her own stuffed toys—a bunny rabbit, a hedgehog—with which she played snarly, shaking games in the evenings. Fliss was impressed by Carole's authority over the animal. She herself was afraid of it, and knew that it sensed her fear.

Carole was a good lodger. She was helpful and unobtrusive. Everything interested her Fliss's embroidery silks, her saved children's books from when she was young, her mother's receipts, a bizarre Clarice Cliffe tea-set with a conical sugar-shaker. She made Fliss feel that she was *interesting*—a feeling Fliss almost never had, and would have said she didn't want to have. It was odd being looked at, appreciatively, for long moments. Carole asked her questions, but she could not think up any questions to ask in return. A few facts about Carole's life did come to light. She had travelled and worked in India. She had been very ill and nearly died. She went to evening classes on classical Greece and asked Fliss to come too, but Fliss said no. When Carole went out, Fliss sat and watched the television, and Cross-Patch lay watchfully in a corner, guarding her toys. When Carole returned, the dog leaped up to embrace her as though she was going for her throat. She slept upstairs with her owner in the big bed. Their six feet went past Fliss's bedroom door, pattering, dancing.

Carole said the dolls were beginning to fascinate her. So many different characters, so much love had gone into their making and clothing. "Almost loved to bits, some of them," said Carole, her treacle eyes glittering. Fliss heard herself offer to lend a few of them, and was immediately horrified. What on earth would Carole want to borrow dolls for? The offer was *odd*. But Carole smiled widely and said she would love to have one or two to sit on the end of her big bed, or on the chest of drawers. Fliss was overcome with nervous anxiety, then, in case Cross-Patch might take against the selected dolls, or think they were toys. She looked sidelong at Cross-Patch, and Cross-Patch looked sidelong at her, and wrinkled her lip in a collie grin. Carole said

"You needn't worry about her, my dear. She is completely well-trained. She hasn't offered to touch any doll. Has she?"

"No," said Fliss, still troubled by whether the dog would see matters differently in the bedroom.

When they went to bed they said goodnight on the first floor landing and Carole went up to the next floor. She borrowed a big rag doll with long blonde woollen plaits and a Swiss sort of apron. This doll was called Priddy, and was not, as far as Fliss knew, alive. She also borrowed—surprisingly—the rigid Sarah Jane, who certainly was alive. I love her disapproving expression, said Carole. She's seen a thing or two, in her time. She had painted eyes, that didn't close.

Other dolls took turns to go up the stairs. Fliss noticed, without formulating the idea, that they were always grown-up or big girl dolls, and they never had sleeping eyes.

Little noises came down the stairs. A cut-off laugh, an excited whisper, a creak of springs. Also a red light spread from the door over the sage-green staircarpet.

One night, when she couldn't sleep, Fliss went down to the kitchen and made Horlicks for herself. She then took it into her head to go up the stairs to the spare room; she saw the pool of red light and knew Carole was not asleep. She meant to offer her Horlicks.

The door was half open. "Come in," called Carole, before Fliss could tap. She had put squares of crimson silk, weighted down with china beads, over the bedside lamps. She sat on the middle of her big bed, in a pleated sea-green nightdress, with sleeves and a high neck. Her long hair was down, and brushed into a fan, prickling with an electric life of its own. Cross-Patch was curled at the foot of the bed.

"Come and sit down," said Carole. Fliss was wearing a baby-blue nightie in a fine jersey fabric, under a fawn woolly dressing-gown. "Take that off, make yourself comfortable."

"I was—I was going to—I couldn't sleep . . ."

"Come here," said Carole. "You're all tense. I'll massage your neck."

They sat in the centre of the white quilt, made ruddy by light, and Carole pushed long fingers into all the sensitive bits of Fliss's neck and shoulders, and released the nerves and muscles. Fliss began to cry.

"Shall I stop?"

"Oh no, don't stop, don't stop. I—

"This is terrible. Terrible. I love you."

"And what's terrible about that?" asked Carole, and put her arms around Fliss, and kissed her on the mouth.

Fliss was about to explain that she had never felt love and didn't exactly like it, when they were distracted by fierce snarling from Cross-Patch.

"Now then, bitch," said Carole. "Get out. If you're going to be like that, get out."

And Cross-Patch slid off the bed, and slunk out of the door. Carole kissed Fliss again, and pushed her gently down on the pillows and held her close. Fliss knew for the first time that terror that all lovers know, that the thing now begun must have an ending. Carole said "My dear, my darling." No one had said that to her.

They sat side by side at breakfast, touching hands, from time to time. Cross-Patch uttered petulant low growls and then padded away, her nails rattling on the lino. Carole said they would tell each other everything, they would know each other. Fliss said with a light little laugh that there was nothing to know about her. But nevertheless she did more of the talking, described her childhood in a village, her estranged sister, her dead mother, the grandmother who had given them the dolls.

Cross-Patch burst back into the room. She was carrying something, worrying it, shaking it from side to side, making a chuckling noise, tossing it, as she would have tossed a rabbit to break its neck. It was the baby doll, Polly, in her frilled silk bonnet and trailing embroidered gown. Her feet in their knitted bootees protruded at angles. She rattled.

Carole rose up in splendid wrath. In a rich firm voice she ordered the dog to put the doll down, and Cross-Patch spat out the silky creature, slimed with saliva, and cowered whimpering on the ground, her ears flat to her head. Masterfully Carole took her by the collar and hit her face, from side to side, with the flat of her hands. "*Bad* dog," she said, "*bad* dog," and beat her. And beat her.

The rattling noise was Polly's eyes, which had been shaken free of their weighted mechanism, and were rolling round inside her bisque skull. Where they had been were black holes. She had a rather severe little face, like some real babies. Eyeless it was ghastly.

"My darling, I am so sorry," said Carole. "Can I have a look?"

Fliss did not want to relinquish the doll. But did. Carole shook her vigorously. The invisible eyes rolled.

"We could take her apart and try to fit them back."

She began to pull at Polly's neck.

"No, don't, don't. We can take her to the dolls' hospital at the Ouse Bridge. There's a man in there—Mr Copple—who can mend almost anything."

"Her pretty dress is torn. There's a toothmark on her face."

"You'll be surprised what Mr Copple can fix," said Fliss, without complete certainty. Carole kissed her and said she was a generous creature.

Mr Copple's shop was old and narrow-fronted, and its back jutted out over the river. It had old window-panes, with leaded lights, and was a tiny cavern inside, lit with strings of fairy-lights, all different colours. From the ceiling, like sausages in a butcher's shop, hung arms, legs, torsos, wigs, the cages of crinolines. On his glass counter were bowls of eyeballs, blue, black, brown, green, paperweight eyes, eyes without whites, all iris. And there were other bowls and boxes with all sorts of little wire joints and couplings, useful elastics and squeaking voice boxes.

Mr Copple had, of course, large tortoiseshell glasses, wispy white hair and a bad, greyish skin. His fingers were yellow with tobacco.

"Ah," he said, "Miss Weekes, always a pleasure. Who is it this time?"

Carole replied. "It was my very bad dog. She shook her. She has never done anything like this before."

The two teachers had tied Polly up into a brown paper parcel. They did not want to see her vacant stare. Fliss handed it over. Mr Copple cut the string.

"Ah," he said again. "Excuse me."

He produced a kind of prodding screwdriver, skilfully decapitated Polly, and shook her eyes out into his hand.

"She needs a new juncture, a new balance. Not very difficult."

"There's a bite mark," said Carole gloomily.

"When you come back for her, you won't know where it was. And I'll put a stitch or two into these pretty clothes and wash them out in soapsuds. She's a Million Dollar Baby. A Bye-Lo Baby. Designed by an American, made in Germany. In the 1920s."

"Valuable?" asked Carole casually.

"Not so very. There were a large number of them. This one has the original clothes and real human hair. That puts her price up. She is meant to look like a real newborn baby."

"You can see that," said Carole.

He put the pieces of Polly into a silky blue bag and attached a label on a string. *Miss Weekes's Polly.*

They collected her the next week and Mr Copple had been as good as his word. Polly was Polly again, only fresher and smarter. She rolled her eyes at them again, and they laughed, and when they got her home, kissed her and each other.

Fliss thought day and night about what she would do when Carole left. How it would happen. How she would bear it. Although, perhaps because, she was a novice in love, she knew that the fiercer the passion, the swifter and the harsher the ending. There was no way they two would settle into elderly domestic comfort. She became jealous and made desperate attempts not to show it. It was horrible when Carole went out for the evening. It was despicable to think of listening in to Carole's private calls, though she thought Carole listened to her own, which were of no real interest. The school year went on, and Carole began to receive glossy brochures in the post, with pictures of golden sands and shining white temples. She sat looking at them in the evenings, across the hearth from Fliss, surrounded by dolls. Fliss wanted to say "Shall we go together?" and was given no breath of space to do so. Fliss had always spent her holidays in Bath, making excursions into the countryside. She made no arrangements. Great rifts and gaps of silence spread into the texture of their lives together. Then Carole said

"I am going away for a month or so. On Sunday. I'll arrange for the rent to be paid while I'm away."

"Where," said Fliss. "Where are you going?"

"I'm not sure. I always do go away."

Can I come? could not be said. So Fliss said

"Will you come back?"

"Why shouldn't I? Everyone needs a bit of space and time to herself, now and then. I've always found that. I shall miss the dolls."

"Would you like to take one?" Fliss heard herself say. "I've never given one away, never. But you can take one—"

Carole kissed her and held her close.

"Then we shall both want to come back—to the charmed circle. Which doll are you letting me have?"

"*Any of them*," cried Fliss, full of love and grief. "Take anyone at all. I want you to have the one you want."

She did not expect, she thought later, that Carole would take one of the original four. Still less, that of those four, she would choose Polly, the baby, since her taste had always been for grown girls. But Carole chose Polly, and watched Fliss try to put a brave face on it, with an enigmatic smile. Then she packed and left, without saying where she was going.

Before she left, in secret, Fliss kissed Polly and told her "Come back. Bring her back."

Cross-Patch went with them. The big empty bed remained, a hostage of a sort.

Fliss did not go to Bath. She sat at home, in what turned out to be a dismal summer, and watched the television. She watched the *Antiques Roadshow*, and its younger offshoot, *Flog It!*, in which people brought things they did not want to be valued by experts and auctioned in front of the cameras. Fliss and Carole had watched it together. They both admitted to a secret love for the presenter, the beautiful Paul Martin, whose energy never flagged. Nor, Fliss thought, did his kindness and courtesy, no matter what human oddities presented themselves. She loved him because he was reliable, which beautiful people, usually, were not.

And so it came about that Fliss, looking up idly at the screen from the tray of soup and salad on her knee, saw Polly staring out at her in close-up, sitting on the *Flog It!* valuing table. It must be a complete lookalike, Fliss thought. The bisque face, with its narrow eyes and tight mouth appeared to her to have a desperate or enraged expression. One of the most interesting things about Polly was that her look was sometimes composed and babylike, but, in some lights, from some angles, could appear angry.

The valuer, a woman in her forties, sweetly blonde but sharp-eyed, picked up Polly and declared she was one of the most exciting finds she had met on *Flog It!*. She was, said the purring lady, a real Bye-Lo Baby, and dressed in her original clothes. "May I look?" she asked sweetly, and upended Polly, throwing her silk robe over her head, exposing her woollen bootees, her sweet silk panties, the German stamps on her chubby back, to millions of viewers. Her fingernails were pointed, and painted scarlet. She pulled down the panties and ran her nails round Polly's hip-joints. Bye-Lo Babies were rarer, and earlier, if they had jointed composition bodies than if they had cloth ones, with celluloid hands sewn on. She took off Polly's frilled ivory silk bonnet, and exclaimed over her hair—"which, I must tell you, I am 90% sure is *real human hair*, which adds to her value." She pushed the hair over Polly's suspended head and said "Ah, yes, as though we needed to see it." The camera closed in on the nape of Polly's neck. "Copr. By Grace S. Putnam // MADE IN GERMANY."

"Do you know the story of Grace S. Putnam and the baby doll?" scarlet-nails asked the hopeful seller and there was Carole, in a smart Art Deco summer shirt in black and white, smiling politely and following the movements of the scarlet nails with her own smooth mulberry ones.

"No," said Carole into Fliss's sitting room, "I don't know much about dolls."

Her face was briefly screen-size. Her lipstick shone, her teeth glistened. Fliss's knees began to knock, and she put down her tray on the floor.

Grace Story Putnam, the valuing lady said, had wanted to make a real baby doll, a doll that looked like a real baby, perhaps three days old. Not like a Disney puppet. So this formidable person had haunted maternity wards, sketching, painting, analysing. And never could she find the perfect face with all the requisite qualities.

She leaned forward, her blonde hair brushing Carole's raven folds.

"I don't know if I should tell you this."

"Well, now you've started, I think you should," said Carole, always Carole.

"It is rumoured that in the end she saw the perfect child being carried past, wrapped in a shawl. And she said, wait, this is the one. But that baby had just died. Nevertheless, the story goes, the determined Mrs Putnam drew the little face, and this is what we have here."

"Ghoulish," said Carole, with gusto. The camera went back to Polly's face, which looked distinctly malevolent. Fliss knew her expression must be unchanging, but it did not seem like that. Her stare was fixed. Fliss said "Oh, Polly—"

"And is this your own dolly?" asked the TV lady. "Inherited perhaps from your mother or grandmother. Won't you find it very hard to part with her?"

"I didn't inherit her. She's nothing to do with me, personally. A friend gave her to me, a friend with a lot of dolls."

"But maybe she didn't know how valuable this little gift was? The Bye-Los were made in great numbers—even millions—but early ones like this, and with all their clothes, and real human hair, can be expected to fetch anywhere between £800 and well over £1,000— even well over, if two or more collectors are in the room. And of course she may have her photo in the catalogue or on the website . . ."

"That does surprise me," said Carole, but not as though it really did.

"And do you think your friend will be happy for you to sell her doll?"

"I'm sure she would. She is very fond of me, and very generous-hearted."

"And what will you do with the money if we sell Dolly, as I am sure we shall—"

"I have booked a holiday on a rather luxurious cruise in the Greek islands. I am interested in classical temples. This sort of money will really help."

There is always a gap between the valuation of an item and the showing of its auction. Fliss stared unseeing at the valuation of a hideous green pottery dog, a group of World War I medals, an album of naughty seaside postcards. Then came Polly's moment. The auctioneer held her aloft, his gentlemanly hand tight round her pudgy waist, her woolly feet protruding. Briefly, briefly, Fliss looked for the last time at Polly's sweet face, now, she was quite sure, both baleful and miserable.

"Polly," she said aloud. "*Get her. Get her.*"

She did not know what she wanted Polly to do. But she saw Polly as capable of doing something. And they were—as they had always been—on the same side, she and Polly.

She thought, as the bidding flew along, a numbered card flying up, a head nodding, a row of concentrated listeners with mobile phones, waiting, and then raising peremptory fingers, that she herself had betrayed Polly, but that she had done so out of love and goodwill. "Oh, Polly," she said, "*Get her,*" as Carole might have said to Cross-Patch.

Carole was standing, composed and beautiful, next to Paul Martin, as the tens turned into hundreds and the hundreds to thousands. He liked sellers to show excitement or amazement, and Carole—Fliss understood her—showed just enough of both to keep the cameras happy, but was actually rigid inside, like a stone pillar of willpower and certainty. Polly went for £2,000, but it was not customary to show the sold object again, only the happy face of the seller, so, for Fliss, there was no moment of good-bye. And you were not told where sold objects were going.

All the other dolls were staring, as usual. She turned them over, or laid them to sleep, murmuring madly, get her, get her.

She did not suppose Carole would come back, and wondered if she should get rid of the bed. The headmistress at the school was slightly surprised when Fliss asked her if Carole was coming back—"Do you know something I don't?" Then she showed Fliss a postcard from Crete, and one from Lemnos. "I go off on my own with my beach towel and a book and lie on the silver sand by the wine-dark sea, and feel perfectly happy." Fliss asked the headmistress if she knew where Cross-Patch was, and the headmistress said she had assumed

Fliss was in charge of her, but if not, presumably, she must be in kennels.

A week later, the head told Fliss that Carole was in hospital. She had had a kind of accident. She had been unconscious for some time, but it was clear, from the state of her nervous system, and from filaments and threads found on her swimsuit and in her hair, that she had swum, or floated, into a swarm of minute stinging jellyfish—there are *millions* out there, this summer, people are warned, but she liked to go off on her own.

Fliss didn't ask for more news, but got told anyway. Carole's eyes were permanently damaged. She would probably never see again; at best, vestigially.

She would not, naturally, be coming back.

The headmistress looked at Fliss, to see how she took this. Fliss contrived an expression of conventional, distant shock, and said several times, how awful, how very awful.

The headmistress said "That dog of hers. Do you think anyone knows where it is? Do you think we should get it out of the kennels? Would you yourself like to have it, perhaps—you all became so close?"

"No," said Fliss. "I'm afraid I never liked it really. I did my best as I hope I always shall. I'm sure someone can be found. It has a very uncertain temper."

She went home and told the dolls what had happened. She thought of Polly's closed, absent little face. The dolls made an inaudible rustling, like distant birds settling. They *knew*, Fliss thought, and then unthought that thought, which could be said to be odd.

KRISTIINA EHIN

The Surrealist's Daughter

The first time I went to visit the Surrealist's daughter, I was bitten by the Surrealist's dog. He bit me in the thigh through the mesh gate. "A really surrealistic wound," I thought, feeling my leg. It didn't really hurt, but it was great to see how the Surrealist's daughter and her mother came running with adhesive plasters and a bottle of iodine, how they knelt down in front of me to treat my wound. The Surrealist's daughter looked at me with big, startled, slightly guilty eyes. I smiled at her but she didn't smile back.

The next time we met was several years later. It happened to be St. George's Night and it was the first time that I saw the Surrealist's daughter completely naked. She stepped in suddenly through the door of the smoke sauna and in the darkness I didn't immediately realize who this woman was. She sat down next to me on the sooty bench and we didn't look at each other. Only later, when I saw one of her strange confirmation dresses and her patterned stockings hanging over a beam in the sauna's front room, did I realize who I'd been having a sauna with.

The third time I met the Surrealist's daughter, I talked all sorts of nonsense. I told her that I had been dreaming of a woman just like her, all my life. I smiled at her again and repeated her name several times. In all seriousness. But the Surrealist's daughter turned into a black stork and sat instead on the shoulder of one of my friends. She rubbed her long neck against my friend's cheek. I saw my friend straining not to turn into a frog and he finally managed it, turning into a punk rocker instead. The punk rocker took the Surrealist's daughter, who was still a black stork, as his driver. "I'd like to go to Hiiumaa Island now," the punk rocker said and the black stork sat down behind the wheel right away. I watched for some time as they were driving away. Then I went off to send some e-mails and went to bed. That night I dreamed that I was flying to who knows where in the dark of night on the back of a black stork that was croaking sadly. My friend later told me that in Hiiumaa he hadn't been able to resist the temptation and had gone behind a lilac bush with a blonde, blue-eyed punk rocker to drink beer. At the same time the black stork was supposed to fill the tank and get some synthetic motor oil, mosquito repellent, and something to eat. But when the punk rocker went back to the black stork in the hotel room, none of this had been done. The stork had meanwhile turned back into the Surrealist's daughter. She lay in her thin white dress on the red carpet and wept.

My friend said he didn't know from that moment on whether to take it or leave it. He thrashed around for a long time in some sort of confused and nameless identity crisis and finally decided that the stork was all right, as far as it goes—but the weeping Surrealist's daughter was just too much.

The fourth time I saw the Surrealist's daughter, she was sitting on a tree and combing her long, silky hair. I looked up at her and said that she was so beautiful. I smiled and she smiled back at me. I said that to my mind she was very, very beautiful. I added quite loudly, to be sure that she heard me, that I had always wanted just her sort of woman. I thought about what else I might be able to say. I said that of course I had wanted just such a mother for my children as well. I got quite carried away. When I looked back up at her in the tree, she wasn't there anymore. She had fallen down and broken her rib. When I drove her to the emergency room, she wept inconsolably and said, "Please don't say such things to me. It's more than I can bear." And yet, right after that, she begged, with tears in her eyes, "Say some more, please."

I continued saying just such things to her the entire time. I gave my fantasy free rein. Although I saw that she was barely able to prepare a meal, that she drops plates, uses too much salt, burns the potatoes, I told her that I would like her to be the mistress of my farm, that I admire her ability to look after things and create beauty all around her. I smiled, for from the corner of my eye I saw the Surrealist's daughter's dusty bookshelves, unwashed windows, and other such things. Thereupon she kissed me, as if incidentally, yet more passionately than I had ever been kissed by any woman before that, and then she just as suddenly asked me to go away. She said she needed to get up in the middle of the night and perform.

Perform . . . the Surrealist's daughter knew how to do that. After all, she worked in a cabaret. Her job was frying the hearts and other body parts of her male audience over a low flame. She did that with her dancing and of course with her ability to transform herself. She was a woman of many faces and many bodies.

Next time I told the Surrealist's daughter about my other women. I told her about them as if incidentally, while we were driving around Egypt in a rented jeep. I had invited her on the trip with me. I wanted to completely entangle her mind in tales of my former and present women and then propose marriage to her. It was so good with her, I thought, why shouldn't we go even further.

But entangling the mind of the Surrealist's daughter had very different and more serious consequences than I could have imagined. Between a sphinx and a pyramid in the desert, the Surrealist's daughter turned into a fire-breathing dragon that had wound itself around a trembling maiden dressed in white. The maiden looked exactly like the Surrealist's daughter, but half her age. The dragon sent caustic tongues of fire in my direction and they were very painful to me. The maiden looked on with an anguished air and I wondered with a feeling of revulsion why I should even bother fussing with this Surrealist's daughter and all her conjurings. Of course I left her. And then I left her again. But our paths kept crossing, for in the course of time we had become friends.

One warm, bright night when she had just come from performing and her body was hot and smelled of frying hearts, we met by chance on the street and went up the hill to look at the moon. I just couldn't help myself and again brought up marriage while at the same time making her jealous with stories of my other women. "Yes, I've had innumerable lovers, in the first years I tried to keep count, but now it's all hopelessly muddled," I said as if incidentally. "But you're different, with you I almost want to . . . Yes, with you and only you." I called her by her name again, several times. In all seriousness. "And yet I'm afraid of that," I continued. "Sometimes panic overcomes me when I think that I might have to be with someone for the rest of my life and be faithful to her."

I should have known I was playing with fire. Again the dragon was standing before me and the maiden was still watching me with her beautiful, trembling eyes. First the dragon bit a chunk out of my thigh. Then it ripped out one of my ribs and bit it in half. The maiden was still watching me gravely and beseechingly, and neither the full moon nor she, nor even the black stork that had suddenly landed on a blossoming white lilac bush, were of any help to me. Behind the maiden stood the cabaret dancer rolling her hips and stroking her breasts. It fried my heart and not only that. Then the dragon turned its seven heads toward me and got ready to tear me apart once and for all and then set me alight.

For some reason I wasn't able to run away, for the maiden's innocent, beseeching gaze and the cabaret dancer's rolling hips rooted me to the spot. Blood flowed from my thigh and my side and the dragon mocked me haughtily. I thought it would be good to fall asleep at that very moment, for death wouldn't be so terrible in sleep. I closed my eyes. But in doing so I had freed myself from the spell cast by the cabaret dancer and the eyes of that grave young maiden. I turned into St. George on his white horse, and a sword as long as a ship's mast grew in my hand. I hewed into the dragon. Or did I hew the Surrealist's daughter? In any case, when every last one of its heads had been cut off, we were all dripping with blood. Me, the maiden, the white horse, the black stork, the cabaret dancer, the lilac bush and even the moon—we were all blood red. And so that there would be an end to all this hocus-pocus I rode home to my farm with them, washed them clean, and put them to bed. When the Surrealist's daughter woke in the morning, she was again all of a piece, she still had the moon in her arms, and she smelt of lilac. She told me that she had become pregnant from the blood of her own dragon and we would immediately be having two pairs of three-headed twins who would all look exactly like me.

TRANSLATED FROM ESTONIAN BY ILMAR LEHTPERE

SYLWIA CHUTNIK

It's All Up to You

I'm sitting in an office chair, propelling myself forward, backward, in a circle, with my feet. The girl in front of me is hot, is a babe, and I think she's younger than me, but she looks older, with her French manicure.

You can tell she double-majored and speaks four languages. Plus she's thin, nicely thin, dressed in H&M, but tastefully. Unpretentiously. An element of surprise: dangling felt earrings, handmade. Her teeth shine, her eyes shine, her skin—you'll never guess—shines, like it's printed on coated paper.

Men in bars like babes like this, when it's nighttime. You might just go after work and relax, hang out, have a drink. Girls like this go so well with beer, like nuts or chips. They're happy. Even if they're not happy, they're about to show you that they are happy. Carefree. They bubble over in endless laughter. They laugh with their whole selves, with their whole being, here and now and for all eternity. They just always find something amusing—they're still giggling long after somebody's told a joke. And their shoulder strap slips down, and their svelte shoulders are playing peek-a-boo—sometimes they pull it back up, but not most of the time. Oh my gosh, my shoulder strap slipped off! I guess I'm having that kind of day! Let me just run to the bathroom for a second.

And the lovely body retreats, the men looking it up and down as it goes, saying nothing. Silence at the table.

And at the bathroom mirror a smack of lip-gloss. Her long, pretty hair—which fits her symmetrical facial features like a glove—is as sensational as TV hair. You look her over like you look through a women's magazine, with all its formulas, its mantras of "radiant hair" and "glowing skin." I mean, my God, sometimes they even use the word "taille," instead of just "waist." But the babe has a skinny everything, after all, that's her thing. US scientists and the KGB both have proven that skinny people are fabulous.

Beer isn't full of empty calories when consumed by babes. Sometimes babes actually eat chocolate, but even then, nothing. Other girls have a single sandwich and blow up like blimps, but not a babe.

And she wears thongs. Because her you-know-what is shaved. Because she never really has anything poking out down there, so she can safely wear whatever lingerie she wants. She's so perfect you might even think she's not real, you might think someone had cut her out of one of those magazines, but she lives and breathes, and this poses a problem for me.

She goes back to the table, and people sigh with relief. Everything's fun again. Sheesh, gosh, you know what happened to me in the bathroom? I'm just looking for the bathroom, and I don't know where to go, I forgot if the women's room had the circle on it or the triangle. Which one means women's? So I go in through the first doors I come to, and there's a guy just standing there, peeing. Peeing! Oh my God, I just turn right around and just say, "Sorry!" But I wanted to laugh so bad, God, like, I was in shock. What an idiot!

The babe knows her own worth—she's not an idiot, after all, she double-majored. So why does she say that, does she just not take herself too seriously? She's well read, she's not a nitwit, she knows her way through the bulk of the literary canon, as it pertains to the conversations she might have. She goes to exhibitions, she has friends of the intellectual persuasion. She listens to music, and she cultivates radiance. She has a normal job, which she doesn't like, because of course you're not supposed to like your job.

I'm sitting opposite her, and we're not at some fun club, not at all, we're in a box in an office building. It just about causes me physical pain to look at her. Envy and regret. That she's not just a stupid girl. She's too cool and pretty.

Do I feel threatened? I get chills just thinking I might be thinking that way. If she was just a dumb Barbie doll, then I could just lump her in with all the other imbeciles and rest assured of my own intellectual superiority—at least I would have that. If, on the other hand, she's actually smarter than me (she *does* have a job, and I don't) . . . And if she's prettier and cooler than me . . . What if? What would that mean? I'd rather not look at her. I'd rather nothing.

I try and laugh like her, at the same times. I can't pull it off, I realize only afterward that I'm supposed to, and then all that comes out is a noiseless and imbecilic grimace. Plus I feel like I didn't dress appropriately. I have several skirts, I don't know why I wore my jeans. Ah, it's cold out. Right, the babe has a car, she can come to work wearing ballet slippers all winter. I could have a car, too, but it just so happens that I don't. Basically I'm afraid of getting killed in a car crash. I have nightmares where my entrails are everywhere. Old ladies drive, nuns drive, but I don't drive, because I'm afraid. Obviously she's not afraid, because she's already had two little fender benders, but she was fine, and when she went to the garage the guy told her he'd touch up her paint for free. And she held out her slender hand with her glorious-smelling wrist with its literally as-thin-as-possible gold bracelet. She has air-freshener in her car, plus a teddy bear, but an "alternative" teddy bear that she got off some American website. It's missing one leg, and it has red dots instead of eyes. What a sweet little bear, that's fantastic. Even her toys are awesome, and people like her never sweat, and they don't ever have any problems with their digestive systems. And they don't go into the pharmacy and ask for Lactovaginal in a hushed voice.

"What?"

"Lactovaginal."

"Vaginal discharge?" shrieks the lady at the counter.

God, yes, vaginal discharge.

The babe is looking over my cv and my statement of purpose. "I would like to work in your office because I am interested in advertising." I sneak a peek at it in her hands and try to think how high my fever must have been to come up with that crap. Had I written it in primary school? Had that been my homework back in the first grade? Why hadn't I taken any professional enhancement courses, why hadn't I bought that book *Your Career Will Make You a Hero*? I'm lazy, I don't know how to do anything, and meanwhile the babe is noting something down on a piece of paper. She's already taken her course on how to conduct interviews, which was connected with her Reiki II foot massage and her advanced German classes. She knows what to say. And if ever she doesn't know, she laughs. I don't know anything, and I'm traveling around the carpeting by chair.

Weee'll letyouknow.

Great. Another job I'm not getting.

I turn and look back at the babe through the glass that separates the swells from the plebs, enclosed in their plastic boxes. I feel a terrible hatred, I feel the injustice of it, I feel the shame of it. A woman in a dress suit walks past me and gives my shoulder a friendly clap. "Don't cry, they might still take you as a cleaning lady—they're holding the next interviews in a week."

I exit the office building and go off to buy myself something to drink. The salesguy at the grocery is in the middle of receiving goods. He's got opened-up boxes of fruit everywhere and is setting some of it on the shelves. Oh, to be a salesgirl in a little kiosk by a bus stop. To weigh, to count, to bag.

I ask if I can have an apple.

"That's up to you," says the salesguy, without looking up at me.

So that's how it is. It's up to me.

A wave of near-erotic excitement overtakes me. The voice he said it in. And what was he referring to? "That" meaning *what?*

The longer I stand there astonished, the less I know what to do. Suddenly the little store turns into a vast stage, where each of us must pass naked before a crowd of people. Of men, women, maybe even our own house pets. A disco ball drops from out of the wooden ceiling, and the lights are glaring, and a guy in an Afro wig coos the same refrain into a microphone repeatedly: "That's, oh yeah, up to you." A little choir of older ladies waiting behind me in line begins to fidget. Yes, it's up to you, child, but buy something already, and let us buy our things too.

Women march down the catwalk. Frenzied music comes out of the speakers, and you have to adjust your gait to fit it. Walk to its rhythm, defer to its rhythm. And I'm enchanted by it, I've never walked like that, under other people's gazes, to their rhythm. In rejecting foreign myths about beauty, I let myself fall into the trap of the ugly bitch. Which is great, after all, there are so many of us around, and really we're all terribly attractive after all, we've got that certain something. If we're at all unattractive, it's just what the man on the speakers calls a "unique brand" of beauty. Original beauty, an interesting and expressive face. A body that keeps its secrets.

I want to be like the ones that have known this music for years. They can sing it to themselves when it's not even playing, and contort to it appropriately—at any moment at any point in their lives.

I ask myself excitedly why I haven't really ever hung out with anybody; I'm in last place, with my hair looking terrible, and only even snuggling up to hairy-pitted minor deities in pants from two seasons ago.

"That's up to you"—like a spell. With one sentence I had been liberated from lackluster evenings alone at the movies, three-cheese pizzas ordered over the phone, pads instead of tampons.

Meaning I might become like the babe at the office? I would paint my nails and laugh at everything. Use lip-gloss and shine in high society. It's up to me, I can choose me. Sporty me, elegant me, domestic me. Like a doll. Have a simple life, lustrous in its ordinariness—the straight and narrow. Straight teeth. Stop listening to hard rock and start listening to smooth jazz. Quit thinking so much. Not bite my nails till my cuticles bleed.

I'd rather live like that, I really would!

Do you want the apples or not? Did you decide?

I had decided. I would go straight to the salon to get anything and everything that had ever poked out from under my underwear and that had roots waxed right off. I would get some clothes that were on sale that would show off my tattoos.

I would stop sleeping in an old T-shirt, I would invest in lace. Everything would change, I would get a job. Never again would I go up to the cash register with my cart and be told, "Hmm, transaction declined." Never again would I take my card from the cashier and pretend that, wow, there must be some mix-up, I mean I definitely have money in my account, oh well, I guess I'll just have to get some cash out of the ATM. And she's thinking, sure, I have money, *right*. I have nothing, and I thought nothing would be enough to get groceries. Actual humiliation, degradation, trying to go on a shopping spree before putting one's plastic in order.

No, I don't want the apples, so nothing. I exit the store brimming with my vital resolutions. It's as if the sun is shining brighter, the world is smiling—the wind flares up, snatching at my old jacket.

If this had been a Bollywood film, I would have already been dancing in my pretty sari in the middle of the street. It was more, however, in the style of the American drama, with an accident at the climax.

I basically just wanted to get to my tram as quickly as possible. I didn't notice that there was a street there, a street with cars, one of which was speeding toward me. All I knew was that something had hit me, and that my cigarette had flown out of my hand. And that I tried to get away from the paramedics. I mean I didn't have health insurance—it wasn't like I could go to the hospital and then not pay. Shortly before I passed out (I had every right, my leg had been shattered), it flashed through my mind that this might be a just punishment for thinking ill of the babe, for not feeling feminine solidarity, for only feeling jealous. For planning on fixing myself up, when really I'd never deserved any improvements. That terrible Christian saying about the wages of sin now paralyzed my brain.

Nothing is up to me, Mr. Grocer. As soon as somebody puts together even the outline of their screenplay, they get their leg ripped off, a steamroller rolls right over them, a plane bombards them. They steal your head right off your shoulders and then dunk it in the toilet to boot.

Nothing is up to us, everything takes place in a thick bell jar. Some people are born pretty, some homely. You can bend over backward, go to a plastic surgeon, and all the ugliness will only come to the surface. The great revolt of the hideous against Beauty is always doomed to fail from the very start, because before the ugly people leave their houses, powdering those broken blood vessels of theirs, the pretty people will long since have been laughing their pearly laughs over their glasses of water. Still water. Not sparkling. No calories, no preservatives, no artificial anything.

I wouldn't forget again, now. Making resolutions regarding myself, revamping things, improving things—it just doesn't work for me. I was programmed before birth to be a doormat. Where'd you get that face, was it on clearance, was it on Ebay, did you get it off an old homeless guy? And where'd you find that shaggy body, did you get it in some lake off a drowned guy, did it come from that movie, *La Grande Bouffe*, did it come from that book, *Fat Swine*?

Covering the bathroom mirror and keeping the lights turned off isn't lying. Lying is when some babe says you look so great. I don't believe in looking great, but I have to work, which is why I'm standing here with my legs torn off at an intersection handing out flyers for cosmetic dermatology. Lymphatic drainage massage, whole-body amputation. My hands are rotting, my ashen face winces in pain at the thought of coming into contact with myself. I stink, although I bathe; I howl, although I smile toothlessly at the girl who's walking by now as I hand her her flyer. She, trying not to look at me, throws the flyer into the trash, because it's not like she needs beauty treatments. Then she comes up to me, spits, kicks, snorts, and leaves.

You might well fight the system, you'll get plenty of support. Be opposed, fight, protest. But your worst enemy is always the pretty girl, the hot babe, the working woman with her car. But then it's like I'm protesting Beauty itself, like I'm an enemy to myself above all else. Blinded by embarrassment, ashamed of my own thoughts.

Caught in the trap of my own desires, I bitch about my butt-ugly life. God, but I'd rather not.

TRANSLATED FROM POLISH BY JENNIFER CROFT

men

DANIEL BATLINER

Malcontent's Monologue

In a little country there is a little town, and the townspeople are few in number, and know each other well. They work, go to market, and pause to greet each other on the little square at the center of town. Children play on the square. Small towns are still places where one can feel at home, preserves of identity and character. While not sealed off completely from the other towns in this country, this town is left more or less in peace. The people too. They go about their jobs at the bank, the insurance agency, the town hall, and they wander, dignified and daydreaming, through their little village lives.

One day, the lawyer Joachim Kaiser crosses to the middle of the village square. He is wearing an impeccably tailored business suit and tie. In his right hand he holds a plastic cup from a well-known fast-food chain, and takes, now and then, a self-satisfied sip. A young boy, not more than eight years old, is torn from his game with his fire engine. Having abandoned it now, he frets about the townspeople: that they will fall victim to the very fire his engine should have doused. Joachim bends down to the little boy.

"My name is Joachim. Joachim Kaiser. I'm a lawyer. Twenty-eight years old. My whole life I've been perfectly average. I was trained to be that way by society. Always eager to do what was asked of me. Just don't stand out, that was the accepted slogan, and we all did our best to live up to it."

For a few seconds all is quiet. The boy looks, concentrating, somewhat perplexed, at Joachim. The lawyer, on the other hand, sees before him a long looked-for and understanding interlocutor. In answer to his nonverbal question, the boy motions for Joachim to sit.

"Have you made the acquaintance of Society, my little friend?"

The boy gives the question some thought, but finds no apparent sense in it. The grown-up, though, is undeterred.

"Actually, it's really very charming. I got to know it as a child. Society guided my family. It showed me what morals are, and ethics. I was perfectly average . . . and not just me, but my whole generation . . . we were educated by Society. Very few missed out on the pleasure of that education. And they're the ones we build prisons for. Jail. It's not permissible, in a civil society, to let certain individuals go on opposing the views of the majority. Do you understand?"

He does not. How could he. No one understands it. He doesn't normally talk like this, Joachim Kaiser, but no one understands him today. In the meantime a small throng has accumulated around the boy and the lawyer, who face each other, still cross-legged. At every pause the boy takes up his game with the fire engine again, firstly because the talking has gone on so long, and secondly, it really is about time he saved those people from the burning house. Lawyers aren't necessary, but fire trucks . . . well. Joachim notices, or maybe not; in any case he doesn't lose his footing.

"'What's the meaning of life,' I asked Society once. It answered with speed and certainty: 'The meaning of life is to be a good student, to earn your diploma, find yourself a well-respected position, earn money, and start a family.' Naïve as I was, I believed it back then. I could hardly wait to get to university."

Now Joachim rises and turns, so he can address himself not just to the boy, but to the curious onlookers all around him.

"Naturally it was out of the question that I study theater, philosophy, or any of the humanities. I could improve Society's opinion of me only in business or law or medicine, with their practical qualifications. So I studied law, and now I have a job at a well-respected firm. Such a career demands that I give my all, and use all of my knowledge, each and every day. I have Society to thank for my understanding of law and morality."

Joachim loosens his tie. His cup is empty, so he tosses it into the nearby trash can, which draws some murmurs from the crowd, but nothing more. All stand at attention, waiting for him to go on.

"Yes—yes, justice and morals. I had nothing else in my life. I had no need for anything else. Society lays out the rules for us to follow. Rules for how to act. Rules we grow up with but never speak aloud, just like we don't chat at the urinal. Anyone who does so might as well be drunk; certainly they're annoying. And we wouldn't want to be annoying, would we?"

This whole scenario on the little square has begun to evolve slowly toward further absurdity: the lawyer Joachim Kaiser stands there like a preacher at the center, tense and interested listeners all around him, and now he's talking about urinals. A few grin, but wherefore? Because of the scene? Have they really understood it? Or was it just the bathroom analogy?

"Society doesn't want us to annoy. Such unspoken rules crop up all the time. People who take the bus every day, they know these rules of conduct well. What happens, for example, when a person gets on who you recognize. He comes on through the front door of the bus, you know him only by sight, that's all. Then he comes right up to you. What should you do? Should you stare vacantly out the window, like you haven't even noticed him? Ridiculous, since you've already made eye contact. In which case you're practically obliged to say 'Hello.' And then . . . what if you do and he gives you the cold shoulder? You look like a dope. So you wait, see what he does, do the same. That's how it works in Society. Mostly we hesitate—too late!—and ignore each other. Why didn't he say hello? What a jerk! You didn't say hello, but you were ready to if he did, but he didn't, so neither did you, but you would have, in his position."

The crowd on the little square is larger now, and quieter. Some feel moved, though without quite knowing why. But hardly anyone knows in what spirit to take these words. Glances shift from right to left and back again with increasing haste. Just to monitor how the others might be taking it all.

"Society is a mother to almost all the children of my generation. According to the moral system I grew up with, then, you'd have to call it a whore. That's it—Society is a whore."

A few now suffer a loss of confidence, but nobody speaks, since it remains to be seen whether this heretic might indeed be right. But Joachim is sure. He knows that he's right, though he gains nothing by it. Being right is nothing more than a status symbol; it can't be shared.

"Law and morals. Together they fashion man to fit the dictatorship to which Society subjects the individual. Did I say dictatorship? Yes, that's just the word. Society is a dictatorship over unsuspecting men, it tells them how to act and how to live. Man has, as it were, only two options: either he accepts the drug called 'Society' as though all he desires is exactly what Society has to offer him; or he takes the other option, he rejects the drug and accepts a life on the margins of Society, which will censure and even sentence him for his decision. Justice, and also religion, founded the dictatorship. Justice, because laws make social mores into general rules. That's how the views of Society bind everyone, whether or not they're a part of it. Those individuals blessed with views or talents that don't accord with Society are held in contempt.

Religion, too, must be held accountable. Not for tempting Society to eat from the tree of false knowledge, but because in her naïveté she fell victim to abuse by institutions like the Church. So that the Church has managed to keep the morals of Society rigid, right down to the present day."

Joachim Kaiser now has the undivided attention of this small town's citizens. From time to time, a head shakes in the crowd, indicating disagreement, but then again it's likely that more agree than don't. Joachim is enjoying the performance, his big day. Enjoying his consternation, which he throws off like a mountain shedding sheets of snow in an avalanche. He removes his jacket, his shoes, socks, and trousers, and throws them, to the astonishment of all present, on the ground. He no longer cares to wear them. Plenty of people look terrible without their trousers, socks, shoes, and jacket on, wearing, in other words, only their shirt, tie, and underpants. Joachim Kaiser does, too. But he doesn't mind, since he now thinks that only idiots would mind. The boy, still sitting there, watching the show, suddenly giggles out loud. It is not the giggling of ridicule, but the innocent giggling of a child pleased by a prank that had been successful beyond his expectations.

"We must strip off the ties by which Society binds us. That's an order, ladies and gentlemen! You may think to yourself, oh but Society is a swell thing. Why free yourself when we all stand to benefit? Intoxicants, it just so happens, have the effect of increasing one's momentary sense of well-being. And why, may I ask, has this 'swell Society' banned drugs?"

He himself can't really say. Well, drugs are bad. They wreak havoc upon body and mind. That's why they're illegal. This is confirmed by several voices.

"You might argue, and rightly, that such substances are addictive, they are harmful, both psychologically and physically. But Society? Who among you could claim not to be addicted to Society and its morals? Hobbled, even, by its social mores! I wouldn't believe anyone here who says he's remained untouched. Because in that case you wouldn't stand around here conforming. You'd be like me, half-naked, on this little square, in this little town, in this little country, running around and saying just whatever came into your head without thinking. But I know I can't ask that of you. Because if you did something like that, what would everyone think?"

He pulls off his tie and shirt and throws them into the garbage can. Now he has nothing on but his underwear. He touches the cotton fabric and thinks a moment. No, he won't do it. He doesn't quite dare. The bystanders know their own minds, but no matter, they want to see what he does, and above all, if he'll really do it.

"Starting now I will call myself a refugee. I'd like to live. Really to lead the life I would have had without Society: run to India barefoot, dance naked on the Champs-Élysées, tear up train tracks, smoke weed on an airplane, be Napoleon."

He laughs and enumerates the other feats he'd like to carry off. Now a man steps forward from the fifth or sixth row, where he'd been listening. It's Julius. Joachim's colleague in the small town's well-respected law firm and beyond.

"Joachim? What are you doing here? We've been getting worried about you. Shouldn't you have been back at work hours ago?"

"Leave me alone, Julius. I'm not coming back."

"What's that, Joachim? Why don't we forget the whole thing and you come along with me."

"Don't you see that you're one of them?"

Julius thinks about it. Joachim wants to tell him something, apparently, but Julius doesn't understand what he means.

"One of who? Joachim, what are you talking about? And why are you practically naked?"

"Because I don't care anymore what your sort thinks of me. I've spent long enough in your little club and I've played along with your game. But now I want to do what I want with my life, whatever I feel like."

"Joachim, I have no idea what you're talking about."

"Of course you don't, because you haven't perceived the game."

"What game?"

"You're a puppet of Society. Can't you see that?"

"Cut this out. There's no such thing as 'being a puppet of society.' Society is nothing but a social construct that eases the task of collective living."

"Society is a cult. Yes, that's right. And you're one of them."

"Don't make a complete fool of yourself, Joachim."

Julius stands very close to Joachim and tries to placate him. Joachim, though, goes dancing around Julius, and mimics him, and won't be reasoned with. He laughs, apes Joachim's movements, and produces indefinable noises.

"You're one of them. You're so good about doing your job. You've got a wife, and a family, and on Sunday you go off to Church, just like you should. Now tell me: Why do you do all that? Because you really want to? Or because Society has you completely conditioned?"

Julius is at a loss. He's lost his connection to Joachim. And Joachim, in turn, has lost his connection to Reality.

"What are you getting at, Joachim? Of course there are days when I don't feel like going to work. But all things considered, I'm satisfied with my life."

"That's not what I mean. Is the content of your life what you want it to be?"

"Yes, I think it is."

"Wrong!"

"Wrong?"

"Wrong! You only think it's what you want it to be, but really you have no free will at all. Your actions and your will are determined by Society. The only escape is to break free altogether."

"We're born into society. It's not something you can just undo."

"Not just like that, maybe, but it's possible."

Julius doesn't know exactly how to handle this talk with Joachim. You can't force someone to understand. It's just not that simple.

"I don't believe in the predetermination of my life by society. I feel like I'm a free individual."

Joachim laughs. Julius has stepped into a trap he seems not to have recognized.

"Because Society wants you to feel that way. Everyone feels like a free individual, but tell me—really—is that so unique?"

Joachim pulls off his underpants and throws them in the trash, cheered by the looks on the bystanders' faces. A few think it's funny. Others are outraged. Julius most of all, because it's up to him to deal with Joachim. What's more, he is now visibly uncomfortable in his role, and wishes he'd never gotten involved. But it's too late for that.

"Joachim! Pull yourself together. You can't do this, just running around naked."

"Oh yes I can. I can and Society can kiss my ass. Not my ass with powder and pants on it, but my bare-naked ass, shitty and hairy and tooting at all of you."

"Joachim, I'm sorry—I can't condone this."

Julius goes running off. A middle-aged woman fights her way through the crowd and pulls the boy from the circle that's formed there. Disappointed, he allows himself to be dragged off. For him it was an outstanding show, a rare sight on the little square, in the little town. Joachim, visibly moved by the departure of his former friend Julius, turns naked to the crowd and begins his victory speech.

"Julius can't take it: he can't take freedom. Hardly anyone can. But even if they come and get me, even if they lock me up, even then I'll still be freer than all of you."

Joachim runs in a circle, whoops, giggles, enjoys the attention of the embarrassed onlookers, whose interest has yielded to disgust. Who should be the one to pull the plug? More and more embarrassed glances cast about for the hero who has yet to arrive. No one wants to be the hero. But the catastrophe is stopped midstream by Julius, returning in the company of two policemen. Julius indicates Joachim, still shrieking, spewing more testimony in favor of freedom. The policemen take hold of him and lead him away. Julius turns and faces the throng.

"His name was Joachim. Joachim Kaiser. He was a lawyer. Twenty-eight years old. His whole life he was perfectly average. He was trained to be that way by society. Always eager to do what was asked of him. Just don't stand out, that was the accepted slogan, something to live up to."

At the pauses in his speech he gathers the items of Joachim's clothing scattered on the ground.

"Joachim never understood that one can be happy and know society is a cult. Even conscious of that fact—one can enjoy the advantages of society. Do I believe society has predetermined my desires? Perhaps, but as long as it's possible to call oneself free, I don't really care."

Mumbled agreement. Still, this scene with its average lawyer has made an impression. The people have been made to think. Even Julius is no longer so certain. He tosses a lit match, and the pile of clothing springs up into cheerful flames.

The next morning, the front page of the small town's small-time newspaper carries the story of a little boy who used his toy truck to rescue imaginary people from the blaze of an imaginary house fire.

TRANSLATED FROM GERMAN BY AMY KERNER

BERNARDO ATXAGA

Pirpo and Chanberlán, Murderers

Neither of them knew what "carte blanche" meant, but if, during the Spanish Civil War, someone had bothered to explain it to them, they would both have replied in unison: "That's us! That's what we've been given!" And they wouldn't have been far wrong. These two friends— famous for their robberies and for the raids they used to make on village fiestas, picking up villagers in a truck and carrying them off to the city's brothels—were capable of killing a person purely on the say-so of some Don or Doña. In fact, they killed as many people as they could, because they were murderers and because there was always someone to give them a good reason for murdering.

Pirpo had the slender build of a dancer. Chanberlán looked more like a lion-tamer. Whenever they chanced upon some hapless clown, the three of them formed a charming circus act, whose motto was: "One performance only. See it and never live to tell the tale." It was said that among those who had attended such a performance were Portaburu, a farm-worker from Obaba kidnapped in San Sebastián, and Goena Senior and Junior, killed in Obaba itself, near the house where they lived. It was also said that when Chanberlán shot them in the head, Pirpo had been only a few feet away practicing the steps of a waltz.

However, after 1940, it suited the Dons and the Doñas to act with more discretion. By then, Pirpo and Chanberlán's circus had become old hat; they had put on one performance too many, and, besides, their act, it seemed, did not go down very well in other countries. "We've had enough of dances and tricks with lions," said the Dons and the Doñas. "Now it's the turn of the courts; mind you, they put on a pretty good show as well." From then onward, Pirpo and Chanberlán's situation changed considerably, and they began to feel rather worried, as if they had lost something. "We've lost our carte blanche," Pirpo tried to say to Chanberlán one day, but, since he did not know the expression, he had to keep quiet, and the worm—that sense of unease—remained inside him. For a while, he even lost the desire to dance.

Pirpo loved champagne and dining on lobster and crayfish and on seafood in general at tables adorned with linen cloths; Chanberlán, on the other hand, spent most of his money in dimly lit clubs and brothels. Women did not, as they did with Pirpo, succumb to him because of his pretty face. Because there was nothing pretty about it.

In this new situation, a shortage of funds soon became a serious problem. They had no talent for business, whether underhand or aboveboard; they had no training or experience, and so could not take up respectable posts in government enterprises; they found it hard to imagine themselves working in a tobacconist's or driving a taxi and unhesitatingly rejected the offer of such employment from one of their former sponsors.

They resumed their circus act and took up smuggling Portuguese emigrants into France. They would collect ten or twelve of them on the Spanish-Portuguese border, usually in the Salamanca region, and having stowed them away in a truck and driven them as far as the Pyrenees, would drop them off while they were still on the Spanish side, in the valleys of Ansó or Hecho. "This is France," they would tell them. "Just follow that road and in a couple of hours you'll reach the town of Tarbes." Two hours later, the Portuguese would find themselves instead in a Spanish police station, and three days later, they would be back in Portugal, in Trás-os-Montes or the Alentejo. Back where they started, but minus their money.

Occasionally, there would be some hitches in the performance, and the Portuguese emigrants would give voice to doubts, would protest or else demand proof that they really were in France. Pirpo— for he was the more communicative of the two—protested as much or more than they did and bemoaned their lack of trust. Then he would turn to Chanberlán. "If you don't believe me, ask him," he would tell the emigrants. And when they saw the gun in the hand of that man who looked like a lion-tamer, not only would they stop complaining, they would lower their eyes and apologize.

Time passed and 1944 arrived, and Pirpo began to grow bored and to miss the old days when, without any need for all this hassle, fortune had smiled on them, and they had enjoyed comfort and wealth and the freedom to do as they pleased—"carte blanche," he would have said, had he known the expression. He didn't want to spend the rest of his life travelling from Portugal to the Pyrenees and from the Pyrenees to Portugal. They had to do something. Otherwise, they would have no option but to close the circus down. But if they did that, how would they pay for the champagne, the crayfish, and the lobster? How would Chanberlán pay for the love of women?

Then, out of the blue, one of the Dons or Doñas sent them a message. An elderly couple in France, in Lourdes to be precise, were in need of a guide. They wanted to cross the Pyrenees into Spain as soon as possible and would pay handsomely for any help they were given. As soon as he got this message, Pirpo began to dance: he had a good feeling about this new job. A day and a half later, when he went to Lourdes and learned more details, he not only danced, he skipped and sang. If he could, he would have leapt into the air and flown.

In the dingy hotel at which they were staying in the holy city, he set out the details to Chanberlán: "Do you know what they call this old man who wants to cross into Spain? *Le Roi du Champagne!* The King of Champagne! And he's loaded. If what his maid told me is true, they'll be traveling with a suitcase stuffed with jewels and money . . ."

Chanberlán did not like to be rushed. "If he's so rich, why does he want to escape from France?" he asked. Pirpo explained that France was now in the hands of a general called De Gaulle, and that the King of Champagne had collaborated with the Nazis and with Pétain, De Gaulle's enemy, and that his collaboration could now mean him facing either the gallows or a firing squad. "And how come the maid told you about the suitcase?" Chanberlán wanted to know. "Because she liked my face," replied Pirpo, executing a few waltz steps. Chanberlán shrugged. It was always the same with women. Him they asked for money, but they happily gave it to Pirpo or else told him where to find it. "Oh, great! It's snowing!" exclaimed Pirpo, looking out of the window. "What do you expect, it's the end of November!" said Chanberlán grumpily. "But you do see what good news it is, don't you?" Pirpo said. "Of course I do. We take the suitcase off them and then we kill them." They had worked together in their circus for a long time and knew each other intimately.

Pirpo thought deeply and that night—the night before they were due to set off—he was worried. They had to take the suitcase from the old couple and kill them, but how? He was aware of the situation they were in: it wasn't 1936 or 1937, it wasn't even 1938, 1939 or 1940, and they lacked something that had been most useful to them during the war, something he could not quite define. Anyway, the fact was that they could not kill as they had in the old days. Still less someone as important as the King of Champagne.

When it grew light, he got out of bed and went over to the window. It was still snowing. And the snow was getting heavier and heavier. All the paths in the Pyrenees would be blocked, impassable. He suddenly launched into a very merry dance and went bounding over to the room where Chanberlán was sleeping. "Eureka!" he would have cried had he known the expression, but, as with "carte blanche," he did not, and so had to make do with ordinary words. "I've got a plan!" he said to his companion. Chanberlán was still half-asleep and didn't want to waste his time on silly stories. "So have I!" he retorted angrily. "We whack them over the head with a stone and that will be that!" "Listen to me, you idiot!" said Pirpo, grabbing his arm and shaking him. "Don't push your luck, Pirpo!" warned Chanberlán, opening his eyes, and Pirpo immediately apologized for calling him an idiot. He and Chanberlán may have worked for years together in their circus, but Chanberlán's eyes still frightened him.

Pirpo's idea was an excellent one and very easy to carry out. They would set off into the snowy mountains and would lead the King of Champagne and his wife along the wrong path. "Oh, sorry, this isn't the right way," they would say after a couple of hours, when they had already walked a fair distance. "It's easy to get lost in weather like this. We'll have to turn back." And so they would turn back and take another path. And once more: "We've got lost again." And off along another path and another few hours in the snow, uphill. Frozen and drenched. And once more: "Oh, no, this is the third time we've gone wrong!" "I've seen them, Chanberlán," explained Pirpo. "They must be getting on for seventy. Eight or ten hours of walking in the snow will do our work for us. They'll die of exhaustion." "But why the big performance? Why don't we just bump 'em off as soon as we're out of Lourdes?" insisted Chanberlán. "They're French. They've got money. If we kill them ourselves, someone might come asking questions. And in France we have no protection." He didn't use the expression "carte blanche," but he came very close.

Two months later, toward the end of January 1945, the two friends, quite untroubled, were making the journey to Paris. They were accompanied by the police, but this fact did not bother them. Chanberlán was annoyed—"right fools we were, fancy not killing the maid first"—but he wasn't worried. And Pirpo could see no reason to feel alarmed either. "We didn't do anything," he said. "It was the cold and the mountains that did it." Later, when the jury found that the slow, calculated way in which they had killed the Roi du Champagne and his wife had been particularly cruel, and sentenced Pirpo and Chanberlán to life imprisonment, the two friends were most surprised, especially Pirpo. "I don't know why you find it so odd," the judge said to him. "Did you think you had carte blanche to murder?" Pirpo said nothing, but, along with his anxiety about the sentence passed down, he felt a kind of relief. He had finally found the expression he had been looking for all this time. He would never forget it.

Chanberlán died four years later in a Martinique jail during a brawl among prisoners. It was another fourteen years before Pirpo could rejoin his circle of friends. Some Dons and Doñas did not hesitate to welcome him back into the family, since, after all, despite certain shared political sensibilities, the Roi du Champagne and his wife had been foreigners, not Spaniards. Besides, these were difficult times, and it was always good to have a loyal servant like Pirpo on hand. Strikes were becoming ever more frequent and the enemies of the political regime ever bolder. Pirpo, however, had grown wary. He would not commit himself so easily again. He had learned his lesson. Before doing anything, he would demand to be given the carte blanche that had saved him so much bother in 1936 and in the three or four years that followed.

TRANSLATED FROM BASQUE BY MARGARET JULL COSTA,

IN COLLABORATION WITH THE AUTHOR

BORIVOJE ADAŠEVIĆ

For a Foreign Master

One morning the postman brought me an unusual letter. *Mutatis mutandis*, this was it:

Dear friend, don't be angry with me for addressing you like this even though we have hardly ever spoken, I am obliged to do so for the sake of the truth. Here, in Sent Andreja, I am holding your book again, having read it the dear lord knows how many times, and I can't get over my astonishment that you should still be there, looking for heaven knows what in that crazy country! What sort of trouble drives you to stay sitting in a town that does not know you, nor will it ever know you, writing for a country that isn't even sure it can look without envy at the most ordinary scribbler, let alone a serious man and writer of conscience! That's Serbia, my friend, Serbia, and it has always lured the devil, and the devil never refuses to come for its own kind. From the moment I took your book in my hands—it was given to me by my friend Kaplan Refika, an Albanian from Belgrade who lives with his family in a Budapest B&B—from that moment I knew that I would always consider you a friend, no matter how hard it would be for you to bear that. My name is Milan Almaši . I'm exactly four years older than you, and when I decided to leave Serbia for good, I had behind me a university degree, a first, second, and third war, and a good fifteen months of work experience as a teacher in school, I left all that behind me, I don't myself know how. Those years of hunger in Belgrade, when I was a student, that poverty which shackled me like ancient prison chains, then arrests, demonstrations, call-up papers, someone knocking the barrel of a pistol on my door in the small hours—all that comes back to me now in nightmares, persecuting me, the evil stamp of the past, like a darkness that wants to gnaw through my eye. You think it's happening to someone else, surely it's all happening at a great remove, people like you have always distanced themselves from everyone. That comes from sensitivity, a person simply has to protect himself, to protect his jangled nerves, and I understand that. But I tell you, when it comes to people like you and me, we all share one destiny. The only differences are in the paths that lead to the crushing realizations that drive us mercilessly to something like this, drive us into exile. For years before I fled, I hadn't wanted to hear about so much as setting foot out of my town, not even out of my street, I'd never even allowed anyone to embark on any story of any length on that topic, but in the end I fled headlong, running as fast as my legs would carry me, tripping over the splinters of our lives. Now, when I look back, I see only the very end of the string that was long ago wound into a ball and which I intend to unwind, but not now, now I will dwell only on some of the main events of my life, which I have enough courage to call appalling. You have to measure the depth of a person's experience not only by the sum of whatever's been survived, but also by the degree of sensitivity possessed by the survivor . . .

But I don't want to drag things out unnecessarily. I left Serbia two months after the end of the 1999 war. It was August, it was terribly hot. I was taking my wife and children, Stefan and Sofija, on a rather risky journey, but it was our journey and we accepted it, wholeheartedly, as such. Had our departure been like the departures of others at that time, I would be very happy, and now I'd be able to write to you about anything other than that, and I'd be more cheerful for sure—but it was not. Our departure was preceded by certain events, which affected you too, as well as all other honorable people in our country, but there were also events that affected only my family and myself, and which were in fact the straw that broke the camel's back, such as it was. At the beginning of everything, like an epic preamble, stands an honorable obelisk erected in all our names to the memory of *Lazar and Kosovo*—much abused, and therefore now tilting, but propped up by the threadbare platitudes of many stale national bards. Throughout the country, joy in honor of the bloodletting grew, students in Belgrade and other university centers were arrested, laws were routinely repealed. Then came the beginning of mobilization—real fear began to rise in people, first a little timidly, but later with increasing ferocity. Then came March and with it war, and on the second day my call-up papers arrived. What could I do? I went. Mother—and this is where she solemnly enters the story—wept. She burned my father's shirt, as she was ironing it, while he and I said good-bye outside the front door.

I left late in the evening and reported for duty. The men around me were stressed, half-drunk, singing nonsense while snot poured into their mouths. On the radio an announcer was holding forth about the courage of the Serbian army, and one of us shat himself with fright when we heard rumbling over our heads. I made my way through the crowd to a telephone to call a relative who lived near the airport. He said: "They hit damn close last night, I was rigid with shock for ten minutes." I could see at once where it was all headed. I didn't know how long the demon would hang on and how many of us he would push into the abyss before his final end.

The process I want to tell you about began to develop in me roughly a week and a half after the beginning of our campaign. All of a sudden I began to feel hatred toward everyone. Or more exactly, hatred and disgust. A kind of muffled nausea, revulsion at all those creatures, that whole heap of rotten human material around me. I should say that, despite my degree from the Arts Faculty in Belgrade, I've always been hostile to our so-called *elitists*, and I still am today. *Elitism* in our country always taking the form of a not-particularly-modern version of snobbery and racism combined. But for a long time that hostility made me foster a kind of sympathy for the common people in our country, who seemed to me to have been almost entirely innocent in all the tragedies that we had experienced throughout our history, everything that pulled us apart as a people and scattered us around the world. Indeed, I cultivated a kind of contempt and even a mild sneer of revulsion toward the Serbian intelligentsia, xenophobic philistines, conceited and bigoted from the outset—the kind of sneer one cultivates toward the particularly stupid and vain. I thought—rightly, I believed—that the ordinary person on the one hand and the pseudointellectual on the other were unbridgeably dissimilar, as though they hadn't sprung from the same roots but had perhaps, one or other of them, landed on our soil from somewhere else, was entirely alien to it. But, some time around my induction, I realized that I had been seriously mistaken. Not only had both parties sprung from the same roots, they were the same people, in no way different—except, perhaps, in the number of years they had spent at school, but even there the disparity was often minimal. Something fundamentally at variance, a complete rift had now been established between them and me, and there was no longer any prospect of reconciliation. Now I looked at these people, ordinary, conceited, and uncontrollable, realizing at a certain moment that everything—the story I listened to every day on the radio or television and the one I listened to in the streets and the suburbs, dressed in my army uniform—had merged, to form one picture, one single, ugly figure. Our whole multicolored country was becoming for me a kind of Ireland in the eyes of an Irishman leaving it forever, it was becoming the *old sow that eats her farrow* and which had opened its hideous jaws, determined no doubt to finish us off. But enough of that. What's important is what was happening in me, that definitive rupture with the Fatherland, however painful I found it. And when a person steps into the next stage of his destiny, there is no way back to the last.

When a person finds himself in a state such as mine, everything around him takes on a different aspect: people seem to laugh differently, walk differently, react to you differently, and you, for that matter, react differently to them. In a word, the world and the people who walk in it appear hostile to you. I would like it not to be so, but that's how it is and now I don't know what I can do about it, apart from describe it. Somehow, I say, everything changes, which means that even the landscape around you seems to change as well. In keeping with all that hatred and that disgust, my life had in store for me an event that would contribute to the further development of those fundamentally negative feelings, which are more a reflection of a man's inherent weakness than the consequence of any repressive social system. Here, with the aforementioned event, I am already nearing the end of my story, because after it things moved quickly, leading right to our exile. Briefly, this is what happened:

The machinery of war had not really gotten going yet when about ten soldiers moved into my parents' house. It had become the custom at that time for the army to take shelter in private houses, while their owners put up with this honor without a word. Well, those ten of ours were the most utterly vile individuals imaginable, and drunkards to boot, so the house resounded with banging and crashing all day long. None of my family had ever been particularly quick to anger— they were always mild people. My father, but particularly my mother, put up with various insults at first—admittedly, still on the edge of the tolerable, but eventually developing into something really unpleasant. Up until the moment that I'm about to describe to you, right up to that moment—or, more exactly, right up to the third day after it—I knew almost nothing about what was going on in that house. I too had been mobilized and billeted in someone else's house, and I considered it my duty to endure that burden silently as well, although the knowledge that soldiers were occupying my parental home was never far from my thoughts . . . (I even carried the key to the locked room in which I still kept most of my books and other personal effects, with me, just in case some stranger found his way in there.) It turned out that those soldiers did whatever they liked. They turned the house into a real pigsty. A certain Brekalović particularly excelled at this—a true alcoholic with a pale, drawn, ghostly face. Only the thin, blue veins on his nose disturbed the eerie pallor of it. He was particularly talented, I say. And he had several serious quarrels with my folks. You can imagine, I suppose, that they were about politics. He didn't fail to mention, during every argument— for he had presumably heard me talking during one of my visits home—that their son, despite being in the army, was a traitor to his nation. Brekalović wanted, also, in the name of said nation, for my room to be unlocked so that he could personally see what I was hiding in it and what kind of books, if you please, the philosopher reads. Mother demanded that Brekalović leave the house. God only knows all the things she'd already learned about Brekalović—but, in any case, she didn't dare share any of this with father and me. One evening, finally, that loathsome figure from our nightmare life broke down the locked door of my room and found himself among my things, among the books and papers of my philosophical work and essay-writing. He stood, the obscurantist, in the middle of the room with Kadare's *The Castle* in his hands, God knows how he managed to hit on that, of all things, among all the works by Nietzsche, Kant,

Spinoza, or Hegel . . . The author's name was probably just what he was looking for—Albanian—for, at the height of the war and its atrocities, he was looking for a straw to cling to, and then . . . do what he did. Seeing him there, my mother screamed, and my father wasn't at home just then, and I don't think that I'll ever forgive him for that. "Bitch, you spawned one treacherous bastard!" hissed Brekalović before he set about raping my forty-nine-year-old mother, who, apart from anything else in her life, had married her very first boyfriend, I mean the man who later became my father.

I stopped by three days after Brekalović's crime and found the house in silence. The soldiers had left, and my mother was sitting hunched up on her bed with a pillow clutched to her stomach. My father, broken. He was crouching in the corner of the room. Silent. Hardly fifteen minutes passed from the moment I heard what had happened till I found Brekalović in front of a nearby bar, led straight to him by some animal instinct. I beat him senseless. His injuries were severe enough that he will never be able to walk normally again, and the four months he spent in hospital are a testament to what happened that afternoon. I admit, I was wholly out of control, there was no voice of reason left in my consciousness then to point out the barbarity of my action. I'm writing this to you today, God help me, to report that a sentence kept resounding in me that day, as in an empty church, a simple, harsh sentence, as though read in some cheap novelette: "So you thought you could fuck an old woman and not pay for it, did you? Well, guess again!" And, over and over again, that sentence filled me, completely, with hatred. I had avenged my mother, and remained just aware enough not to take my action to its ultimate end. I left Brekalović alive and later I told the police and the judge the truth, down to the last word. What happened then, however, simply confirmed some of the attitudes I've already expressed over the course of this letter, I mean about our people and our country.

It turned out that Brekalović was related to the dean of the school where I taught. There followed pressure, telephone calls. Soon I was summoned to have a "talk" with my superior. Briefly, I was told that if I did not withdraw my accusation of rape, I would lose my job. Which would be fatal for my family and myself—or so I was told. After all, I no longer lived in my parents' house, which meant that I could hardly know what went on there in every detail. If I retracted my claim, they would, they said, for their part, *do what they could*. (In the office at that moment, I should say, in addition to the dean and myself, was Brekalović's lawyer.) I repeat, they would, for their part, *do what they could*. As though it was I who had raped Brekalović's mother, as though my mother had not been so viciously, cruelly humiliated! We did not withdraw the accusation. But now, thanks to you won't believe what pressures, here we are, my wife, my children, and I, in Szentendre, outside that country—although, I have to say, not far enough away from those people there. At a certain moment my mother demanded that we go, because the threats and blackmail could no longer be borne. The judicial process is still going on and will continue to go on, no doubt, for a while longer yet. As long as it takes, I hope, for Brekalović to see the inside of a prison. And then, of course, I know that one day he will get out of jail. As though nothing had happened, he'll stroll along to the first bar for a double brandy, he'll knock it back, maybe pinch the waitress's behind, or tell some drunk that he'd done time just because he humped some traitor's mother. That his beloved country had punished an innocent man; that it was he, in fact, who was the victim and not that stinking old whore who could have given him a nasty disease. But there we are! Everyone gets what he deserves. He'll go to prison, while I'm already in exile. Voluntary or not—that's a different question. Besides, I am not myself blameless as regards the country in which I spent virtually all my life up to now.

Incidentally, it's nice here. This "little bit of Serbia" is extraordinarily good for my nerves, and it seems to me that, although there aren't many of them, the Serbs here live quite differently from those there. Or perhaps I should say "you there"?

Tomorrow we'll be getting money from Stockholm: a relative is sending us German marks to buy supplies for the coming three months, which I believe is as long as it will take for us to get Swedish immigrant visas for my family and myself. Refika brought me your collection of stories and one dreadfully bad volume of poems, translated into Serbian, by one of his countrymen, which I intend to throw in the trash. He laughs, the bum, and says, pointing at the book of poems: "Read one every night, before you go to sleep." "All right," I say, putting it aside. And he falls onto the bed, roaring with laughter. He told me I was a "Serbian cultural racist." Once in a while, I do feel better. We were right to leave Serbia, because of the children, because of my wife, because of my mother. That's how it is in a foreign land, my friend. Here, my hand writes of its own accord: "Waging war, shedding blood for a foreign master . . ."

TRANSLATED FROM SERBO-CROATIAN BY CELIA HAWKESWORTH

marriage

MIRANA LIKAR BAJŽELJ

Nada's Tablecloth

Fucking complicated, you think to yourself, as you walk along the smooth, slippery, shining surface and beneath your thin leather soles feel every joint between the paving stones. You're afraid that you will get tangled up in this dress, to which you are not accustomed. If you do, that will be a sign, and if you do not, likewise; the whole street is somehow bulging, because of fear, rainwater, or time, certainly because of something. A few months ago you would have described this moment with the word paradoxical; now that word, along with several others, is stuck somewhere behind you, somewhere in time. Tell me which words you use and I'll tell you with whom you spend time and what you are. You can still change your mind, in spite of the fact that the world has been speeding up from month to month, from week to week, from day to day; today it's speeding up from hour to hour, and that's all you can think of, that there's no time left, and of how everything is so fucking complicated.

In front of you is the red, white, and blue flag with the checkerboard, probably there's also one somewhere at the back, not to mention those left behind in the parked cars; around the flag are hired musicians who sing of the beauties of our homeland and about the beautiful Dalmatia that they will defend with their last drop of blood;

everyone is singing along, Goran is walking beside you and behind you are a whole lot of people. All your folk from back home are here and you know exactly what they're thinking, that this isn't our kind of climate, it's too hot. They're mixed in with Goran's people, brown, green, and washed-out pastel shades among black, blue, and colorful modern; your folk aren't used to being away from home, the most elegant colors for them are brown and moss green, they're not made for these hot white stones on this hot Saturday afternoon, but for you they'd do anything and what our Nuša does is always right. You don't even know that at the pub your father is known as OurNuša because he begins every sentence with your name. OurNuša, he says, adjusting his glasses. Goran's people are also dressed up. The men in elegant suits, on their feet sharp Italian shoes but no socks. This is another reason for that pain in your diaphragm. What kind of world is it where men dressed for a special occasion are not wearing socks? What's wrong with them?

You go along the seafront, there's a smell of salt in the air, mixed with a smell of oil and, come on, let's admit it, a smell of sewage. On your right yachts are moored, flags hang in the still air like limp rags: the foreigners on deck watch and size you up. A small man on an Italian yacht stretches to take a picture of the men. You are somehow floating but you notice all this, your eyes take in all this confusion. You see yourself walking on the centuries-old stones, you know you're hot, you're afraid that something isn't quite right, you also see the camera in the Italian's small brown hand. It's possible that as early as the autumn some male models with icy, imbecilic looks will be stalking down the catwalk without socks, a nice trick, skin against skin, he'll be dreaming about these tall Dalmatian men, flags, this scene. In memory of this summer day he'll dress the models in shorts and raincoats, he'll put a flag in their hands, your wedding will be frozen in the bizarre images of an upside-down world. Damn queers, Goran will say one day sitting in front of the television, and change the channel. But where will you be then?

Even last year you yourself would also have said they were good looking, these Dalmatian men, and they sing nationalist marches at weddings, interesting, and they have flags with them, which isn't all that strange when you think how those madmen from the hills bombarded them . . . But last year is last year, while this year is this year and this is no longer just a bit of exotica for you to photograph and keep for a rainy day. Now those flags are above and below you, and the questions have only increased, they're multiplying and getting under your feet, and it's not the best time for questions to which you don't have answers, although in reality you do, otherwise you wouldn't feel so bad. Over a couple of days a whole arsenal of images has appeared, each bad in its own way, while the moment is approaching when all the questions will be combined into one and there will be only one answer.

Suddenly, for instance, you noticed Nada's tablecloth, Nada and the kind of things she said . . . Goran wasn't at home. Two days before the wedding and he hadn't been home all night. He had said he was just popping out, that he'd be right back, and that right back had stretched until morning. His mobile phone stayed at home, you see, that's what life with him is really like, and you sat with Nada in the kitchen waiting for him, quiet more than anything, strangers. You noticed that her tablecloth was plastic and worn and, come on, admit it, also dirty. It wasn't as if you had never seen a plastic tablecloth before, it wasn't that. It was that you would be living with Nada, Goran has already told you. And will you rip the tablecloth that has suited her all these years right off the table? That's what your home will be like. Will such a home help make you a new homeland?

Nada was looking at you in despair; through the cigarette smoke you heard those words that threw a new light on everything. What can I say, she said, you know where he came from, and with disgust she gestured somewhere between her legs. Now you're asking yourself if this is hereditary. From mother to son. Forever. Can it be fixed? What do you do with despair?

The most frightening thing about your own mother's reaction was the hint in the words look here, plus the same desperate look, plus the same silence. Look here, she said to you, when you told her. Look here. Is this what you studied for? Is this what you worked so hard for? Your father won't be able to bear it. He used to get up at night just to check that you were still breathing. Who's going to give you a job there? And you hadn't even told her the half of it. Now your mother and father are somewhere at the back asking themselves whether this is really happening, and what's going to happen next.

Your mother is so afraid. Last year she showed you a holiday photo in which there were some female refuse collectors. Female refuse collectors seemed a safe and neutral theme; there are donkeys here, a cathedral damaged by shelling, but women on a garbage truck, yes, it's terrible that in Dalmatia they have women refuse collectors. It seemed good that in your world at least that wasn't the case. Nor was it the case that men came home in the morning, saying give me a glass of mineral water, dear, I drank a bit too much, and went to bed without another word, and you weren't even allowed to ask them any questions because the answer was always the same. That's what I'm like, you know what I'm like, so what now? Is the first pain not better than the last?

You told him immediately that you were pregnant; you could have waited and made your own decision, but you went charging in there regardless. Bam. Did you think he'd make the decision for you, or what? You know what his outlook on life is. What happens happens. It's all the same to him. If you decide you should get married, then you will; if you decide differently, then you won't. But if that's what you decide, then you'll live here with him and Nada, he's not moving anywhere. He's not exchanging a weekend lover for a weekend wife.

Very soon now you will enter the church, it's still full of holes outside, they haven't repaired that; you're increasingly afraid, the nave is decorated with white tulle and white flowers, while you experience moments in which you've decided and moments in which you've changed your mind. Your life is now made up of these moments; quite a few of them have already built up, creating something that could even be called fate. Are you thinking of that architect? When you met him he had just gotten divorced. I knew, he told you, I knew it would end badly, even when I went to get married at the town hall. But I didn't have the strength to stop the wedding, everyone dressed up to the nines, the presents bought, the apartment furnished. Everything would have been better if I'd followed my instincts. When you heard that you thought you would never let yourself be dragged that far, that you and your inner voice were one, and now look at you.

Even a year ago . . . The upper floor at your parents' house to begin with, some colleague from the legal world who would be transformed overnight into an ideal lover and wonderful husband; on Saturdays you'd leave the kids with mother and go off on your own: skiing in the winter, Egypt in the summer; a billable hour of a lawyer's time costs such and such and each day has so many working hours, multiplied by two . . . That's why you went sailing with colleagues from work. To try to draw from the drabness of office life some kind of color picture, some kind of opportunity . . . which became null and void in that moment when, after seven days, somewhere in the middle of your intellectual love games, Goran crawled across your bed toward the space where the autopilot was kept. When it broke down you didn't know that it was there in your cabin, at the end of the bed, behind a small door. The only one in the town who might be able to fix it is Nada's Goran, they said in the marina when you told them how your holiday had been spoiled. But he's hard to get, at this time of year he's always at the Kornati Islands. Without any real hope you took the phone number.

You've got no instructions, you've got no circuit diagram, you've got no idea, he noted and swam across your sheets to look at the autopilot which had gone crazy so that the yacht went its own way regardless of what the men up on deck typed on their screen. They should have steered manually, but how can you do that and drink beer at the same time? Fucking useless, he decided, electronics are always fucking useless, without a diagram there's only logic and give me a screwdriver. After two hours the sheets were wet with his sweat but he had fixed it. Logic won the day. So where has that day gone? And what about now? You have no instructions for yourself, you have no circuit diagram, you're no longer thinking logically.

You gladly offered him a beer. He drank it without any particular enthusiasm for you all or for himself among you. He said he was heading for the Kornati, to sleep a bit in the shade, swim a bit, and maybe grill a fish, that's all he was interested in. He played with the golden cigarette lighter over which your eyes first met and because of which you thought Leo, he's a Leo. You should have fled then, but you couldn't because after that look his tone of voice changed almost imperceptibly. When I was still going to maritime college small boats didn't have these things, he told you, but two years ago I was sailing a boat for some rich guy where the system was even more complicated, but with logic you can sort everything out. When he was still a kid he had used logic to dismantle his moped and put it back together again. There were just two parts left which he didn't know what to do with, but the moped went faster.

Rich guy, boat, logic . . . You were all eyes and ears. Yes, you all know the name of the famous person Goran was working for, so he won't tell you who it was, only that it was really hard-earned dough, not that it was physically demanding, but the atmosphere was terrible because to that sort you're always, regardless of what they pay you, just a second-class citizen. It's hard to take if you have even an ounce of self-esteem and Goran, after all he's experienced, has a great deal of self-esteem. What's more, he had been responsible for the entire crew. When one day on Malta he was instructed to tell them to clean the grooves in the white soles of the shoes of the boss's guests, which the ordinary sailors polished every morning in any case, he simply packed his bag and left. He doesn't give a damn about money, when he can't take something anymore he's off. He's a free man and no one is going to take that freedom away.

At that point you wanted only one thing, to lie with him on the Kornati Islands, just as freely. And now, at this moment? How much freedom do you still have? And you simply can't tell anyone that the very same day you really did lay with him there. And after that there was no going back, not to the yacht, not to your old, nothing-special story, not to your life. When you lay with Goran you had to immediately take on the whole of him. He told you there and then that he would never do much more in his life than lie around like this, and now and then fix this or that fucked-up thing and get well fucking paid for it. He told you then, but it's only these last few days that you've understood what he was actually telling you. That he had already seen all there was to see and that there was nothing more to see than what he was looking at now. He had volunteered to fight in the war and no rich faggot was going to tell him about life. He was in an outfit that hadn't been mentioned in any military documents, there was nothing in his service record to show that he had fought in the war for his homeland. Officially, he had never had any contact with the Croatian army. They reported directly to the minister of the interior and the minister only passed on to his detachment a general order about what they should do and how. And they did. They did everything right. Every time. They thought that the homeland would be grateful, but the homeland had lost all their papers, if there had ever been any, and so it was that Goran and his comrades in arms preferred to look at the Kornati Islands and the calm sea, and so it was that little else interested them. A nonexistent unit, he said. When you asked him what they had done, he said everything. They'd done everything. Everything they believed they had to do. While other, ordinary folk had been refugees dependent on foreign aid, burning parquet flooring in the dark, Goran and his comrades from the detachment that didn't exist had stayed in the most protected building around, with their own generator, their own fuel, good food, whisky, cigarettes, and everything else in abundance, as well as the most up-to-date weapons that had ever come to Croatia. Every comfort for those who did everything. Last year you still thought that Goran had piloted a Black Hawk in the Platoon that saved Private Ryan, you were in love, but now, girl, now you know what he meant by everything and what he meant by detachment, because you looked online, where it clearly states: a detachment is a special military unit or formation of indeterminate size made up of squads and companies set up to perform a specific task. In this case, everything. And now you somehow know that he didn't charge around against a background of sound and light effects, he operated more in the dark, in silence. Since he cries out in his sleep it could be that above all else he crawled. But what did he have in his hands, then? They don't make films about Goran's everything. Sometimes, when he closes his eyes, you know that it isn't all over yet, that the year he spent on a fishing boat immediately after the war to erase everything and then live normally erased nothing, because it can never be erased. Is this what you wanted? To spend your life with a man who drags with him something that cannot be erased? Who has no illusions? Who has already seen everything?

In front of the altar the priest awaits you. He's learned some Slovenian words for the occasion, but who cares, you're not marrying the priest, if you marry at all. You come back down to earth; now beneath your shoes there's red coconut matting, the ceiling is high, that's what cathedrals are for, to make people yearn for the heights, for the heavens. They are playing the wedding march and you're still weighing your options. You stand on the right; on the benches behind you are your people and on the benches behind Goran, his, and they all know what's going to happen, everyone does, apart from you. Near the ceiling a bird flies silently; the windows in the cupola, which seems to be sinking beneath the evening light, are open, and the bird too is seeking a way out. If you wrote that down somewhere no one would believe it, what a stale metaphor they would say, but the bird really is there and it really is seeking a way out. If it finds one, you think, if it finds one that will be a sign and you will say no, and try to salvage what can be salvaged. If it doesn't, you'll say yes and all the mothers in the church will cry, moved, and all the men outside the church will then shout she's ours . . .

The priest is saying something, Goran is swaying almost imperceptibly, people are clearing their throats, flashes are flashing. When the priest asks you, Nuša, do you take . . . you forget to look at the bird and you say . . .

TRANSLATED FROM SLOVENIAN BY DAVID LIMON

CHRISTINA HESSELHOLDT

Camilla and the Horse

> *. . . and the blood of love welled up in my heart with*
> *a slow pain.*
> SYLVIA PLATH

[CAMILLA]

First we go into an expensive Italian restaurant across from the strip club and drink a bottle of wine to kill time, it soon becomes clear that the waiter is attracted to my husband, who's getting older but is still hot-blooded. The waiter's getting older too, he's been photographed with both Sophia Loren and Helmut Kohl *in this restaurant*, and that arouses my husband's interest. By now it must be nine o'clock, and we cut across the intersection to the opposite corner. We go in. I start by asking whether it's okay for me to be there even though I'm a woman. I do that to ingratiate myself and make contact. It's perfectly okay, and we're also the only guests. The girl behind the bar is from Romania and strong with short hair. My husband thinks I'm good at making contact and taking things easy. You have to be careful not to praise me too much, because it really gets me going, and then I can cross the line and become totally unstoppable. There are so many hookers I can't even tell you how many; we're the only guests and weren't planning on buying sex, I tell the bartender this several times. That's perfectly okay too, we can just drink, three drinks are included in the price of admission, I take the strongest one and down it fast. Up on stage the show begins, a mulatto girl makes the expected movements and gestures with and around a pole until she's naked. I think about the circus and great fatigue, wearying routines, because I'd rather not say "like a tired circus animal." As soon as she's leaving the stage she gets self-conscious, she bows her head and presses her costume against her stomach.

Meanwhile, at the bar: a woman has taken the stool beside me, another Romanian (from here on I'll refer to her as my darling), I ask her if she's familiar with Herta Müller, she asks for titles, I mention *The Fox Was then Ahead of the Hunter*, it's not an easy title in German, not for me, with my German; her German isn't so great either, she's taking courses and claims she speaks German that's 85% correct. I don't know how to respond, "the modal auxiliaries, you know," she says. Those I know. But then I realize that I've completely forgotten how articles and nouns are declined, and that nothing I've said has meant a thing. In effect I've spoken German that is 0% correct, so I switch to English. I'm sitting with my back to my husband, he's very interested in hearing what we're talking about, and once in a while I turn around and give him a summary. Then he nods and puts some additional questions. I ask my darling if she sends money home to her elderly parents, because you always read about that, but no, they didn't help her, so why should she help them. "Is that a bit harsh?" my darling asks. It seems harsh to me. It seems that way even to my darling. Each time we slip my husband into the conversation, she treats him with great respect, he gets all the time he wants. This makes me jealous, I really want her full attention.

"Do you want to buy him," I ask, "for 300 euros?"

She looks at him to see if he's amused, and he is.

"Oh, that's expensive, that's expensive," she says.

"He's a little old, but he's good," I say, "he fucks like a stallion."

"Ah, a stud-boy," she says.

"Some boy," I say.

"Prince Charles," she says to him, and he likes that.

My husband leans back on his bar stool and laughs, my darling laughs, I laugh. It occurs to me that I'm using her time and I ask if she wants to be paid for talking to me.

"Nah, Camilla," she says to me, "money, money, money isn't everything."

I make to hand her a bill and can clearly see she doesn't think 50 euros is a whole lot, but the bill disappears into her clothing. She's dark and could easily be a gypsy. Now my husband starts getting bored, he gets up and saunters over to a group of girls at a table, among them the Romanian bartender, who's studying mathematics, she's the one he'd like to chat with. He takes an interest in Romania's standard of living, differences and similarities before and after Ceausescu. It makes me a bit insecure that my husband talks to other women; "Nun, mein Schatz," says my darling, "let him do it anyway, that's how it goes now and then, everyone needs to." "Mmm." Then I ask her if she has a boyfriend. Yes, but she doesn't sound enthusiastic. I ask whether it's hard to have a love relationship when you're a prostitute. She takes a deep breath and says something about orgasms, she's about to deliver a lecture on various types of orgasms, or the absence of orgasms, when some clients arrive, three short Chinese, and she has to run. I feel abandoned. She wraps herself around them. I get up and go over to my husband and the women at the round table.

"This'll cost," I say to him. "This is an expensive conversation you're having."

"No," he says, "this is the staff table. And I'm talking to the bartender."

"Trust me," I say, "it's going to cost. It's like riding in four taxis at once."

"Bull," he says, "we're talking about Romania."

"Bull," say the girls.

"Then we're agreed," I say, "we're agreed that I'm paranoid."

I join the little circle, which consists of:

1. The mulatto girl, 24 and skeptical
2. A fair-haired woman who introduces herself as an alcoholic
3. One with short hair and a small face that she's just had lifted
4. The bartender

"Mein Schatz," my darling says when she catches sight of me (the Chinese are about to leave) and climbs onto a stool behind me and flings her arms around me. "Camilla and the horse," she says to the others, pointing at my husband and me. Then she wags a finger in the air in front of her nose and corrects herself: "Prince Charles," she says, pointing at my husband.

I pay a suitable compliment to the mulatto girl's performance and then ask her: "Would you like to buy him? He's a little old, but he's good."

She hasn't yet managed to reply when the alcoholic leans across the table and introduces herself again as an alcoholic. I tell her that she is highly talented and very beautiful and encourage her to stop drinking and feel good about herself. I show her how I pat myself on the shoulder every day, unfortunately I can't remember what this maneuver is called, but it works (with each passing day I am more and more at peace with myself), I got it from an article in *Reader's*

Digest. I make her promise not to go back to drinking the next morning, I start seeing myself as a sort of barfoot doctor, walking from bar to bar, I order champagne for the whole table to celebrate the alcoholic's decision, and my darling kisses me, her tongue is very pointy, mine is very dry, this will be expensive, and I tell them that my love life with my husband is like a looong German porno film, he is a stud-boy, he's cracking up, I'm totally cracking up too, one of my darling's breasts has fallen out of her blouse and her skirt has twisted halfway around, she's on the verge of cracking up too but she strokes me and strokes me, now she wants to go home, so I slap her but not really hard.

"She hit me," my darling says, astonished.

"It's on account of love," says the one with the small face, "I prefer men, but once in a while I have a woman."

"Sorry, sorry, sorry," I say, it's dawn and I ask what it would cost for her to stay just one more hour, oh please-please-pretty-please but she lives faaar out in the suburbs. I picture my darling alone in the subway, alone on the suburban train. I want to buy more champagne for her, for everyone.

We have to leave now, the club is closing, it's seven o'clock, I have a husband who fucks like a stallion, I weep, and "Oooh," they coo at the sight of the tears: "It's true love," I give the alcoholic a final admonition, now she's got to manage without her coach, because now Camilla and the horse are leaving, "No no wait: Prince Charles," my horse is my crutch on this piercingly bright morning; it's suddenly the last summer ever.

I wish I were Žižek. Žižek can get everything to hang together, if I were Žižek then right now I would be lying in a Punic bordello and having a fucking match with Houellebecq, the hookers wouldn't be trafficked, merely glob-al-ized neigh-bors at sex-u-al la-bors—can't you *hear* that as sung by Gregorian monks, or maybe a castrato: glob-al-ized neigh-bors at sex-u-al la-bors.

Aaah, that very human, that all too Žižekian urge toward coherence where there is none. What is it that I can't get to hang together? My memory? My love life? We'll have to examine all this more closely.

I miss my Romanian darling. I never found out her name. My husband says: if you want to see her again you'd better hurry back there, these people move around a lot. By which he means that she may already be working at a different club, in a different city; or that so many people have glided through her hands that she's forgotten me, or stands a good chance of soon doing so.

"These people move around a lot": the statement surprised me. As if he were in possession of experience I didn't know about—and now he was lifting a corner of the curtain.

At first *I* couldn't remember *her* either. I mean: I couldn't picture her. And I couldn't really remember what had happened.

First of all, when I woke up a little later that day after only a couple of hours' sleep (we left the club at seven o'clock and stepped out into a morning whose light was like a needle, I weeping over my lost love, over parting as such, over life's brevity) and with a terrible hangover, or sooner, still drunk perhaps—first of all I found in my purse her address and phone number, which I'd forced out of her and which she'd handed me with a shrug (maybe they were fake), and I quickly tore the note into tiny shreds and flushed them down the toilet so as not to be tempted to contact her. A memory arrives, on Platform Cortex, as somber as a freight train. One loss hauls the thought of another along with it. One loss opens the door for another that opens the tear ducts. Even as a child I always feared the worst. I was secretly in love with a boy in my class and wrote him love letters that weren't intended for his eyes, never never, my love was hopeless, I wrote the letters (*well, they weren't exactly Shakespeare, were they*) because he felt closer and closer as I wrote them, while I was communicating, while I put his name and mine together inside a heart. Out of fear that these letters might nonetheless fall into his hands, or into anyone's hands, for that matter, immediately after writing them I tore them into shreds and threw them into the toilet. No sooner had I flushed them down than the nightmare began. I imagined him coming into his bathroom many kilometers away from mine, only to find, backed up into his toilet—my ripped-up letters, which he would immediately fish out of the water, dry out, and paste together. After which he would throw his head back and laugh, and I would switch schools. A fatal flaw in the sewage system was to blame for this horror: his pipes and mine were connected! The next time I burned my love letter. The breeze caught a few scorched flakes and blew them out the window. After that I took to daydreaming and in this way avoided leaving any evidence. Now the memory is departing from Platform Cortex, do not cross the tracks. And take care to secure your valuables.

We found ourselves on the twenty-fifth floor of a hotel on Alexanderplatz, at the same height as the restaurant on the TV Tower. I could draw the curtains and make the small hotel room darker, even more enclosed, or I could provide a clear view of my misery. Not that I believed anyone could peer into our hotel room from the restaurant on the TV Tower; that would require binoculars. Not that I believed anyone would think of doing that. No, it was just that the TV Tower itself seemed observant, a stout observer with blinking red eyes right outside the window.

The toilet and shower were located inside a glass room with walls of green mottled glass *in* the hotel room—a shower cabinet with toilet. I threw up for a long time, disgustingly, inside this small cage where it was hard to get on your knees and where the sounds you made were in no way blocked from reaching the surrounding room (I hoped that Charles was deep asleep). Who could puke without a sound, like silent rain. Like the expression, "the life running out of you." As if life were a little stream. I did it in convulsive jerks, kneeling, in the most humiliating position, arms flung around the white bowl, embracing it (how much more I would have preferred to be kneeling among sheep at a stream and drinking; among sheep).

Come to that, I have always imagined that my death would play out in a bathroom, a very clean bathroom, an almost antiseptic death, I'd be leaning against white enamel, a foretaste of the coffin's white tranquillity, but I hope my death bathroom will be larger than the cabinet in the hotel room on Alexanderplatz, with a bit more space, a bit more *Totesraum*, if you please. After I'd thrown up I lay down in my bed with closed eyes and tried to remember. Beside me was the snoring of Prince Charles.

The first thing Charles did when he woke was to squeeze my hand. A little squeeze that means: we belong together, we two, even though other people captured our interest last night. Or it could also mean: I didn't hear you throwing up. Very reassuring, very loving. I squeezed back. After that he leapt up and started rooting around in his pockets and pulling out all the receipts from the night's party. His credit card had been swiped quite a few times. We hadn't been able to use the card in the club, they wanted cold cash, and the bartender had offered to have Charles driven to an ATM in the club's white six-door Cadillac with tinted windows, the kind that looks like an oversized hearse (if I could choose my own death, I would be run over by a hearse, Death is as close as a *wife* / the hollow-cheeked attendant of my *life*, tra-la-la, it sounds like one of my friend Alma's limping, foot-dragging verses, the undertaker would pick me up from the street and put my bruised body on top of a coffin, skip the hospital and the funeral parlor too, straight to the point, right into the grave), or more precisely, at least in this instance, like a bordello on wheels. Charles had declined. He was quite capable of walking. And that's what he had done—a good many times—back and forth between the club and the ATM, and here was the evidence of all his promenades, a mound of crumpled receipts.

"Uh-oh," he said, "it was an expensive night."

"Let's just see how much cash we have lying around in our pockets," I said optimistically.

But there wasn't much.

"We spent 9,000 last night."

"Euros?"

"Kroner."

"How much is that in euros?"

"Why do you want it in euros?"

"How much is it in yen?"

He looked at me. And I knew we were thinking the same thing. He had claimed it was gratis, free and clear, to talk to the girls at the staff table about Romania's standard of living etcetera, etcetera, and I had known it would be expensive, we would end up paying for all their drinks as long as the conversation continued. I didn't say anything. I thereby doubled my pleasure: not only had I been right, but now I could show my magnanimity by not saying anything. I smiled at him. And raked in my chips. After that we started discussing whether there was any possible way to deduct the expense. Charles is a food reviewer. But even though we'd sat in the club and dipped nachos into avocado dip (from a can), the place could hardly be called a restaurant. I felt sick again and said, "Dear, sweet Charles, would you mind going out for a good long while?"

"Out into the corridor?"

I nodded: "Yes, but hurry."

He quickly pulled on pants and a shirt and opened the door to the corridor. As I squeezed into the cabinet he said, "You know, don't you, that a party carried all the way to its conclusion is a suicide."

The Balcony. Genet.

"Yes," I answered, "we should have chosen the boring lilies of the field."

"Genet," he said and closed the door.

We've just read *The Balcony.* We read aloud to each other before we go to sleep. I read novels, poems, plays aloud to Charles. And Charles reads recipes to me. In the preface to one of his cookbooks it says that there's nothing to prevent people from living to the age of 140. That's the book we cook from. When he's done reading aloud, we're terrifically hungry. We run out to the kitchen, and that's why we've grown a little—just a little—too heavy. As long as we travel together down the heaping highway of life, where your spare tire is mine and my spare tire is yours.

My only keepsake of her is her lighter. Charles found it in his jacket pocket and gave it to me. It's black. With palm trees. And a couple in evening dress, dancing. You can make out a bungalow behind them. Slim and elegant, they dance away the bottomless tropical night. He in a tuxedo, she in a white cocktail dress. He with one hand on her back, which arches alluringly, the hand placed precisely there, in the arching small of it. She with a hand on one of his shoulders, broad in the tailor-made jacket. A waiter holding a tray is about to cross the bungalow's patio. Bungalow from *bangla,* a one-storeyed house for Europeans in India. It's another era. All in all, I gather, very colonial (it's as if the only thing missing is some pillars, there should have been a house with colonial columns), very hot, the ocean isn't very far away, and there are snakes in the grass. It happens that a snake gets into the bungalow. Then the servants start screaming, and the woman in the white dress screams even louder. Small underdeveloped men wearing kurtas, men as spindly as crickets, come running in from the garden with sharp instruments and make short work of it. The chauffeur is leaning against the large car, bored, he's lit one of his master's cigars and has to smoke it furtively, hidden in his hand, if that's possible with cigars. The couple are in an early phase of their marriage. It still occurs to them to dance out on the patio at night.

I keep the lighter. It's a memento. At one point I drew her onto the dance floor—I danced out onto it first and, deeply intoxicated as I was, spread my arms like a figure skater and cried, "I'm an architect!" Though I'm not.

Charles and the little gathering at the staff table, consisting of the alcoholic, the mulatto girl, the bartender, and the short-haired woman who'd recently had a facelift and whose small face reminded me of a taut raisin, observed us, cooing. I had an awful lot of clothing on. A calf-length skirt, flat-heeled boots, and a thick black sweater. She was more suitably dressed—more lightly. I probably resembled an aging, somewhat overly plump panther. Still possessed of a certain litheness. But. By that time she was already longing to get home. When we sat down the bartender said, pointing at Charles: "He has children."

"He got them in Hamburg," said the alcoholic.

"Uh, a person shouldn't go to Hamburg."

"No, avoid going to Hamburg."

"I've never been to Hamburg," Charles said and stuck his wallet into his pocket. Obviously he'd shown them pictures of his grown sons. Two enterprising men in their twenties. Business, that slightly fishy word. The younger one earned his first million when he was seventeen. A happy story. He isn't my son. But I too have expectations of him.

Charles fell back in his chair laughing and looked at me, shaking his head: we had landed among surrealists. (I thought of Gulliver and what he'd been subjected to, how surprised he was. As a kid I could never look long enough at the illustration in which the giant Gulliver wakes up among the Lilliputians and finds himself tethered to the ground by countless thin threads, while on and around his body there swarm an army of miniature humans, as industrious as ants, all of them carrying some useful object or other in their hands, on their way to carrying out useful tasks.)

"He's a stallion."

"Unnnh, a stud-boy," my darling said, pulling a chair up behind mine and embracing me.

"You devil," she said.

It was a short while later that she took my head in her hands and kissed me. And I started to believe that she was falling in love with me. Our acquaintance lasted from about nine o'clock, when we arrived at the club and she sat down on a chair next to me, to seven A.M., when we left the place, unwillingly (I, in any case, was unwilling).

Every single time she left me in the course of the ten hours, for example to be with the short Chinese, I felt like I was missing something. As if my existence were a clutching at empty air (which it quite possibly is). That's exactly how it was when, over fifteen years ago, I met Charles. Empty, lonely, hollow, all wrong—if he wasn't close by.

TRANSLATED FROM DANISH BY ROGER GREENWALD

DAN LUNGU

7 P.M. *Wife*

He left the tinted-glass high-rise building without looking back. Not once. He was walking with resolute, unhurried steps, his eyes trained on the impeccably shined toecaps of his Timberland shoes. He hadn't even bothered to reply to the doorman who had probably wished him well, smiling like someone in a dental-floss ad. He'd had enough of smiling and talking nicely. Being polite. Not being able to afford to lose his temper. That was what he did all day long. "Hell's fuckin' bells," he hissed in spite of himself. He jumped into his car and took off his jacket and tie. Meaning it was Friday. On regular weekdays he'd only loosen his tie.

He nosed into the traffic instinctively, his mind void of all plans. He drove with the flow.

It was Friday after all.

The images around circled his brain like so many soap bubbles around a fan.

He reached the outskirts of the city and pulled over. He didn't want to go anywhere. Well, he did, sort of, but not all that badly. Some other time.

He got out of the car to look at the hills.

Everything was so beautiful. Nothing was ever beautiful.

Still two hours to go until seven.

How long till seven? He glanced at his watch again. Two hours.

Sometimes he'd ask himself something and forget what it was.

Alternately, he'd answer his own questions and forget the answer.

"Hell's fuckin' bells" echoed through his mind.

His own voice. Or the memory of his own voice.

His temples were throbbing. The weekend headache. Nothing out of the ordinary. Everything was under control. Sales were doing well. What sales? He started. The memory of his boss's voice.

He went into a bar and ordered a double shot of brandy. Closest bar to where he'd parked.

He eavesdropped on the patrons' conversation, but their words circled his brain like so many soap bubbles around a fan. He liked the thick smoke. He liked the squalor in there. He liked the people—ugly, toothless, unshaven. Come to think of it, it was a good thing sales were doing so well. What sales? Installment sales, what else . . .

"Hell's fuckin' bells," his voice snapped back at the memory of his boss's voice.

A tumble with Carolina, a tumble with Carolina, kept ringing through his head.

One hour to go till seven.

It would have been nice if it had started raining out of the heavy smoke. A downpour of beer into the mugs of the toothless. Let the losers have a field day. Let 'em dance in the rain.

As for him, Carolina was going to save him. She was going to suck all the headache out of his head.

It was Friday after all.

How long till seven?

He drained his brandy and called her, though she was expecting him. No one answered. He left no message. Could be she was with another one of her johns.

"Hell's fuckin' bells."

7 P.M. was booked exclusively for him; no one could take that away. He was paying for it. He was a faithful customer. He didn't take anything on credit.

A tumble with Carolina, a tumble with Carolina.

He was a paying customer, wasn't he? No one could take his hour away from him.

Frantically pressing the keys of his cell phone, he finished a second glass of brandy. Carolina wouldn't answer. He panicked. It was the first time anything like this had happened to him. As a rule, Carolina was always waiting for him. There, in her rented flat.

He felt cheated.

Without fail, at the beginning of the weekend, he'd come to Carolina. She'd be waiting for him in lingerie he'd bought her himself. Sand-colored. 7 P.M. was his hour. He didn't care about anything else.

He felt double-crossed. It just wasn't fair. He had never ever barged his way in at any other hour. He didn't care who she was screwing the rest of the time. But at 7 P.M. she was supposed to be at home for him. At 7 P.M. she was as good as his wife.

Carolina knew him well. Knew all his whims.

After a tumble with Carolina, he was back on his feet.

His temples throbbed.

Everything is under control. Nothing is ever under control.

Carolina had been unfaithful to him.

Like the cheapest whore.

Carolina was screwing another guy at *his* hour. She didn't give a fuck about his headache. About his tiredness. About his having to go back to work on Monday. Having to talk nicely and keep smiling. Not losing his temper. Boosting sales.

"Hell's fuckin' bells . . ."

Carolina is a bitch in heat, he chalked on an imaginary wall.

He made up his mind to call Renata. She was a friend of hers, sort of. Well, to the extent two women working in that profession could be friends. She used to talk to him frequently enough about Renata, whom she had kind of adopted. Taught her the tricks of the trade. She'd given him her phone number the moment they started seeing each other. If you can't reach me, you should try Renata, she'd told him back then. There'd never been any need to.

Renata answered the phone.

He didn't have to go into any details about who he was before she said: oh, right, the 7 P.M. customer, aren't you? No, she knew nothing about Carolina. Nothing whatsoever. They hadn't seen each other in days. But she was available herself. Sure, right away.

He jumped into his car and drove back to the city.

A tumble with Renata, a tumble with Renata, kept ringing through his head.

It was getting dark.

On his way, he drove past Carolina's block. All the lights were off. Totally off. He groped his way around the neighborhood till he found the right address.

Renata was waiting for him in a satin gown. Her curves hinted she was naked underneath. She was medium height, plump, and she looked somehow mischievous.

"While you undress, I'll go to the bathroom," she said.

He listened to her peeing for a long time.

The flat was dingy—two adjoining rooms. Probably rented. Sparsely furnished with odd pieces. A country rug for a bedspread. He lowered himself into a loose-springed armchair and started undressing listlessly. The atmosphere of impoverished improvisation depressed him. Not an ounce of warmth, not an ounce of imagination. Not one flower. At Carolina's place everything had been shipshape.

He listened to Renata washing her hands and spraying herself. He didn't hear her flush the toilet, though.

He watched her enter, brisk and roly-poly, crotch shaved. She'd left her gown in the bathroom.

"What's up? Are we feeling a bit grumpy today?"

He nodded his assent. She started undressing him expertly.

"We can't afford to be grumpy," she grumbled.

She stood him on his feet as for some kind of physical and moved into gear. She started by nibbling at his nipples with her teeth, then little by little glided down towards his pubis. She was giving off a strong odor of cheap deodorant. Yet he had to admit she was adroit at using her tongue, she was almost as good as Carolina. When performing the act of fellatio, Carolina had once explained, unless you can make good use of your tongue, you'll just botch the whole thing. Ever since, he'd been always alert to that particular skill. He felt his member beginning to get stiff and his tiredness seemed to disperse. While getting on with her business, Renata watched him with her big blue eyes and attempted to smile at him, which made her face look rather sinister: like a snarling dog fiercely defending its bone.

"Now, that's more like it . . . Who's a pretty-pretty baby? Let's put a nice hat on, so we don't catch cold." She went on talking to his sex while completely ignoring the rest of him.

She pulled one of the chest drawers open and produced a condom. She ripped the package open with her teeth. She caught its tip between her lips, dropped to her knees, and before unrolling it down his penis, she started chomping on it the way babies do a pacifier—imitating a baby's gurgling cries all the while: ngwa-aa! ngwa-aa! ngwa-aa! He found it quite funny. He smiled.

"You liked my toy, didn't you?"

He nodded his assent.

"Let's get down to business and chase all your troubles away," she said, bursting with optimism and cheerfulness, as if it'd been ages since she'd last done it.

He positioned himself behind her. Her back was broad and powerful.

"You're from Transylvania?" he asked, panting slightly.

"How did you know?" she replied with another question, her voice muffled by a pillow.

"I could tell by your accent," he went on, a barely audible tremor in his voice.

"If you don't like it this way, we can change position . . ."

"Nah, this suits me fine . . . we can talk while we're at it . . ."

Her groin, not quite recently shaven, prickled him a bit. He found she had rough skin in that area, somewhat leathery. Professionally calloused, flashed through his mind.

"You from somewhere in the country?" he asked, no hint of disdain in his voice.

"Yea, a village not far from Cloo-oojj . . . but how'd you figure that out?" she queried him earnestly, her voice seeming to rise from the bottom of a well.

"Well . . . it was that rug . . . gave me the clue," he said in a quiet voice.

"Yup, it's from Mom. It's very precious to me. I take it along wherever I go working . . ."

Then they both gave up talking as things were moving to a crescendo.

When he was spent, he eased himself onto his back in satisfaction, eyes closed. His headache was beginning to let up. Renata sprang to her feet to walk off her accumulated stiffness.

"What about having another go?" she asked him cheerfully.

He signaled to her with his finger: he wasn't game.

"Maybe next Friday," he added a moment later, forcing the words out.

"I didn't want to tell you right away, but since you're bound to find out anyway . . . looks like Carolina might have found herself someone. She might leave the profession . . . At least that's what people say . . ." she said, ill at ease.

He said nothing. She joined him in his silence.

A few moments later he heard her going to the bathroom again. A series of obscene plops, this time followed by the sound of a flush.

He rose heavily and started getting into his clothes.

He left her money on the table and cleared out while he could still hear the shower.

Back home he jumped into bed with his clothes on, a glass of brandy in his hand.

Eyes boring into the ceiling.

All that remained in his head was the echo of that prolonged piss, followed by obscene plops.

TRANSLATED FROM ROMANIAN BY JEAN HARRIS AND FLORIN BICAN

sons

BERNARD COMMENT

A Son

"Orange juice." The label in red letters on a white placard seemed decisive, rather too much so for this mixture of concentrate and water. That's the most deplorable thing about chain and low-scale hotels: breakfast, this simulacrum of luxury divested of any attention for the guest. A flabby croissant, a jar of marmalade, two strips of cheese under plastic, an apple that's too green and too smooth, sometimes some grapes out of season, looking Botoxed, with thick, flavorless skins, and coffee, there's a coffee machine, we always have a slightly stupid look before a clipped conversation, especially in the morning when we haven't slept well.

The notary public saw me first, it's not charming at all, but you're close to it all, to the cemetery, to the house, if you took a room that looked out on the courtyard, it wouldn't be too noisy, the Périphérique is still far away, and in this weather the windows stay shut, he sniggered. It's been raining for about an hour, with a low sky, everything is gloomy. The ceremony takes place at ten. I would have liked to get an umbrella at the reception desk, the lady looked confused, no, monsieur, we don't have those, she might as well have said, this isn't a palace, you'll have to take care of yourself here, go on and find a store that sells those, I went out into the drizzle, going down side streets whenever I could. When I came to the cemetery entrance, it was early, too early.

I crossed the paths between the graves, thinking about going out the other exit, in this long narrow rectangle between the lanes of the Périphérique and the boulevards des Maréchaux, but the second door, black and solid iron, was shut, I had to retrace my steps and then go around the surrounding wall almost to the Châtillon gate where I finally found some newspapers. I couldn't start the day without having read the paper, the sports scores, the major political events, that night's TV shows, like a promise against boredom, but I told myself right away that this wouldn't be smart, to show up at a father's funeral with a newspaper in my pocket. I scanned the headlines, the general information predating what I'd heard on the radio this morning, the sports pages were boring, I discreetly threw the folded-up paper in a trash receptacle, one of those green plastic bags fluttering in the wind. I only had to wait ten minutes, we were meeting at the entrance, I hadn't had any desire to be present for the closing of the coffin, in any case I would be alone, for whatever might happen.

In 1998 he decided to come live here, for the convenience of a ground-floor apartment, the notary public said, he lived entirely on the ground floor, the upper floors were only useful for storing things, this house was a nice setup, and he joked about no longer being in the center of Paris, but he didn't go there much anymore, the attached garage was how he made his decision, you'll get a great price for it, the market's up again, the neighborhood to the south's getting trendy, there's a few celebrities in the area. I replied that we were going to bury my father, and as for the rest, we would see to it later, this was without question the first time I'd used the phrase "my father" out loud. The notary public understood, but he kept talking, the layout was simple, everything was ready for us, no possible contestation, there wasn't anybody left in his family, you're the last and sole representative. I thought that my mother must have been the last, at the time, she had been the last since her childhood, an orphan at three years old, malnourished, anemic, and graceful, with a fragile beauty, terribly fragile, but he was the one who would know.

The hearse started up, an elegant Mercedes, the red and black gate rose, I followed on foot, the burial plot wasn't too far to the right. When the notary public came, I had to greet him, we were the only ones there aside from the two funeral home employees, but also because he had a face that matched his voice, and a raincoat on, I told myself. We could have asked for a priest, or an old friend, surgeons always had stories to tell, they thought of themselves as saviors, playing with the line between life and death, but it seems that he hadn't been in touch with anyone for three or four years, was completely isolated, even from myself, he had stopped sending these pathetic letters that arrived more or less frequently for all five years, the memories, the regrets, how he had loved my mother, and how that love had been stronger than he had been, I remember that about him, he couldn't sustain it anymore, I had every reason to bear a grudge against him, but he would have loved to see me again, to know more about me, about my studies, about my life now, the last letter must have come in 2002, with forceful handwriting that had pressed down on the paper with a Bic pen, like a prescription, contrary to what somebody might have said to me he didn't really know the risks, or the seriousness of the risks, she wanted a baby at any cost, only motherhood would give structure to her life, jobs in healthcare were rarely careers, no matter what people claimed, it was just a way to earn some money, or to ward off one's fears, but for her, it was a full commitment, such determination that life gave her, what destinies followed, he put together sentences like that, an exceptional midwife, who wanted to have that same experience, he doubted that any other baby in the world had been more wanted than I was, this lachrymosity disgusted me, and then, for five years, silence, no more news, not one letter. It's true that with Carole and her children we had moved abroad in 2003 without any forwarding instructions for the mailman. But I doubt that he wrote. I'm sure he let it pass.

The notary public walked with me to the cemetery exit, he was parked nearby, and when he went his way he told me, you've seen that the burial plot is set aside for two people, your father insisted it be like that, I don't know what your intentions are, and this isn't the time, but for what it's worth, the fee's been paid for a very long time, you know your father, he liked to plan for the long term, not to have to depend on anybody else. I replied curtly that no, I didn't know my father. I didn't have any memories of the first four years. Or they were hazy.

I came back to the boulevard Brune, inexplicably calm at this late hour in the morning, in the middle of the week. A tram passed, almost silently, then a few cars, going slow. I walked nonchalantly, aimlessly, in the emptiness of the hours to come. A new tram came toward me, it gave out a little chime. A strange chime, in juxtaposition with the machine's modernity. It reminded me of the milkman's van, elsewhere, at my aunt's, in Switzerland, she who I called my aunt, anyway, by some strange convention, she's been dead for several years, by a lake, I believe that she was happy at the end of her life, alone, sipping aperitifs and watching television or putting together the pieces of a jigsaw puzzle, she wrote me every week, I went to see her three or four times a year, then my kids were born, we moved away from Europe, didn't get back in touch when we returned, after so much time it would have been too difficult, I learned about her death from a neighbor to whom she always spoke highly of me and my family, her words filled with pride. I took the milk can and went down the stairs whenever the piercing chimes pealed far off so I wouldn't miss the truck, and I loved the noise of the ladle that brought up milk from the huge *boille*, that's the word we used there, the *boille*, there was a steel footboard at the back of the truck so kids could get up enough to see over the counter, we tipped him, then we put the other coins in our pockets, a secret we all shared, it was a little bit of money for candy, sometimes lollipops, usually chewing gum.

The small Hungarian cemetery was unusually beautiful the day I went, I had just turned eighteen and gotten my driver's license, it was nearly the end of spring, my aunt had given me access to my bank account, enough in there to keep up my studies, long years of studies according to my father's instructions, I had taken a bit out for this short trip. There were trees everywhere in there, the forest was beyond, a big forest of slender, leafy trees swaying in the wind, like a sonata of souls. Right below my mother's name were the two dates, 1953 and 1978, in a big square where other members of my family lay side by side: her parents born in 1934 and 1935, died in 1956; uncles, aunts, grandparents on my father's side. I thought that I would have liked to be buried there as well, one day, near the one I'd cost so dearly, and with all these people I'd never known, but later, several years ago, with Carole, we discovered the Tadoussac cemetery, close to where we lived, on the left bank of Saint-Laurent, and there as well I thought it would be nice, or peaceful, to spend my afterlife there, with small steles covered in red tiles, as if that mattered in the least. But here at Montrouge, in this tangled earth between rent-controlled apartments and the Périphérique? No, thank you.

The notary public insisted that I had to have the keys to the house, he had a copy just in case. I had to at least stop by, get some idea of the place. The keychain was weighted with an iron ball, which sagged in my vest pocket. I ordered some skate with capers, the pub was nearly empty, a few old women also alone at their tables, or a few possibly illicit couples kissing over their wine glasses, and businessmen, all part of an old world that still exists. My mother couldn't swallow the smallest bite of meat, it seemed. Those were the only kinds of memories I'd retained. Or, well, not memories, but rather information, picked up here and there. The letters I received didn't include any concrete details. Once, shortly after my wedding, he sent me a few pictures, including one of my mother, with long black hair, a few gray streaks already, at least this was a problem with the picture, a long and very thin nose, a large mouth with thin lips, she wore a red-and-green-and-yellow-checkered dress, the colors were a bit dated, it was a Polaroid, her shoulders were thin, bony, the bags under her eyes betrayed her sadness, but her body was lively, there was a clear strength, maybe even some happiness, something hidden but joyous, I like this picture that I've moved each year into yet another daily planner, maybe this is the reason I don't want a tablet computer, not even the iPad that Carole pressed on me just before this trip, she had downloaded two or three movies to kill time, and pictures of our kids, from our last vacation, it's clear we're happy, tranquil days in store.

He must have known the risks that she was incurring, she'd consulted him because he had a good reputation, he was well-known, a very big deal, in a slightly different field, but he inspired confidence, people talked about him, attributed miracles to him, so she did everything she could to arrange a meeting, and that's how they met, because she worked in a different department in a different building, there was barely any chance, if any at all, that their paths would cross by accident. He would have to wait months until a decisive meeting. Her overwhelming desire for a child must have touched him, or unexpectedly awakened a similar desire in him, one of those groundless desires that spontaneously appears and stubbornly develops into reality, come hell or high water, her fragility, his age, fifty-three years old, and soon came the wedding, a small ceremony, few friends, mostly colleagues, this mix of professors and nurses that almost seemed like a cliché. A few months later, she became pregnant. Her gift, her fate. I don't really know how he got by during the three or four years he had me with him, when I was with him, when we were together, nannies I suppose, or babysitters, a few of whom probably ended up in his bed, my aunt always said he was a seductive man, people didn't say no to him, the surgeon's charm, both financial and metaphysical, I didn't understand that word when I was a child and a teenager, I'm not sure I understand it today, it's a word that inspires a little bit of fear.

As I left the pub, it wasn't raining anymore, but the clouds were still heavy, very heavy, and a faint fog loomed. I debated about taking the avenue Jean-Moulin, and finally decided on the noisy and chaotic avenue de Général-Leclerc, they said the liberation had come from the south, but the disembarkation happened in the west, even the northwest of Paris, I was lost among my reflections when suddenly I found myself struck by a new calmness. There wasn't any more traffic around me, men were stopped, seized by fear, and there was nothing but the emergency lights of two ambulances facing each other and two fire trucks across the street. I saw first a motorcycle frame that was still smoking under the fire-fighting foam that glazed it with a drab gray, then the raised stretcher that two firemen were carrying to their truck, without any IVs or other signs that the victim would live. They had just left the scene, clearly, and put aside the body wrapped in a silvery cloth and covered again with a sheet over its legs. Everything was quiet, the nurses had a haggard look in the cold, one of them grimaced, the police took action, assessed the scene around the car that had struck him, and suddenly I felt death, the brutal and sudden weight of death, with sadness, despondency, and some kind of compassion, a deep compassion for this man that they had slid into the back of a fire truck and who was probably my age and had children as well and a stupid move, the wrong decision, a pointless attempt, an accident, bang, it was all over in minutes. I was afraid, standing there on the sidewalk. Afraid to walk, afraid to cross streets, afraid of the noises that returned little by little as I approached the Périphérique. I had wanted to buy a little something for the kids and for Carole, but I wasn't in the right frame of mind for something like that, I couldn't think about anything other than the accident, or that femme fatale named Fate, or that woman who was perhaps getting a phone call right now that would bring about the collapse of her life, of the work she had dedicated so much of her life to. I was almost ready to cry, but it was cold, a cold wind came, followed by rain that was turning to snow, just as they had said this morning in the weather report.

I called Carole on my cell phone, it did me good to hear her voice, our kids in the background, I heard their laughter, their screams, I didn't really know what to say. I talked about the funeral, about my unease there, the house, she said let it go, don't worry about the past, it's okay to give it up, I know it, you can say no, after all you've certainly got the right, he's not going to be bothered, your father, you don't owe him anything, we don't need his shit, I was surprised to hear her using that word, not because of the word itself, but because it meant she was annoyed, or even outraged, she who was always so calm, so gracious around people, I told her I would call in the evening, because I needed to lie down now, I hadn't slept well the night before.

When I walked out of another, lighter drizzle into the hotel, there was a message from the notary public for me to call him back. His secretary told me that he was busy, that she would leave him a note because she had to leave early today to take care of her son. I turned on the television, without paying any attention, I switched from one channel to the next. I almost dozed off, and when the phone rang, when I answered, I could tell from his voice that the notary public was embarrassed, that he didn't know how to tell me, it's a secret, there wouldn't be any red tape, the rooms have never been listed and as such no one else could have any legal claim on them, and anyway none of that changes anything, nobody has any idea, but after all, I thought that I should let you know, you seemed so distant this morning, so closed-off, but listen, your father ran some tests, I don't know exactly when or why, you were very little, it was when you were still living with him, and these tests, how should I put this, these tests completely changed things, I think he wasn't able to handle it, it was impossible, you know, in any case, he couldn't handle it at all, you weren't there for no reason, of course, but he named you as his heir, his sole heir, as you know, that makes you a pretty rich man, believe me, and so I thought it was important that you knew, now you can do what you want, it's none of my business anymore. I hung up the phone carefully.

The skate isn't enough to hold me over. I'm hungry, but it's too early for dinner. I'll sleep a bit first, in the darkness of the room, with the tune of rainfall against the window.

TRANSLATED FROM FRENCH BY JEFFREY ZUCKERMAN

RAY FRENCH

Migration

We're standing on the banks of the Humber river, my father and I, the two of us enjoying the sun, the pleasant breeze. This is a rare outing for him. His loss of memory, a gradual loosening of his grip on the world, making him increasingly reluctant to leave home, where he's surrounded by things that are familiar, that can be named. But, today, he is coping well with the unfamiliarity all around him, remarkably well in fact. Who knows when there'll be another day like this—I'm determined we make the most of it.

To our right is the Humber Bridge. He gazes at it admiringly and says, "That must have taken some work, boy."

The cue to take my notebook from my pocket, flip to the page where I'd scrawled some notes while reading the display about the bridge at the Information Centre. He likes facts, cherishing their lack of ambiguity—clear and solid signposts in a shape-shifting world.

"It took 480,000 tonnes of concrete and 11,000 tonnes of steel wire to build it," I tell him. When I glance up at him he's alert, focused; nothing grabs his attention like detailed information about construction. He worked as a labourer all his life, this is his currency, these are things that still bring him satisfaction.

"That's enough wire," I continue, "to stretch one and a half times across the world."

"Fecking hell!"

I knew he'd love that one. He shakes his head and looks back at the bridge.

"That took some work alright."

It's good to see him re-engage with the world. There should be more days like this.

"When the winds reach eighty miles an hour," I say, encouraged by his reaction, "the bridge bends by up to three meters in the middle. That's close to ten feet—amazing, isn't it?"

Bad idea. His face grows taut, worried, a nerve begins to jump under his eye. This drags him back to some dark and threatening place.

"Nature is fierce, boy. It doesn't matter how hard he tries, man will never beat it." He shakes his head emphatically, "Never."

I wonder if he's remembering the pitch and roll of the British navy destroyer on which he served in the Second World War. It must have been a terrifying experience, toiling away as a stoker in the bowels of the ship, knowing that if it went down, he would go down with it.

He looks at the bridge again and says, "I wouldn't want to be on that on a windy day."

"You'd be safe," I say gently, "you wouldn't actually feel the bridge moving."

He looks doubtful. When I was young he was brave to the point of recklessness, burning with manic energy, refusing to ever compromise.

I'll fecking show the lot of 'em.

In fact, while we're on the subject of bridges, he once got into a scuffle with a Military Policeman while crossing one in Berlin shortly after the war—it ended when my father threw him into the Spree. Oh yes, he was a tough character back then, well able to stand up for himself. But, as he grew older, something lurking inside that he'd kept at bay for so long by sheer willpower, some dark and twisted thing, grew stronger, began to corrode his spirit.

No more talk about bridges bending in high winds, I change the subject.

"Did you know there used to be brickyards all along here?"

There's little evidence of that now, instead a thick band of reeds, standing pale gold in the sun, then mud, beyond that the brown, churning Humber. I make a sweeping gesture with my arm, encompassing the bank from the bridge right up to where we're standing.

"At one time there were thirteen firms along here making bricks and tiles. In the mid 1930s they were making over a million bricks a year."

"Is that so? Hard work too, I'll bet."

Dad's expression lightens; he liked hard work, knows what it means. I could have taken him to one of the museums in Hull, but they would never have held his interest. He looks around, picturing this as a place bustling with activity—people digging clay, shaping it into bricks in wooden moulds and stacking them to dry, others firing the kilns. I tell him about Blythe's Tile Yard, nearer the bridge, about ten minutes walk from where we're standing, which has been reopened and makes bricks and tiles using the old methods, without using toxic chemicals. From there you can, if you look hard enough, make out the marks where the train lines once ran just below the Humber bank. Further along are the remains of the posts which held up the jetties once dotted along this stretch of the Humber, the river filled with sloops and keels collecting cargoes of bricks, tiles, and rope. It must have been a stirring sight—the Humber was one of the last places in the country you could see working boats under sail. These days Hull is just another desolate northern town, its streets crammed with drunks every weekend.

"Shall we walk down that way a bit?" I ask him.

"Aye, we will—come on."

Though slow, he's steady on his feet today. So different to how he is at home, a pale, bent, shuffling figure, head down, arms wavering, as he makes his way painstakingly across the room. Here he's alert to his surroundings, looking around, noticing things.

"What are those yokes?"

I explain that the broken chunks of bricks and tiles lying in the grass and reeds are the remains of the long gone industry. I pick up a jagged half-brick and hand it to him, watch him turn and examine it, run his thumb along the edge.

"You could build yourself a house out of all the bricks lying around here."

"You could."

He weighs it in his hand, enjoying the solidity, the connection with his working life, back when he was young and strong, before so many things frightened him.

He nods approvingly, "They knew what they were doing in those days. They built things to last."

"They did."

We walk on another few hundred yards, but I can see he's beginning to tire a little now. This has been a long day for a man who rarely ventures beyond the circuit of bedroom, living room, bathroom, and kitchen.

"Shall we go back?"

"Aye, I think we will."

At that moment the sun, obscured by clouds for the last few minutes, emerges again, and he stays where he is and he lifts his head to the sky and closes his eyes. He always loved the sun. When I was a boy he would be brown as a berry all summer from working outdoors, never burning like so many other Irish people. I follow his example and close my eyes too. There's no sound except the water lapping, the stiff breeze, the occasional cry of a bird. You could be back in Ireland, in Cullenstown, County Wexford, right back there on the strand, on a fine spring day. I wonder if that's where Dad is thinking of now, back at the beginning of his journey, his life before him, knowing nothing of this country, of what it is to be a husband, or a father, what it feels like to grow old and frail.

As we're walking back to the Information Centre, I tell him that I'll show him where I work afterwards, then we'll get something to eat before driving back home.

"Where is it you work?" he asks sharply, as if I've been hiding it from him.

"The University."

"A university?"

"Yes, Dad."

"Which one?"

"Hull."

He stops to stare at me, wide-eyed.

"Jayzus, doesn't that beat all. A university? You've done well for yourself, boy."

I can't help smiling. If he had any idea of the enormous expectations, the hopes he'd carried on those narrow shoulders. That he still carries, despite everything.

"What do you do there?"

"I teach."

"A teacher. That's grand. What is it you teach?"

"Creative Writing."

I watch him mulling this over, but growing a little impatient now. I get fed up of repeating myself, wanting him to retain some information about my life, for it to have some meaning for him. A smile begins to form on his lips.

"Writing?"

I nod and he laughs scornfully, "You'd think they'd be able to write properly by the time they got to University. Christ, what's the world coming to?"

I agree that it's gone to hell in a handcart. When we start walking again, he's still chuckling to himself, convinced I've pulled a fast one—what a way to make a living.

I must try to get him out more often. At home, the house is always overheated, the television on, way too loud, all day long. Sometimes, as he looks around him, I'm sure he's wondering how he got here, sitting next to this middle-aged man he believes is probably his son, he certainly looks familiar, struggling to make conversation with him. I am careful to call him Dad often, frequently mentioning my mother, reminding him that this woman, this child that I have brought with me are my own family. What I'm trying to do, what I want, so much, is to place him in a familiar network of associations and meanings. Native Americans speak of having a map in the head, a way of knowing where one is in relationship to the land, its history, society, and all living beings. Most days now, my father has no map, all meaning draining away from his surroundings.

Yes, I really must try to get him out more often.

Back at the Information Centre I get two teas from the machine, bring them across to one of the tables. We sip our drinks looking out at a couple of swans gliding across one of the flooded clay pits. Here at Far Ings, they have created a nature reserve reclaimed from an industry based on digging up the land. In fact this visit is partly a reconnaissance mission, I had the idea of bringing my Creative Writing students here for inspiration, getting them away from the seminar room and out into the world. Unlike the quarries that I visited recently, where you could feel the poignant absence of what is no longer there, here a kind of balance has been restored. When I explain how this place came about my father is delighted. It's a process that chimes with his belief that the land was here before us, and would survive our tenancy, still be here long after we have gone.

"If I had my way," he says, "I'd turn every factory, every site that I'd ever worked on into a place like this. They've done a good job here, a damned good job."

We sit for quite some time without the need for conversation, at ease in each other's company.

Before we head off, we look at the display about the various birds it's possible to see at Far Ings, and the incredible journeys that they make to reach here. The pink-footed geese coming from Arctic Russia, the swallows and sedges from South Africa, the sand martins from Chad.

"Isn't it amazing?" says Dad, "the journeys these birds make."

We read the panel informing us that scientists still don't fully understand why birds migrate.

"What about you, Dad? Why did you migrate?"

I watch him thinking about this for a while, then he says, "Half the people I went to school with left too, sure there was nothing for us at home." He starts to laugh, "A great flock of Paddies migrating, that's what we were—thousands of the buggers descending on Britain."

This a glimpse of his old self re-emerging—irreverent, scornful. It used to get him into trouble sometimes, when people tried to have a serious discussion about the burning issues of the day.

We look through the window, see a man below with a pair of binoculars and a camera strung around his neck.

"Bird watching, aye, there's plenty of fellas who love it. I never did it meself. It looks a grand hobby, though, very relaxing."

But he did do it. Sometimes I'd catch him standing utterly still and silent back in Wales, riveted by the flocks of swallows gathering on telegraph poles in September, before wheeling away in formation and heading back to Africa. Hard not to think he was envying them their return to their homeland, while he was stuck here for another year. Unlike the swallows and sedges, the sand martins and pink-footed geese, he never made it back to where he came from.

You move for work or education, for what you think are short-term goals, but before you know it you are putting off your return home for another year, then another. There is a sense of exhilaration whenever I cross the Severn Bridge to Wales and leave England behind. For a few days I feel that I finally belong somewhere—I rediscover my map in the head. So why the surge of relief when I leave again a few days later? I wonder if Dad used to feel something similar when he was departing Ireland, shrugging off myriad obligations, feeling suddenly weightless?

My father asks, "What is it you do again?"

I explain about teaching at Hull University once more.

"Where's that?"

"Just there, across the river."

He looks to his right, over the murky water into Yorkshire.

"Does your mother know?"

I tell him she does.

"Has she told them in Ireland?"

"She has. I'll take you there later, to the University. I'll show you my office."

"You have an office?"

The wonder in his voice reminds me how when I got my degree, many years ago now, he said, "Christ, you're made, boy, bleddy well made. You'll never have to work outside in the rain and the cold again."

When we're back outside and heading for the car park I realise that I've left my notebook on one of the tables. I suggest that he waits in the car while I run back and get it.

"Ah no," he says, "I think I'll go and sit on that bench over there next to the water."

For a moment I'm worried about leaving him outside on his own like that. But he looks so happy at the prospect that I dismiss my fears.

"Okay, Dad, alright. If that's what you want."

"I think I'll do a bit of bird watching while I'm here."

I'm not sure if this is a joke or not.

"Are you going to take it up as a hobby?"

He hesitates, looking across the water into the reeds.

"I think I will."

He seems serious.

"I'll get you a pair of binoculars for your birthday then, shall I?"

"Aye, just the job."

I'll buy us both a pair, and we'll come back and look for bitterns and marsh harriers. We'll stand side by side in one of the hides, I'll bring a flask of tea, a pack of sandwiches. We'll make a day of it. I walk over to the bench with him, watch him settle down, stretch out his legs and turn up his face to the late afternoon sun.

"You sure you're alright?"

"I'm grand," he replies, "go on, take as long as you want, I'm in no hurry, sure."

As I walk back up the stairs to the Information Centre I'm humming. If he's feeling this good then maybe we can go for a drink. Suddenly I have this desire to see him supping a pint of Guinness, a thread of the creamy head coating his lips, him gripping the glass and savouring the aftertaste.

"That's a grand pint."

Yes, that's what we'll do. We passed a pub on the way, The Sloop Inn, that looked old-fashioned, friendly, unthreatening—we'll go there, have an early drink and get something to eat while we're at it.

The notebook is where I left it, lying on the table, I pick it up, pop it in my bag and amble back downstairs and into the car park.

The bench is empty. Of course it is. I look around, just to be sure, but he's nowhere to be seen. When it's clear that he's gone, that our brief time together is over, I feel a hole opening up inside me. For a long time I just stand there in the middle of the car park, slowly getting used to the world without him all over again. It felt so very good to have him back, even for such a short time. We get on much better now he's dead.

It's impossible to predict when he'll return again. The one thing I can be sure of, it won't be when I expect him to, it's not something that can be planned. The last time I was back home I walked the length of the road where I grew up, clotted with memories from the railway line at one end to the dock gates at the other. Halfway down I stopped outside the site of the Whitehead Iron and Steel factory, where Dad worked for many years, now a waste ground awaiting development. It was not so difficult to close my eyes and smell, once again, the hot oil and chemical stench, to hear the piercing scream of metal being sliced at high speed. But there was no hint of my father's presence there. I stood outside our old house until the new owner drew back the curtains and peered at me suspiciously and I turned away and left. No hint of him there either. At the end of the road I turned left, following the map in my head, and walked down Coomassie Street. When I was a boy my father and I found the name thrillingly exotic and mysterious, we would turn it over in our mouths, elongating the vowels. I closed my eyes and strained to hear his voice—nothing. Then on to Mill Parade, with the Transporter Bridge to my right—how many times did Dad and I take that to the far side of the river, leaning over the rail to look down onto the muddy banks of the Usk below? In Church Street I came to a pub where the two us would sometimes go when I was back from University. These were expeditions prompted by my mother—*why don't you two go out for a drink together?* These father/son outings were filled with awkward silences, our eyes wandering to the TV perched high on the wall. There, in the nearly empty lounge, I lingered over my drink, sure that this would be the place, but I was wrong again. No, his appearances are just as impossible to predict as that sudden, urgent desire to ring home, before I remember there's no one there now, both of them gone, the house sold.

But, whenever I think of him, the memories still so alive, his presence still so powerful, it's impossible to believe that he's no longer in this world. And I think of him often. I know that I'll think of him the next time I'm sitting in my office at the University, the rain beating against the window.

MIKE MCCORMACK

Of One Mind

Sometimes I feel young and sometimes I feel old and sometimes I feel both at the same time. This trick of being in two minds, of weighing things on the one hand and then again on the other, has never been a problem for me. But, while I can hold two warring ideas in my head at the same time, and even retain a clear idea of what it is I am thinking about, I am sometimes less sure of who or what it is that is doing the thinking. This weightlessness takes hold of me, this sense that somehow I am lacking essential ballast. I suspect it's one of the gifts of my generation, a generation becalmed in adolescence, a generation with nothing in its head or its heart and with too much time on its hands.

Lately however I'm experiencing something new and it has taken me a while to recognise it. Obscured behind amazement and something like awe it has taken me weeks to see it clearly as the thing it really is. When I finally did get it straight in my mind I could hardly believe it. To the best of my knowledge I have never experienced anything like it before, nor, living the type of life I've done, is there any reason why I should have.

Take this example, an incident with my eight-year-old son only last week . . .

It was, on the face of it, a simple enough disappointment involving a school trip to an open farm outside the city. Giddy with anticipation, Jamie had talked about nothing else in the days leading up to it and, when I had met his questions with memories of my own upbringing on a small farm in west Mayo, his expectations had soared; the chance to see something of his Dad's childhood promised to be a rare treat. But now the trip lay in ruins. Traffic congestion and a radio alarm clock flummoxed in the small hours by a power cut conspired to have us arrive at the school fifteen minutes after the bus had left. Now we stood in the stillness of his classroom, gazing at the neat rows of tables and seats and I thought to myself that surely there was no place in all the world so full of absence as an empty classroom.

And Jamie's disappointment was huge. I had no need to look down at him to know it—I could feel it rolling off him, deep noxious waves of it. Just to have me in no doubt he told me so himself.

"I'm disappointed," he said solemnly. "I can feel it here, right here." He placed his hand low on his chest and rubbed it up and down as if trying to relieve some digestive ache.

"Next week Jamie," I assured him. "We can all go next week, the three of us. I promise."

"I'm in pain," he persisted. "Severe pain."

"You'll get over it," I replied shortly. "Next week I said. Let's go."

I took him by the hand and led him out to the car. January light hung low in the sky, oppressive and tightening the muscles across my chest. I hated these winter months, the gloom that rose in my heart; summer seemed an infinity away.

"This isn't the first disappointment like this," Jamie said, as I held open the door for him. "They're beginning to mount up. I can feel the pressure."

"That bad?"

He nodded and sat in it. "Yes, that bad. I'm only telling you for your own good."

"Be a man," I blurted. My own disappointment at letting him down now made me brusque. "Put on your seatbelt."

There is of course no such thing as a simple disappointment, a small disappointment to an eight-year-old child. I've seen enough of fatherhood to know that feelings like these only come man-sized, brutally disproportionate to the job in hand, never calibrated to the dimensions of a child's world. They come with crushing intent, fully capable of annihilating their fragile universe. The wonder is that any child can survive even the slightest of them.

We drove back towards the city centre, the traffic loosened up now after the early rush hour. Jamie sat silently in the back seat. A glance in the rear-view mirror showed him gazing out the side window, his moon pale face pinched with the effort to hold back the tears.

He happened into my life over eight years ago, waking a dream of fatherhood which took me completely by surprise when it presented itself out of the blue some time before my thirtieth birthday. Before that all my visions of children came with a completeness about them which Jamie's arrival had totally confounded. Nothing in my idea of fatherhood had warned me against the fact that children do not drop fully formed out of the sky, nor of the ad hoc nature of fatherhood, which is its day-to-day idiom; basically, nothing had warned me against screw-ups like this.

"Someday," he called suddenly from the back seat, leaving the word hanging in the air.

We had pulled into the first of the two roundabouts on the western edge of the city. Rain was now falling, that resolute early morning drizzle which tells you there will be no let up for the day.

"Someday," he repeated, eying me in the rear-view mirror.

"Someday what Jamie? Speak up, don't be mumbling back there to yourself."

"Someday," he said, "when you're sitting in the visitors gallery of the criminal court listening to the jury returning a guilty verdict on all charges and hearing the judge hand down the maximum sentence with no recommendation for bail you will probably be asking yourself where did it all go wrong. Well, just to set your mind at rest, you need look no further than this morning."

"That bad?"

"I'm only telling you for your own peace of mind."

"Thank you, that's very kind of you. I'll remember that when I'm organising your appeal."

Eight years ago I blundered out of my twenties, a feckless decade of drink and dope smoking, a decade of late nights and videos lived out against a soundtrack of white boy guitar bands, a decade funded by various under the counter jobs and the most gullible welfare system in the whole country. The setting up of the nation's second-language TV station rescued me, drew me out, pallid and blinking, into the light. Being fluent in Irish scored me a contract subtitling the German and Scandinavian cartoons which bulked out the station's Irish-language quota in its early days. A month-by-month contract had opened out to a yearly one and all told I had now turned in seven of them. Each year I resolved to find something permanent and each year the relevant deadlines passed me by. This last year the cartoons had given way to captioning the station's twice-weekly soap opera which now, in its fifth year, was responsible for a big percentage of the station's advertising revenue. A job which took me all of thirty hours a week left me with more than enough time with which to split the child-minding duties with Martha, Jamie's mother.

Back then the advent of a new TV station on the outskirts of this city had drawn a new type of female into the light. Upmarket and eager, all short skirts and high boots, they had a radiance about them which gave them allure in a city which till then had seen heavy boots and woolly sweaters as the uniform of bohemian aspirations and left-wing politics. That the majority of these new sirens were merely continuity announcers, weather girls, and bit-part players in soaps did not diminish their glamour one bit; the city was grateful for their new colour and the open optimism they shed about them. This was Martha's milieu. She too had the looks and the standoffish poise of a young woman with plenty of choices. Therefore, when I met her, it was somewhat gratifying to find that in fact her status was almost as lowly as my own. She too worked temporary contracts, honing scripts for continuity announcers and weather girls, all the time dreaming of an alternate world where she wrote code for video games, specifically tactical world-building games. At the time she was working out the end of her current contract and thinking of moving to London where she hoped to find work in one of the design studios that had sprung up after the launch of the PS2.

Six months after we met a casual affair was brought to its senses by an unbroken blue line running through the window of a pregnancy test kit. Much solemn talking ensued, once more the old weighing of things against each other only this time between two minds equally adroit at seeing both sides of any story without ever necessarily reaching a decision. Finally however we did rent a semi D in one of the new estates on the city's outskirts and settled down to bringing up a child between us. After three years however we had to face up to the fact that we were hopelessly out of love with each other. With the leaking away of all physical desire, our relationship bottomed out to a colourless haunting of each other, a leaching away of all feeling from our togetherness. We woke up to the conclusion that, were it not for the child between us, we would long ago have gone our separate ways. Some time in Jamie's third year we sat down and tallied up the cost of our lives together. All things considered it hadn't been too expensive. One beloved child and the enrichment of sense and soul he had brought to us more than offset any regrets for dreams we had set aside on his account. Speaking for myself it was the kind of balance sheet I could live with. We talked into the night, mapping out the details of an amicable separation, the terms of which would come into effect three years down the road when, we blithely reasoned, Jamie would be more of an age to cope with the trauma. We gave each other the love-you-but-not-in-love-with-you speech, agreed on the you-deserve-better postscript, and then sat there ashamed of ourselves, quietly appalled that in our early thirties and after three years and a child together this was the best we could do by way of a row. How could we have felt so little? Then, in a rush of gratitude toward each other, we made love for the first time in months. The following morning, embarrassed by these faltering intimacies, we renewed the vows of the night before.

When the three years were up we sat Jamie down between us and told him that his family would now be divided between two houses. His reaction was muted, no hysterics or anxious pleading, no face down pummelling of pillows. He walked into his room, pulled the door behind him, and was not seen or heard of for the rest of that day. He came out later that evening and asked for something to eat, his face flushed, his whole being pulsing in a haze of anxiety.

A couple of weeks after that he began wetting the bed.

Lately he's got this idea, more accurately an obsession. How this idea has taken hold of him I cannot properly say but Martha dates it to the time of our breakup, the weeks and months after I moved out of our semi D and into a two-bedroomed flat in the city centre. Martha speculates that it's all part of the break-up trauma, a childlike but nonetheless canny ploy with which to win treats and privileges off both of us. I listen to Martha because she is smarter than me and more attuned to the nuances of our child. Also, with her background in game programming, she is always likely to see chains of cause and effect. But just this once I have a feeling she's wrong. Jamie's conviction runs deeper than the circumstances of our breakup; it seems to come from the very depths of him, stirring something bleak in his young soul, putting him in the way of words and ideas completely out of scale with his age.

Another example: one day he stepped into the kitchen draped in one of my old T-shirts and wearing a baseball cap back to front. His hands barely poked beyond the cuffs of the short sleeves and the baseball cap threatened to fall down over his eyes. It was a flashback to my grunge past, to a time at the beginning of the caring decade when, paradoxically, serial killers were valorised by a section of my generation as great countercultural heroes, heroic transgressors. The image leaped out in red ink, Michael Rooker in the title role, *Henry: Portrait of a Serial Killer.*

"Where did you get that?" I asked.

"The box."

"I thought I told you."

"Yeah, yeah—look at this." He held up a newspaper and tapped a headline in the middle of the page. *Playgrounds designed by SAS,* it read.

"Tell me what it says. Sit into the table, this spaghetti is done."

He pulled out a chair and sat in, spreading the paper out in front of him. "It says that children have become bored with swings and slides, too girly they think, no thrills in them, no danger. They were lying deserted all over Britain. Then someone had the idea of bringing in SAS instructors to design these assault courses and now kids can't get enough of them."

I laid the plate on the table and handed him the fork and spoon. "Eat up. Those playgrounds will be closed down in a year. Injuries and litigations, they'll be lucky to stay open a year."

Jamie shook his head. "That's where you're wrong. One broken elbow and a concussion—that's the injury list for a year in one of those playgrounds." He folded up the newspaper, took off his cap, and fell to eating. "What do you make of that, what does it mean?"

"Not with your mouth full." I handed him a napkin and he drew it across his mouth, streaking an orange blur halfway to his ears. "What would I know, kids are daft. Who knows what goes on in their heads?"

"That's true, look at me."

"Look at you indeed. Do you want to stay the night?"

"Yes."

"Finish your spaghetti and then call your mam."

"I already have."

A couple of weeks after we split up Martha told me that Jamie had begun wetting the bed. Martha took him aside and asked him about it. If fear and disappointment come only in man-size dimensions so too does embarrassment. He bolted from the kitchen and slammed the door on his bedroom. Martha bought a rubber sheet and told me not to mention it to him. A week later he brought the subject up himself.

"I need something," he said. "I'll come straight out with it."

"Yes."

"No beating around the bush or anything."

"I'm all ears."

"A request."

"Which is?"

"You won't like it."

"Jamie!"

"A beating."

"A what?"

"A beating."

He was framed in the doorway, a little study in misery. Once more he was the child wrestling with outsize miseries which threatened to engulf him.

"What have you done Jamie? Whatever it is it can't be that bad."

"It's not what I've done, it's what I'm going to do."

"And what exactly are you going to do that warrants a beating."

He pulled the chair out from the table and sat in. This is his way of late whenever he has something big to get off his chest. It seems to give him confidence, putting him in a position of strength insofar as a child is ever in such a position. But just then he looked hesitant, teetering on the threshold of a great disclosure but unsure of how to begin.

"What is it you are going to do?" I persisted.

"I come from a broken home," he began.

"No Jamie, you come from a home divided between two houses, you spend an equal time with each of us. Whoever you want."

He shook his head, the flaw in the argument too obvious even to him. It was at times like this I had the feeling Jamie was streaking ahead of me, gaining on truths and ideas which by right I should have been handing down to him.

He spoke irritably, "By any definition of the normal family I come from a broken home."

"Jamie, I'm only guessing but I don't think this is what you want to talk about."

"I wet the bed," he blurted desperately.

"Yes, I know, it's not a big thing, you'll get over it."

"I can't stop, each night I say my prayers and each morning I wake up covered in wee."

"God has a lot on his mind Jamie. He's a busy man, you might have to wait your turn. But wetting the bed is no reason for a beating."

"I'm going to do something bad, something really bad."

"We all do something bad at one time or other. What is it you're going to do?"

"I'm going to kill someone."

"That is bad," I conceded. "Do you know who this someone is— it's not me by any chance."

He threw up his hands in a gesture of unknowing. "I don't know," he said with some exasperation. "You'd want to take this serious because you'll probably blame yourself later on and I wouldn't want that."

"How do you know you're going to kill someone?"

"There are signs," he said, "indications."

"This is that T-shirt. I told you before about going through my stuff."

"It's not the T-shirt," he yelled suddenly, "you're not listening."

I held up my hands. "Okay, I'm listening now. What signs?"

"Like I've said I come from a broken home and I've started wetting the bed."

"And that's enough to turn you into a killer?" I felt distinctly odd discussing this with my eight-year-old son. Once more this sense of weightlessness came over me; I felt buoyant, unmoored from myself. From what I remembered none of the parenting manuals Martha showed me had ever covered this kind of situation. However I was certain also I had to see this conversation through to the end. "What has this to do with wanting a beating?"

"The broken home and the bed-wetting are two of the classic signifiers of serial killers in their youth. The third one is parental abuse. In order to have a complete profile I need to have a beating. That is where you come in."

"Why would you want to kill anyone?"

"It is not that I want to kill anyone—it's just that that is the way it is going to be."

"This is ridiculous Jamie. I'm sorry, there are no beatings here today."

He looked at me sadly and sighed. "You have a responsibility," he said softly. "Sooner or later the corpses will start turning up. Two with the same MO and signatures might be a coincidence but three points to a serial killer. We have to give the investigation every chance. A full profile would put a halt to me before I get into my stride."

"This is nonsense Jamie. This conversation is at an end now." I got up from the table; he grabbed my wrist.

"He was quiet," he said fervently, "he kept to himself a lot." He fixed me with a glum stare. "That's what the neighbours will say when I'm being led away. Of course long before that there will be all the other signs—the low self-esteem, the sexual inadequacies . . ." His voice trailed away.

"I'm sorry. There's no beatings here today. Or any other day for that matter."

He raised his voice. "I'm only telling you, the child is the father of the man."

I talked to Martha about this the following day. She had finally moved her computer into the small box room I'd used as a workspace when I'd lived there. A couple of personal items around the room claimed the space as her own. One of Picasso's blue women hung on the wall to her back and a series of little marble Buddhas stood ranked along the windowsill that looked down over the back garden. She knew nothing about Jamie's big idea.

"He hasn't mentioned anything to me about it. It sounds like a father and son thing."

"Does he spend much time on the Internet?"

"Only an hour or two each day, the laptop on the kitchen table where I can keep an eye on him. John, he's a good boy, I can't stop him doing everything his friends are doing at the moment. He has it tough enough as it is."

Every time she talks about Jamie I can see him in her face, the ghost of him flitting through her features: the same wide spacing of her eyes across her nose and the freckles on her forehead which stand out so vividly during these winter months. And it is clear also that if Jamie keeps growing at his present rate he is going to meet the same problems buying clothes as his mother—the narrow hips on which skirts and jeans drape sullenly and the skinny wrists which protrude beyond every sleeve no matter how generous. It pleases me to see these shades of Jamie in her; the sense of continuity gladdens me. Sometimes though I wonder if the causal chain always runs from parent to child; since Jamie's birth I could have sworn I noticed in Martha a flightiness which lay at odds with her usual downbeat moods. As for myself, while I take it for granted that there is indeed something of myself in my son, I can never quite put a finger on what this something is. If ever I press Martha on the subject she tells me airily that we are both the same age.

"This worries me Martha. You should have heard him, all these technical terms and a rationale as well. And, this beating thing."

"Did you give it to him."

"For Christ's sakes Martha!"

She grinned openly. "I know, I'm winding you up. You're so easy."

"Let's talk to him together, this has me really spooked."

She pivoted from the chair and kissed me on the cheek. Over her shoulder I could see her computer screen locked in pause, two tiny figures arrested in their progress across some heroic landscape of rolling hills toward a gloomy forest.

"Leave it to me," she said, "it might need a woman's touch."

I nodded to the screen. "What is it this time?"

She waved a narrow wrist.

"Orcland. A centuries-long dispute between elves and orcs, border violations, mineral rights, it goes back to the dawn of time. I have to tip the balance of power toward the elves, upgrade their ordnance for the second edition add-on. Market research has shown elves' approval rating has risen across all demographics. The gaming community has responded badly to seeing them getting their arses kicked so easily. I have to help tip the balance of power for the next add-on."

"They're still not going to win, the template is fixed."

"I know, I can only help them make a better fight of it. Well, fairer at least."

"What sort of job is that for a grown woman," I teased.

"The type of job that puts food and rent on the table."

I sat on her chair and gazed at the screen. Two elves were streaking toward a great forest where they would find refuge and a cache of arms. Tipping the balance of power, squaring the odds, this is the type of thing Martha did.

"Martha, how did we get to be this trivial, elves and subtitles? How did we ever get sidetracked into this shite?"

She shrugged, shook her head. "Don't ask me. But you show me another job that comes up with rent and crèche at twenty hours a week and I'll consider it. Till then I've got elves to arm." She giggled suddenly, put her hand on my shoulder. "John," she said, "don't worry, his name is Jamie, not Damien."

"Jesus, Martha."

"Sorry, I couldn't help it."

Whatever way she broached the subject she made no headway with Jamie. And whatever he said to her in reply left her in no doubt that this was something between men. No, there was no drawing him out on the subject—he'd talk it out with Dad he said. So I left him to it, hoping he might put the whole thing behind him, thinking that if he needed to talk about it badly enough he would bring the subject up in his own good time. And sure enough he did. We were sitting together on the couch after a double episode of *The Simpsons*.

"You haven't given my request any more thought?"

"No, I can't say I have, how about you?"

He squirmed round to face me, tucking his feet in under him.

"Yes, I have it all figured out. Yesterday I killed a frog, I wrote it into my diary—that covers the cruelty to animals part. One beating now and I will have a complete profile, every box ticked off. Any investigation would have to be blind not to be able to track me down. But I need that beating. One beating registered with the childcare authorities and the job will be complete." He rolled up his sleeves revealing his skinny upper arms. "You could confine your work to areas of soft tissue, my thighs and arms, places where the bruising will be obvious but not dangerous. But nothing around the head, I'd like to keep my wits around me."

"And how's that going to make me look, a registered child beater?"

"I'll clear your name. I'll say it was totally out of character, I pushed you to the end of your tether."

"You're a serial killer, who's going to believe you?"

"I'm under oath, I won't lie."

"This profile thing, that's an American template."

"So?"

"I'm saying that it may not translate across the Atlantic."

He shook his head sadly. "Dad, the world is of one mind. That's the way it is."

"No, it doesn't have to be like that. These things aren't fixed."

I put my arm round him and drew him into my side. There wasn't a pick on him, the bones in his shoulders dug into my ribs. "How do you know these things Jamie, where do you get these ideas from?"

"How does anyone know anything? I just pick them up along the way, same as anyone. This is all common knowledge."

"It's not common to me. Why don't you turn yourself in now, before you do any damage?"

"Who would believe an eight year old?" He turned his face up to me. "Would it kill you?"

"I'll never know."

He lowered his face. "It's only for your good," he said, "you'll thank me for this later on."

I sat there long after he'd gone to bed, the TV on mute.

Someone told me once that you know nothing of love till you have a child of your own. You know nothing of its unconditional demands nor the lengths you will go to protect it. And this is what I've been feeling these last few weeks, this is what spooks me. I've seen enough to know that wherever there is love there are opportunities for guilt also. It has something to do with more laws and prohibitions, more opportunities for transgression and omission.

What spooks me now is that his fear will become my fear, his terror my terror. One day it might spread from him, slip through his narrow boundaries and become mine. And, as ever, being in two minds, that old sense of weightlessness comes over me when I think these things; once more I am at a remove from myself . . . One night, at the end of your tether, the world really might be of one mind. And because you haven't the courage to be scared, the courage to take up the full duty of love, you find yourself pitched into a place beyond marvelling that you could be pushed this far. And because this is the age of reasoned hysterics and because you are haunted by his pale arms, you find yourself walking down the hall to his bedroom, to where he is tucked up fast in his dreams. And sitting on the side of his bed, lit by the light streaming in from the hall, you run through your reasons once more, squaring your story against the day when you will stand up and tell the truth, the whole truth, and nothing but the truth. And then, these things straight in your mind at last, you reach out to touch his shoulder, touch him gently, calling his name in a whisper that barely reaches into his sleep . . . "Jamie," you call, "wake up Jamie, wake up, good boy . . ."

And that you could even think these things, that for these moments you are in two minds and so divided from the better part of yourself leaves you with this question—to whom or where do you turn to now?

Americans

GYRÐIR ELÍASSON

The Music Shop

I visited a most unusual music shop the other day. Actually, it wasn't "day"; it was night and I was sound asleep during my visit. Yet in my dream I was wide-awake and walking down Vesturgata on a sunny spring evening. The air was perfectly still and all the gardens were a fresh new green. I walked almost to the end of the road, then turned off, only to find myself in a small side street. Not only had I never been down there before, as far as I knew, but I hadn't even been aware it existed.

There was a tall, blue building ahead with a flat roof and a shop on the ground floor. The sign over the door said ALADDIN'S MUSIC STORE. I couldn't quite see what Aladdin had to do with music but it had been so long since I'd read the story that I didn't give it another thought.

I'm constitutionally incapable of walking past a music shop without taking a look inside, and this time was no exception, so I climbed the low flight of steps and went in. A jangling at the door announced my entrance and a young girl emerged from a back room and said good evening.

"I just wanted to take a look at your music."

"Go right ahead," she replied. She had a lovely voice; dark hair, dark eyes.

"You're open late," I said.

"We're always open."

I walked over to the racks of CDs. For its size, the shop boasted an extraordinarily wide selection. I flicked quickly through the racks. Beethoven's Eleventh Symphony: I was pretty sure he'd never composed it, yet here it was, in a very fine German edition. It was the same with Satie's Military March for 203 Pianofortes: I knew this piece had never been performed. When Satie died, three hundred and fifty-four dirty shirts were discovered behind his piano—perhaps because he'd sweated so much when composing this work.

I moved over to the Blues section and before long found a CD by Mississippi John Hurt that got me excited; he was playing the electric guitar and singing songs by Neil Young. The evening sun shone in through the large window at the front of the shop and there was a bluish radiance inside, though no lights were on. The girl was still standing by the counter, gazing absentmindedly into the evening light.

"I'd like to listen to this one."

"Of course."

She went round the back and re-emerged with a machine that I took at first for some kind of vacuum cleaner. It reminded me rather of one of the old cylindrical Hoovers; silver like them, with a long, gray, concertinaed windpipe.

She put the CD in the machine and handed me a pair of headphones: "You're welcome to go outside in the sunshine and listen there. Just drag the windpipe with you and carry the machine in your hand."

I thanked her and opened the door, with the machine in one hand and the earphones on my head. The door closed gently on the windpipe, which stretched across the threshold as I went out.

I met no resistance when I pulled on the windpipe; it yielded every time. The weather was so glorious that I decided to walk a little farther, down to the corner at the western end of the street, where I could sit on a bench bathed in evening sunshine. I listened, blown away by the sound of Mississippi John performing songs by Neil Young, although I knew perfectly well that he had never played those songs, and that Neil Young had probably never even composed them—at least not to my knowledge.

Shortly afterward another customer came out of the shop bearing the same kind of machine as me. He dragged the windpipe after him like a fireman wielding his hose and for a moment I was afraid he was going to extinguish the blazing sun.

But he just took a seat on the bench beside me, plainly absorbed in his listening. I didn't want to disturb him so we just nodded at one another, with those gray metal cylinders lying between us and the windpipes trailing back up the street, gleaming in the fading light. I never see anything without being reminded of something else, so my thoughts strayed to divers' breathing tubes. It was such a short distance down to the shore in this western part of town, and the sun was about to sink into the sea.

The man took off his headphones, staring into the middle distance. Behind us the shadows of the houses were deepening. I turned off the CD player and removed my headphones as well.

"What were you listening to?" I asked.

"Oscar Peterson on the recorder," he replied.

At first I thought he was joking but then I noticed the CD case on the bench beside him and there was no mistake: Oscar Peterson, solo recorder recital, recorded New York, 1967. The man was middle-aged, graying at the temples, and a little overweight, in a green shirt, with a large pair of sunglasses in the breast pocket. After a moment or two he took out the sunglasses, put them on and now seemed to be gazing straight into the fiery-red sun.

"It's a good shop," I said.

He nodded in agreement, then, putting his headphones back on, he picked up the CD case, gripped the player in one hand, and stood up. As he made his way slowly back toward the shop, the windpipe swayed and coiled behind him like a snake dancing to a fakir's pipe.

I got to my feet as well. A cool breath of wind had begun to blow in from the sea and everything had taken on a twilight hue. Walking back I didn't listen to anything except the low hissing of the machine's windpipe as it dragged over the tarmac. I returned the music apparatus to the shop and told the girl behind the counter that I would be back later to buy the CD. Could she reserve it for me?

She said she was afraid she couldn't do that.

I left the shop, heading back the way I had originally come; walked all the way home, got into bed and fell asleep and didn't wake up until the dream was over. I haven't managed to go back to the shop to buy Mississippi John Hurt in spite of repeated efforts every night to return.

I hope it won't go out of business.

TRANSLATED FROM ICELANDIC BY VICTORIA CRIBB

ARI BEHN

Thunder Snow AND
When a Dollar Was a Big Deal

THUNDER SNOW

It was days before we talked to each other. We slept one on each side of the scruffy room we had been allotted by Madame Rosa in the guesthouse in Tangier. We were two Norwegians who, independently of each other, had decided to explore North Africa. I wasn't at all shy in those days and spoke to anyone, which is precisely why I avoided my fellow countryman. I hadn't come here to hang out with Norwegians.

One evening he was standing on the terrace speaking in a low voice to Madame Rosa. He was wearing a shirt and waistcoat, had long hair and a hat. There was a tangle of beads around his neck and on his feet he wore pointed boots that must have been much too hot. He was a tall, handsome man who called himself Thunder Snow. I was short and sloppily dressed in jeans and a T-shirt with *Ramones* printed on it over a faded picture of four guys lacking any charisma. A few months earlier I had cashed in my student grant and dropped out of university. Madame Rosa beckoned to me, I went over reluctantly to join her and my fellow countryman.

"Madame says you know Paul Bowles," said Thunder Snow and shook my hand. His grip was strong, and he held on.

"You mustn't believe everything she says," I said.

"Fine," he said. "Then I'm certain you know him."

Next morning we ate breakfast at the Café Metropole and a few hours later went down to the beach to bathe. In the evening we visited Paul Bowles. He served us tea and offered us thin, hand-rolled cigarettes. They were in a small metal case. This was the first time Thunder Snow had smoked kif. He sat wide-eyed in the American writer's tiny bedroom and spoke dreamily of travelling to Timbuktu. This fabled desert town was the one place in the world he wanted to see more than any other. Bowles laughed genially.

"I've never been to Timbuktu," he said.

A few days later we said good-bye to Madame Rosa and took the train to Casablanca. From there we travelled on by bus to West Sahara. At Laâyoune we decided to join a convoy that was heading to Nouakchott in Mauritania. Several times over the course of this drive we saw caravans. The Tuaregs pass freely back and forth across borders in the world's biggest desert, they trade with people of different nationalities, it's a clever way of moving goods and traffic around in the Sahara.

"The Tuaregs will take us to Timbuktu," said Thunder Snow. He was clearly entranced by all the tales of the desert town. "I've always known that the Sahara is my home. Here in the desert is where I belong. I'll spend the rest of my life in Timbuktu."

"That's funny," I said. "I was thinking just the same thing."

"You're kidding, right?" He looked at me, happy and surprised.

"No," I said. " Why else would I go along with this ridiculous idea of yours to go to Timbuktu?"

It took us over a month, by car, bus, truck, and in the end camel, to get from Nouakchott to Timbuktu. Both of us came down with dysentery on the way, and when we finally reached the remote little town in the depths of the Sahara we were so exhausted that neither of us had the energy to celebrate. We booked in at Le Bouctou and slept for twenty-four hours straight.

When we woke it was evening and we were served soup in the almost deserted restaurant. Afterward we had a beer in the bar. It was full of tourists from France, Germany, and America.

"I never thought there'd be Americans and Germans here," said Thunder Snow.

Next morning we woke early. Sand blown in under the doorway had gathered in a fine-grained pile on the floor. It was like the snow in the mountains back home in Norway. Thunder Snow and I got dressed and went out to take a closer look at the town.

Timbuktu is a con. It's just a bunch of houses on a desolate rise in the middle of an endless ocean of sand. There was nothing to be gotten from that town.

"This place stinks," I said. "What the hell are we going to do in a place like this?"

"Nothing," said Thunder Snow. "That's why it's perfect."

I had been tricked, that was what it felt like, without ever quite knowing what it was I had actually been expecting. I was restless and ready for adventure, that was about it. To be there, hidden away in an enormous desert with a bunch of scruffy tourists and a weird guy like Thunder Snow, that didn't suit me at all.

"I'm off," I said. "I can't stay here, that's for sure."

"Don't you realize that Timbuktu is just as much a place that's inside of you?" Thunder Snow seemed genuinely moved. "The town is a dream and an idea. Every kid growing up has heard of Timbuktu as the most remote place on earth. Now we're here, you and me. We made a big effort to get here. You mustn't be disappointed that the streets aren't paved with gold or that there's no university bursting with infinite wisdom. Because that's what the first explorers thought they would find in Timbuktu. They were just as disappointed as you when they finally got here."

"Jesus Christ," I said. "You sound like a tourist guide."

Thunder Snow hummed to himself, strolled along the dusty streets with his hat at an angle, had himself photographed with tourists, and clearly fancied himself one of the attractions. It made me even more depressed. Timbuktu was absolutely no kind of a place to stick around.

I packed my rucksack and bought a ticket for a seat on an old propeller plane that flew to Mopti twice a week. My plan was to travel on to Bamako, the capital of Mali.

I left without saying good-bye.

I've been back to Timbuktu twice to look for him, and failed both times. When I meet people who've been there I ask whether they have seen an enigmatic and inscrutable Norwegian wearing a hat, beads, and a waistcoat. The answer is always no. People who know Timbuktu say that no Norwegian has ever lived there. Now I've more or less come to terms with the fact that I must have invented him.

WHEN A DOLLAR WAS A BIG DEAL

He let his beard grow and travelled to America, read Arthur Rimbaud, and wrote poems. On the bus from New York to Los Angeles he met a girl who was on the run. The girl said the childcare people were after her. Her mother was a junkie and her stepfather hit her. He stroked her crotch. When she got off next morning in Knoxville she gave him her father's address. He stayed on the bus until late the next morning holding that little note in his hand. He flew home from Los Angeles after losing all his travel money in Las Vegas and hitchhiking across the Mojave Desert. Back in Norway he sent a letter to the girl who had got off the bus in Tennessee. "You're the best thing that ever happened to me," he wrote. "Maybe we belong together . . . ?" Three weeks later the letter came back. ADDRESS UNKNOWN was printed in capital letters across the envelope. The American postal service paid the return postage. This too was written in capital letters. As though a dollar was such a big deal.

TRANSLATED FROM NORWEGIAN BY ROBERT FERGUSON

Index by Country

Index by Author

Author Biographies

BORIVOJE ADAŠEVIĆ was born in 1974 in Užice, now in Serbia. His first books were collections of short stories entitled *Ekvilibrista* (Balancer, 2000) and *Iz trećeg kraljevstva* (The Third Kingdom, 2006). These were followed by a novel, *Čovek iz kuće na bregu* (The Man from the House on the Hill, 2009). He lives and works in Požega.

BERNARDO ATXAGA was born Joseba Irazu Garmendia in Gipuzkoa, Spain, in 1951. After receiving a degree in economics from the University of Bilbao, he studied philosophy at the University of Barcelona, and worked as an economist, bookseller, professor of the Basque language, publisher, and radio scriptwriter until 1980, when he dedicated himself completely to writing. He lives in the Basque Country, writing in both Basque and Spanish, and many of his works are available in English translation, including *Obabakoak* (1988, 1992), *The Lone Man* (1992, 1996), *The Lone Woman* (1996, 1999), *The Accordionist's Son* (2003, 2007), and *Seven Houses in France* (2009, 2011). Among several Basque prizes for literature and criticism, he was awarded the Premio Nacional de Narrativa in 1989, the Millepages Prix in 1992, and the Prix des trois Couronnes in 1995.

MIRANA LIKAR BAJŽELJ was born in 1961 in Novo Mesto in what is now Slovenia. She is a professor of Slovenian language and literature and has a degree in the same subject, as well as degrees in education and library science. She started writing a few years ago and published her first short stories in the magazines *Literatura, Mentor, Sodobnost,* and *Vpogled.* She has received a number of awards for individual stories. Her first short story collection *Sobotne zgodbe* (Saturday Stories) came out in October 2009 and her second book *Sedem besed* (Seven Words) was published in 2012.

RUMEN BALABANOV was born in 1950 in Sofia, Bulgaria. His works include *Someone Has Gone* and the play *Beyond the Curve.* He received the prestigious "Southern Spring" prize for young writers with his first novel, *Honey Dew,* and has received numerous other awards, including the Chudomir and Golden Youth prizes. He worked as an editor for *Hornet,* Bulgaria's sole humor newspaper, was editor-in-chief of the *Literature Front* newspaper, and published the *Psycho* newspaper. He is best known as the founder of Bulgaria's "gutter press." Balabanov became a TV producer and owned Channel 2001 from 2000 to 2006. He is currently editor-in-chief of *Word Today,* the official newspaper of the Union of Bulgarian Writers.

BALLA is a highly original voice on Slovakia's literary scene, the author of absurdist short stories populated by a gallery of lonely, alienated, and peculiar characters unable to relate to other human beings and undergoing bizarre, often frightening experiences. A recipient of several literary awards, Balla shuns the spotlight and continues to live in the provincial town of Nové Zámky. He published the first of his seven short story collections, *Leptokária,* in 1996. His recent books include the collections *De la Cruz* (2005) and *Cudzí* (Strangers, 2008). In 2011 he published a novella, *V mene otca* (In the Name of the Father), followed by another, *Oko* (The Eye), in 2012.

DANIEL BATLINER was born in Eschen, Liechtenstein, in 1988, where he spent most of his childhood. He began to write while very young, predominantly for the stage. Though many of his works had already been performed in Switzerland, where he lived until recently, spring 2012 found his first full-length plays *Wodka Nicotschow* and *Once Oberland, Please!* debuting to great acclaim in his native Liechtenstein, where he now resides.

ARI BEHN was born in 1972 in Aarhus, grew up in England and Northern Norway, and is currently a resident of Bærum. His debut story collection *Trist som faen* (Sad as Hell) appeared in 1999 to great acclaim; he has since published three novels. His most recent publication is a collection of short fictions, *Talent for lykke* (Talent for Luck, 2011). He married Princess Märtha Louise of Norway in 2002, and they have three daughters.

KRIKOR BELEDIAN is an Armenian writer, literary critic, and translator living in France. He was born in Beirut in 1948 and teaches Armenian Studies at the Université Catholique de Lyon and the Institut national des langues et civilisations orientales in Paris. He is the author of six novels and multiple volumes of critical essays and poetry.

LASHA BUGADZE was born in 1977 and is a Georgian novelist and playwright. He has won an award from the BBC International Radio Playwriting Competition (for his drama *The Navigator*) as well as the SABA Awards for Best Novel and Best Play of the Year. Bugadze is also a cartoonist, screenwriter, producer, and TV personality with the Georgian Public Broadcasting Company.

A. S. BYATT is internationally acclaimed as a novelist, short story writer and critic. Her books include *Possession*, *The Children's Book*, and the quartet of *The Virgin in the Garden*, *Still Life*, *Babel Tower*, and *A Whistling Woman*. She was appointed Dame of the British Empire in 1999.

DULCE MARIA CARDOSO was born in Trás-os-Montes, Portugal, in 1964. She spent her childhood in Angola and returned to Portugal in 1975, after which she studied law and wrote film scripts. *Campo de sangue* (Field of Blood, 2002) was her first novel, and it won her the Grande Prémio Acontece. In 2009 she was awarded the European Union Prize for Literature for her novel *Os meus sentimentos* (My Feelings). In 2010 she won the PEN Prize for her novel *O chão dos pardais* (Sparrow Ground).

SYLWIA CHUTNIK was born in 1979 in Warsaw. She graduated with a degree in Culture and Gender Studies from Warsaw University, and is currently a social worker and the President of the MaMa Foundation, which promotes the rights of mothers in Poland. She is also a member of the feminist group Porozumienie Kobiet 8 Marca, and she works as a Warsaw city tour guide. She is the author of *Kieszonkowy Atlas Kobiet* (The Pocket Atlas of Women, 2008), a book that was nominated Book of the Year by the Polish Radio Programme Three, awarded the Polityka Passport Prize in literature, and longlisted for the Nike Literary Prize in 2009.

VITALIE CIOBANU was born in 1964 in Floresti, Moldova. He is a novelist, essayist, literary critic, and president of Moldova PEN Centre. He is editor-in-chief of *Contrafort* literary magazine, contributes articles to numerous cultural and political magazines in Moldova and Romania, and works as an analyst for the Chisinau bureau of Radio Free Europe. He received the Union of Romanian

Writers Essay Prize in 1999. His short stories have been translated into English, German, and Spanish.

BERNARD COMMENT born in Switzerland, lives and works in Paris, where he directs the prestigious Fiction & Cie imprint at Éditions du Seuil. He is the author of numerous books of fiction and nonfiction, including the story collection *Tout passe* (Everything Passes), which received the Prix Goncourt de la nouvelle in 2011.

ZEHRA ÇIRAK was born in 1960 in Istanbul, Turkey. She moved to Germany with her family in 1962 and has lived in Berlin since 1982. Among other awards, she has won the Adelbert von Chamisso Prize (1989 and 2001) and the Hölderlin Prize (1994). She is the author of *Vogel auf dem Rücken eines Elefanten: Gedichte* (Bird on the Back of an Elephant, 1991); *Fremde Flügel auf eigener Schulter* (Stranger Wings on One's Own Shoulder, 1994); *Leibesübungen* (Abdominal Exercises, 2000); and *Der Geruch von Glück* (The Scent of Happiness, 2011), among others.

KRISTIINA EHIN was born in Rapla, Estonia in 1977. She studied Comparative and Estonian Folklore at the University of Tartu, and in her native Estonian has to date published six volumes of poetry, three books of short stories, and a retelling of South-Estonian fairy tales; she is also the author of two plays. She has won Estonia's most prestigious poetry prize for *Kaitseala* (Protected Area, 2005), a book of poems and journal entries written during a year spent as a nature-reserve warden on an otherwise uninhabited island off Estonia's north coast. Her work has been translated into numerous languages, including, in English, six books of her poetry and three of prose, with her work making frequent appearances in English-language journals. She is a highly acclaimed performer of her own writing, and travels extensively around Estonia and abroad to perform her work, sometimes accompanied by musicians.

GYRÐIR ELÍASSON was born in Reykjavik in 1961, but spent most of his childhood in Sauðárkrókur in northwest Iceland. He is a poet, fiction writer, and translator: his first poetry collection was published in 1983, and since then he has published poetry collections, novels, and collections of short stories—the latter including 2003's *Steintré* (The Stone Tree), which was published in English translation in 2008. Elíasson is also a diligent translator, mainly from English, and has translated works by William Saroyan and Richard Brautigan. He has been labelled "the great stylist" in Icelandic contemporary literature, and won the Icelandic Literary Prize as well as the Halldor Laxness Prize for Literature in 2000 for his short-story collection *Gula húsið* (The Yellow House). He was nominated twice for the Nordic Council Literature Prize before he won the prize in 2011. He currently lives in Reykjavík with his wife and three children.

PAUL EMOND was born in Brussels in 1944. After obtaining a degree and a doctorate of letters at the University of Louvain (with a thesis on the novels of Jean Cayrol), he spent three years in Czechoslovakia and wrote his first novel, *La danse du fumiste* (The Dance of a Sham, 1979). Returning to Belgium, he published other novels and worked for the Archives et usées de la littérature in Brussels, eventually becoming a professor at the Institut des Arts de Diffusion, in the Graduate School for Theater and Film, where he teaches now. An accomplished dramatist as well as fiction writer, Emond's first play debuted in 1986, with more than fifteen to follow, these being performed in numerous countries, including France, Quebec, the United States, England, Romania, and Bulgaria.

RAY FRENCH was born in Wales. His first book was *The Red Jag & other stories* (Planet, 2000). His novel *All This Is Mine* (2003) was translated into Italian and Dutch, and he was a co-author of *Four Fathers* (2006) a collection of stories about fatherhood, which was translated into Spanish. His second novel *Going Under* (2007) is about a middle-aged man who, faced with redundancy, buries himself alive in his back garden and refuses to come up until everyone's job is saved. The *Sunday Times* said, "Given that our hero spends most of its three hundred pages in a box, the pace and plotting of this novel are remarkable . . . " It was translated into French and German, and adapted for German radio. His forthcoming novel *Welcome To The Reservation*, is about a Native American who arrives in a desolate ex-mining town in the Welsh Valleys, pledging to save an ancient yew from being chopped down to make way for a supermarket. He teaches at the University of Hull.

CHRISTINA HESSELHOLDT, born 1962, has been called "one of Denmark's finest prose writers" by the major daily *Information*. After early work in poetry and experimental prose, she has published eight novels, one collection of short stories, and three volumes of linked stories: *Camilla and the Horse* (2008); *Camilla—og resten af selskabet* (Camilla—and the Rest of the Party, 2010); and *Selskabet gør op* (The Party Breaks Up, 2012). Various of her books have been published in Norwegian, Swedish, French, Spanish, Serbian, and Arabic.

KIRILL KOBRIN was born in 1964 in Nizhny Novgorod (then Gorky), Russia. He writes both fiction and nonfiction, co-edits the Moscow magazine of sociology, history, and politics *Neprikosnovennij Zapas* (Emergency Rations), and conducts research into the cultural history of Russia and the Czech Republic. Kobrin is the author of twelve books, of which the latest is a tribute to Flann O'Brien entitled *Tekstoobrabotka* (Bookhandling). He has been hailed by critics as the "Russian Borges" and is considered one of the founders of Russian psychogeography. His work has been translated into several European languages. Kobrin lives in Prague.

ŽARKO KUJUNDŽISKI was born in 1980 in Skopje, Macedonia. His first novel *Spectator*, was published in 2003 and went through five editions. His later works include (in Macedonian): *Andrew, Love, and Other Disasters* (2004), *America* (2006), *Found and Lost* (2008), and a collection of short stories, *13* (2010). He has also published award-winning short stories and essays, several of which have been translated. In 2009 he received his MA in World and Comparative Literature from Sts. Cyril and Methodius University in Skopje. He is editor-in-chief at the Antolog publishing house and e-zine *Reper* (reper.net.mk). He also writes weekly columns for the daily newspaper *Dnevnik*.

DAN LUNGU was born in 1969 in Botoani, Romania. A sociologist by training, he is one of Romania's leading authors today. To date, he has written four novels, two volumes of short stories, and he has edited several collections. His books have been translated into ten languages, and his novel *Sînt o babă comunistă!* (I'm a Communist Old Hag!, 2007) is currently being made into a film. He has founded the literary group Club 8, playing an important part in the literary life of postcommunist Romania. He has been nominated for the Jean Monnet European Literature Prize and received many other literary prizes.

TOMÁS MAC SÍOMÓIN was born in Dublin in 1938. He received his doctorate in biology from Cornell University and has worked as a biological researcher and university lecturer in the USA and Ireland, as well as a journalist, editor of the newspaper *Anois*, translator (from Catalan), and editor of the literary and current affairs journal *Comhar*. His collection of short stories, *Cinn Lae Seangáin* (The Diary of an Ant, 2005) won the award for best short story collection in the Oireachtas competition in 2005, and his novel *An Tionscadal*

(The Project, 2007) won the main Oireachtas award in 2007. His most recent novel is the futuristic science fiction *An bhfuil Stacey ag iompar?* (2011).His work has been translated into many languages, most recently into Slovenian, Romanian, and Catalan. He now lives and works in Catalonia, Spain.

TANIA MALYARCHUK was born in 1983 in Ivano-Frankivsk, Ukraine, and is considered one of Ukraine's most talented young prose writers. Her first novel, *Adolpho's Endspiel,* or a Rose for Liza, appeared in 2004. Her later collections of short fiction include *From Above Looking Down: A Book of Fears* (2006), *How I Became a Saint* (2006), *To Speak* (2007), and *Bestiary of Words* (2009). She is the only Ukrainian writer under thirty to have had her collected works published in a single volume (as *The Divine Comedy*, in 2009). In 2012 she published her second novel *The Biography of a Chance Miracle.* She splits her time between Vienna and Ivano-Frankivsk.

MIKE MCCORMACK was born in London in 1965 and grew up in Ireland. His first collection of short stories, *Getting it in the Head* (1996), won the Rooney Prize for Irish Literature in 1996 and was New York Times Book of the Year in 1998. He co-wrote the screenplay for an award-winning short film adaption of one of the stories in the collection, "The Terms." He has also published two novels, *Crowe's Requiem* (1998) and *Notes from a Coma* (2005), which was shortlisted for the Irish Book of the Year Award in 2006. He is currently writer-in-residence at the University of Ireland in Galway and teaches fiction writing for the MA program there.

SEMEZDIN MEHMEDINOVIĆ was born in 1960 in Kiseljak, Bosnia. He is a writer, filmmaker, and editor, and is the author of five books, two of which—the poetry collection *Nine Alexandrias*

(2003) and the acclaimed novel *Sarajevo Blues* (2001)—are available in English translation. When the war in Bosnia began in 1992, he and his family remained as "internally displaced" persons in besieged Sarajevo. Together with friends, he started a new magazine *Dani* (Days), in an effort to support the spirit of democratic rule and pluralism during what soon became a systematic genocide against his compatriots. The magazine remains Bosnia's leading news and cultural venue. His articles, poems, and essays have been translated and published in leading European and American newspapers and magazines, including *The Village Voice, Conjunctions, TriQuarterly, Der Spiegel*, and others. He and his family arrived in the US in 1996 as political refugees and currently live in Alexandria, Virginia.

LYDIA MISCHKULNIG lives in Vienna, Austria. She has won numerous prizes, including the Bertelsmann Literature prize, the Elias Canetti Award, the Austrian Literary Scholarship, and the Joseph Roth Award. Her publications in German include *Umarmung* (Embrace, 2002), *Hollywood im Winter* (Hollywood in Winter, 1996 and 2012), *Macht euch keine Sorgen* (Don't Worry, 2009), and *Schwestern der Angst* (Sisters of Fear, 2010). She maintains a website at www.lydiamischkulnig.net and publishes essays in Spectrum (*Die Presse*) and Album (*Der Standard*).

DRAGAN RADULOVIC was born in Cetinje, Montenegro, in 1969. He published his first collection of short stories, *Petrifikacija* (Petrification) in 2001 and his first novel *Auschwitz Café*, in 2003. He also published two collections of short pieces, *Vitezovi ništavila* (Knights of Nothingness, 2005), and *Splav Meduze* (The Raft of the Medusa, 2007). Dragan Radulović currently lives in Budva, where he teaches philosophy at the Danilo Kiš Secondary School and writes essays and literary reviews for Montenegrin periodicals.

TIINA RAEVAARA was born in 1979 in Kerava, Finland. In 2005 she received her doctorate in genetics from the University of Helsinki. Her first novel, *Erääna päivänä tyhjä taivas* (One Day, an Empty Sky) was published in 2008. Her first collection of short stories, *En tunne sinua vierelläni* (I Don't Feel You Beside Me, 2010) won the prestigious Runeberg prize. Her most recently work is a scientific exploration of the relationship between dogs and humans *Koiraksi ihmisille* (About Dogs and Humans, 2011). Her fiction, which draws on elements of science fiction, fantasy, and surrealism, stands apart from the largely realistic mainstream of contemporary Finnish literature.

MARIE REDONNET was born Martine l'Hospitalier in 1948 in Paris. Her first publication was a volume of poetry, *Le Mort & Cie*, in 1985 (*Dead Man & Company*, 2005). Her works since include short story collections, novels, and dramatic works, are available in English translation: *Forever Valley* (1992), *Hôtel Splendid* (1994), *Rose Méllie Rose* (1994), *Candy Story* (1995), and *Nevermore* (1996). In 2006-2007, she was visiting professor at the University of Colorado in Boulder. She currently divides her time between Morocco and Aix en Provence.

GUNDEGA REPŠE was born in 1960 in Riga, Latvia. A graduate of the Latvian State Art Academy, Repše made her literary debut at nineteen with her short story "A Camel in Olde Towne of Riga." Since then, she has authored five short-story collections and seven novels, and she is considered one of contemporary Latvia's most brilliant writers. Repše's interest in cultural processes and art are apparent in her biographical novel-essays on Latvian artists and countless reviews and columns in major literary magazines and newspapers. Repše's work has also been adapted for the stage in Latvia—the play *Stigma* at the Daile Theater; the play *Smagais metāls* (Heavy Metal), based on the novel *Alvās kliedziens* (The Tin Scream), at the New Riga Theater; and the play Juras velni (Sea Devils) at the National Theater.

ELOY TIZÓN was born in Madrid in 1964. His novel *Velocidad de los jardines* (1992) was hailed by critics as one of the most interesting Spanish novels of the last 25 years. His novel *Seda salvaje* (1995) was finalist for the Thirteenth Premio Herralde prize. Excerpts of his work have been translated into English, French, Italian, German and, Finnish. His most recently novel is *Parpadeos* (2006).

IEVA TOLEIKYTĖ was born in 1989 in Vilnius, Lithuania. She is currently studying Scandinavian philology at Vilnius University. She became interested in literature in early childhood and began writing quite young—at first some abstract sketches and poems before going on to short stories. In 2009 her first collection of short stories, *Garstyčiųnamas* (The House of Mustard), was published; "The Eye of the Maples," which comes from that collection, is her first piece to be translated into English. She has also published poems and short stories in various Lithuanian magazines.

MIKLÓS VAJDA was born in 1931 and is editor emeritus of *The Hungarian Quarterly*, for which he worked from 1964, becoming editor in 1990. His "essay-memoir" *Anyakép, amerikai keretben* (Portrait of a Mother in an American Frame) was published in Hungarian in 2010. He has translated numerous American and British plays into Hungarian, and he currently lives in Budapest.

Translator Biographies

ANNA ASLANYAN is a journalist and translator. She co-edits *3:AM* magazine and writes for various publications, mainly on books and the arts. Her translations into Russian include works of fiction by Tom McCarthy, Martin Amis, Peter Ackroyd, Mavis Gallant, and Zadie Smith. She has translated a number of essays and short stories from Russian into English.

SHUSHAN AVAGYAN is the translator from Russian of *Energy of Delusion, Bowstring,* and *A Hunt for Optimism* by Viktor Shklovsky, and, from Armenian, *I Want to Live: Poems of Shushanik Kurghinian.* She currently teaches at the American University of Armenia.

FLORIN BICAN has published English translations in Britain, Ireland, the United States, Singapore, and Romania. His translations from English into Romanian include Lewis Carroll's *The Hunting of the Snark* and T. S. Eliot's *Old Possum's Book of Practical Cats.* Since 2006 Florin Bican has been in charge of the Romanian Cultural Institute program "Translators in the Making."

ALISTAIR IAN BLYTH lives in Bucharest and has translated fiction, poetry, and philosophy by writers from Romania and the Republic of Moldova. The authors he has translated include Max Blecher, Gellu Naum, Ion Creanga, Filip Florian, Lucian Dan Teodorovici, Bogdan Suceava, Iulian Ciocan, and Constantin Noica.

CHRISTOPHER BUXTON first came to Bulgaria in 1977 as an English teacher. He has had three novels published in Bulgaria: *Far from the Danube, Prudence and the Red Baron,* and *Radoslava and the Viking Prince.* He has translated a significant number of classic and contemporary Bulgarian texts including new work for the Elizabeth Kostova Foundation. He maintains a website at www.christopherbuxton.com.

MARGARET JULL COSTA has been a literary translator for over twenty years, translating, among others, Javier Marías, Eça de Queiroz, and Bernardo Atxaga. Her work has brought her various prizes, the most recent of which was the 2011 Oxford Weidenfeld Translation Prize for *The Elephant's Journey* by José Saramago.

VICTORIA CRIBB was born in England but lived in Iceland for several years. Her translations from Icelandic include *Stone Tree* by Gyrðir Elíasson and *From the Mouth of the Whale* by Sjón, which was shortlisted for the UK Independent Foreign Fiction Prize in 2012. She is currently pursuing a doctorate at the University of Cambridge.

JENNIFER CROFT is a writer and translator of Spanish, Polish, and Ukrainian. She is a founding editor of *The Buenos Aires Review.*

ROBERT FERGUSON is a renowned translator of Scandinavian literature. He has also written biographies of Nobel Laureate-winning author Knut Hamsun, author Henry Miller, and playwright Henrik Ibsen.

WILL FIRTH was born in 1965 in Newcastle, Australia. He studied German and Slavic languages in Canberra, Zagreb, and Moscow. Since 1991 he has been living in Berlin, Germany, where he works as a freelance translator of literature and the humanities. He translates from Russian, Macedonian, and all variants of Serbo-Croatian.

MARGITA GAILITIS was born in Riga, Latvia, and grew up in Canada. In 1998 she returned to Latvia to work on a Canadian International Development Agency-sponsored project translating Latvian laws into English. Her poetry has been published in Canada and the US, and she is the recipient of Ontario Arts and Canada Council awards. In 2011, she was awarded the Order of the Three Stars by the President of Latvia.

ROGER GREENWALD, an American poet and translator based in Toronto, has won the CBC Literary Award twice (poetry, travel literature). His books include *Connecting Flight* (poems); and the translations *Through Naked Branches: Selected Poems of Tarjei Vesaas; North in the World: Selected Poems of Rolf Jacobsen*, winner of the Lewis Galantière Award; *Picture World*, by Niels Frank; and *A Story about Mr. Silberstein*, a novel by Erland Josephson.

JEAN HARRIS has published fiction, literary criticism, translations, book reviews, and literary dispatches. She won a translation grant from UC-I's International Center for Writing and Translation for her work on Ştefan Bănulescu's Misţretii erau blazi. She has directed the Observer Translation Project at translations.observatorcultural.ro, which translates Romanian fiction into numerous languages.

CELIA HAWKESWORTH is emerita Senior Lecturer in Serbian and Croatian at the School of Slavonic and East European Studies, University College, London. She has published numerous articles and several books on Serbian, Croatian, and Bosnian literature, including the studies *Ivo Andrić: Bridge between East and West*, *Voices in the Shadows: Women and Verbal Art in Serbia and Bosnia*, and *Zagreb: A Cultural History*. She has translated numerous works from Serbo-Croatian, including Vedrana Rudan's *Night* and several books by Dubravka Ugresic.

HILDI HAWKINS is a writer and translator and the London Editor of Books from Finland. She is also the editor of things magazine, a journal of writings about objects, their pasts, presents, and futures.

ELIZABETH HEIGHWAY is a literary and medical translator. She was educated at the Universities of Oxford and Chicago, and holds an MA in Translation Studies from the University of Birmingham. She translates from Georgian and French, and is the editor and translator of Dalkey Archive Press's *Contemporary Georgian Fiction*.

AARON KERNER is a freelance writer and translator from German, French, and Spanish.

AMY KERNER lives in Rhode Island, where she is working toward a PhD in Modern European History at Brown University. She translates from German and Spanish.

VIJA KOSTOFFF is a linguist by education, and a language teacher, writer, and editor by profession. She has been collaborating with

Margita Gailitis for more than ten years in translating the novels, short storeis, plays, film scripts, and poetry of many of Latvia's major writers. Born in Latvia, she now resides in Niagra on the Lake, Ontario, Canada where she exercises her secondary passions for gardening and painting.

SOILA LEHTONEN is a journalist and theater critic, and currently Editor-in-Chief of *Books from Finland*. She edited a collection of writings about the city of Helsinki together with Hildi Hawkins, *Helsinki: A Literary Companion*.

DAVID LIMON translates literature for children and adults from Slovenian into English. His translations include the prize winning novels *Fužine Blues* by Andrej Skubic and *Iqball Hotel* by Boris Kolar. He is Associate Professor at the Department of Translation at the University of Ljubljana.

ILMAR LEHTPERE is Kristiina Ehin's official English-language translator. He has translated nine books by her, both prose and poetry, including the Poetry Society Popescu Prize winner *The Drums of Silence* (2007) and the Poetry Book Society Recommended Translation *The Scent of Your Shadow* (2010). He has also translated her dramatic works and radio broadcasts. His translations of Kristiina Ehin's work appear regularly in leading English-language literary magazines and his collaboration with her is ongoing.

OKSANA MAKSYMCHUK was born in Lviv, Ukraine. She moved to the United States when she was fifteen years old. She began translating Ukrainian and Russian poetry as a student at Bryn Mawr College, and has also published two books of her own poetry in Ukrainian: *Gifts to the Host* (2005) and *The Chase* (2008). In 2004 and 2007 she was the recipient of prestigious Ukrainian literary awards for young authors; since 2006, she has been living in Chicago and pursuing a doctorate in philosophy at Northwestern University.

RHETT MCNEIL has published numerous translations from Portuguese and Spanish, including short fiction by Machado de Assis and Enrique Vila-Matas, and novels by Gonçalo M. Tavares, A. G. Porta, and António Lobo Antunes.

RACHEL MCNICHOLL studied, lived and worked in Switzerland and Germany before returning to her native Ireland. Her career path has covered academic research, teaching translation at university, journalism, in-house book editing, and literary translation. Recent short-story translations from German include "England, I Set Foot on You in Heels" by Lydia Mischkulnig, in *Zwei Wochen England*, and "Belyed: A Fishy Story" by Gabriele Haefs in *Short Fiction in Theory and Practice*. She has also translated work by Klaus Modick, Nadja Spiegel, Yoko Tawada, and Sigrid Weigel.

NIKOLCHE MICKOSKI teaches at the Faculty of Philology at Ss. Cyril and Methodius University in Skopje and translates from English, German and Serbian. His translations include, among others, Ford's *The Good Soldier*, and Faulkner's *The Sound and the Fury*, and *Absalom, Absalom!* into Macedonian, as well as Simon Drakul's *The White Valley* and *Žarko Kujundžiski's Spectator* into English.

MAX POPELYSH-ROSOCHYNSKY was born in 1986 in Simferopol, Crimea. He moved to the United States in 2006. He is currently writing a dissertation about Marina Tsvetaeva's poetry and criticism at the Department of Slavic Languages and Literatures at Northwestern University. He is also working on his first book of poetry in Russian.

MARILYA VETETO REESE is Professor of German at Northern Arizona University. She was among the first US Germanists to interview and write about Turkish-German writers. The recipient of Fulbright, DAAD, and Goethe Institut support, Reese works with, translates, and has numerous publications on contemporary German authors such as Zehra Çirak and Kemal Kurt as well as on Holocaust poet Hilda Stern Cohen and on foreign language pedagogy.

BRENDAN RILEY was born in Dunkirk, New York. He has worked for years as a teacher, translator, writer, and editor. Among other works, he has translated Álvaro Enrigue's *Hypothermia*, Carlos Fuentes's *The Great Latin American Novel*, and Juan Filloy's *Faction*, all for Dalkey Archive Press.

KATINA ROGERS holds a PhD in Comparative Literature from the University of Colorado. In addition to translating contemporary francophone literature, she works on graduate education reform and emerging models of academic authoring and publishing at the Scholarly Communication Institute.

JULIA SHERWOOD was born and grew up in Bratislava, then Czechoslovakia. After studying English and Slavic languages and literature at universities in Cologne, Munich and London, she settled in the UK. Since moving to the US in 2008 she has worked as a freelance translator from Slovak, Czech, Polish and Russian. Her literary translations include Daniela Kapitánová's *Samko Tále's Cemetery Book* (from the Slovak), published in 2011, and Petra Procházková's *Freshta* (from the Czech), published in November 2012.

GEORGE SZIRTES was born in Budapest in 1948 and came to England as a refugee. He was brought up in London and studied Fine Art in London and Leeds. For his poetry, he has won the Faber Memorial prize and the T. S. Eliot Prize. He has also worked extensively as a translator of poems, novels, plays, and essays and has won various prizes and awards in this sphere. His own work has been translated into numerous languages. He lives near Norwich with his wife.

ELENA MITRESKA WEISS resides in New York City and had worked for two renowned publishers, HarperCollins and Penguin Group (USA), focusing on author contracts. She has worked to scout Macedonian authors for publication in English, including Goce Smilevski. She was educated at Hunter College, New York City, and Ss. Cyril and Methodius University in Skopje, Macedonia.

JAYDE WILL is a lecturer at the Department of Translation and Interpretation Studies at Vilnius University. His translations of Estonian, Lithuanian, and Russian poetry have appeared in a number of anthologies. He has also translated Lithuanian plays for the London stage. He splits his time between Vilnius and Tartu.

JEFFREY ZUCKERMAN works in book publishing. He holds a degree in English with honors from Yale University, where he studied English literature, creative writing, and translation. He has translated several Francophone authors, from Jean-Philippe Toussaint and Vassilis Alexakis to Édouard Levé and Frédéric Beigbeder.

Liberté · Égalité · Fraternité
RÉPUBLIQUE FRANÇAISE
AMBASSADE DE FRANCE
AUX ETATS-UNIS

Service culturel

CYNGOR LLYFRAU CYMRU
WELSH BOOKS COUNCIL

elic
Estonian
Literature
Centre

N O R L A

HUNGARIAN BOOK
FOUNDATION

POLISH
CULTURAL
INSTITUTE
www.PolishCulture.org.uk

MINISTRY OF CULTURE
AND MONUMENT PROTECTION
OF GEORGIA

DG
LB
DIRECÇÃO-GERAL
DO LIVRO E DAS
BIBLIOTECAS

Bókmenntasjóður
The Icelandic Literature Fund

swiss arts council
pro helvetia

SPAIN
FOREIGN
CULTURAL
COOPERATION

PRINCIPALITY OF LIECHTENSTEIN

etxe
pare
EUSKALINSTITUTUA
INSTITUTOVASCO
BASQUEINSTITUTE

FILI
FINNISH LITERATURE EXCHANGE

STATENS
KUNSTRÅD
DANISH ARTS COUNCIL

LITERÁRNE
INFORMAČNÉ
CENTRUM

J A K   JAVNA AGENCIJA ZA KNJIGO REPUBLIKE SLOVENIJE
SLOVENIAN BOOK AGENCY

Acknowledgments

Publication of the *Best European Fiction 2013* was made possible by generous support from the following cultural agencies and embassies:

The Arts Council (Ireland)

Communauté française de Belgique--Promotion des lettres

Cultural Services of the French Embassy

Cyngor Llyfrau Cymru--Welsh Books Council

Danish Arts Council

DGLB—General Directorate for Books and Libraries / Portugal

Elizabeth Kostova Foundation

The Etxepare Basque Institute

Embassy of the Principality of Liechtenstein
to the United States of America

Embassy of the Republic of Macedonia in Washington D.C.

Embassy of Spain, Washington, D.C.

Estonian Literature Centre

Finnish Literature Exchange (FILI)

Hungarian Book Foundation

Icelandic Literature Fund

Literárne informačné centrum (The Center for Information on
Literature) Bratislava, Slovakia

The Ministry of Culture and Monument Protection of Georgia:
Program in Support of Georgian Books and Literature
NORLA: Norwegian Literature Abroad, Fiction & Nonfiction
The Polish Cultural Institute of London
Pro Helvetia, Swiss Arts Council
Romanian Cultural Institute – New York
The Slovenian Book Agency (JAK)

Rights and Permissions

Semezdin Mehmedinović: "My Heart" © 2011 by Semezdin
Mehmedinović. Translation © 2012 by Celia Hawkesworth.

Lydia Mischkulnig: "A Protagonist's Nemesis" © 2009 by Haymon
Verlag Ges.m.b.H. Translation © 2012 Rachel McNicholl.

Dragan Radulović: "The Face" © 2007 by Dragan Radulović.
Translation © 2011 by Will Firth.

Tiina Raevaara: "My Creator, My Creation" © 2010 by Tiina
Raevaara. Translation © 2010 by Hildi Hawkins and Soila
Lehtonen, originally published in Books from Finland.

Marie Redonnet: "Madame Zabée's Guesthouse," excerpt from
Diego; original French text copyright © 2005 by Les Éditions de
Minuit. Published by permission of Georges Borchardt, Inc., on
behalf of Les Éditions de Minuit. Translation © 2012 by Katina
Rogers.

Gundega Repše: "How Important Is It to Be Ernest?" © 2009 by
Dienas Gr-mata. Translation © 2012 by Margita Gailitis and Vija
Kostoff.

Eloy Tizón: "The Mercury in the Thermometers" © 2006 by Eloy
Tizón. Translation © 2012 by Brendan Riley.

Ieva Toleikytė: "The Eye of the Maples" © 2011 by Ieva Toleikytė.
Translation © 2011 by Jayde Will.

Miklós Vajda: "Portrait of a Mother in an American Frame," excerpt
from *Anyakép, amerikai keretben* (Portrait of a Mother in an
American Frame) © 2009 by Miklós Vajda. Translation © 2010
by George Szirtes.

◪ SELECTED DALKEY ARCHIVE PAPERBACKS

PETROS ABATZOGLOU *What Does Mrs. Freeman Want?*

MICHAL AJVAZ *The Golden Age* ▪ *The Other City*

PIERRE ALBERT-BIROT *Grabinoulor*

YUZ ALESHKOVSKY *Kangaroo*

FELIPE ALFAU *Chromos* ▪ *Locos*

IVAN ÂNGELO *The Celebration* ▪ *The Tower of Glass*

DAVID ANTIN *Talking*

ANTÓNIO LOBO ANTUNES *Knowledge of Hell* ▪ *The Splendor of Portugal*

ALAIN ARIAS-MISSON *Theatre of Incest*

IFTIKHAR ARIF AND WAQAS KHWAJA, EDS. *Modern Poetry of Pakistan*

JOHN ASHBERY AND JAMES SCHUYLER *A Nest of Ninnies*

ROBERT ASHLEY *Perfect Lives*

GABRIELA AVIGUR-ROTEM *Heatwave and Crazy Birds*

HEIMRAD BÄCKER *transcript*

DJUNA BARNES *Ladies Almanack* ▪ *Ryder*

JOHN BARTH *LETTERS* ▪ *Sabbatical*

DONALD BARTHELME *The King* ▪ *Paradise*

SVETISLAV BASARA *Chinese Letter*

RENÉ BELLETTO *Dying*

MARK BINELLI *Sacco and Vanzetti Must Die!*

ANDREI BITOV *Pushkin House*

ANDREJ BLATNIK *You Do Understand*

LOUIS PAUL BOON *Chapel Road* ▪ *My Little War* ▪ *Summer in Termuren*

ROGER BOYLAN *Killoyle*

IGNÁCIO DE LOYOLA BRANDÃO *Anonymous Celebrity* ▪ *The Good-Bye Angel* ▪ *Teeth under the Sun* ▪ *Zero*

BONNIE BREMSER *Troia: Mexican Memoirs*

CHRISTINE BROOKE-ROSE *Amalgamemnon*

BRIGID BROPHY *In Transit*

MEREDITH BROSNAN *Mr. Dynamite*

GERALD L. BRUNS *Modern Poetry and the Idea of Language*

EVGENY BUNIMOVICH AND J. KATES, EDS. *Contemporary Russian Poetry: An Anthology*

GABRIELLE BURTON *Heartbreak Hotel*

MICHEL BUTOR *Degrees* ▪ *Mobile* ▪ *Portrait of the Artist as a Young Ape*

G. CABRERA INFANTE *Infante's Inferno* ▪ *Three Trapped Tigers*

JULIETA CAMPOS *The Fear of Losing Eurydice*

ANNE CARSON *Eros the Bittersweet*

ORLY CASTEL-BLOOM *Dolly City*

CAMILO JOSÉ CELA *Christ versus Arizona* ▪ *The Family of Pascual Duarte* ▪ *The Hive*

LOUIS-FERDINAND CÉLINE *Castle to Castle* ▪ *Conversations with Professor Y* ▪ *London Bridge* ▪ *Normance* ▪ *North* ▪ *Rigadoon*

HUGO CHARTERIS *The Tide Is Right*

JEROME CHARYN *The Tar Baby*

ERIC CHEVILLARD *Demolishing Nisard*

MARC CHOLODENKO *Mordechai Schamz*

JOSHUA COHEN *Witz*

EMILY HOLMES COLEMAN *The Shutter of Snow*

ROBERT COOVER *A Night at the Movies*

STANLEY CRAWFORD *Log of the S.S. The Mrs Unguentine* ▪ *Some Instructions to My Wife*

ROBERT CREELEY *Collected Prose*

RENÉ CREVEL *Putting My Foot in It*

RALPH CUSACK *Cadenza*

SUSAN DAITCH *L.C.* ▪ *Storytown*

NICHOLAS DELBANCO *The Count of Concord* ▪ *Sherbrookes*

NIGEL DENNIS *Cards of Identity*

PETER DIMOCK *A Short Rhetoric for Leaving the Family*

ARIEL DORFMAN *Konfidenz*

COLEMAN DOWELL *The Houses of Children* ▪ *Island People* ▪ *Too Much Flesh and Jabez*

ARKADII DRAGOMOSHCHENKO *Dust*

RIKKI DUCORNET *The Complete Butcher's Tales* ▪

For a full list of publications, visit: www.dalkeyarchive.com

The Fountains of Neptune ▪ *The Jade Cabinet* ▪ *The One Marvelous Thing* ▪ *Phosphor in Dreamland* ▪ *The Stain* ▪ *The Word "Desire"*

WILLIAM EASTLAKE *The Bamboo Bed* ▪ *Castle Keep* ▪ *Lyric of the Circle Heart*

JEAN ECHENOZ *Chopin's Move*

STANLEY ELKIN *A Bad Man* ▪ *Boswell: A Modern Comedy* ▪ *Criers and Kibitzers, Kibitzers and Criers* ▪ *The Dick Gibson Show* ▪ *The Franchiser* ▪ *George Mills* ▪ *The Living End* ▪ *The MacGuffin* ▪ *The Magic Kingdom* ▪ *Mrs. Ted Bliss* ▪ *The Rabbi of Lud* ▪ *Van Gogh's Room at Arles*

FRANÇOIS EMMANUEL *Invitation to a Voyage*

ANNIE ERNAUX *Cleaned Out*

LAUREN FAIRBANKS *Muzzle Thyself* ▪ *Sister Carrie*

LESLIE A. FIEDLER *Love and Death in the American Novel*

JUAN FILLOY *Op Oloop*

GUSTAVE FLAUBERT *Bouvard and Pécuchet*

KASS FLEISHER *Talking out of School*

FORD MADOX FORD *The March of Literature*

JON FOSSE *Aliss at the Fire* ▪ *Melancholy*

MAX FRISCH *I'm Not Stiller* ▪ *Man in the Holocene*

CARLOS FUENTES *Christopher Unborn* ▪ *Distant Relations* ▪ *Terra Nostra* ▪ *Where the Air Is Clear*

WILLIAM GADDIS *J R* ▪ *The Recognitions*

JANICE GALLOWAY *Foreign Parts* ▪ *The Trick Is to Keep Breathing*

WILLIAM H. GASS *Cartesian Sonata and Other Novellas* ▪ *Finding a Form* ▪ *A Temple of Texts* ▪ *The Tunnel* ▪ *Willie Masters' Lonesome Wife*

GÉRARD GAVARRY *Hoppla! 1 2 3* ▪ *Making a Novel*

ETIENNE GILSON *The Arts of the Beautiful* ▪ *Forms and Substances in the Arts*

C. S. GISCOMBE *Giscome Road* ▪ *Here* ▪ *Prairie Style*

DOUGLAS GLOVER *Bad News of the Heart* ▪ *The Enamoured Knight*

WITOLD GOMBROWICZ *A Kind of Testament*

KAREN ELIZABETH GORDON *The Red Shoes*

GEORGI GOSPODINOV *Natural Novel*

JUAN GOYTISOLO *Count Julian* ▪ *Exiled from Almost Everywhere* ▪ *Juan the Landless* ▪ *Makbara* ▪ *Marks of Identity*

PATRICK GRAINVILLE *The Cave of Heaven*

HENRY GREEN *Back* ▪ *Blindness* ▪ *Concluding* ▪ *Doting* ▪ *Nothing*

JACK GREEN *Fire the Bastards!*

JIŘÍ GRUŠA *The Questionnaire*

GABRIEL GUDDING *Rhode Island Notebook*

MELA HARTWIG *Am I a Redundant Human Being?*

JOHN HAWKES *The Passion Artist* ▪ *Whistlejacket*

ALEKSANDAR HEMON, ED. *Best European Fiction*

AIDAN HIGGINS *A Bestiary* ▪ *Balcony of Europe* ▪ *Bornholm Night-Ferry* ▪ *Darkling Plain: Texts for the Air* ▪ *Flotsam and Jetsam* ▪ *Langrishe, Go Down* ▪ *Scenes from a Receding Past* ▪ *Windy Arbours*

KEIZO HINO *Isle of Dreams*

KAZUSHI HOSAKA *Plainsong*

ALDOUS HUXLEY *Antic Hay* ▪ *Crome Yellow* ▪ *Point Counter Point* ▪ *Those Barren Leaves* ▪ *Time Must Have a Stop*

NAOYUKI II *The Shadow of a Blue Cat*

MIKHAIL IOSSEL AND JEFF PARKER, EDS. *Amerika: Russian Writers View the United States*

GERT JONKE *The Distant Sound* ▪ *Geometric Regional Novel* ▪ *Homage to Czerny* ▪ *The System of Vienna*

JACQUES JOUET *Mountain R* ▪ *Savage* ▪ *Upstaged*

CHARLES JULIET *Conversations with Samuel Beckett and Bram van Velde*

MIEKO KANAI *The Word Book*

YORAM KANIUK *Life on Sandpaper*

HUGH KENNER *The Counterfeiters* ▪ *Flaubert, Joyce and Beckett: The Stoic Comedians* ▪ *Joyce's Voices*

For a full list of publications, visit: www.dalkeyarchive.com

⑤ SELECTED DALKEY ARCHIVE PAPERBACKS

For a full list of publications, visit: www.dalkeyarchive.com

SELECTED DALKEY ARCHIVE PAPERBACKS 🔲

For a full list of publications, visit: www.dalkeyarchive.com

⅁ SELECTED DALKEY ARCHIVE PAPERBACKS